# IT ALL COMES BACK TO YOU

BOOKS BY MELISSA WIESNER

*Her Family Secret*

*The Girl in the Picture*

*Our Stolen Child*

*His Secret Daughter*

# IT ALL COMES BACK TO YOU

MELISSA WIESNER

bookouture

Published by Bookouture in 2023

An imprint of Storyfire Ltd.
Carmelite House
50 Victoria Embankment
London EC4Y 0DZ

www.bookouture.com

Storyfire Ltd's authorised representative in the EEA is Hachette Ireland
8 Castlecourt Centre
Castleknock Road
Castleknock
Dublin 15 D15 YF6A
Ireland



ISBN: 978-1-83790-820-2
eBook ISBN: 978-1-83790-819-6

*To Sid. This book could only be for you. Thanks for the inspiration.*

# PROLOGUE

## SUMMER, PRESENT DAY

Dr. Anna Campbell had spent the last decade and a half trying not to go home. But just beyond those airport exit doors loomed Pittsburgh, Pennsylvania—the city she'd spent her childhood trying to escape.

For courage, Anna gripped the gold pendant that had hung around her neck for the past two decades, rubbing her thumb on the delicate lines etched on the surface. She wasn't a scared, desperate kid anymore, and this trip was her chance to finally find the answers she'd spent half her life chasing.

To finally put the past behind her for good.

Anna squared her shoulders and followed the other weary travelers off the escalator, hesitating as they veered toward baggage claim or out the sliding doors, where friends and family would pick them up. She didn't have any bags. All of her belongings fit in the pack on her back, and nobody was coming at this late hour to get her. So, instead, she scanned the overhead signs for one that would point her to the Uber stand.

She was about to head out the doors when a low voice, from somewhere behind her, called out, "Can somebody call a doctor?"

Anna whirled around, her apprehension forgotten as her gaze jerked to one of the most beautiful men she'd ever seen, a few feet away, watching her. She stood there, immobile, as her bag slid off her shoulder and fell to the floor.

The man's mouth curved into a smile.

"Gabe!" she gasped, launching herself at him. He met her halfway, picking her up off her feet and swinging her around.

Gabriel Weatherall, her best friend in the world.

"I can't believe you're here," she said when he finally put her back on the ground.

Her plane had landed after midnight, and she'd told him she planned to grab a hotel room near the airport and get some sleep. She should have known better than to believe he'd listen to her.

"You didn't honestly think you were going to sneak back into the country after all this time, did you?" he asked.

"Well, not sneak." She flashed him a crooked smile. "Maybe just tiptoe."

Gabe shook his head and sighed, the gesture laced with amusement but also a hint of something else. Exasperation, probably. "You know my family's been counting down the days until your arrival, right?"

Anna's heart gave an unexpected lurch: Gabe's family, the Weatheralls. Gabe's huge, loud, sweet, loving, overbearing family. They'd been in her life since she was a kid, and having been embraced by them was the best thing that had ever happened to her. Still, there were times, like today, that she knew she'd never be the same as them. They viewed every transition in life as a cause for celebration, the louder and more crowded, the better. While Anna wanted nothing more than to hide out until she could figure out what to do next.

As if he could read her mind, Gabe said, "You're lucky the whole family didn't show up at baggage claim with a marching band and fireworks." He raised his eyebrows and looked at her sideways. "I suggested that might overwhelm you."

He was exaggerating, but only by a little. And just as he always had, Gabe knew her better than anyone. He understood her past, her childhood, and all the reasons why it was hard for her to open herself up to people as freely as his family did.

Well, he understood most of it. There were some things she'd never told anyone.

Even still, she knew her reserve sometimes frustrated him.

She snuck another glance at him as he grabbed her backpack. It had been four years since she'd seen him. Now in his mid-thirties, there were a few laugh lines around his eyes, and while he was still lean, he'd filled out a little since she'd been away. Of course, that only made him more attractive.

He turned around and caught her staring.

From somewhere far away, a low hum resounded, beginning quietly and building in intensity. For a second, Anna thought the luggage belt had started up over in baggage claim, but no. It was just her—just that shaky, buzzy feeling that took over her limbs when she was around Gabe.

From the tiny twitch in the corner of his eye, he felt it, too.

Just like that, she was transported to the last time she'd seen him, on that early June evening, four years ago. To the two of them on his parents' front porch, those few wooden planks that separated them a wider gulf than the ocean she'd just traversed. To that stunned expression on Gabe's face and the hurt reflected in his eyes as she'd retreated from all the lines they'd almost crossed.

She retreated again now, bending to pick up her jacket and riffle through the pockets as if finding her passport was suddenly urgent. Gabe breathed out a quiet huff, and there was that exasperation again.

For about the millionth time since the stormy spring night when she'd left the country, she wondered how time and distance had shaped Gabe's feelings about their last encounter. Was he equally glad they'd stopped before anything happened between them?

And equally sorry?

She'd never ask him.

They talked about everything. Everything except this live wire thrumming between them. That subject was so off the table, it wasn't even in the room. Because if there was one thing that mattered more to her than anything, one thing she would throw herself in front of a rushing train to protect, it was her friendship with Gabe.

It was the only thing in life she'd ever been able to count on.

# PART I

# ONE

## FALL, FIFTEEN YEARS AGO

Anna took a shaky breath to calm the jackhammer in her chest as her professor rattled off a list of names from the podium. The guy seated to her right shot a pointed look at her worn-out sneaker, and she pressed a hand to her leg to still the nervous tapping.

The person whose name her professor was about to call had no idea that Anna's future was riding on them. As one of only a handful of high school kids who qualified for this free college program, this project was her shot at a scholarship, at a life where she wasn't always looking over her shoulder.

The sharp crinkle of paper in Dr. McGovern's hand echoed through the lecture hall as her finger slid down the list and then stopped.

Anna clutched the hem of her hand-me-down T-shirt as she waited for her new project partner's name.

"Gabriel Weatherall."

Her gaze flew across the room to the tall, dark-haired guy slouching in his chair, idly rolling his pen between his fingers.

He hitched his chin to acknowledge her and then looked away. Less than a second later, his head whipped back, and his mouth dropped open in an almost comical enactment of a double take.

Well, it would've been comical if her whole life wasn't at stake.

She forced herself to flash him a friendly smile.

As his eyebrows rose and his lip curled in disdain, Anna felt her scholarship slipping from her grasp.

Dr. McGovern paired off the remaining students on her list and then started her lecture, but Anna didn't hear a word of it. She perched an elbow on the desk and pulled her brown hair in front of her face as if she cared about things like split ends. Gazing past her long bangs, she took in Gabe's thick black hair, fraternity T-shirt, and arms folded across his broad chest in a posture of complete self-confidence. Half the girls in the class would kill to work with Gabe for the next two semesters, but, oh my God, she wished she'd gotten almost anyone else.

This was her second class with him, not that he ever noticed her in the back of the room. But she knew who he was. Gabe was the poster boy for having it easy. He moved and spoke too confidently to have ever experienced hardship, and he was the kind of guy whose parents had told him he was smart and special from the day he was born. Everything he did reflected this, from how he jumped right into arguing a theory with a professor, to the way the sorority girls flocked to him, and he paid them just enough attention to keep them coming back—but never enough to limit his options.

Okay, so Gabe *was* smart, and more than once, she silently agreed with him when he was making a point in class. But he was too attractive, too arrogant, and too unrestrained. She needed a partner who would put his head down, not draw any attention, and work like crazy. Or better yet, back off and let her take over. Gabe Weatherall wasn't going to do either of those things.

After class, Gabe headed for the door surrounded by the

group that he always sat with, not bothering to spare Anna a glance. She took her time as she carefully put her books in her backpack. Hopefully, Gabe would be too distracted to remember to wait for her, and maybe she could sneak away and contact him later about the project. If she did some research first, she could plan out what she wanted to say when they actually met up in person.

But when she stepped from the room, Gabe was leaning against the wall, alone, and watching the door. His eyes met hers, and her stomach did a slow roll. They were the palest blue, bordering on silver. Eyes like that didn't belong on a person with hair that dark, and yet, there they were. Staring back at her like storm clouds with the sun peeking through. How had she never noticed them before?

She gave herself a mental shove.

*Storm clouds? Stop it.*

Gabe flashed his palm in a half-assed wave, and she slowed her steps.

"Hi." She stopped in front of him and forced her lips to curve upward. "I guess we're partners on this project."

Gabe didn't bother to return her smile. Instead, he looked her up and down. "How old are you?"

She clutched her notebook to her chest to hide her oversized hardware store T-shirt. One of her mom's boyfriends had left it behind after her mom kicked him out. He was a plumber, and she'd been sorry to see him go. He was one of the few nice ones, and it was the only time the radiator had worked without having to bang on it with a can of peas. The T-shirt was too big, but that's what she liked about it. It was easier to hide behind.

But why hadn't she remembered that today was the day they'd be getting their partners and tried a little harder? Now she was conscious of swimming in that enormous T-shirt, especially since she was pretty sure she'd lost some more weight recently. And being over five foot nine didn't help either. Most of the time her height only highlighted her awkwardness. A boy in her high school once told her she reminded him of Bambi, all knobby knees and giant brown eyes. He'd thought he was giving her a compliment.

Well, the best thing to do was act confident. Luckily, she'd gotten pretty good at acting lately. She cleared her throat. "Nice to meet you. I'm Anna Campbell."

Gabe blinked. "Are you a freshman?"

"And... what was your name again?" Anna pulled her shoulders back and stood up to her full height. That always worked at her job at the grocery store when she was dealing with an angry customer. *But damn it.* Gabe was still six inches taller and didn't look the least bit intimidated. Though he did look amused.

"Gabriel Weatherall. My friends call me Gabe."

"Well, Gabriel. It looks like we'll be working together for the next two semesters. So maybe we should swap emails and make a plan to meet."

Gabe hesitated for long enough to make her squirm. Was he considering how he could get out of this? Finally, he plucked her notebook from her hand and opened it to a blank page. Scribbling his name, email address, and phone number, he murmured, "Best way to reach me is to text."

He handed her notebook back, and she slowly wrote down her phone number and email address. He held out his hand to take it, but she hesitated.

Anna couldn't text him. She didn't have a cell phone, just a crappy cordless landline that had been in the apartment when they moved in. She curled her toes inside her sneakers and forgot she was supposed to be acting confident. "I, um... Email is really better for me, if that's okay..." She didn't have a computer either. Or Wi-Fi. But she practically lived in the library and could use the computer lab there.

He took the paper with her information and studied it as if

it contained some clue to who she was. "Sure, whatever. So, when can you meet?"

She pressed her lips together. He wasn't going to like this. "Well, I can't really meet during the week. I'm only on campus on Tuesdays for classes."

Gabe ran his hand through his hair, making it stick out sideways. At least he wasn't the kind of guy who used fifty pounds of gel in his hair. "Okay. I have a car," he said. "Where do you live? I can meet in your neighborhood, or we could work at your place."

Her breath caught at the idea of this attractive, confident, clearly wealthy college guy coming to her *apartment* to work on their project. He'd think... Her cheeks burned. She couldn't even imagine what he'd think. It didn't matter because it was never going to happen. But they *were* going to be spending a lot of time together over the next two semesters. So, she had to tell him at least a little bit about herself, as much as it pained her. "Look, I can't meet during the week. I'm in school all day. And after school, I work."

She watched the confusion spread across his face. "You're in school all day. School, like..."

"School, like, high school."

"*High school?*" His head jerked back like she'd taken a swing at him. "What are you doing in global economics? Usually seniors take this class." Gabe laughed, but his face was grim. "*College* seniors."

"I'm in a free program for promising high school students." Anna didn't mention the part of the program aimed at "low-income" or "at-risk" students. She hated the phrase "at risk." She didn't need a reminder of all the risks involved in her situation right now. "It's really competitive. I've been taking classes since I was a sophomore. When I graduate from high school, I'll be able to use the credits toward my bachelor's degree."

Not to mention if she aced this project, she'd be on every professor's radar when she applied for honors scholarships.

Guys like Gabe didn't have to worry about scholarships.

"Since you were a sophomore," he repeated. "And now you're a...?"

She sighed. "I'm a junior. I'm sixteen." Gabe was a college senior, probably twenty-one already, so Anna could sympathize with his surprise at ending up with a high school student as his partner. But surely he knew Dr. McGovern wouldn't have let her in the class if she didn't belong there.

He pushed away from the wall and took a step toward her. "Seriously? Sixteen? The most important project of my college career, and my partner is still waiting to hit puberty?"

Maybe Anna was only sixteen, but suddenly her body ached like an old lady's. She'd unloaded boxes at the grocery store until ten o'clock the night before and then stayed up past midnight doing homework. Every night that week would be the same. She didn't need to stand here and listen to this.

Pressing her hands to her hips, she glared at him. Up close, those eyes weren't so special. Calling them silver had been a stretch. They were nothing but gray. Murky, dishwater gray.

"Look, I can do the work. I've gotten As in every class I've taken. I work hard. You won't have to carry my weight. So you'll still have time for hazing freshmen and getting sorority girls wasted on cheap beer, or whatever it is you Theta Chis do in your spare time."

She regretted the words as soon as they came out of her mouth.

Gabe took a step back. "Wow."

Could this have gone any worse? It wouldn't surprise her if he went to Dr. McGovern and demanded a different partner. She'd practically had to beg to get in the class, and if Gabe switched to another group, she'd really be screwed.

Gabe's eyebrows knitted together. "I'm sorry to disappoint

you, but you've got it all wrong." Anna was about to stammer out an apology when his mouth twisted into a smile. "Theta Chis are way too classy to offer girls cheap beer. We usually go with mixed drinks."

Anna stared at her sneakers to hide her smile.

Gabe sighed. "Look, we're stuck with each other, so we might as well get to it. Do you work on Sunday?"

She shook her head.

"Let's meet at the library. Noon?"

She nodded, still half expecting him to try and switch partners.

"I'll do my best to drag my hungover ass out of bed." He took off down the hall and, without turning around, called back, "Try not to get grounded between now and Sunday."

As Anna watched his tall frame round the corner, she slumped back against the wall. How were the two of them going to work together without killing each other?

If the past five minutes were any indication, it was going to be a very long year.

# TWO

On Saturday evening, Gabe's roommates rolled in with a group of girls from their fraternity's sister sorority. They hung out on the front porch of their old brick fraternity house, drinking beer out of plastic cups and soaking up what might've been the last rays of summer sunshine before fall blew in.

Normally, he would have been right in the mix—talking shit with Jake and the other guys, crushing it at beer pong—but it was senior year, and as his dad liked to remind him, time to start thinking about the future. That meant getting his grad school applications in early to qualify for the best research positions.

Gabe headed out the front door with his bag slung over his shoulder, giving his friends on the porch a wave. He was halfway across the lawn when one of the sorority girls called his name. He turned as she tapped down the porch steps in her high-heeled sandals and tossed her blond hair over her shoulder, showing off the tan she'd probably perfected by the pool over the summer.

"You're not leaving, are you?" The girl fiddled with one dangly earring.

He dragged his gaze upward, to her face, and then flashed

her a grin. "Sorry, sweetie, I'd love to stay and hang out with you, but I've got work to do."

Behind the girl, Jake rolled his eyes and made a gagging motion. Gabe was pretty sure he knew what that was about. All the guys gave him a hard time because when he forgot a girl's name, he called her "sweetie."

This particular girl didn't seem to mind. She gave him a wide grin. "It's Saturday night. You can do your work tomorrow. Stay and have a drink." Her fingers grazed his forearm.

It was a gorgeous evening, and the idea of staying with her was pretty appealing. But tomorrow was Sunday, and he was supposed to meet that high school girl about their project. He didn't even want to think about it. And then after, he had family stuff.

"Sorry, but I should go." He checked her out from the corner of his eye. "But, hey, I'll do my best to get my stuff done and make it back in time to hang out later."

She flashed him a satisfied smile. "Great. I'll be here."

With one more wave, he took off down the street toward campus.

When Gabe got to the library, he made his way to the main study area. A group of students wearing hip glasses and scarves draped around their necks sat in one corner debating the merits of a recent best-selling novel. Three skinny kids, probably computer science majors, occupied another corner, geeking out over a program someone was developing on their laptop.

The only other student sat with her back to the room. Her long, dark hair swung over her shoulder as she sifted through a huge pile of books and scribbled in a notebook.

It was beautiful weather and still early in the semester. Most students had something better to do than hang out at the library on a Saturday night. If his grad school applications weren't so important, it was the last place he'd be.

Gabe rubbed the back of his neck and sighed as he pulled his laptop from his bag. He was applying for PhD programs in economics and considering some of the best schools—Harvard, MIT, the University of Chicago, Stanford. Gabe was one of the strongest students in his undergrad program. If he went to the top PhD program and published his research with the most respected economists in the field, he could pretty much write his own ticket after that. But first, he had to pass global econ, which suddenly wasn't looking like such a sure thing.

He'd thought about going to Dr. McGovern and asking for a new partner, but whining wasn't Gabe's style, and it wasn't going to impress anyone. So, he'd sucked it up and agreed to meet with the high school girl. *Anna.* He wasn't about to call her "sweetie."

What he needed was a plan. He could take charge and assign Anna some easy tasks—basic research on topics he identified, formatting charts and graphs, that kind of thing—and steer the project in the direction he wanted. It could work out in his favor. A nervous and intimidated high school girl might be easier to deal with than one of the other econ majors. He could tell Anna what he wanted her to do, and she'd go along with whatever he said.

Gabe rubbed his temples as the weight lifted slightly. Time to get to work. He turned to his applications and started an outline of his personal statement.

Three hours later, he snapped his laptop shut and stretched back in his chair. The computer geeks were long gone, but the dark-haired girl's head was still bowed over her notebook, and her massive collection of books had tripled in size.

Out the window, a couple of guys in hoodies and jeans walked past, headed in the direction of Greek Row. Probably freshmen recruits on their way to welcome parties at the fraternities they hoped to pledge. His fraternity would be having those parties in the next few weeks. A group of girls strolled by, and the sound of their laughter drifted in through the open window. They wore sundresses, or jeans and tank tops, unconcerned that the temperature would plunge after midnight, and they'd be freezing on the walk home.

He checked the time on his phone. The party would just be ramping up back at his house. Maybe he could still get there in time to hang out with that girl from the sorority.

Gabe packed up his bag and headed for the door. Right as he passed behind the dark-haired girl, she reached out and yanked a book from the middle of the stack. The pile swayed, and the books toppled over and scattered to the floor. The largest volume landed right on his shoe.

"Jesus!" He grabbed his foot as pain shot through it.

"Oh my God, I'm sorry!" The girl covered her mouth in horror and dove under the table to gather the books.

"It's fine. I'm fine," he said, limping over to help her. Bending down, he caught a glimpse of her flushed face and rocked back on his heels.

*Well, hell. Of all people.*

He should have expected Anna the high school girl to be the one throwing books at him. He had a feeling she'd be causing him a lot of pain in the coming months.

"Hey, kid."

Anna's head jerked up and she turned even redder. "Hi." She bit her lip. "It's Anna, by the way."

He smirked. "I know."

Anna cleared her throat and reached down to pick up the rest of the books. He helped her, and soon they'd built two neat stacks on the table.

"What are you doing here so late?" Gabe turned over the book he was holding in his hands and looked at the cover.

*Banker to the Poor: Micro-Lending and the Battle Against World Poverty* by Muhammad Yunus.

"Muhammad Yunus, huh?"

Anna grabbed the book from his hand. "Yes. So?"

He knew Muhammad Yunus was one of the pioneers of modern microfinance—the practice of lending small amounts of money to help poor people start businesses who didn't have access to typical loans. What class was she working on?

There were a few more books on microfinance, and then he picked up one called *The Making of Haiti*.

Wait—Haiti? Dr. McGovern had assigned each group a country, and their project centered around researching and designing a strategy to improve economic growth.

An email with their assignments had come in earlier that week, and they'd been assigned to Haiti.

"All this is for *our* project?"

"Yes." She made a grab for the book, but he held it out of her reach. "I'm still thinking it through." She squared her shoulders and looked him in the eye. "But... yeah. I think we should consider focusing on microfinance."

"Hmmm..." he murmured, cocking an eyebrow. "Yeah, I don't know." He already had some ideas for their project, and microfinance wasn't on the list.

This time she managed to snatch the book away. "Hey, don't dismiss it because it's not your idea."

"It's not about whose idea it is—"

"Look," she interrupted. "I've seen a bunch of projects from past years, and most of the time, they focused on national economic growth—things like bringing manufacturing and jobs to cities."

Yeah, that was along the lines of what he was thinking.

She shook her head as if she could read his mind. "But in a place like Haiti, many people are living in rural areas. They don't have the access to do those jobs, so the poorest people are still left behind." Her voice picked up speed. "I think we should focus our plan on microfinance—empowering women in rural areas to increase their incomes through small businesses. This will lead to education for their children, who will be qualified to do higher-level jobs, building a stable middle class." Her eyes met his and didn't waver. "I planned to look over a few more books tonight and have an outline for you tomorrow. But you get the idea."

Gabe's gaze skimmed across this girl who suddenly had his academic career in her hands, and the word that came to mind was *mousy*. She was skinny—too skinny—or maybe it was that she was swimming in another too-large T-shirt and baggy jeans that pooled around her ankles. The purple smudges under her eyes seemed more pronounced than they had earlier that week, and her dark hair hung too long down her back, kind of trailing off at the ends the way her voice did when she talked.

Well, the way her voice trailed off when she talked... before she started talking about their project.

He squeezed the ache in the back of his neck. Her suggestion, well, it made sense. In fact, it was a pretty good idea. It would be different from what the other groups were doing and would help them stand out. It was also not a direction he would have gone in on his own.

Maybe she wasn't as nervous and intimidated as he thought.

He sat down in a chair and picked up one of the books. "Okay. Tell me more about what you're thinking."

Anna smiled and dropped down in the chair next to him. "Well..." She laid out what she'd read and showed him several pages of notes. He asked questions, made a few comments, and threw out a couple of his own ideas, which she added to the notebook.

They sat and talked for three more hours.

When they finished, they had an entire plan for the project

written out in Anna's notebook, with a list of next steps and a timeline for when to complete everything.

Gabe sat back in his chair and studied Anna with grudging respect. Not only did she have some decent ideas, but she was organized, too.

They agreed to still meet the next day, but the library wouldn't be as empty tomorrow as it was tonight, and they wouldn't be able to talk and spread out without bothering people. Gabe briefly considered the study room at the frat house, but taking Anna there on a Sunday after a big party was out of the question. The house would be a disaster of liquor bottles, pizza boxes, and people passed out on couches in the living room. Anna already thought he was an irresponsible frat boy.

Not that he cared what she thought about him.

"We can work at my parents' house. They live nearby, and my dad has a home office. We can talk and spread out our stuff, and nobody will bother us."

Anna bit her lip. "Your parents' house? We won't bother *them*?"

It never occurred to Gabe that his parents would mind if he went over to work with a partner from class. He and his siblings had been in and out of the house with a steady stream of friends for his entire life. His mother wouldn't know what to do without a regular crowd to feed and entertain. "No, of course not. I go over every Sunday anyway."

"Really?" Anna's eyes widened. "Why? Does your mother do your laundry?"

He sighed. After three hours of collaborating—very amicably—on their project, he hoped she would've developed a little more respect for him. "I do my own laundry, thank you."

Anna's lips twitched in what might've been a smile. Was she messing with him?

"Actually, I go over for dinner." Gabe stood and packed up

his bag. "My brother and sisters are usually there, too. Sunday dinner is kind of a family ritual." He shrugged. "What about your parents? They don't mind that you're out until..." He checked his phone. "Jeez. One in the morning?"

Anna stared at the books she was holding. "Oh, it's just my mom and me. And she usually works nights at a nursing home, so..." She spun on her heel and carried the books to a library cart.

Gabe raised his eyebrows. He and his siblings used to have a strict curfew when they were in high school. And where was her dad? He followed with another pile of books. "How do you usually get home?"

"The bus. I think it'll still be running since it's Saturday night."

Maybe if her mom worked nights, she didn't know Anna was out so late. No way she'd want her daughter riding with all the creeps on the bus at one in the morning.

"I'll drive you."

Anna looked up sharply. "Oh, no, you don't have to. The bus is fine, honestly. I take it all the time."

"Listen, kid. I know you think I'm an asshole frat boy—"

"I don't think that!"

"—but I'm not about to let you go home on the bus all by yourself at one in the morning, okay?"

Anna hesitated and then nodded. "Okay. Thanks."

They headed out the library doors and down the street. The temperature had dropped about fifteen degrees since the sun went down, and Anna folded her arms across her faded T-shirt. Gabe shrugged out of his zip-up sweatshirt and held it out to her. She looked at him sideways and then slowly reached out and took it.

"Thanks."

They walked for a few minutes, and then Gabe broke the silence. "So, how did you manage to get McGovern to admit you into the class? I know you're the best and the brightest and all that, but most of us have been taking prereqs for three years."

"Oh, you know." Anna flashed him a crooked smile. "I had an affair with her."

He let out a startled laugh. Dr. McGovern had married one of her former graduate assistants, and rumor was the entanglement had started while the assistant was still a student. He wouldn't have expected Anna to pay attention to gossip, let alone make a joke about it.

"That plaid couch in her office is more comfortable than it looks," Anna deadpanned.

Gabe shook his head, still chuckling. "I'll never look at that woman the same way again."

They walked in silence for another minute, and then Anna said in a low voice, "Actually, I read her book."

Gabe stopped walking. "Now I know you're lying. No way you read *The New Principles of Economics.*"

Dr. McGovern's book was legendary among the economics students. Many had tried to read it, including Gabe, but nobody he knew had gotten past the second chapter. At 750 pages, it was long-winded, rambling, full of obscure terms, and impossible to follow. Gabe's copy was currently propping open his bedroom window.

"Yep, and then I went and asked if we could discuss it. I sat on that couch in her office for *two and a half hours*. I take it back. It is *not* more comfortable than it looks."

Gabe grinned with admiration. She'd impressed him just by reading that awful book, but actually going in to discuss it took way more nerve than he'd given her credit for.

"I *did* take some of the prerequisites, so I asked if I could take her class. She signed my paper right away." Anna giggled, reminding him of his little sister, which was kind of refreshing. Anna seemed so serious and reserved, it was easy to forget she was just a kid. "Believe me, having an affair with her would have been easier."

He laughed. "I'll keep that in mind when I have to ask for grad school recommendations."

They arrived at Gabe's car, and he opened the door for her. Anna directed him to her neighborhood and then asked about grad school. He told her about his applications and the personal statement he'd written. For the second time that evening, Anna surprised him. She was easy to talk to and had some pretty smart ideas. Most of his friends in the fraternity were engineering or computer science majors, so they weren't really equipped to talk about econ theories. Plus, he and the guys didn't have that kind of relationship.

The ten-minute drive to Anna's house passed quickly. As they crossed the Bloomfield Bridge into Pittsburgh's Lawrenceville neighborhood, Gabe realized he'd grown up only a few miles from where she lived, but he'd never had a reason to go there before.

He'd heard from somewhere that, thirty years earlier, Lawrenceville had been a nice neighborhood with sturdy brick row houses. But Gabe knew that these days it was mainly known for its drugs, crime, and prostitution. As he steered his car up her street, they passed more than a few boarded-up windows and crumbling porches.

Gabe stopped the car, and as Anna shrugged out of his sweatshirt and grabbed her bag, he studied her house. She lived in a large Victorian that years ago had probably been the home of a wealthy family, but at some point, it had been cut up into apartments, which was evident by the number of battered mailboxes nailed to the brick wall. The porch hadn't seen a coat of paint in at least three decades, and the steps leading to the front door looked like they'd blow away in the next strong wind.

Gabe tried not to be a snob. Maybe it was very nice inside.

They made plans for him to pick Anna up the next day, and

she climbed out of the car. He stayed in park to make sure she got in okay. As she made her way to the door, he watched her hop over a treacherous plank of wood on the stairs and sidestep an old can of instant coffee that looked like it was doubling as an ashtray. She put her key in the front door and waved as she went inside.

As she was about to close the door, he rolled down his window. "Hey, kid."

She swung the door back open. "Yeah?"

He grinned at her. "Nice work today."

"You, too." When she relaxed, her smile really lit up her face.

He watched her disappear inside and drove off, chuckling at her story about McGovern's book.

It wasn't until he was halfway home that he swore under his breath and smacked the steering wheel. He'd completely forgotten about that sorority girl he'd meant to meet up with back at the frat house.

# THREE

Less than twenty-four hours later, Anna was back in Gabe's car on the way to his parents' house.

The neighborhood was only fifteen minutes from her apartment, but it was like traveling to another planet. What did people even do with all that space inside those giant mansions?

It was mortifying to imagine what Gabe must have thought of the state of her apartment building when he dropped her off last night, especially when she had a feeling his family lived in one of these fancy houses. She could've insisted on taking the bus so he wouldn't have to see it, but it hadn't seemed like he'd been willing to take no for an answer, a fact that surprised her. Anna would have guessed he'd be eager to ditch her and get back to whatever parties or bars he usually frequented on a Saturday night.

She crossed her arms over her chest, remembering the unexpected softness of his sweatshirt and the woodsy scent that had enveloped her when he'd handed it over. Was it possible she'd been wrong about Gabe? The truth was that the guy she'd dismissed as a careless frat boy only days earlier had worried more about her well-being last night than anyone had in—

Well, in longer than she wanted to think about.

Anna hadn't pushed very hard to take the bus last night because she was so tired of looking over her shoulder. Just once, she wanted to know someone was checking to make sure she got home okay.

Gabe turned the car onto a quiet side street and then into a driveway, stopping next to a big, sprawling maple tree. While he gathered his books, Anna studied the house.

Gabe's childhood home was a three-story brick Victorian with an enormous porch that spanned the entrance. In beds in front of the house, plants and flowers grew randomly, as if someone had tossed handfuls of seeds just to see what would pop up. From her attempts to grow the yellowing, limp ivy in cracked terracotta pots on her narrow apartment windowsill, Anna knew someone had put a lot of time and love into making that garden look effortless.

She got out of the car, stepping onto a red brick driveway set in a herringbone pattern that led to a detached garage in back. A basketball hoop hung on the wall above the garage doors, and a basketball sat in a flowerpot at the edge of the yard. A little girl's bike leaned against the wall with pale-yellow and white streamers waving from the handlebars.

It took Anna a moment to recognize the boulder sitting on her chest.

*Longing.*

What would it have been like to grow up this way?

It wasn't a feeling that she indulged in very often. Dwelling on what other people had didn't do her any good. And she knew better than anyone that something might look nice on the outside, but who knew what was really going on beneath the surface?

They climbed the porch steps and headed for the front door. Anna didn't notice the older woman sitting on the wicker loveseat until the diamonds on her mottled hand glinted in the sunlight.

The woman gazed into the front yard, nodding her gray head over and over.

"Hi, Grandma," Gabe said, leaning down to kiss her wrinkled cheek.

Gabe's grandmother blinked and stared up at Gabe, her expression blank. She blinked a few more times and then cocked her head. "What did you call me?"

"I called you Grandma." Gabe adjusted a corner of the blanket sliding off her lap. "I'm your grandson Gabe."

The woman stared for another moment, and Anna had a feeling she wasn't really seeing him. Then she gave a tiny shrug and shook her head.

"This is my friend Anna." Gabe gestured in Anna's direction. "She's here to work on a school project with me. Anna, this is my grandmother, Dorothy."

"Hi, it's nice to meet you."

Dorothy looked at Anna, nodded with a faint smile, and then turned back to the garden. She rocked gently back and forth as if the loveseat were a porch swing.

"We're going to get to work," Gabe said. "But we'll see you later, okay?"

He tilted his head toward the front door, indicating Anna should follow him.

"Alzheimer's?" Anna whispered, when Dorothy was out of earshot.

Gabe nodded. "It started a few years ago, but it's gotten worse in the past year. She used to be the most energetic, involved grandparent, always coming to our games and school plays, and having all the kids stay with her for the weekend, you know?"

Anna didn't know. Not even close. But she nodded anyway.

"Now she doesn't even know who any of us are. It's been really hard on my mom."

"I'm sorry," Anna murmured, watching Dorothy pluck at the blanket. "It must be sort of like you lost her already, even though she's still here."

Gabe shot her a sideways glance, and Anna's face flushed. God, she should stop talking. Was it rude to imply that his grandmother was already gone when she was sitting right in front of them? She'd spent so much time trying *not* to talk to people, now she was clueless about how to actually do it.

"Yeah." Gabe's silver eyes clouded with sorrow as he took in a slow breath. "That's exactly what it's like. How did you know that?"

*Because that's how I felt about my mother for years.*

Before she blurted that out loud, Anna shrugged and mumbled, "Oh, I-I guess I can imagine." Yeah, definitely time to stop talking now.

But on her way across the porch, Anna paused and took one last look at Dorothy. She'd read a little bit about Alzheimer's once, when she'd missed the last bus home and gotten stuck at the library late at night. She liked to wander the section with all the medical books and daydream about being a doctor someday. Should she tell Gabe what she'd read?

"You coming?" he called to her.

Anna shook off the idea. Gabe probably wouldn't appreciate a sixteen-year-old thinking she knew anything about his grandmother's condition.

Gabe opened the front door and gestured for Anna to go first.

She stepped inside, and her grubby sneakers sank into a lush throw rug stretched across a gleaming hardwood floor. Kicking off her shoes, she took in as much as she could with a casual glance. To the left was a living room that Anna vowed to steer clear of. Even standing in the doorway, she was nervous around all that spotless cream-colored and pale-blue linen. But then again, maybe she'd take her chances if it meant she could check out the framed photographs showcasing a younger Gabe, and presumably his siblings, on the mantel. Gabe *must* have gone through an awkward phase. Otherwise, it just wasn't fair.

The room to the right with the huge mahogany desk and big, shiny computer had to be his dad's office. An upholstered chair sat in a corner with a reading light perched over it, and a shelf of books spanned an entire wall. Gabe wasn't kidding when he said his parents had plenty of space for them to work.

He led Anna straight down the hall to the back of the house where they came to a bright, sunny kitchen with white cabinets, dark countertops, and an island surrounded by barstools. Large windows overlooked the backyard, and French doors led out to a deck. Tucked away in one corner was a cozy breakfast nook.

The kitchen was about as big as her entire apartment, and it was the warmest, most inviting place Anna had ever been. Fresh herbs and a colorful bowl of fruit sat on the island, glass panels gleamed in upper cabinets displaying neat stacks of handmade pottery, and linen curtains fluttered in the windows.

A middle-aged blond woman stood over a pot at the restaurant-grade stove, stirring something that smelled delicious. She looked up as they approached, and her face broke into a grin. "Gabriel!" She wiped her hands on an apron decorated with little-kid handprints and hurried over to hug Gabe.

Gabe hugged her back. "Hi, Mom."

Another fragment of longing slid into Anna's heart. What she would've given to go home and find her mom waiting, happy to see her.

Gabe let go of his mother, and his hand brushed Anna's shoulder. "Mom, this is Anna."

Even though Gabe's mother was dressed casually in a pair of black yoga pants, a turquoise zip-up workout jacket, and had an apron tied around her waist, she carried herself with the elegance of someone who was used to being wealthy and comfortable. There wasn't a hint of gray in her chin-length blond bob or an extra pound on her lean, muscular frame. A gold necklace hung below her throat, and a pair of diamond studs glinted in her ears.

Anna subconsciously touched the pendant hanging around her own neck before tugging her cardigan around her, glad she'd thought to put on her best jeans and sweater that morning. But Gabe's mother didn't spare a glance at Anna's clothes. Her pale-blue eyes found Anna's, and her wide smile radiated warmth. "Gabriel told me about your project. Welcome."

"Thanks for letting us use your office, Mrs. Weatherall," Anna said.

"Oh, call me Elizabeth. I'm happy to have Gabe and his friends here anytime. You'll stay for dinner, won't you?"

Anna wanted to curl up in the breakfast nook and stay forever. But she hadn't grown up in a world where people invited her to anything. Was Elizabeth just being polite?

"Oh... I don't want to... impose."

Gabe smiled. "Stay for dinner. My mom always makes enough to feed fifty people. And she loves to have guests because then my obnoxious siblings have to behave."

"You mean because then my obnoxious *son* has to behave." Elizabeth rolled her eyes at Anna, as if she were in on the joke. "Please stay. We have plenty of food, and we'd love to hear more about this college program that you're enrolled in."

A tantalizing garlic-and-tomato smell wafted from the pot on the stove, and Anna's mouth watered. The only food she had at home was a box of cereal and a couple of cans of tuna. There wouldn't be anything else until she got paid on Friday, so that was pretty much dinner for the week.

"I'd love to. Thanks."

Gabe grabbed a couple of sodas from the fridge and handed one to Anna. "We'll be in the office. Thanks, Mom."

. . .

They sat in front of the computer, going over the details of their project, searching the internet for data to back up their ideas, and occasionally arguing over a point. Just as Anna's stomach growled, and she wished she'd had a granola bar or something at home to bring in her bag, Elizabeth tiptoed in and placed a tray of sandwiches and fruit on the desk next to them.

Anna didn't want to seem greedy, so she slid two sandwich halves and a small bunch of grapes on her plate. But later, when Gabe left to go to the bathroom, she grabbed another sandwich, wrapped it in a napkin, and stuffed it in the bottom of her backpack, along with an apple.

She settled back into the reading chair in the corner and looked around the room. Above the computer hung a vintage map of the United States, and Anna's attention was drawn to the left side of the frame, almost but not quite to the Pacific Ocean. *California.* Every time she walked past the globe in the lobby of the library, she gave it a spin, her finger sliding to the little black dot that marked the city of San Francisco.

Gabe's footsteps thumped down the hall, and Anna sat up straight, yanking her attention back to her present location. "What do you think; have we done enough for today?" Gabe asked when he returned to his chair.

At that moment, the office door flew open and a girl a few years older than Anna burst into the room. "Gabe! Mom said you're bringing a *girl* to dinner!" She spotted Anna. "Oh, oops... sorry."

Anna blinked as she took in the girl's combat boots, baggy camouflage pants, and fitted black T-shirt with the words *Girls just wanna have fun-damental rights* printed across the front. Her platinum-dyed pixie cut was almost as short as Gabe's hair and stood up in carefully crafted spikes. Thick black eyeliner circled her silver-blue eyes, and rows of tiny hoop earrings lined both her ears. She had to be Gabe's sister. It wasn't just the eyes that matched; she had his same inordinate good looks and confident way of carrying herself.

Gabe gestured to the girl. "Anna, this is my sister Rachel. Rachel, this is Anna from my econ class."

"Hi." Anna pushed a lock of hair behind her ear and then regretted the nervous gesture. She dropped her hand into her lap.

Instead of greeting her back, Rachel turned on Gabe, her eyes flashing. "Jesus, Gabe!" She walked over and smacked him hard on the arm.

"Ouch! What the hell, Rachel?"

"What is the matter with you? She's, like, fourteen years old! This is a new low, even for you. What, did you run out of girls your own age?"

Anna looked back and forth between Rachel and Gabe. Oh my God, Rachel didn't know they were working on a project. She thought Anna was *dating* Gabe. She shook her hair around her face to hide her burning cheeks.

Gabe sat back in his chair and rolled his eyes. "Calm down, Rachel. She's my partner for a class project. We were *working*, until you barged in and interrupted us."

Rachel stepped back and surveyed the papers strewn across the desk and the spreadsheet open on the computer. "Oh." She flashed them a tiny, chagrined smile. "Well. Mom didn't mention that part." She turned to Anna and looked her up and down.

Anna squirmed under the scrutiny.

"How old are you?" Rachel demanded.

"I'm—"

"She's sixteen," Gabe said shortly.

"Really?" Rachel peered at Anna again. "Are you, like, some kind of genius?"

Anna opened her mouth to explain, but before she could,

Gabe barked, "Yes, she's a child prodigy." He waved his hand in the general direction of his sister. "Anna, Rachel is a freshman at the all-girls college in Shadyside. A women's studies major, of course. And in the month that she's been there, she's decided that I represent the evil patriarchy."

Anna pulled her shoulders back, determined to get control of this conversation. Before she could think too much about it, she blurted out, "Isn't it usually referred to as a women's college, not *girls'*? It's not a preschool."

Rachel snorted.

Gabe raked his hand through his hair, making it stick out sideways, and turned to his sister. "Rachel, as you can probably tell, Anna also has a deep contempt for fraternity guys and is only working on this project with me because she thinks I can help her get an A in the class. Otherwise, she wouldn't be caught dead with me. So you two have a lot in common."

*Really?* Anna raised her eyebrows. "Actually, I'm helping *him* get an A in the class. But everything else he said is pretty accurate."

Gabe flopped his head against the back of the chair and sighed as Rachel bent over with laughter.

"Oh, this is priceless," she said with a gasp. "Are you guys done here? Anna, come sit with me on the porch. I think we're going to be friends."

Gabe waved his hand in a motion to go, and Anna followed Rachel into the hall. Behind her she heard Gabe call out, "Rachel, she's too young for you to date, too, so don't even think about it!"

"Shut it, Gabe!" Rachel called back.

Anna's face flushed again.

Anna and Rachel sat on the porch chatting about Rachel's major in college, Anna's plans to apply next year, and all the favorite books they had in common. In another world, Rachel was exactly the kind of girl she would've been friends with. Anna curled her legs under her as they gossiped about classes and teachers and let herself pretend for a little while.

Pretty soon, though, Rachel asked about her parents. It was a regular kind of curiosity about where she came from and what her mom and dad did for work, but the questions snapped Anna from her fantasy. This was why she avoided making these kinds of connections. Friends expected to know normal stuff about your life, and nothing about Anna's life was normal. Rachel wasn't deterred by her vague, mumbled answers and attempts to change the subject, so Anna escaped into the house, making excuses about finding a bathroom.

Elizabeth found her hovering in the hallway and, as if sensing her unease, asked if she wanted to help make a salad. Anna gratefully accepted. She was standing at the kitchen island, chopping carrots and peppers, when a man who had to be Gabe's dad came in through the back door and stopped at the stove to kiss his wife. They chatted for a minute about his golf game, and then he turned to Anna.

"Gabe mentioned he'd be bringing a friend. I'm John." He held out his hand to shake hers.

Anna blinked in surprise at the formality and then dropped her knife on the cutting board, reaching out to return John's firm handshake. She tried not to stare as he settled on a stool across the island.

Gabe had mentioned his dad was a doctor, but John was more like a doctor on a TV show than any doctor she'd seen in real life. He was as tall as Gabe and only slightly more filled out, with a solidness that comes with age. His blue eyes were darker than Gabe's, and his almost-black hair showed streaks of silver, but his straight nose and strong jaw matched his son's. It was like she was looking at Gabe thirty years in the future.

John stared intently from across the kitchen island as he

peppered her with questions. *Where do you go to high school? What is the college program you're doing? What are your grades like? SATs? Where are you applying to college?* He nodded as Anna stammered out her responses. It felt more like a job interview than Sunday dinner conversation, and she hoped she was giving the right answers.

After a nerve-wracking couple of minutes, John got up to get a beer from the fridge and told her that it sounded like she had good prospects, so she assumed she'd passed the test. Still, she was glad when Gabe wandered into the kitchen, giving John one of those half-hug, half-back slaps, and taking the focus off her.

"How are your applications coming?" John set the beer down on the counter.

Gabe's smile faded. "Good."

"Your personal statement done?"

Gabe walked to the refrigerator, opened it, and then closed it without taking anything out.

"Gabe?" John prompted.

Gabe sighed. "Wrote a draft yesterday."

Anna peeled a cucumber and followed him with her eyes. He'd seemed pretty eager to talk about his applications on the drive home last night, so she wondered what this sudden reluctance was about.

John nodded. "Well, make sure you get some eyes on them before you send them in."

Something flashed across Gabe's face—annoyance maybe? And then almost imperceptibly, he rolled his eyes. "Of course."

Anna was so busy wondering about that exchange that she didn't notice the tall, stocky man walk into the kitchen until he was halfway across the room. He wore a paint-spattered T-shirt, well-worn Carhartt work pants, and brown work boots. Anna's first thought was that he'd been hired to work on the house. But then he greeted Gabe with a punch on the arm, and when they stood next to each other, she saw the resemblance.

Gabe's brother. He was unexpected, especially next to John in his golf shirt, and Elizabeth in her diamonds. She felt slightly better about her own jeans and thrift-store cardigan. He leaned in to give John one of those half hugs, but it ended up being more of an abrupt pat on the back.

"Do you think you could clean up a little before you come into the kitchen?" John muttered in a voice so low she almost missed it. "At least take off those dirty boots."

The brother and Gabe shared a glance, and Gabe shook his head. Elizabeth walked over and squeezed the brother's shoulder.

Before Anna could spend much time wondering about the exchange, he noticed her behind the island. "Hey, I'm Matt."

"Anna. Hi. I'm working with Gabe on a class project." She blurted it out before anyone else assumed that Gabe was some kind of pervert, bringing teenage girls home with him.

Gabe was quick to jump in and add, "Anna's a junior in high school. She's doing a special program where she takes college classes."

Matt wrinkled his nose and shook his head. "Oh, man, I'm sorry. You must be pretty smart to do a program like that. How'd you get stuck with the dumbest guy in the class as your partner?"

Anna shrugged, biting her lip to hide her smile. "I pulled the short straw."

Matt laughed as Gabe looked at her with feigned outrage, turning his palms upward in a *what-the-hell?* motion.

A few minutes later, Rachel came into the kitchen. Matt grabbed her in a hug, shifting his arm around her platinum head until he had her in a headlock. "Anna, have you met Rachel yet?"

Rachel shoved her elbow into Matt's side, and he let her go with a grunt.

Anna leaned against the counter, taking in the teasing and banter between the siblings. She'd always wanted a brother or sister, but it had only ever been her and her mom. What would it have been like growing up with a whole big group looking out for each other, instead of being alone all the time? Would things have turned out differently? Or would her mom have only ended up in even more desperate circumstances with more kids to care for?

She felt movement next to her and looked down to find a little girl about eleven years old. Her hair matched Elizabeth's blond, and she had the same blue eyes as the rest of the family. Probably the owner of the yellow bike in the driveway. How many family members were there? It seemed like every time she turned around, another person appeared, like they belonged to some sort of giant sitcom family where zany things happened but, by the end of the thirty-minute episode, everything turned out okay.

And maybe for some lucky people, everything *did* turn out okay.

"Who are you?" the girl demanded.

"Anna. I'm Gabe's friend."

"I'm Leah." She stepped back and studied Anna. "You don't look like Gabe's other girlfriends."

Anna wasn't sure whether to laugh or take offense. She settled for a wry smile. Leah was only telling the truth. "Yeah, we're just friends."

Leah nodded as if that made more sense.

"Leah, honey, can you wash your hands and set the table, please?" Elizabeth cut in. "Dinner will be ready in ten minutes."

Anna pushed away from the kitchen island. "Let me help you." She followed Leah into the dining room with a stack of dishes while Gabe and the others stayed in the kitchen, pouring drinks and dressing the salad. Anna was grateful for the momentary reprieve. There'd been more conversation, laughter, and noise in the Weatheralls' kitchen in the past ten minutes than in her own apartment in the past year. It was overwhelming. And wonderful.

All day, she'd been struggling to do and say the right thing, to come up with smart, creative ideas for their project, to keep up with Gabe's siblings' jokes. And then there was that grilling by John. Somehow, in the past few hours, she'd developed a strange desire to impress Gabe and his family, and she had no idea where it was coming from.

She'd never cared about fitting in before. Usually, she hoped nobody would pay any attention to her at all. The more she blended into the background, the less likely it was that anyone would ask questions about who she was.

Or go poking around in her life and find out what she'd done.

# FOUR

*Thunk. Thunk.*

Anna did her best to concentrate on the economics book in front of her, but it was impossible with Gabe pacing the office and taking shots at the garbage can with crumpled-up pieces of paper.

*Thunk.*

Earlier that week, when they'd talked about working on their project, Anna had suggested they meet at the library. They could get their work done and then go their separate ways without getting sucked into all the jokes and family stuff at his parents' house. But Gabe had argued that the library would be uncomfortable. They'd have to whisper, or they'd bother other students, and there'd be no place to spread out.

A discarded to-do list banked off the wall and landed in the garbage can with another *thunk*. Gabe spread his arms and jumped up and down as if he'd just scored the winning point in the championship game.

Maybe he was right about them bothering people in the library.

"Can you focus here?" Anna waved a book at him, and a handful of crumpled papers came flying at her.

"Loosen up, kid," he said with a grin. "We've been working for hours."

She scooped the balled-up papers with both hands and tossed them back. He ducked, and the papers sailed past him. In a swift move, he spun around and picked up the garbage can. Before she could react, he tipped it over her head. Balls of paper rained down and landed in her lap.

Her mouth fell open. "Oh my God!"

His silver eyes shined with laughter, and her stupid, stupid heart fluttered.

None of this would've happened in the library.

Anna stood up, letting the papers slide to the floor. "I take it this means we're done working?" She grabbed the garbage can and crouched down, focusing on the rug as she scooped up the mess.

Still laughing, Gabe moved in to help her, and his shoulder bumped hers. A flush slowly traveled up her cheeks. His woodsy scent drifted across her, and she quickly stuffed the last of the papers into the can and scrambled to her feet.

She needed to get it together and stop acting like a silly teenager with a crush. Gabe was her project partner, and that was it. So what if he was the smartest guy she'd ever worked with, and they were on the exact same page about their project? Or if he laughed at her stupid jokes and actually seemed to think she was funny. It didn't mean they were friends. Gabe was older, popular, confident in ways she couldn't even begin to imagine. Guys like Gabe weren't friends with girls like her, and she knew better than to get distracted by him. She had less than two years until graduation, and she'd be an idiot to lose sight of that because some cute boy was nice to her.

Or because he had the kind of family she'd always dreamed about.

Gabe's mother asked her to stay for dinner again, and Anna knew she should politely decline and grab the next bus home. But the smells coming from the oven were too tempting to pass up, and soon she was back in the kitchen, laughing with Gabe and his siblings.

Matt's girlfriend, Julia, was there, too, giving her a warm smile and murmuring, "Welcome to the circus, Anna."

And Anna felt welcomed, and warm, and comfortable in a way she couldn't explain but that she hadn't experienced since before everything fell apart.

But she didn't belong here, and as the jokes, teasing, and general pandemonium continued through dinner, a heaviness settled in her chest. She could get used to this. And she was smart enough to know that would be a terrible idea.

After they'd cleaned up the dinner dishes, and the family broke off into smaller conversations, Anna slipped out of the kitchen and tiptoed down the hall. She knew she'd find a quiet place out on the front porch next to the garden. Gabe had said those flowers and plants were Dorothy's doing, and she'd lovingly tended them for longer than they'd expected after her diagnosis. Now, John and Elizabeth hired a gardener to come once a week. But Dorothy still liked to sit there in the evenings after dinner and gaze at the flowers she could no longer remember planting.

With that thought, Anna grabbed her backpack from the office before she headed out the front door to follow Dorothy to her usual spot. When she'd met the older woman last week, something had flashed in her mind that she'd been thinking about ever since. Anna had run to the library that morning, and now she had a gift of sorts for Dorothy.

"Hi." Anna stopped in front of the older woman, twisting the strap of her bag in her hands.

Dorothy turned to Anna, expressionless. "Hello," she murmured, and then gazed back out at the front yard.

"Do you like music?" Anna sank down on the chair across from her.

Dorothy nodded, but Anna didn't know if she was answering the question or doing that rocking thing again.

Anna dug in her bag and fished out a couple of old music CDs. She held up the plastic cases. "Do you know them? Frank Sinatra? Dean Martin? Ella Fitzgerald?"

Dorothy reached for a CD and traced her finger down the cheek of a smiling Dean Martin. She nodded faintly.

Anna had bought an old Discman at a yard sale on her way home from school last year, and it was worth every penny; if she kept her headphones on in the lunchroom at school, she could study without hearing the other kids' comments about the backpack she'd been carrying since middle school, the shoes that went out of style two years ago, or her free-lunch tickets.

That CD player had helped her through a lot of lonely times, and nobody could be lonelier than an old lady trapped in her memories.

"Do you want to listen?" Anna reached over and slid the headphones over Dorothy's ears, taking care not to snag her silver perm.

Dorothy's hands flew up to feel the cushiony ear covers, but she remained silent.

Anna pushed the play button, and the first few notes of a piano jingled faintly through the tiny speakers. Dorothy continued to press the headphones against her ears and stared out into the yard. After a minute passed, she looked at Anna with a warm smile.

Anna was so surprised she dropped back into her chair. Dorothy rocked back and forth, but this time she seemed to be moving to the music. A minute later, a rumble came from Dorothy's direction. A low, throaty hum. The song ended, and the next one started. Dorothy continued to hum, and when the song got to the chorus, she opened her mouth and began to sing.

Anna gasped, and her hand flew up to cover her mouth. Dorothy's voice was hoarse, probably from lack of use, but her tone was warm, and the notes were on key. Her whole face changed as she sang, cheeks flushing and eyes shining. Anna pressed her hands to her temples to will away the unexpected burn in her eyes.

Dorothy was in the middle of the next verse when Gabe's muffled voice inside the house yanked Anna back to reality. "Have you guys seen Anna?"

"She was here a minute ago," Elizabeth replied. "Do you hear someone singing?"

A pair of footsteps tapped down the hall. Anna sucked in a breath and sat up straighter. Elizabeth appeared in the screen door, her eyes blinking at a still-singing Dorothy, over at Anna, and then back at Dorothy. Her mouth dropped open, and her hand grasped the front of her apron. "Oh, my goodness!"

"Mom? What?" A heavier pair of footsteps raced down the hall, and Gabe appeared next to his mother. As he took in his grandmother singing, his eyes widened. "Wow."

Anna eyed Gabe and Elizabeth as they opened the screen door and walked onto the porch in stunned silence. Her heart pounded, and her mind whirled, searching for an explanation. But there was no explanation. She didn't know Gabe's family at all. Just because they'd been so welcoming last week, it didn't give her a right to mess with their sick relative. What had she been thinking?

Gabe turned to Anna. "Frank Sinatra?"

Anna rubbed her sweaty palms on her jeans and picked up the CD case with a shaking hand. "I thought it might be from her era."

At that moment, Rachel appeared in the doorway. "Who's singing?" she demanded. And then, "*Grandma?*" She shoved the screen door open.

Dorothy's song came to an end, and for a moment, the porch

was deathly silent. Not even a car passed on the road or a bird chirped in a tree. Anna shrank back into her chair and wished there was a way to sneak away with nobody noticing. But she was stuck, and it was her own fault.

Then Dorothy looked right at Elizabeth, smiled, and said, "Do you remember that song, Lizzie? Your daddy and I used to dance to it in the living room."

Elizabeth gasped behind the hand that was pressed to her mouth, and her face crumpled. Tears streamed down her cheeks as she hurried over to her mother and sat down next to her on the loveseat. Taking Dorothy's hand, she whispered, "Yes, I remember, Mama."

From the doorway, Rachel muttered, "Holy shit!" and then turned and ran into the house, probably to tell the rest of the family.

Anna was overwhelmed by the urge to cry, and she took a deep, shaky breath to get herself under control. Maybe it was Dorothy's unexpected awareness, or the way Gabe was staring at her, his expression unreadable. She longed to go back to two weeks ago, before she was assigned to work with Gabe, before she started acting like this impulsive person she didn't recognize.

"Maybe we should give them a few minutes?" Anna stood up, stumbled past Gabe, and fled into the house. She could sense him following her, but she picked up her pace down the hall. She didn't know where she was going; it wasn't like there was anywhere to hide. But she kept walking until he took her by the elbow, gently tugging her around to face him.

"How did you know the music would spark her memory like that?"

Anna shifted her weight and looked at his hand on her arm. "I-I didn't." She wrestled to keep the tremor out of her voice. "Not really. I mean, I once read in a neuroscience book that the receptors of the brain that remember and respond to music are the last to deteriorate when someone has Alzheimer's. So I thought maybe the CDs would help her connect to something." Anna studied her feet. There was a hole in her sock she hadn't noticed before.

"You just read that in a neuroscience book?"

It sounded even weirder when he said it out loud like that. "Yeah."

Gabe was quiet, and when she glanced up, he was looking at her oddly.

"What?" she asked warily.

"Nothing. You're just... unexpected."

Anna had no idea what he meant by that, and she was too afraid to ask. She slipped away, into the office to pack up her things and, when she couldn't avoid it anymore, shuffled down the hall to the kitchen to say goodbye.

The conversation dropped off when she walked in. Obviously, they were talking about her.

She hovered in the doorway, and finally, Rachel broke the silence. "That was seriously cool."

Leah jumped up and down. "You're just like the miracle worker in the book we're reading about Helen Keller at school!"

John pulled her aside and told her she had no idea how much this meant to Elizabeth, and they'd never forget it.

And as she and Gabe were leaving, Elizabeth grabbed her and crushed her in a hug. Then she squeezed Anna's hand and said, "Please come back next week. You're welcome, always."

Anna clutched Elizabeth's hand, feeling translucent and fragile, like leaves in a garden after the first frost. One strong wind would tear a hole right through her. She longed to come back next week. She longed for a place where she was welcome, always.

. . .

Gabe was quiet on the drive back to her apartment. Anna stared out the window, chewing on her thumbnail and wondering what he was thinking. He stopped the car in front of her house, and as she bent down to get her backpack from the floor of the car, she peeked at him through the hair falling across her eyes.

"Thanks for the ride." She turned to leave but gave a start when he touched her arm.

"Anna."

She stopped with her hand on the door handle. "Yeah?"

"Thanks for what you did for my grandmother."

"Thanks for..." What? *Being nice to me? Paying attention to me?* God, what did it say about her that she was just so damn grateful for a little bit of kindness? "Thanks for bringing me to hang out with your family. They're really great."

"They have their moments." His mouth twisted into a wry smile. "They're pretty big fans of *you*. As we were leaving, my mom made it clear that if I didn't show up with you next Sunday, I might as well not show up at all."

A warmth spread through her. *Careful,* a little voice in the back of her head warned, but even before the word was fully formed, she was opening her mouth to respond. "I'd love to go back next week."

Despite her late hours at the grocery store on Monday night, Anna got up early to meet Gabe at the library before their class on Tuesday. They found a quiet corner in one of the lounges where they could talk about their project and make a plan for Sunday, when they'd do their research at his parents' house before dinner with his family.

Sundays were usually her day off from the grocery store, when she caught up on studying, so hanging out with the Weatheralls was going to cut into her other work. To make up for it, she'd have to get up early to study before school the rest of the week. She told herself it was no big deal; she could sleep when she got into college.

When Anna arrived at class with Gabe that Tuesday, the girls he always sat with waved him over. He started to move in their direction and then stopped short, causing the student behind him to stumble and swerve to avoid collision.

Gabe glanced from the lone seat in the middle of the group of girls to Anna, and then his eyes shifted away from her.

Anna stood awkwardly next to him. *Oh, right.* Even though they were friendly when they worked on their project, it wasn't like they were *friends*. Especially when there were pretty sorority girls with long, shiny hair around.

Whenever she saw him across campus, Gabe was always surrounded by stylish, beautiful people, and that definitely didn't describe her. Although she was tall, she was skinny, practically flat-chested, and had drab brown hair she trimmed herself whenever she got around to it. Her high cheekbones and large brown eyes might've been attractive if she had the time or money to play them up with makeup. Which she didn't. And she'd never be able to pass her thrift-shop clothes off as the trendy outfits the college girls wore.

Not that she wanted Gabe to think of her like the steady stream of girls he flirted with. *No way.*

Anna stammered that she'd see him later and fled to an empty seat across the room. None of it mattered. What was important was to do well on the assignment, get an A, and move one step closer to a free ride to college and then medical school. One step closer to a better life.

Before she could stop it, the image of a rickety staircase descending into a dark basement flashed in her memory.

And one step closer to putting it all behind her.

She wasn't going to let Gabe distract her.

Anna sat down and dug through her backpack, pretending

to look for something important so she wouldn't be tempted to stare at him across the room.

Someone jostled her leg, jerking her from her thoughts. She glanced up from her bag to find Gabe grinning as he slid past her into the next seat. Anna's gaze flew across the room to the shocked expressions on his friends' faces, and then she looked down at her desk to hide her smile.

# FIVE

Gabe sat back in his chair and watched the cursor on his dad's office computer spin. *Application, transcripts, GRE scores, personal statement.* With one final *click*, there went his last grad school application.

After all the energy he'd put into them this fall, he expected fireworks, or music to play, or something. But nope. Just a generic message: *Thank you for your application. You will receive a confirmation email shortly.*

It was okay. He knew he'd see Anna later, and she'd be appropriately excited. Funny how that awkward, mousy girl he'd barely been able to talk to without an argument had turned out to be his biggest supporter when it came to his grad school stuff. She'd read his essays, offered some pretty smart suggestions, and even encouraged him to apply to the long-shot fellowships.

At first, they'd spent every Tuesday morning and Sunday afternoon working on their project. As it started to come together, though, they really didn't need to meet every week. But hanging out with Anna had become part of his routine, and he liked talking to her about other stuff.

He knew his friends were pretty confused about how much time he'd been spending with her. The guys in the frat liked to joke, calling her *your girlfriend* and making cracks about him being into younger women. Mostly, he ignored the taunting because he wasn't about to give them the satisfaction of seeing him get worked up.

Anna was in high school, and he'd never in a million years think of her as anything other than a little sister. But it bugged him that most people only saw what was on the surface—the timid, dowdy girl hiding behind her hair—and didn't bother to get to know her and find out how brilliant and hilarious she was. He was ashamed he'd almost made the same mistake.

Gabe rolled back the desk chair and headed into the kitchen to grab some coffee from the pot his mom made before her walk in the park. He could've submitted his applications at his house, but his parents' internet connection was more reliable since they weren't downloading porn like his roommates probably were. He laughed under his breath. At least he hoped his parents weren't downloading porn.

He was about to head back to the office to clean up his papers when his dad walked in through the back door. Gabe hadn't expected him home until that afternoon.

His dad stopped and did a double take, probably equally surprised to see his son standing there. "Gabe!" He chuckled. "I was expecting your mother. I thought you and Anna wouldn't be coming over until later."

"I'm just here to submit my grad school applications. I'll pick up Anna in a little while."

His dad's eyebrows rose. "You're submitting your applications today?"

Gabe blew out a breath. "I submitted. They're done."

"You didn't tell me you were doing that today."

"Didn't I?" Gabe knit his eyebrows together. "I thought I did. Last week, or..." Yeah, so that was a lie. He didn't want his dad up his ass about his applications, so he'd called the house before he came over that morning, making sure his dad was already out running errands.

"Well, congratulations." His dad slapped him on the back. "So, what's the plan now?"

"What do you mean, what's the plan? I wait to hear if I got in."

"And if you don't? What about job prospects? Setting up some interviews?"

Gabe opened his mouth and then closed it. Jesus. He'd hit "send" on his applications five minutes ago. Did his dad think he wouldn't get in? Or was he afraid if he loosened his grip for one minute, Gabe would start ripping up floorboards and installing drywall like his brother? What would his dad tell his golf buddies if both his sons ended up in working-class jobs?

It wasn't like Matt was screwing around. He owned his own business, made a good living, and his work was in high demand. But Matt had given up an opportunity for a career in medicine, and his dad had never gotten over it.

Shocking everyone, Matt had gone the blue-collar route, career-wise. He'd been all set to enroll in the pre-med program at Johns Hopkins when he took a summer job installing kitchen cabinets and reproducing antique moldings for house renovations in up-and-coming neighborhoods around the city. He had a real talent for it, and Gabe could still remember how happy Matt had been that summer, without the pressure to get straight As and ace the SATs weighing on his firstborn shoulders.

Once Matt had decided to defer college to make a go of his business, the expectations had shifted to Gabe. All of a sudden, his dad was grilling him about studying for exams over dinner and wanting to have conversations about how he saw his future. Gabe was well aware that studying economics at the local university wasn't quite up to par with medicine at Hopkins, at least in his dad's eyes. But it made his mother happy that he stayed close to home, and he'd pledged the same national fraternity his dad had been in at Yale.

John Weatherall's dream had always been for one of his kids to follow in his footsteps and go into medicine. Gabe wanted to please his dad, but when it came down to it, he found himself avoiding going home freshman year, changing the subject when his dad wanted to talk about declaring his major.

And then that C in organic chemistry had pretty much sealed the deal. Gabe had never gotten less than an A in any college class before—or since. But for some reason, he couldn't wrap his brain around those resonance structures and reaction mechanisms in o-chem.

It was almost like he was *trying* not to do well, his dad remarked, when the grades came out.

Gabe wasn't a psych major, so he didn't know what Freud would say about that.

And now his dad was right back to the same old refrain.

"There's still time to consider retaking that organic chemistry class next semester. Just to leave the option open."

Gabe had to get out of there. "Anna will be waiting for me to pick her up."

His dad nodded. At least he approved of Anna. "Sure. We can talk more about this later."

*Great. Can't wait.*

Gabe took off for Anna's house. He was early, so he sat in the car and waited. The front door opened, and a middle-aged guy with greasy hair and patchy stubble on his face wandered out. He lit a cigarette and popped open a can of beer.

Beer at eleven-thirty in the morning.

Gabe squinted at the house. The guy was probably another tenant. Gabe hoped he wasn't Anna's mom's boyfriend or something.

The guy went back inside, and a few minutes later, Anna came out. She ran across the porch and swung the car door open. The cold November air hit him as she slid into the seat. "Hi."

"Hey. How's your morning?"

"Good." She shrugged. "Just studying."

He inclined his head toward the house. "Is it just you and your mom living in your apartment?"

"Yes." She glanced at him sideways. "Why?"

"I don't know. You never talk about your dad."

She looked away. "I never met my dad."

Not having a dad didn't sound so terrible. But then Gabe felt like a total shit. His dad was a good guy and Gabe loved him. He just wished he'd lay off once in a while.

Anna turned in her seat to face him. "Hey, how was *your* morning? Did you do your applications?"

He started the car and busied himself with checking the mirrors. His earlier excitement was gone. "Yep."

"Gabe! That's great! Are you done?"

"Yeah."

"Wait until they *all* accept you, and then you have to make a decision about where to go."

See? Why couldn't his dad have reacted like that? Even if it was a little optimistic, his dad could have at least shown some enthusiasm.

"Yeah, we'll see." He pulled out onto the road and focused on the car in front of him. Anna didn't say anything, but he could feel her watching.

"What's going on with you?" she asked after a few minutes of silence.

"What do you mean? Nothing."

She reached over and poked his hand gripping the steering wheel. "You can loosen up there; it's not going to roll away."

He jerked the car to a stop at a red light and then turned to look at her. "I submitted all my applications today, and you know the first thing my dad said? *What if you don't get in?*"

She gasped.

"And the second thing he said? *Med school.*"

The light turned green, and he pressed his foot on the gas pedal, peeling into the intersection.

"When I was thinking about what programs to apply for, he was adamant I only try for the top schools. No safety schools like Penn State or Michigan. It's almost like he doesn't want me to get in because then he could start pushing for med school again."

"Hey." She shoved on his arm. "Pull over. You're driving like a maniac."

Gabe jerked the steering wheel to the right and pulled to the side of the road. He raked his hand through his hair. "Sorry."

"You know what? Let's not go over there today. To your parents'."

"Really?" He wasn't up for another chat with his dad. Chances were, he'd end up saying something shitty he'd regret later.

"Yeah. Can you drive without killing us? I'm going to take you somewhere."

He gave her the side-eye. "Where are we going?"

"You'll see."

She directed him toward the university but at the last minute had him make a right onto a road winding behind campus. When she told him to park, he stopped the car in front of a huge domed building made of glass and steel: Phipps Conservatory, a greenhouse and botanical garden.

"Have you been here lately?" she asked, her voice tinged with excitement.

"Ummmm, not since a school trip in about fourth grade."

"Really? You know our student IDs get us in for free, right?"

He was vaguely aware they had access to all the museums

and stuff, but he usually had other things to do with his free time.

The frigid wind cut through him as soon as they got out of the car. Hard to believe that, even last week, it still felt like fall. Now, the gray clouds on the horizon looked like they might bring some snow later. Anna's coat wasn't zipped, but she pulled it closed around her, and they ran for the entrance to the building.

They checked in at the desk, and then Anna led him through a large, domed room, full of trees and flowers. In the center, garden workers decorated Christmas trees and hung poinsettias for the holiday display.

"You should bring your grandmother here. I bet she'd love it," Anna mused.

Gabe stopped walking. Damn. Why hadn't he thought of that? His grandmother *would* love it. "That's a great idea. You should come."

"Really?"

Anna and his grandmother had formed a special bond since the music incident. Dorothy had mostly retreated into her own world again, but she'd become more animated when Anna sat with her on the porch.

"Yeah, let's do it next week."

She gave him that smile that lit up her whole face and led him through a couple more rooms to a door with a sign that said *Tropical Forest*.

The other rooms had been cool, but the tropical forest was a sauna, and the humidity seeped into his windburned cheeks and still-numb fingers. They strolled down a path lined with palm and banana trees, fat orange-and-purple birds of paradise, and pink bougainvillea. Crossing a bridge over a pond bursting with some kind of reedy plant and koi fish, they made a right behind a thatched hut displaying tropical spices.

It looked to Gabe like they'd hit the end, but then Anna

flashed him that grin again and stepped off the main walkway onto a small dirt path leading into a cluster of trees. She pushed aside a couple of giant leaves and disappeared behind them. Intrigued, he followed her.

After fighting his way through the palm fronds, he made it to the other side and came to an abrupt stop.

Anna sat on a stone bench in the center of a small clearing, surrounded by tropical flowers. The din of building mechanics, other visitors walking by, and the tropical bird noises piped in over the speakers were fainter back here. If he didn't know he was in the middle of the city, he would have easily believed he was deep in a jungle somewhere.

"Wow."

"I know. It's my favorite place. I like to come here and read."

He sank down on the bench beside her. "Thanks for sharing your secret spot with me."

"I can trust you with it, right?" She narrowed her eyes. "Don't bring any girls here to make out, okay?"

He laughed because he might've considered it. Except this was too special to share with just anyone, and he wouldn't have felt right doing that to Anna. "Never. I promise."

They sat for a while in the warmth and stillness. Tension seeped from Gabe's shoulders, and he tilted his head to the expanse of glass overhead. The sky was a pale, dull gray, but tiny white snowflakes swirled, shimmering and glinting as they hit the warm glass and turned to water droplets.

After a few minutes, Anna's voice cut through the silence. "If it makes you feel any better, I think you'd make a terrible doctor."

He let out a surprised snort and swung his head around to her, expecting a joking grin on her face. She gazed back, expressionless. Was she serious? The thing with Anna was she probably was. For some reason, her honesty struck him as hilarious.

"Well, thanks, I guess. I'm not sure that makes me feel

better, but I appreciate the effort." His shoulders shook as he tried to contain his laughter.

"I didn't mean it as an insult!"

"Sure."

"No, really." She elbowed him in the side. "Stop laughing. What I meant was, being a doctor is actually a job for an introvert. I know you're supposed to have a bedside manner and all that, but it's a lot of having your head buried in books and patient charts. I mean, can you imagine sitting in some med school basement dissecting a corpse for eight hours a day?"

He gave an exaggerated shudder.

"Right?" She continued. "I see how you are in class. You're in your element when you can jump into a big discussion or argue over some theory or other. Dr. McGovern says something controversial, and you start humming with excitement. You belong in an economic think tank where you get to be the expert who comes up with brilliant theories. And then argue with the other experts."

He stared at her. *Well, hell.* She was right. And it did make him feel better to think that just because he wasn't doing what his dad wanted, it didn't mean he wasn't doing the right thing.

He grinned and nudged her in the arm. "Well, what does that say about you? You want to be a doctor, but you love to argue."

She nudged him back. "I only love to argue with *you*. Everyone else thinks I'm that quiet girl who'd probably get along great with corpses."

He met her eyes, and they both started laughing. But deep down, something nagged at him. It was almost like she wanted people to think that. Not the corpses part, of course. But a few months ago, he'd had no idea Anna was one of the smartest people in their class. She wasn't really shy—she'd proved that on the first day when she'd told him off—so why didn't she speak up more? Why wasn't *she* the one arguing about economic theories, or at least raising her hand when she knew the answer?

They'd spent so much time together these past few months, and somewhere along the way, he'd started to consider Anna a good friend. In some ways, he knew her so well, but in others, he didn't know her at all. Her family, for instance. She'd said she'd never met her father, but she rarely mentioned her mother except to say she was working at the nursing home. And Anna never really talked about friends or going out with people at her high school. Was she as aloof there as she was in her college classes?

He glanced in her direction, and she gave him a crooked smile. "I'm glad we ended up working together on our project," she said.

"Me, too, kid." He bumped her shoulder with his.

Maybe he was reading too much into things. Anna was super smart and focused on her schoolwork. Not all teenage girls wanted to chatter on about friends and parties. Look at Rachel. She spent her weekends at political protests and volunteering at the women's shelter.

If there was something important going on in Anna's life, she'd say something. They were good enough friends now that she could open up to him.

# SIX

A cold wind buffeted Anna's threadbare coat, and she clutched the hat on her head to keep it from blowing away. Maybe it would snow later. Gazing up at the ashen clouds in the sky, a small thrill ran through her. A real Christmas dinner around a big dining table, complete with falling snow outside, would be like something out of a movie. Definitely not something she'd experienced in real life.

When Gabe's mother had asked about her plans for Christmas, Anna had been so flustered she'd blurted out that she and her mom were planning a quiet day at home. Elizabeth immediately invited them to dinner, and Anna didn't know how to say no, didn't *want* to say no, even though she should have.

Another gust of wind blew, and she tugged her coat closed. The sleeves slid past her wrists. She was going to have to buy a new one soon, and it put a damper on her Christmas cheer. Coats were expensive, even at Goodwill. She sighed and pushed the thought out of her mind as Gabe's car pulled up. She ran out and hopped in the front seat. The heat from the car and his grin drove away her gloomy thoughts. "Merry Christmas!"

"Merry Christmas. Is your mom on her way down?"

Anna's smile faltered. "Oh. Uh. No. I'm sorry. My mom can't come."

Gabe raised his eyebrows. "Oh. Is she okay?"

"Yeah. She"—Anna examined her hands as she ran through the excuse she'd rehearsed earlier that day—"had to work. Someone called in sick at the nursing home, and they asked her to fill in. I feel bad because your parents were so nice to invite her, and your mom's cooking extra and everything."

"It's fine. You know my mom cooks for an army anyway. She'll send leftovers home." Gabe gave her arm a little shove. "And, hey. I'm glad you're coming. Otherwise, you'd be sitting home alone on Christmas when your mom went to work."

"Yeah." Anna shrugged. She didn't want to talk about her mom anymore.

The snow began to fall in earnest as they walked in the Weatheralls' door. Elizabeth had decked out the house in garlands and white Christmas lights. Candles twinkled on the fireplace mantel, and a ten-foot tree filled an entire corner of the living room.

Anna bit back a gasp as she took in the scene. It really was like a movie. Snow fell in fat flakes outside the window, glittering on the tree branches and covering the yard in a white blanket.

The family gathered around the Weatheralls' enormous dining table to eat more courses of food than Anna had ever seen in her life. Afterward, they played a raucous game of charades that, this being the Weatheralls, was more competitive than a normal game would have been.

Anna soaked it in, happier than she'd ever been. Only once did a little voice pop up to diminish her joy, reminding her that someday she was going to regret this. That it would hurt like hell when she was all alone again. She shoved the voice aside.

At least she'd have happy memories, which was more than she could say before this.

It was close to midnight by the time Gabe drove her home. When they pulled up at her house, they were still laughing over the game of charades. As Anna turned to thank Gabe for a great Christmas, she spotted someone sitting on her front porch, and her laughter trailed off.

A man lounged on the beat-up couch someone had tried to pass off as patio furniture, his feet up on a plastic crate. Anna watched him take a drag on his cigarette and blow it out slowly. Smoke swirled around him, glowing in the amber porch light.

Anna's stomach clenched at the sight of him: Don, her landlord who lived in the apartment downstairs. She did her best to avoid him, and a few times she'd even climbed down the fire escape at the back of the building when she heard his voice in the hall.

Anna gave Gabe a bright smile and grabbed her bag. If she hurried, she could escape into the house before Gabe noticed him there. But as she swung the door open, Don stood up, yanking a Pittsburgh Steelers sweatshirt down over his gut and popping open a can of beer.

"I'll walk you in," Gabe muttered, grabbing his door handle.

"Oh, uh, you don't have to," Anna stammered. "It's just our landlord. He's harmless."

"It's fine. I'll walk you in," Gabe repeated in a firm tone, and Anna knew it was useless to argue.

Resigned, she got out of the car and shuffled up the porch steps with Gabe right beside her. She put her head down and nodded at Don. Maybe the holidays had warmed his heart enough to leave her alone.

But no, that was too much to ask. Halfway to the front door,

Don stepped in front of them. "Hey, genius, where's your mother?" he grunted, in a voice thick with smoke.

Anna gave him a hard look. "She's working."

Don scratched his belly and took a swig from his can of Iron City. "She'd *better* be working because she stiffed me on rent again this month."

Anna stole a glance at Gabe, who watched their exchange with narrowed eyes.

"I—" She pushed her shoulders back and used her dealing-with-an-angry-customer-at-the-grocery-store voice. "I'm sure it was a mistake. We'll get you the rest by the end of the week."

Anna tried to step around Don, but before she could make a move toward the door, his hand snaked out and closed around her upper arm. She winced and tried to wrench free. But despite the pain shooting to her shoulder, her first thought was, *Oh my God, this is* not *happening in front of Gabe.*

In less than a second, Gabe was between them, yanking Don away from her.

"*Don't touch her.*"

Don took a step back, his eyes scanning Gabe's Patagonia jacket, high-end Levis, and trendy sneakers. Then he turned to Anna with a chuckle. "I see you got yourself a rich college boyfriend. You always thought you were better than us here in the neighborhood, didn't you? Well, you still owe me the rest of my rent, and I want it now. A hundred bucks."

He held out his grubby paw like she was going to pull it from her pocket and hand it to him.

*Yeah, right.*

She didn't have a hundred dollars, and she wouldn't get paid for a few more days. Rubbing her arm where Don had grabbed her, she glanced at Gabe. She'd give anything not to have this conversation in front of him. "We'll have it to you by Friday."

"Friday's not good enough. I want it tomorrow, or I'm throwing you out on your ass."

"But—it's Christmas," Anna said, stalling for time. "The banks won't be open. Surely you can give us an extra day—" Or *three*. But she'd worry about that later, when Gabe wasn't standing there taking it all in.

"Bah. Freaking. Humbug," was Don's reply.

Gabe reached into his pocket and pulled out his wallet. "How much did you say? A hundred?"

"No." Mortified, Anna grabbed Gabe's arm and tried to shove his wallet away. "Gabe, I don't need your money. I can handle this."

But Don was already reaching for the bills. He took the money, made a display of counting it, and stuffed it in his pocket. "That should cover the rest of what you owe this month. Don't be late again next month."

Gabe nudged her toward the front door, and she went along because what else could she do? Wrestle the money from Don and give it back to Gabe?

"You didn't have to do that," she whispered, thankful for her anger because it was the only thing keeping her from crying. She pushed the key in the lock. "He was just bluffing to show off in front of you. I had it under control."

Anna shoved the front door open, and the stale smell of cigarette smoke wafted around them. There was another smell, too, something strong and sour. Her chest tightened as she imagined how Gabe saw the building. Ancient peeling wallpaper covered the hall, leaving the walls bubbled and textured like they'd developed some sort of skin disease. Water stains mottled the ceiling from the winter when the pipes had frozen and then burst, and a single yellowing light bulb swayed back and forth on a cord above them, casting eerie shadows on the walls.

She stomped up the stairs with Gabe following close behind

and stopped on the landing. "I'm going to pay you back on Friday," she muttered.

"I don't care about the money. I just don't want that guy harassing you."

Anna glared back at him. "*I had it under control.*" She was being rude, but she couldn't help it. Being rude saved her from facing her mortification.

Before Gabe could respond, she turned and marched to her apartment door. She fiddled with the lock—it always stuck, but she wasn't about to complain to the landlord—ignoring Gabe as he leaned his shoulder against the wall next to her.

"Look," he said. "Maybe you could handle it by yourself. But you didn't *have* to."

Anna concentrated on jiggling the key in the lock, tilting her head so he couldn't see her eyes fill with tears. She needed to get it together. If she started crying now, it might be the most humiliating thing that ever happened to her. Plus, Gabe would start asking questions she wasn't prepared to answer.

After a few aggressive turns, the lock popped, and Anna swung the door open. She stepped inside and turned around, holding the door just wide enough to fit her body. "Thank you for a lovely Christmas." She paused. "And for your help with the landlord. Have a good night."

But Gabe didn't take the cue to go. "I don't like leaving you alone with that jerk downstairs. Has he ever done that before?"

"Done what?"

"Manhandled you like that?"

Anna closed her eyes. This was a nightmare.

"He has, hasn't he?" Gabe took a step toward the door, and Anna yanked it closer to her shoulder, hoping he couldn't see inside. "Jesus, Anna. Does your mom know?"

"What? No. The landlord doesn't *manhandle* me. He's—" He's what? Was there any reasonable explanation for this whole scene that wouldn't have Gabe calling the cops? "He's drunk, and it's Christmas."

Gabe squinted at her. "That doesn't even make any sense."

"I mean, he's not *normally* drunk. He was probably celebrating the holiday and had a few too many. I'm as surprised as you are."

He didn't look like he believed her for one minute, and Anna's frustration grew. She'd become an expert at diverting attention these past few years. Why did Gabe have to be the one to see through her?

"Maybe I should stay until your mom gets home?" He leaned down to meet her eyes. "We can tell her what happened."

"No!" She immediately regretted the desperation in her voice when Gabe took a step back in surprise. But there was no way she could have him hanging around her run-down apartment, waiting for her mom. "She'll be home late, and I'm really tired. Honestly, the landlord is harmless. I'll dead-bolt the door, just in case."

When Gabe hesitated, she smoothed her face into a calm, neutral expression.

*Please. Please go.*

If he refused, she didn't know what she'd do. Finally, he nodded, and relief washed over her.

"You'll call me if you need anything?"

"Of course." Anna nodded. "Thanks again. For everything."

Before he could change his mind, she closed the door. Through the cheap aluminum, she heard him take a few steps and then shuffle to a stop. Anna jingled the chain lock and clicked the dead bolt with extra force so the noise would carry out into the hall. Then she pressed her ear to the door and listened as his footsteps slowly faded down the stairs.

With a sigh, she flung her coat over a chair and pulled on the thick wool sweater and brown Grandpa-slippers she wore all winter to keep the heating bills low. Then she flipped on the light, surveying her dingy apartment. The inside wasn't much better than the outside. She tried to keep it clean and neat, but there wasn't anything she could do about the worn gold carpeting, the dark brown cabinets coated in forty years of cheap lacquer, or the yellow cigarette-smoke stains on the walls.

She cringed, imagining Gabe there, shivering on the lumpy plaid couch, a relic from the 1980s, while he waited for her mom to come home. What would he think when he compared it to the warm, inviting house they'd just left? And what would he do when her mom never arrived?

# SEVEN

A few weeks later, Gabe stepped into the front hall of his parents' house and kicked off his shoes as his dad's voice drifted out from the living room. "Make sure you begin studying for the MCAT in your junior year, so you can take it in the spring."

"Okay," Anna replied. "That makes sense."

Gabe stepped into the living room doorway and found his dad and Anna sitting together on the couch, John leaning forward while Anna scribbled something into a notebook. Gabe's mom had sent him to the store to buy an onion for that evening's dinner, and it looked like Anna had ended up talking to his dad while she waited for him.

"Then submit your primary application as soon as the portal opens," John continued.

"Got it." Anna nodded, writing that down.

"Next... Oh, hello, Gabe. I didn't see you there." His dad nodded to acknowledge him.

"How's it going?" Gabe propped one shoulder against the doorframe.

"Anna and I were just chatting about medical school. Did you know she plans to apply after college?"

Of course Gabe knew Anna planned to apply to medical school. He'd only spent at least two days a week with her for the past five months, and this was a big deal for her. "Yeah, I think I heard something about it," Gabe said, unable to keep the hint of sarcasm out of his voice.

But it didn't matter, because this was John's absolute favorite subject, and he'd already turned back to Anna.

"As I was saying, next, you'll receive the secondary application."

Anna shot Gabe a tiny smile, acknowledging that *she*'d heard him, before adding John's information to her list in her notebook. She was obviously just humoring his dad because Gabe knew she'd already researched the medical school process extensively. But then, a minute later, John offered to go over some interview questions with her, and her eyes widened hopefully. So maybe she wasn't just being polite. "Really? You'd do that for me?" she asked, almost breathless.

"Of course I would." His dad gave her a smile. "I think you show a lot of promise."

Anna bit her lip and blinked. "That would be amazing."

John nodded. "Come over early next Sunday, and we'll talk about it then." He stood up and finally looked back at Gabe. "I'll let you two get back to your project now."

Anna stood, too, clutching her notebook to her chest. "Thank you so much for this. It means..." She paused, looking down at her striped socks. "It means a lot."

John headed out, and as Anna packed up her backpack so they could head across the hall to start their project, her brow furrowed. "Do you think your dad really meant it? That he wants to advise me?"

Gabe cocked his head, surprised by the question. "He wouldn't have offered if he didn't." If anything, his dad was a little *too* eager to help out when he ought to back off. But then Gabe immediately took that thought back. Anna didn't have a dad, and her mom was obviously working crazy hours just to pay the bills. Anna probably didn't have any adults in her life helping her with applications, or—if the number of times he'd found her working in the library at midnight were any indication—paying much attention to her at all.

Gabe promised himself he'd pull his dad aside and thank him for helping Anna out. It really was nice of him. Maybe he'd mention the thing that happened with her landlord at Christmas, too. Just to get his dad's take on it. For the past few weeks, since it had happened, the memory of that guy grabbing Anna's arm had left Gabe's heart racing every time he thought of it.

"Hey, Anna," Gabe said now, following her across the hall to his dad's office. "Can I ask you something?"

"Yeah?" She dropped her backpack on the chair.

"February first is coming up. I know your rent will be due soon, and I just wondered if the landlord is giving you any more trouble."

Anna froze, her face flushing crimson. "No." She turned away from him, pulling her economics book from her bag and banging it on the desk. "Don had been drinking because it was Christmas. I told you he's not normally like that."

"But what about rent this month? Do you need any hel—"

Her head started shaking back and forth before he could finish the sentence. "*No.*"

"Okay, well, if you do..." He had plenty of savings from working last summer for his brother's construction company. If it would get the landlord to lay off Anna, he'd happily give it all to her.

"We're fine. We've got it covered."

"Are you sure? Because—"

Anna whirled back around to face him, her hands flying to her hips. "Seriously, Gabe. I appreciate your concern. But I promise you it was all just a misunderstanding. My mom took care of it, and we're good now."

"She did?" Gabe searched her face. "So, you told her about how he cornered you on the porch? And"—he cringed—"grabbed you like that?"

Anna stared over his shoulder. "Yes." She finally sighed. "I told her."

"What did she do?"

"She went and talked to him." Anna waved a dismissive hand. "He won't give us any more trouble."

Gabe wasn't convinced. He'd seen the creepy look in Don's eyes, heard the mockery in his voice, and none of that was the result of him imbibing a couple of extra Christmas cocktails. The guy was a mean drunk, and probably mean when he was sober, too. Gabe hated to think what would happen if Anna and her mom were late on rent again. "You've got it covered for this month? But will you have enough for next month?"

"Gabe," Anna said, her voice measured. "I appreciate your concern, but—" She glanced around his dad's spacious office. "I have a feeling you've never lived paycheck to paycheck or have any idea what that's like. This is *normal* for us." She flushed even redder than before, and Gabe realized it had taken her a lot to admit that to him. "We always make it work, and we don't need to rely on other people to swoop in. My mom and I are fine. Please just let it go, okay?"

Gabe watched her press her hands to her bright red cheeks. Anna and her mom had been surviving for a lot longer than the few months he'd been in her life, and maybe she was right. They didn't need him to try to save them. Finally, he nodded. "Okay." He'd respect her wishes and let it go. For now. But Gabe wasn't making any promises that he'd let it go forever. From now on, he'd be keeping an eye on Don, and if that jerk even came near Anna, he would definitely be stepping in.

He didn't trust that guy for one minute.

# EIGHT

A few Sunday afternoons later, Anna wandered into the Weatheralls' kitchen to offer to help with dinner and found Elizabeth buried in a pile of recipe books.

Elizabeth looked up with her brow furrowed. "Can you believe Leah *just* told me she's supposed to bring cookies for the spring party tomorrow at school?"

Anna gave her an exaggerated cringe. "Tomorrow? That doesn't seem like much notice."

"You're exactly right," Elizabeth said with a laugh. "I was just looking for a recipe so I can throw something together." Of course, Elizabeth wouldn't have dreamed of sending anything store-bought, even if it *was* the night before the party.

"What can I do?" Anna slid onto the nearest stool and picked up a cookbook, eager to help. Elizabeth had been so welcoming these past few months, inviting Anna to stay for dinner every Sunday. Anna had yet to find a way to really thank her, other than offering to help out with dinner. Even that seemed more for her own benefit than Elizabeth's, though, since there was almost no place Anna would rather spend her time than in that warm, inviting kitchen.

"Aren't you and Gabe still working?"

Anna waved at the back door. "Matt dragged him outside to play basketball in the driveway."

"Well, if you're sure." Elizabeth opened one of the recipe books she'd been holding and slid it toward Anna. "If you can mix up this dough, I can get started on dinner."

In Anna's world, cookies came in a package labeled "Chips Ahoy," so she read and re-read the well-worn, butter-stained recipe and measured each ingredient twice. Eventually, she had a bowlful of dough that she rolled out and cut into the shape of flowers and baby chicks while she chatted with Elizabeth.

"Next week is Easter Sunday," Elizabeth reminded her, as she chopped a pile of herbs. "I was hoping your mom could join us for dinner. Do you think she might be available?"

"Um." Anna stared down at her cookie dough, concentrating on sprinkling the shapes with colorful sanding sugar. She probably shouldn't be surprised by the invitation. After all, they'd invited her mom for Christmas, too. "I think she'll probably have to work. Holidays are busy at the nursing home." How long would they continue to buy that excuse?

Elizabeth nodded. "Maybe you could ask her to look at her calendar and see if there's another day she could make it? We'd really love to meet her. Any Sunday would work."

The idea of her mom there, laughing with everyone around the Weatheralls' dining table, getting to know this family who had become so important to her, left a giant-sized ache in Anna's heart.

Her mother was never going to come to dinner.

And soon, the project with Gabe would be over, and Anna's own dinner invitations would come to an end. She hated to even think about it, but she knew it was better that way.

Every time she came to this house, sat down to dinner, allowed herself to grow a little bit closer to a member of the family, she was putting her future at risk. The more she dragged this out, hanging around the Weatheralls like she deserved the kindness they'd offered, the more they wanted to know about her homelife and her mom. The more questions they asked.

Questions with answers that could ruin her life.

Luckily, a timer over the stove beeped, alerting Anna that her first batch of cookies was done. With a relieved sigh, she ran for the oven. She pulled out a baking pan and plunked it on the counter, nudging a shaker of sprinkles aside with her elbow.

"Those look beautiful," Elizabeth said with a smile.

Anna stood back and surveyed the golden cookies shimmering with pink and yellow sanding sugar. She had a 4.0 GPA and over a dozen college credits to her name, but she was swelling with pride because Leah would have beautiful cookies for her party.

A moment later, Gabe came through the back door to wash his hands and help make a salad, and he was quickly followed by Rachel and Leah. Anna rolled out some more cookies and hoped that now that the family was filtering in, Elizabeth would forget about her mom's dinner invitation.

Rachel leaned against the counter and surveyed Anna's cookies. "These look nice," she said, picking up a still-steaming flower and juggling it from one hand to the other. She took a bite but, before she even started to chew, made a horrible gagging noise and ran for the sink.

Bracing her hands on the counter, Rachel gasped and coughed, spitting out the cookie and then grabbing a paper towel to scrub at her tongue.

Anna's eyes widened as she watched Rachel's display. "Oh my God! Are you okay? Did you burn your mouth?"

Elizabeth looked at her with disapproval. "Really, Rachel. Is all this drama necessary?"

Rachel faced the sink, her shoulders shaking, and Anna worried that she was actually hurt. But before she could run over to check, Rachel turned around and collapsed sideways against the counter. It slowly dawned on Anna that Rachel was laughing so hard she'd doubled over.

Anna's confused face swung to Gabe, who shrugged.

"What is...?" Rachel gasped, trailing off as hysterics overtook her again. She took a deep breath and tried again. "What is *in* those cookies?"

Anna looked at the pan on the counter, where her beautiful cookies sat cooling. "What do you mean?"

Gabe walked over to the island, picked up a cookie, and examined it. He slowly raised it to his mouth and took a tentative bite. Gabe's show of gagging wasn't as dramatic as Rachel's, but he did lunge for a paper towel to spit out the bite.

"What? What's wrong with them?" Anna held her hands to her cheeks as a slow flush crept across them.

Gabe pressed his lips together and had the courtesy to hide his smile. "Um. Is it possible that you used salt instead of sugar?"

"No!" Anna mentally reviewed the ingredients she had found in glass canisters in the pantry. The white powder in the big canister was obviously flour, and the white sandy stuff in a smaller canister next to the flour had been sugar. Hadn't it? It looked like sugar. But now that she thought about it, she hadn't actually tasted it or looked in the other canisters. And what did she know about baking? Her hand flew to her mouth in horror.

Gabe lost the battle to suppress his laughter and collapsed next to Rachel. Anna slumped against the opposite counter and tried to blink away the burning in her eyes.

"Okay, that's enough laughing," Elizabeth's voice cut in. She crossed the room to Anna and slid a comforting arm around her shoulder. "It's okay. Don't worry about it at all."

"I'm so sorry," Anna murmured. All those ingredients wasted, not to mention that she hadn't been any help to Elizabeth. She knew it was ridiculous to be so upset over a batch of cookies, but she was crushed. "I should have told you that I don't know how to bake. But"—Anna swiped at her wet cheeks —"I wanted to help."

"It's my fault. I didn't mention the salt and sugar containers look alike." Elizabeth gave her shoulder a squeeze. "Please don't feel bad; it could have happened to anyone."

Leah ran across the room and threw her arms around Anna's waist. "Don't be sad, Anna. I'll teach you how to make a new batch."

Anna gave a watery laugh. "You will?"

Elizabeth nodded. "That's a great idea. Why don't we let Gabe and Rachel clean up this mess and finish making dinner" —she shot them a pointed look across the room—"and the three of us can have a baking lesson."

Anna stepped back to look Elizabeth in the eye. "I don't want to be any more trouble."

"Of course you're not any trouble. We'd love to, right, Leah?"

Leah nodded enthusiastically. "It'll be fun!"

Anna washed her hands, and they got to work greasing baking pans and measuring out ingredients for a fresh batch of cookies. And it *was* fun. Hanging out in the kitchen with Elizabeth giving her baking tips and Leah helping her to decorate cookies was the most fun she'd had in a long time. It reminded her of how she and her mom used to be when it was just the two of them.

Back then, she'd had no way of predicting that life could change in an instant. But Anna knew now.

She took a sweeping glance around the kitchen, determined to savor every moment while she still had the chance.

# NINE

One late April afternoon, Gabe pulled his car in front of Anna's building and put it in park, his gaze roaming over the front porch. He'd continued to keep an eye out for Don when he picked Anna up to work on their project, and once or twice he'd spotted the guy smoking on the front step. But Anna always crossed the porch and jumped into the car without a glance in Don's direction, and she'd claimed that he hadn't bothered her since Christmas.

In a couple of months, Gabe knew he wouldn't be around to look out for Anna anymore, so he hoped that her mother had handled the situation for good.

It was strange to think he wouldn't be seeing her every few days or know what was going on in her life. Six months earlier, Gabe had been upset to learn Anna would be his partner on the project, and now he almost dreaded the end of their time arguing over economic theories and whose turn it was to analyze a spreadsheet. Earlier that month, he'd sent his enrollment paperwork to the University of Chicago. In the fall, he'd be starting the joint masters-PhD program and work as a graduate assistant for one of the most prestigious professors in the field. But, sometimes he wondered if he'd find someone there he'd work with as well as Anna.

With that thought, he took another glance at the front porch. She wasn't waiting for him in her usual spot, so Gabe got out to wait for her. He headed up the walk but lurched to a stop when he heard an argument coming from inside the building.

Someone was yelling, and it sounded a lot like Anna.

Gabe bolted up the steps and shoved his shoulder into the front door, tripping over a book propped in the frame. He stumbled forward, sending the door flying into the wall with a crash.

Anna and the landlord didn't even glance in his direction.

"You *know* it was all there!" Anna yelled as Gabe charged in. She stood at the other end of the hallway with her hands on her hips and a murderous expression on her face.

Don had his arm braced on the wall in front of her, blocking her path to the door. "What I *know* is there were only two hundred dollars in the envelope. That means you owe me two more." Don wobbled toward her, and she jerked back, crashing into the wall behind her.

Gabe took off down the hall, shoving past Don until he was by Anna's side. "*Hey*. What's going on here?"

Anna continued to glare at Don. "I saw you open the envelope and look through it!"

"Yeah, but I didn't count it." Don's voice had a distinct slur around the edges. "When I got home later, I counted and realized some of the money was missing."

"You're lying! The money is missing because *you took it*!"

"Oh yeah? And how are you going to prove it?" Don took a drag on his cigarette and blew the smoke in her direction.

Anna had one arm crossed over her stomach and the other pressed to her mouth. The tears that threatened to spill down her cheeks burned a hole in his gut.

"Anna." He reached for her arm.

She stared at Don as if she didn't hear him. "I gave you—we

gave you everything we have. It was the full amount. I—we—can't pay you any more."

Gabe turned to Don. "Is this about the rent again?"

"That's right." And then it was like a light bulb flickered on in Don's head. "You got any cash on you?"

Finally, Anna acknowledged Gabe's presence, and she whirled around. "Don't you dare give him any money! I already paid him! He's lying!"

Gabe eyed Don, pretty sure he was drunk. He should just pay the guy whatever he wanted so he'd leave Anna alone. But Anna would kill him if he pulled out his wallet. He shook his head. "Look, when Anna's mom gets home, she'll come and talk to you about it."

"Sure she will. Where's your mom, genius?"

"She's at work."

"I don't care if she joined the goddamn circus. I want my money. And you didn't pay it all this month."

"Yes, I did!"

"Well, it looks like we have three options." Don counted off on his fat fingers. "One, you can pay me the money you owe. Two, I can kick you out on your ass. Or three..." He paused as a grin spread across his florid face.

Gabe had a pretty good idea where this was going. He took Anna's elbow and tugged her toward the door. "Anna, let's go."

Don reached out to grab for Anna's arm, but he missed and stumbled forward. The guy wasn't just drunk—he was wasted. "Or three," he slurred, "you can work it off. Come by my place later tonight, and I can show you an easy way to earn a few hundred bucks. I hope your mother taught you her tricks."

Without stopping to think, Gabe swung around and slammed Don against the wall. The cigarette flew out of his mouth and slid across the floor.

"Are you a goddamn pervert?" Gabe shoved his forearm

into Don's chest, pinning him against the wall. "She's sixteen years old!"

"Gabe. Stop!" Anna wrenched his arm, but he shook her off and didn't budge.

"Get off me!" Don yelled as he began to struggle. He outweighed Gabe by at least fifty pounds, but Gabe had about eight inches on him and was in much better shape.

"Stay the hell away from her," Gabe warned in a low voice, leaning in even harder.

"Gabe, stop it." Anna gave his arm another yank. "Gabe! *Please.*"

Something about the way she said "please," as if she could barely breathe, made him turn his head to her.

"Please. Let's just go," she whispered, looking about as defeated as he'd ever seen her. Something stirred in his chest, and he nodded.

With a hard shove, Gabe pushed himself away from Don and took Anna's arm. "Come on." He hurried her down the hall and out the door.

Don grabbed his cigarette and followed them, stumbling to the porch railing. "You better give me my money, or I'm going to come and get it." There was no mistaking the threat in his voice.

They ducked into the car, and Gabe threw it into drive, tearing off down the street. A few blocks from Anna's house, he veered to the side of the road and slammed on the brakes.

"Anna." He twisted in his seat to face her.

She sat with her arms crossed and her bony shoulders hunched to her ears.

"Anna," he tried again, in a gentler tone. "I know your mom works a lot, but why isn't she dealing with this stuff? You're just a kid. This shouldn't be your problem."

Her chest hitched. "I'm *not* a kid."

"You're sixteen. You shouldn't be dealing with that guy's bullshit."

"That guy's bullshit isn't even *close* to the most I've ever dealt with." She finally looked at him. "I have *never* been a kid."

He studied her face for a clue to what he was missing. "What's going on here?"

Clearly something dark and agonizing. But she shifted away from him and stared out the side window. "Nothing. Never mind."

Whatever was going on, he hated that she was dealing with it alone. "Hey." He reached out and took her hand.

She claimed she wasn't a kid, but right then she looked like a lost little girl. She was so skinny, her clothes practically hung off her, and there was fear in her eyes.

He felt like shit for how he'd grabbed her and dragged her away from Don earlier. He could've hurt her.

She jerked away from him. "Can we please stop talking about this? I'll handle it, okay? Let's talk about our project."

"I don't give a damn about our project."

"Well, I do! Finishing our project is *all* I care about. Just drop it."

Gabe opened his mouth to argue, but then he snapped it shut. She glared at him with her arms crossed in front of her, and he knew her well enough to know he wasn't going to get anywhere at the moment. He shook his head and started the car. She didn't speak again on the drive to his parents' house.

When they arrived, Anna wordlessly turned on the computer and flipped through their presentation. They discussed a few minor changes to the layout, but her voice was flat and emotionless, as if she didn't really care. As soon as they finished, she fled from the room to talk to Rachel, and he headed for the kitchen to help his mom with dinner.

Gabe took Anna home, relieved the landlord was nowhere in sight. He insisted on walking her to her apartment and made her promise she'd dead-bolt the door and talk to her mom about what had happened earlier that day. Maybe he was wasting his breath. Talking to her mom clearly wasn't helping, and he had a feeling there was a lot more to Anna's story than she was revealing.

He'd spent more time with Anna in the past two semesters than with any of his other friends, but he still didn't know much about her homelife. It was pretty obvious she was poor. Aside from the run-ins with the landlord over the rent, there was the shabby apartment building, and the fact that she worked almost every evening at the grocery store in addition to her schoolwork.

His family had never met Anna's mother after she couldn't make it to Christmas dinner. She'd been invited a few times, but Anna always made excuses. It was strange her mother didn't care that her sixteen-year-old daughter was out until all hours of the night, or that she never wanted to meet the college guy Anna was spending so much time with.

And then there was the thing with the landlord. The way he bullied and harassed Anna was disturbing, but the threats and disgusting sexual comments seemed downright dangerous.

As Gabe drove back to his own house, he wondered if maybe he should've called the cops earlier. After all, the landlord had been drunk and threatened Anna, a minor. But it was the landlord's word against theirs, and no actual crime had been committed. Gabe didn't want to piss off the guy even more and put Anna on his radar the next time she came home alone late at night.

No, he didn't need cops to do a whole lot of nothing.

He needed answers. Ones that would help him make sure Anna was safe and that someone would be looking out for her after he left town.

. . .

The next morning, Gabe parked his car in front of the nursing home where Anna said her mother worked. She'd only mentioned it once, when his mother wondered if it was the same place they'd briefly considered for his grandmother. For some reason, it had felt important to tuck the name of the place away in his memory.

And now here he was.

Gabe walked through the glass doors into the lobby and smiled at the woman at the front desk. She was probably in her mid-fifties with short, graying hair, a sensible pair of khakis, and a pale-blue cardigan. She put down the phone and patted her hair as he approached. He turned up the volume on his smile.

"I bet people tell you all the time that the color of your sweater makes your eyes pop," Gabe said, propping a hip against the desk and inwardly cringing a little at his shameless flattery. But desperate times...

The woman let out what could only be referred to as a girlish giggle, and Gabe's smile grew wider.

"I was wondering if you could help me."

"Well, I'll sure try, honey."

"I'm looking for a woman who works here. I think she's a nurse's aide. Last name Campbell?"

"Campbell?" A crease appeared between her eyebrows. "You sure? I don't know any nurse's aides named Campbell. Is she new?"

Gabe had no idea.

"Well, let me take a look at the staff phone directory. Maybe I'm forgetting someone." She pulled a binder from under the desk and slid her finger down a list of names. "Hmmm, let's see... Callahan... Cataldo... Nope, there's no Campbell listed here."

He hadn't expected that. "Are you sure?"

"Sorry, honey. It's right here." She tapped the binder.

"I was positive this was the right place," Gabe muttered.

"Well, what's her first name? Or maybe she's listed under a maiden name?"

He didn't have a clue. Maybe he should've thought this through before rushing down here without any information. But Anna was so closed off and secretive about her life; it wasn't like he had much of a choice.

The woman's smile shifted from flirtatious to pitying. "Mind if I ask why you're trying to track down a woman whose name you don't even know?"

"Ummm. She's the mother of a friend. Maybe one of the nurse's aides mentioned having a daughter named Anna? Sixteen years old?" It was a stretch.

The woman shook her head. "Sorry. It doesn't ring a bell."

Gabe sighed. "Well, thanks anyway." Frustrated, he turned to leave. Maybe Anna's mother did have a different last name. Or maybe she didn't work there at all. This was going nowhere unless he could find a way to get a little more information out of Anna.

*Yeah, good luck with that.*

As Gabe moved toward the front door, the woman behind the desk called out to him. He whirled around, and she gestured toward a middle-aged woman in scrubs pushing an old man in a wheelchair.

"Maybe Barbara can help you. She's been working here for almost twenty years and knows everybody."

Gabe took a few eager steps toward Barbara.

The woman behind the desk pointed at Gabe. "This young man is looking for a friend's mother. Last name Campbell. Has a daughter named..." She trailed off and looked at him.

"Anna."

Barbara's brows knit together. "You don't mean Deb Campbell, do you?"

Yes! Maybe. He leaned in eagerly. "Does she have a daughter?"

Barbara nodded and rubbed her chin. "Deb has a daughter named Anna."

Gabe exhaled the breath he'd been holding. "Is she working today?"

Barbara shook her head. "I'm sorry, you must be confused. The last time Deb worked here was maybe five or six years ago. Her daughter, Anna, was probably about ten back then."

*Wait a minute.* "Five or six *years* ago?"

Barbara nodded.

Gabe was sure Anna had said this place, but maybe he'd heard wrong. "Well, do you know what nursing home she went to after she left here?"

Barbara blinked. "Oh no. She wasn't able to get another job as a nurse's aide after..." She glanced at her patient in the wheelchair and then the woman behind the desk.

"After what?"

Barbara cringed, and the fine lines around her eyes deepened.

"Please?" Gabe pressed. "It's really important that I find her."

She hesitated for another moment and then sighed and shook her head. "I guess it's no secret. And it was a long time ago. Deb couldn't get another nurse's aide job after she was fired for stealing some of the patients' pain meds."

Gabe's muscles stiffened. "Oh. Wow."

Barbara frowned. "We were old high school friends actually. The thing with the pills wasn't the first time. She had a problem with drugs. I tried to get her to go into a program, but a person's got to want to change, you know?"

Gabe nodded, still trying to process it all. Anna's mom used to be addicted to pills. Or maybe she still was, and Anna had been hiding it this whole time. His stomach clenched at the thought of her going home to that every day. Dealing with it all by herself. He wished she'd trusted him enough to talk to him.

"We did keep in touch for a while." Barbara gazed off across the lobby. "But the last rumors I heard around the neighborhood, Deb had moved away. Somewhere out West? To California maybe? That was a while ago. I haven't heard from her since then, but I hoped it'd be a new start for her." She paused, searching Gabe's face. "Is her daughter in some kind of trouble?"

Anna's mom was in *California*? What the hell? How was that possible?

Except it made sense. It explained why her mom was never around, why she left Anna to deal with the landlord, why she never gave a damn that her daughter was at the library until one in the morning with some college guy. Because she'd taken off. And it explained why Anna was so secretive about her homelife. Having a parent addicted to drugs was one thing, but not having any parent at all was an even bigger mess. How was Anna living there all by herself? Who was paying the rent and bills?

Barbara cleared her throat. She was staring at him, probably because he was standing there practically muttering to himself. She'd asked if Anna was in trouble. *Yes*. But he had no idea how much, or what other secrets she was keeping from him.

"Oh no. Anna's not in trouble. I was just hoping to talk to her mother about—" He flashed Barbara his most charming smile and told her the first story he could think of. "It's silly. Anna's birthday is coming up, and we were planning a surprise." He forced a laugh. "Thanks for the information. I should probably go. I've got class soon."

Barbara seemed satisfied with that. "Sure. Hey, if you talk to Deb, tell her to give me a call. I'd love to hear how she's doing."

"Oh, absolutely. Definitely. Thanks again."

Gabe headed across the lobby. He waved to Barbara, trying to appear casual, but then he turned around and narrowly missed crashing into a potted plant. He flashed Barbara a grin and then swerved around the plant to hurry for the door.

# TEN

As soon as Anna walked into her pitch-black apartment, she knew the electricity had been shut off again. She cursed and stumbled around in the darkness, bumping her head on a cabinet while she searched for a candle under the kitchen sink.

Just as she lit the candle and put it on the coffee table, there was a knock at the door. Anna's heart dropped as her mind flashed to the landlord. On her way home, she'd paid him the money he claimed she owed, even though she *knew* she'd paid it the first time. But she couldn't prove it, and not having electricity for a while was nothing compared to being evicted. She'd have no place else to go.

Anna took a deep breath. Don was probably at home gloating over his windfall. He'd leave her alone for a couple of weeks, at least until the rent was due again.

Another knock echoed, and Anna's chest constricted painfully. Before she could stop it, her mind flashed to her mother.

*No.* Her mother wouldn't knock, would she? Even after all this time? It was probably just Mrs. Janiszewski, the older lady from upstairs. Sometimes Anna helped her out with things, and

Mrs. Janiszewski liked to drop off cookies to thank her. Cookies would be pretty nice since she had almost nothing to eat in the apartment. Along with her overdue electricity payment, most of her food money had gone to Don that month.

Anna opened the door, and a shock ran through her.

It wasn't Mrs. Janiszewski.

Gabe stood silhouetted in the doorway, the dim fluorescent light in the hall behind him turning his dark hair to blue-black. What was he doing here?

"Gabe! How did you get in the building?" She leaned on the doorframe and pulled the door closed against her shoulder.

"Someone propped the door open downstairs with a book again," he grumbled. "I'd tell you to talk to the landlord about how that's not safe, but I get the feeling he won't give a shit. Can I come in?"

"Um..." *Oh my God. No.* Anna glanced behind her. The lone candle flickered on the table. She did *not* want him coming in, especially right then. "Now's not really a good time."

"Now's perfect," Gabe said shortly, and before she could stop him, he brushed past her into the apartment.

She took a deep breath, and the churning in her stomach had nothing to do with the fact that she hadn't eaten.

Gabe stood in the middle of the living room, blinking to adjust to the darkness. One benefit of having the electricity shut off was at least he couldn't see what a dump the place was.

"Why is it so dark in here?" Gabe stomped to the wall and felt around for a light switch. He flipped it on and off, but nothing happened. Then he tried a lamp on the side table. "Why is there no electricity?"

"It'll be back on in a few days." *Or next month.* Thank God it was spring or she'd freeze to death.

"Why isn't it on now?"

Anna crossed her arms and glared at him. What right did he have to show up at her apartment barking questions at her?

Gabe met her eyes and glowered back at her until—*damn him*—she finally looked away. "I couldn't pay the bill, okay? I had to pay the landlord the money he said I owed, or he was going to kick me out."

"Kick *you* out? What about your mom?"

*Right.* "Kick us out, I mean."

"Uh-huh." Gabe wandered over to the bedroom and stood in the doorway, peering into the darkness. "And right now, she's at work?"

"Yes," Anna answered warily.

"At the nursing home?"

"Um. Yes."

"Really?" Gabe swung back around and faced her again. "That's funny because I stopped by there, and they said she hasn't worked there in years."

The blood rushed from her head, and she grabbed the back of the couch before she fell over. "*You what?*"

"Where's your mother?" Gabe asked in a low voice.

"She's—it's none of your—" Anna sputtered. "*What right do you have to go digging around in my life?*"

"Anna. Where is she?" Gabe's voice was gentle now, which somehow made it even worse.

She looked away. *He knew.* There was no point in denying it. "I don't know, okay?"

"What do you mean, you don't know?" He gazed at her steadily.

Was he really going to make her spell it out? She flung her hand in the air. "She left. She took off. Last I heard, she was in California."

"When did she leave?"

"A while ago." Anna pressed her hands to her temples as her head started to pound. *This isn't happening.*

Gabe stood there, arms crossed, not backing down.

She sighed. "Two years ago."

Gabe took a step back. "So, you've just been living here by yourself *for two years*?"

Anna shrugged.

"And the rent and bills and everything?"

"I've worked at the grocery store since I was thirteen. They pay me under the table."

"Jesus, Anna."

It wasn't like she had a choice. Why was he looking at her like this was her fault? "What do you care? We're going to get an A on our project. You don't have to worry about my messed-up life. It hasn't gotten in the way of my schoolwork yet."

Gabe narrowed his eyes. "I'm not worried about a *grade*."

"So why do you even care?" Her voice was rising.

"At the moment, I'm really not sure."

Anna slammed her hand down on the back of the couch. "Well, stop it! My life is none of your business!"

"It's my business when some drunk guy is threatening you, and I have to step in and make him back off."

"Nobody asked you to do that!"

Gabe paced a groove through her living room. "You know, for a smart girl, you're being pretty damn stupid."

"Because I don't want you sneaking around behind my back and stirring things up! If someone figures out my mom..." Anna lowered her voice. The walls in the old building weren't that thick. "Look, my mom is gone, and I'm living by myself. How do you think that's going to end up? Where do you think *I'm* going to end up?"

He came to an abrupt halt. "I don't know, Anna. But you can't keep living like this."

She stared at him in disbelief. Was he really that sheltered? "Are you serious? What would you suggest I do? What are my alternatives here, Gabe?"

"Don't you have any other family?"

Anna had a flashback to the day they were assigned to be

partners in class, when she thought of him as a pampered rich boy who had no idea about hardship. "My mom ran away from her abusive family when she was sixteen. And as far as my dad —" She laughed, because even the thought of having a dad was absurd. "Well, you can take your pick. He might have been a married doctor my mom had an affair with when she worked at the nursing home. Or maybe one of the many deadbeat boyfriends in and out of her life. Or I could be her drug dealer's kid. Who the hell knows?"

Gabe eyed her for a moment. "My money is on the doctor."

"Well, thanks. That's helpful."

They glared at each other across the living room until Gabe spun on his heel, grabbed the candle off the table, and marched into the kitchen. He yanked opened the refrigerator door. Anna thought about yelling at him to stop, but it was useless. She stood helplessly as Gabe peered in the empty refrigerator and then opened and closed a couple of cabinets full of mismatched dishes and dented pots.

He stopped when he found a lone can of peas and a box of generic macaroni and cheese. "You have no electricity. And is this all the food in the house?"

She pressed her lips together and stared at the flickering candle reflected in the window.

"And then there's your landlord. Who knows what could happen some night when you get home late all by yourself? You're not safe here."

"I'll have plenty of food when I get paid in a few days." But that wasn't exactly true. She had to save most of the money she made for next month's rent. And the electricity bill. She pushed it out of her mind. "The electricity is just temporary."

"And what about the landlord?"

"I can *handle* the landlord."

"How are you going to do that? By paying him every time he cheats you? Or by doing him the "favors" he wants in place of payment?" He used his fingers to make air quotes, his voice thick with disgust.

How dare he use that mocking tone when he had no idea what it took to survive? *No idea.*

"Maybe! If that's what it takes!" If her voice grew any louder, the neighbors would hear, but she was beyond caring. It wouldn't be the first time the neighbors heard fighting coming from her apartment. Usually, they just turned up the volume on their TVs to drown it out.

"I have one year left. *One year.* And then I'll be almost eighteen and done with high school. If I can get through this one year, I *know* I can get a full ride to finish college. That's my one shot." Her voice turned cold as she narrowed her eyes at him. "But you wouldn't know anything about how that feels. You've never had to work for anything. So don't lecture me about *my* life when you've lived yours with your parents handing you everything."

Gabe reeled back. "Wow."

Her rage spilled over before she could stop it. "You can stop treating me like your goddamn community service project now. I don't need you. I've been taking care of myself for my entire life."

"Are you kidding?" Gabe's voice was rising. "You think I'm just hanging out with you because you're some 'project' for me?"

"I don't know. I don't care. Just leave me alone."

"Anna..."

She whirled on him and yelled, "Get out right now, or I swear to God, I'm going to call the police!"

She was lying. There was no way she'd call the police. The first thing they'd do was ask where her mom was. Gabe had to know it, too, but he didn't argue. He just stood there with his hand balled into a fist and a muscle twitching in his jaw. Then he dropped the candle on the coffee table and stalked out of the apartment, slamming the door behind him.

Anna sank down on the couch, dinner forgotten, her appetite gone. The throbbing in her head had morphed into a full-blown migraine as the gravity of what had happened started to sink in. Not only did Gabe know she'd been lying about her mother, but she had no idea what he was going to do with that information.

What if he did something stupid like turn her in to protective services, thinking he was looking out for her? He had no idea it would literally ruin her life. Legally, she was still a minor, and they'd send her to foster care to live with some family she didn't know and couldn't trust. But that wasn't even the worst part.

The worst part was what might turn up if anyone started poking around in her mom's past. In Anna's past.

What terrible secrets they might uncover.

A half hour later, Anna was in that same spot on the couch, staring at the candle flickering on the table with her mind still whirling. She jumped when someone pounded on the door. Had Gabe called the police already? Or maybe a neighbor complained to the landlord about the yelling earlier.

There was nowhere to hide. She hadn't dead-bolted the door, she wasn't even sure if it was locked, so whoever it was could just walk in. Hands shaking, she hauled herself up and dragged the door open.

Gabe stood in the hallway, this time with two shopping bags in his hands.

She braced herself for another fight with him, but Gabe just shoved the bags into her arms, turned, and left without a word.

Anna hovered in the doorway as his feet pounded down the stairs and the front door slammed shut, and then she closed and locked the door. She sank down on the couch and, in the dim candlelight, pulled things out of the bags and set them on the table. A loaf of bread. A box of crackers. Three jars of peanut butter. About a dozen cans of soup, beans, and vegetables. A bag of apples.

Anna leaned back against the couch cushions and stared at the food covering her coffee table, not even bothering to wipe away the tears pouring down her cheeks.

# ELEVEN

The next day, Gabe waited at their usual table in the library for Anna to show up. He sorted through some notes without really looking at them and checked and rechecked the time on his phone. She still hadn't showed by the time he had to head over to class, and worry was starting to gnaw a hole in his stomach. She didn't answer when he called, and he had no way of knowing if she wasn't home, or if her antiquated phone had been shut off as well as the electricity.

Anna would never miss class a week before their project was due. He watched the other students file into the classroom, but there was no sign of her. When Dr. McGovern moved to the front of the room to start the class, Gabe fidgeted in his seat, willing her to appear.

The girl in the next seat shot him an odd look, so he took a deep breath and tried to concentrate on the lecture.

After what seemed like an eternity, Dr. McGovern stopped rambling and told the class to take a five-minute break. Gabe slammed his notebook shut, grabbed his bag, and was the first person out the door. He pulled out his phone and called Anna's number again.

No answer.

Glancing over his shoulder at the classroom where he was supposed to be heading back to his seat, he made his decision, and took off toward the exit of the building instead. And then on the path outside, he stopped short, nearly crashing into the person he'd been looking for.

"Anna," he gasped, trying to catch his breath.

"Hi." Her huge brown eyes were shadowed by dark circles, reminding him of a scared woodland animal. "Why aren't you in class?"

"Why aren't *you*?" He raised his palms in a questioning gesture. "You didn't show up earlier today."

"Yeah. I, um. Sorry." Anna kicked at a stone on the path with her scuffed tennis shoe. "I just needed some time to think."

"And it didn't occur to you to call me and let me know?" He crossed his arms over his chest. "So I wouldn't worry about you?"

Anna's head tipped up, almost as if that surprised her. "I thought you were mad at me for lying to you. And for the things I said to you last night."

"For the record, I am a little mad." He hated that she'd lied to him, that she didn't trust him enough to tell him the truth. But he'd have to be completely heartless if he didn't understand why. "That doesn't mean I don't care about you though."

Anna took a step closer. "I should have told you I wasn't coming. Honestly, I'm just..." She shoved her hands in the pockets of her hoodie.

"You're just what?"

Anna pressed her lips together. When she spoke, her voice was a whisper. "I'm just not used to someone worrying about me."

The last of Gabe's annoyance evaporated. "Damn it," he muttered under his breath.

"So, what do we do, now that you..." Anna kept her head

down, mumbling it to the pavement. "Now that you know about me."

"Can we sit and talk?" He scanned the quad. A low stone wall stretched along the far side of the lawn, away from the paths that crisscrossed the campus. Nobody would bother them over there.

She nodded and followed him across the grass. They dropped their backpacks and sank down on the wall next to each other. Anna stared at her lap, letting her hair fall around her face, hiding her pained expression.

Gabe leaned forward so he could see her eyes. "Anna, your situation is much more intense than I thought it was. I need to understand what's really going on."

Anna put her elbows on her knees and rubbed her forehead as if she felt a headache coming on. For someone who was so closed off, she could be ridiculously transparent. It was obvious she was weighing her options and deciding how much to reveal.

"I need the *real* story," he said, before she could come up with another fictional version of her life like the one she'd been telling him for months.

Anna's shoulders slumped. "She's not a bad person, you know."

"Your mom?"

"Yeah. Some of the kids at school used to call her a druggie, a junkie, stuff like that. I'd hear them whispering when I walked through the halls." She tugged at the gold necklace hanging by her collarbone. He'd never asked the significance of it before, but in that moment, he had some ideas.

Anna dropped her hands to her lap. "But the worst part was the way they said it, like my mom was a monster, and by association, I was, too."

Teenagers could be so terrible. Gabe hadn't been the kind of guy to bully kids in high school, but looking back, he probably hadn't done enough to step in and defend the ones like Anna either. A sharp pang of regret stabbed him.

"But she wasn't a monster. She *isn't*," Anna continued. "She has an addiction. It's a disease. Her parents really were monsters. It's no wonder she ended up the way she is. She had all these scars on her arms, and one day she told me that when her parents were mad at her, they would burn her with their cigarettes. My mom never did anything like that to me."

Horror curled in his gut. What a terrible thing for her mother to go through. He couldn't even imagine it. But it also hit him that somewhere along the way, Anna's standard for her childhood had become, *At least I wasn't burned with cigarettes.* Her mom had taken off, abandoned her, and Anna was still rushing to defend her.

"What was it like when she was around? Was she high all the time—" He stopped, reeling in his anger. The last thing Anna needed was someone else making her feel like shit about her life. "You know what, you don't have to answer that. It doesn't matter."

Anna was quiet for so long, he wondered if she'd even heard. Finally, she turned and looked at him. "No. She wasn't high all the time. Not in the beginning. After she ran away from her terrible parents, she worked hard to get her life together. She finished her GED and trained to be a nurse's aide. And then she got pregnant with me. My dad was never in the picture. But she was a good mom. Honestly, she *was*." Her eyes pleaded with him. "Even if it doesn't seem like it right now. And I know she loves me."

He was struck by her use of the present tense: "She loves me." The certainty on her face was a knife twisting in his heart, and he couldn't bring himself to point out all the evidence to the contrary. "Of course she does," he said, wanting it to be true more than he actually believed it.

"I have lots of happy memories of her. She used to read to

me before bed." Anna stared out across the campus. "There were birthday parties with cake with sprinkles. She took me to the zoo..." She grasped the pendant she wore around her neck again, and Gabe could see that it was shaped like a half circle with some sort of flower pattern etched into the surface. "My mom gave me this, and she has the other half. She never takes it off. They fit together like puzzle pieces."

He wanted to reach over and put his arm around her, but he didn't know if that would be weird, so he settled for leaning in until his shoulder brushed hers.

"I don't know exactly when she started using. I was probably too young to realize it was happening at first." She gave a quick shake of her head. "I was maybe in about third or fourth grade when she hurt her back helping a patient out of a wheelchair, but the nursing home didn't care. They just fired her because she couldn't work."

Gabe blinked. Anna didn't seem to know her mom had been fired for stealing pain meds from the nursing home residents. He couldn't bring himself to hurt her even more by telling her now.

"She had this guy, Rob, who brought pills for her bad back. But she couldn't always pay for them, so sometimes she'd do things for him. Favors, or... you know." A flush crept from her cheeks all the way into the neckline of her shirt. "They'd turn the TV on really loud and disappear into the bedroom." She shifted on the wall so she could angle away from him. "Her pain made her desperate. And then, it wasn't like there were a lot of people falling over themselves to help a poor, single mother addicted to oxy. She's not a bad person."

Gabe took her by the shoulder—God, she was so skinny—and gently tugged her back around until she was facing him. "Anna, I'm not judging, okay?"

"Gabe, how can you not judge? You come from this perfect family, and your parents are wonderful. If they knew..." She closed her eyes and shook her head. "If they knew everything... I wouldn't blame them if they never wanted me in their house again."

He tightened his grip on her shoulder. "Anna, you can't be serious. You've been handed a lot of shitty circumstances. Nobody blames you for that." His body felt heavy from the weight of all she'd been through. He couldn't even imagine how she must feel having lived it. "I'm in awe of how you've held everything together for so long. There isn't anything you could tell me that would change my feelings."

She leaned back and looked at him sideways, as if she wanted to believe him but didn't. "I don't think you really mean that."

Gabe squinted back at her, trying to read the expression on her face. "Is there something else you're not telling me?"

She quickly looked away. "No. I just mean that my life must seem so sordid."

But Gabe wasn't convinced. Anna's hands were shaking, and she wouldn't look at him. "You can open up to me. Is it something about your mom?" His heart seized. "Or did something else happen with the landlord?"

Anna shook her head. "No, I haven't seen Don again."

Gabe could still feel the man's hot, beer-drenched breath in his face as he shoved him against the wall, away from Anna. "You know it's only a matter of time, right? He's not going to leave you alone. Especially if he knows you're living in that apartment by yourself."

"He doesn't know."

Gabe wasn't convinced of that either.

Anna took a deep breath and blew it out slowly. "The thing is..." She finally met his eyes. "Rob wasn't the only guy who came around. There were a bunch of boyfriends. They brought money and drugs. Those guys were pretty rough, and there were some intense fights when they were high. Or my mom would pass out, and I'd be alone in the apartment with these strange men."

Gabe could actually hear the blood pounding through his veins, rushing to his head. "Did they—were you—" Sweat trickled down his back as he tried to form the words.

Anna would have been close to his little sister's age. The thought of her as a girl like Leah, left alone with the kind of creepy men Anna's mother probably brought home, made him want to kick over the stone wall he was sitting on.

"No." Anna's head whipped back and forth. "No. Gabe, I'm not telling you this to make you think..." She paused, pressing her palms against her temples. "I'm telling you because I want you to understand I can *handle* guys like Don. I've been taking care of myself for a long time. I know my neighborhood isn't the safest—"

She stopped abruptly as two girls from their global econ class strolled by. They waved to Gabe as they passed, and he gave them a quick nod and then averted his eyes so they wouldn't stop to say hello. He couldn't even imagine chatting about end-of-semester parties or whatever else they might want to talk about. Suddenly, all the college stuff that had taken up so much of his time and energy felt incredibly shallow and stupid compared to the life Anna had been living.

Anna watched the girls until they disappeared into the economics building and then continued. "Gabe, I have it all figured out. I know how to get home at night, which streets to walk down, and who to avoid. I carry pepper spray. My landlord is usually too drunk to even walk straight. He's harmless, and I can handle him."

Gabe stared at her as she sat on the wall with her head bowed and her hair falling in front of her face. She hadn't been exaggerating when she told him she'd never been a kid. Anna might come off as meek and mousy at first, but she was the strongest person he knew. He didn't doubt for a second she could handle all of it. But *shit*. He didn't want her to have to handle it anymore. At least not alone.

"Do you have any idea why your mom left?"

"I—" Anna's shoulders tensed. She grabbed her necklace and turned her head away.

Something hollow opened up inside him. She *wasn't* telling him the whole story. "Anna?" Gabe prompted gently. "You can talk to me."

Anna pushed her hair behind her ear, and Gabe caught a glimpse of the sorrow in her eyes. When she finally spoke, her voice was hoarse and shaky. "At some point, it wasn't just pills she was using." Anna shuddered. "All our money was going to drugs, and we were dead broke. My mom had a boyfriend who helped pay the rent and buy a little food. But there was always a price..." Anna wrapped her arms around herself, as if those skinny limbs would protect her from the pain.

Gabe inched closer. They were across from the economics building, and people he knew were all over campus. Any of the guys from the fraternity could stroll by and see them. He might get shit for it later, but Gabe didn't care. He slid his arm around Anna's shoulders and pulled her against his side.

She leaned into him, and her body relaxed.

"One night I came home and—" Her voice broke off, cracking at the end. "And my mom had packed a bag and said she was going to California. She had a job there, an opportunity to make enough money so we wouldn't have to rely on guys like that anymore." Anna took a deep breath and exhaled slowly. "She said she was going to California to take care of us, but that she'd be back."

Gabe could only imagine what kind of job had lured Anna's mom to California. Nurse's assistant jobs certainly didn't pay much money. And if she had drug dealers coming to the house while her underage daughter was there, he was willing to bet she'd take a job doing something illegal.

Anna took a deep breath and exhaled slowly. "A couple of weeks went by, and she never came home. She called a couple of times, promising to send money that never arrived. And then..." Her head dropped forward as if the burden of holding it up was too much. "And then the calls stopped."

"Do you think she's—" Gabe abruptly stopped talking. *She's what?* He had no idea how to phrase the question. Or what he was even asking. *She's dead? In jail? Still living in California without you?* There was no scenario that didn't make his heart break for Anna. Finally, he settled on, "Do you have any idea what happened to her?"

"No." Anna scrubbed her hands across her wet cheeks. "I check the arrest and death records all the time. There's never been any sign of her. But I can't file a missing person report until I'm eighteen, or someone could find out about me." She shuddered. "If they do, they'll send me to foster care."

Gabe knew foster care sometimes had a bad reputation, but there had to be plenty of nice families out there. And Anna's situation in that run-down apartment with a dangerous landlord downstairs couldn't be a better option.

"She could still come back," Anna insisted, her voice shaking. A tear dripped down her cheek. "I just need to keep things up for a little bit longer."

Gabe's heart ached. Despite everything she'd been through, Anna still believed her mom would come home. For her sake, he wanted this story to have a happy ending. But he didn't for one second believe it would.

Gabe pulled her more firmly against his side, and something sparked in his chest, something fierce and primal. An instinct to protect this mysterious girl who'd become so important to him. As she sucked in another shaky breath, he knew she was trying to hold it together and be strong, as usual. He wanted to tell her it was okay to fall apart. That she wasn't alone anymore.

But he hesitated for now. Before he made any promises, he

had to figure out how he'd be able to keep them. Because despite her insistence that she had everything under control, it killed him that she had to carry pepper spray and plot out her route to avoid the creeps in the neighborhood. That nobody was ever waiting to make sure she made it home. That she was skin and bones from having to decide between paying the rent and buying food.

He was leaving for grad school in a couple of months, and there was no way he could go before he made sure she was safe for good.

# TWELVE

Anna leaned into Gabe and breathed in his familiar woodsy scent. If she could just stay there next to him, with his arm wrapped around her, everything would be okay. Just for a little bit.

His voice rumbled against her cheek. "I'm just so sorry, Anna. I had no idea."

"Nobody does. They can't know."

"Do you miss her?"

Her breath caught, and tears pricked the backs of her eyes. Anna missed her mom every single minute of every single day. The sound of her voice, her smile, the way she used to collect goofy jokes from the nursing home residents to make Anna laugh. Even after her mom started using, there were good times, at least at first. That day Anna was home sick from school, and they'd spent hours on the couch eating ice cream and watching old movies. Their evening walks across the railroad tracks to throw stones in the river.

Anna grabbed the pendant around her neck.

She'd never forget the birthday when her mom gave her that necklace. Her mom had said she and Anna would always belong together, just like the two halves of the pendant. Anna stared down at it now. Sometimes that necklace was the only thing that kept the darkness at bay on those cold nights alone in the apartment. "Yeah. I miss her." She still woke up every morning hoping that maybe that was the day her mother would come home. And every night before she went to bed, she'd think, *Maybe tomorrow she'll be back.*

But a year had gone by, and then two. It was agony, every day, wondering what had happened to the most important person in her life—and the only family she'd ever known. It was agony wondering if her mom was out there somewhere, hurt or afraid.

When the addiction had really taken over, their roles had reversed. Anna would take care of her mom, helping her get into bed, running a bath. She could remember digging through her mom's purse, hoping to find loose dollar bills so she could buy cans of soup at the local mini mart. Anna's mom never wanted to eat much, but Anna would sit with her on the couch, gently encouraging her to try a few bites. Even when her mom was totally out of it, she'd mumble about how much she appreciated Anna, how she didn't know what she'd do without her.

"I'm going to find her," Anna said. "She needs me."

Gabe's muscles tensed, and he looked at her sideways. "What about what *you* need? You keep talking about how none of this is her fault. But you've been living all alone for two years. Whose fault is it, then?"

*It's mine. It's my fault.*

Anna pressed her lips together to keep from saying it out loud. Because seeing the worry etched across Gabe's face, feeling his strong arm supporting her, she wanted to close her eyes and bawl into his chest like a little girl. To hand over this burden she'd been carrying around and let him hold it for a while.

But that would be far too dangerous, and Anna knew better.

She'd already revealed more than she should have. If he knew how much she didn't deserve his care, his concern... She shook her head and reluctantly pulled away, sliding off the wall to stand in front of him. "What I need is for you to trust me that I have my life under control. You're not going to tell anyone about my living situation, are you?"

"I—" He winced, and his gaze darted over her shoulder.

Panic slammed into her. "Gabe. Please." She hated that she was pleading with him, hated that her future was in his hands. "You know how hard I've worked. If I can keep up the way I've been, I know I can get scholarships to college. I'll be able to move into the dorms in a little over a year. But if anybody finds out about me now, who knows where they'll try to send me?"

"I know, Anna. But..."

"Gabe, I know you want to protect me, but I swear, I can handle this. Promise me. *Please*."

Gabe winced and rubbed the back of his neck. He opened his mouth to say something but then snapped it shut.

Her control was slipping, and it terrified her.

Finally, he sighed, running his hand through his hair. "Anna, we're not done talking about this. I know you think your landlord is bluffing, but honestly, after the run-ins I've had with the guy, I don't think so."

"I'll be more careful. I promise."

Gabe jumped off the wall. "Look, we missed most of class, so why don't we get out of here? We can go over to my parents' place, put the final touches on the project, and grab some dinner."

Her body sagged with relief. That was exactly what they needed. To go back to their old routine and forget all about this. "Yeah. Let's do that."

He waved her to go ahead of him, in the direction of the frat house where he usually parked his car.

Anna started down the path but then stopped short and turned to face him. "Gabe?"

"Yeah?" He tilted his head to squint down at her.

"Thanks."

He gave her a smile and a nod. Anna spun back around and started walking. Gabe was the best friend she ever had. She could trust him to keep this secret.

That afternoon, they worked on their project for the last time. All that was left to do was present it to the class next week. But Anna wasn't in any hurry for it to be over, so she lingered in John's office going over the smallest details. Since Gabe suggested one more run-through—their third—maybe he wasn't in any hurry either.

When they couldn't find anything more to do, Gabe went to the kitchen to make them some sandwiches, and Anna flopped in the reading chair in the corner. She glanced around the room that had become so familiar these past few months. It might be one of the last times she'd sit there. Their project was finished, and there wouldn't be any more excuses to come over for dinner. Gabe would leave for grad school in Chicago in a couple of months, and she'd focus on SATs and college applications. Not to mention working at the grocery store and continuing to scrape together enough money for rent and bills every month. She sagged in the chair under the weight of it all.

Working on the project had been an unexpected escape from her real life, but all that was over. The next year stretched out in front of her without Tuesday mornings working on the project with Gabe and Sunday dinners with the Weatheralls.

She'd spent so much of her life on her own, but she didn't realize how lonely she'd been until right at that moment.

Anna was so lost in her thoughts that ten minutes had gone by before she realized that Gabe hadn't returned to the office.

Maybe his mom and dad had come home from work through the back door. He'd probably gotten caught up talking to them in the kitchen. Anna sighed and hauled herself to her feet to go say hello. *No more wallowing today.* She was determined to enjoy spending these last few days with the Weatheralls. There would be plenty of time for sadness later.

Anna left the office and headed down the hall toward the kitchen, hearing the low timbre of Gabe's voice as it drifted down the hall, followed by murmurs from John and Elizabeth. It sounded like she was right, and they were home. Anna stopped short when she caught the word "concerned" from Elizabeth, and "trouble" from John. Whatever they were talking about, it sounded serious, and it occurred to Anna that maybe she shouldn't interrupt.

She was about to turn back toward the office when she heard Gabe say her name.

Anna stumbled to a stop. They were discussing *her.* She silently slid her sock-covered feet closer to the kitchen doorway.

"I think Gabe should probably tell her," Elizabeth said in a low voice.

"I agree," John added. "It will be easier if it comes from him."

"She must know she can't keep up her present situation." Elizabeth's voice carried out into the hall.

Anna gasped and then quickly covered her mouth. She knew exactly what this was about. They were planning to ambush her. She'd trusted Gabe, and he'd turned around and reported everything to his parents. Anna stared down at the floor as the tears threatened to spill over. The betrayal hurt almost as much as the realization that she was about to lose everything she'd worked so hard for.

"Surely, in some ways, this will come as a relief," Elizabeth continued.

*A relief?* Oh God. Here it was. The moment they started

talking about protective services and foster care like it was no big deal, like it would be a safe place.

*Like it's not the end of everything.*

It had been the biggest mistake of her life to trust Gabe. The biggest mistake of her life to trust any of them. And the worst part was, she'd known it all along.

Anna spun on her heel and hurried as quietly as she could back down the hall to the office. She paused there, taking it all in for one last time. The computer on the desk was still open to the presentation she and Gabe had been working on moments ago.

All the sacrifices she'd made, the countless hours of work she'd put into that project, thinking it might be the ticket to her future, to scholarships and a chance for a better life. A life like the one the Weatheralls had.

How ironic that they'd be the ones to blow it all up.

She wouldn't be there to make that presentation. She'd fail the class, and all the struggles, the all-nighters, the hours sleeping in the stacks in the library, they'd be for nothing. It wasn't just global econ but everything she'd worked for these past few years. If she took off now, she'd be homeless, a runaway, a high school dropout. What college would ever want a girl like that?

It would be over.

But if she stayed here, it would be over, too. They'd take her away and send her to foster care where she'd be shuffled from place to place with no say in where she ended up. She'd be a statistic in a system that didn't care about poor people like Anna or her mom. If they had, someone would have stepped in to help them a long time ago.

Anna's heart suddenly clenched with another terrible realization. What if the cops came and started asking questions? Someone might be able to trace her and her mom back to that afternoon...

Anna shook her head as if that would banish the thought from her mind. *If they find out what I've done, they'll send me to far worse places than foster care.* It would be over, no matter which path she chose. But if she ran, she might at least have a chance.

Anna grabbed her backpack and threw it over her shoulder. Her hands shook, and her legs threatened to give out, but she had to keep going, to keep moving.

*Just like you always have.*

As silently as possible, Anna pulled open the front door and left the Weatheralls' house. For good.

Out on the street, Anna took off at a run, rounding the first corner she came to and darting into an alley where she was less likely to be spotted if they came looking for her. She kept moving with no real destination, racing through the maze of backstreets until her lungs burned and her calves begged for relief. Panting, she stumbled to a stop and slumped against someone's detached garage. For a few moments, all she could do was hug the brick wall and gasp for air. Finally, when her heart rate began to slow to a normal rhythm, she sat down on the curb and forced herself to focus.

What now?

She couldn't go back to her apartment. That would be the first place they'd look for her. In fact, it wouldn't surprise her if they'd noticed she was gone and were headed over there right now.

Anna wrapped her arms around her midsection, suddenly shivering despite the sweat dripping down her back from her sprint a moment ago. Would she be leaving that apartment behind forever? It might be old and shabby, but it was the only home she'd ever known. All her stuff was in that apartment. Most of it was worthless—her mom had sold anything of value years ago—but what was left was hers. Her favorite books, her CD player, the stuffed bunny she used to sleep with as a little girl. Plus, there were photos of her mom. Not many but a couple of old ones someone had snapped back before Anna had been born.

Could she risk sneaking home and grabbing those things?

It was too dangerous. She'd just have to leave it all behind. Luckily, she'd learned a long time ago never to get too attached to material things.

If only she could have applied that same principle to people, she wouldn't be in this mess.

*Focus. Where can you go?*

She had nobody. *Nobody.*

Except...

Anna reached for the pendant around her neck.

She grabbed her backpack from the curb next to her and dug around in the side pocket until she found a small, folded piece of paper. It had started out white, but after rattling around in her bag for the past couple of years, the paper had faded to a dull gray and frayed at the creases. But she could still make out the address written there. And anyway, she'd memorized it long ago.

*1908 Capp Street, San Francisco, California*

# THIRTEEN

"There's an overnight bus leaving for Chicago in about two hours." The middle-aged woman behind the counter typed something into her computer. "You want to be on it?"

Anna glanced over her shoulder. Whatever bus would get her out of town the fastest, that was the one she wanted to be on. From Chicago, she could easily buy a ticket to San Francisco. She reached for the worn fabric pouch she kept with her at all times—safer than leaving it at home where the landlord might find it. It held $518.92. All her money in the world. She'd planned to pay her rent tomorrow, but Don wouldn't be getting his money this week or maybe ever again.

"*I'll take it.*" Did she sound too eager? Would the woman wonder if she were old enough to buy a ticket? Anna stood up straight and gave the woman her most confident smile, sliding her university card across the counter. "Here's my ID." Nobody would expect a college student to be under eighteen.

The woman barely glanced at her as she took the card and typed the information into the computer. While she worked, Anna turned and performed another casual sweep of the bus station. A young mother sat next to the vending machine, looking at her phone while her child tried to reach into the dispenser and grab for the candy. A homeless man napped on a bench next to a shopping cart full of his belongings. And in a booth across the room, a security guard flipped through a magazine. Nobody seemed the least bit interested in her, and that was exactly how Anna wanted it.

Two more hours, and she'd be gone for good.

As Anna took her ticket from the attendant, her stomach growled. It had been hours since she'd eaten anything at all. She approached the vending machine, and the boy's mother reached out a hand to him.

"Come here, baby. Let's move out of this girl's way."

The child, a boy of about three or four, turned to his mother. "Can I have some M&Ms?" he asked, his little face hopeful.

His mother stood and picked him up, propping him onto her hip. "Not now, sweetie." She sighed, smoothing a hand across her red-rimmed, tired eyes. "I don't have any money for that." She shook her head, and the ugly fluorescent lights overhead seemed to deepen the worry lines around her mouth. "I'm sorry," she whispered, adjusting her grip on the boy and reaching up to push a lock of hair off his face. "Maybe when we get to Grandma's she'll have a treat for you." Her voice was soothing, but her face looked strained, unsure.

Anna's gaze briefly dropped to the woman's scuffed shoes and then slid past her worn gray sweatsuit back to the child in her arms. Instead of throwing the tantrum she expected, the boy propped his head on his mother's shoulder and nodded, almost as if he were resigned. "It's okay, Mommy."

The mother smiled sadly and stroked her child's head again. Anna's heart constricted. Something about the entire scene was achingly familiar. The bone-tired mother trying to hold it together, the child reassuring his mother so she wouldn't look so sad. Anna reached for the pendant around her neck. *Ten years ago, it could have been my mom and me.* Just like this young boy, Anna had known, too, that her mom had it hard, that every single day was a struggle. Anna had done everything she could to make it easier, but it hadn't been enough.

But now, maybe Anna had a chance to find her and fix everything. At least, that's how she liked to imagine it might go. It hurt less than the alternative.

Anna touched her pouch of cash again. She needed every bit of this money. But she'd been scraping by for years, and a few dollars weren't going to make that much of a difference. "Can I get your son a treat?" she murmured to the woman, and the boy perked up.

The woman's mouth dropped open. "Oh, you don't have to—"

"Please?" Anna said. She turned to the vending machine, slid in some money, and bought the M&Ms, a Snickers bar, and a bag of chips. "Here," she said, handing the two chocolate treats to the woman. And then, before she could change her mind, Anna shoved a five-dollar bill into the woman's palm, tucked the pack of chips in her jacket pocket, and fled across the room.

Anna found a seat against the opposite wall, ate her snack, and settled back against the cheap vinyl to wait. The exhaustion came in a wave, and she closed her eyes.

She'd just begun to drift off when the shrill ring of a phone hit her from across the room. Anna sat up straight, and her eyes flew open.

The security guard tossed aside his copy of *People* magazine and picked up the receiver of an old-school black phone. Anna was too far away to hear the conversation, but she watched him nod, and then nod again. And then he abruptly looked up, directly at Anna. Her heart vaulted in her chest, and she pressed back into her chair as if that little bit of extra space between them would help her escape his notice.

The guard nodded at whatever the person on the other end of the phone was saying, and then he slowly set it back in the cradle, still staring at her across the distance.

Anna stood and hurried down a hallway where a sign pointed to the bathrooms. Once she was safely in the women's room, she crossed her arms over her chest and leaned against the back wall. Did that guard know who she was? Is that why he looked at her so intensely? Was she just being paranoid?

The bathroom door swung open, and Anna's heart jumped again until she realized it was only the mother and boy she'd met earlier. The woman smiled at her and nudged her son into a stall.

"Excuse me." Anna held out a hand. "Did you happen to see that security guard outside the bathroom when you came in?"

The woman blinked in surprise, and then her face softened, and she seemed to register understanding. She probably knew that when you were on your own, you could never let your guard down. "He was in the booth a minute ago." The woman opened the bathroom door and peeked down the hall. "There's nobody there now."

Anna let out a heavy breath. "Thanks." She probably *was* just being paranoid. That phone call could have been from anyone. Maybe the security guard's wife wanted him to pick up a carton of milk on his way home. There was no reason to think she was on his radar. Anna glanced at her watch. Thirty more minutes and she'd be on a bus to Chicago. And from there, to San Francisco, where nobody would ever think to look for her.

Anna left the bathroom and headed down the hall. At the entrance to the waiting area, she peeked around the corner to the security booth. The guard sat there, leaning casually back in his chair, staring at his magazine again. Her shoulders relaxed.

*I'm definitely being paranoid.*

She stopped at the vending machine to grab a bottle of water for the bus ride. Just as she was tucking it into her bag, she felt someone's weight shift behind her. Before she could react, the person grabbed her by the arm, wrenching her backward.

# FOURTEEN

"Ow! Let me go!" Anna yelled, wrestling to get free. Bruising fingers dug into her flesh through her thin jacket, and all of a sudden, she was being dragged across the room. "Help!" she yelled, fighting harder to disengage her attacker. She twisted around to get a better look and saw the flash of a gold armband on a navy sleeve.

The security guard *had* been waiting for her all along.

He towered over her, six feet of muscle, and for a moment Anna wondered if he was going to rip her arm from the socket as he hauled her toward the security booth. Heart racing, Anna changed her tack, and instead of pulling away, she shoved all her weight in his direction, landing an elbow under his rib cage. The guard grunted, and for a moment his hand went slack. Anna seized her opportunity, yanking herself free and spinning around to land a hard kick to his shin.

"Damn it!" the guard roared, and before she knew what was happening, he dove, tackling her. She flew sideways, her shoulder hitting the concrete floor with a crack. The air whooshed from her lungs, and she frantically pressed her hands to the ground, trying to push herself to a seated position, fighting to scramble out of the guard's reach. But he was on top of her, pinning her down.

She gasped for air. "Get off me. Please get off me." It was too much. The weight of him on top of her. The feeling of helplessness. It was too familiar. She could almost see the staircase descending into that basement all those years ago, could almost feel the dampness seep into her fevered skin through the open doorway. "Please."

*I can't breathe.*

"Hey!" a sharp voice echoed from somewhere across the room, yanking her back to the present. The next thing Anna knew, Gabe was there, dragging the guard off her, pulling her to her feet. "Are you okay?"

"No." She reeled backward, away from him, her whole body shaking. "No, I'm not okay. Did you send him after me?" She leaned on a chair, gasping for breath, but the movement sent a shot of pain through her shoulder.

"Anna." Gabe approached her slowly. "What were you thinking, running away like that?"

Anna stood abruptly. The burning in her limbs from being manhandled by the security guard ignited into a fire that radiated across every part of her. Anger. Wild, blazing anger. "*What were you thinking, telling my secrets to your family?*"

"I had to. You know I had to."

"You didn't have to do *anything*." The tears welled up again, which only served to fan the flames of her anger. She swiped at her wet cheeks with her palm, took a deep breath, and looked Gabe straight in the eye. "I hate you, Gabe. I hate you, and I will never forgive you for this."

To her great satisfaction, Gabe flinched.

Good. She wanted to hurt him. She wanted to reach inside his chest and tear out his heart like he'd done with hers. But that would require him to care about her. And nobody who truly cared could have betrayed her this way.

The security guard shuffled forward and reached for her again. "Listen, I don't know what's going on here, but I was told this girl's guardians would be coming for her."

"Don't you dare touch me," Anna hissed at him.

"They'll be here any second." Gabe stepped in front of the guard. "They're parking the car."

"Anna!" called a familiar female voice from across the room.

Anna looked up to find John and Elizabeth hurrying toward her.

"Honey, are you okay?" Elizabeth took her by the arms, looking her over, and before Anna knew what to think, the older woman was pulling her into a hug.

For just one moment, Anna closed her eyes and leaned in. She was so tired. *So tired.* But then another sharp pain stabbed her shoulder, and Anna remembered why they were here. She wrenched herself free. "I'll keep running. You'll have to lock me up until I'm eighteen. But I'll still keep running."

"Anna, just listen, okay?"

Gabe held out his hand in a calm-down motion, but the gesture made her feel the opposite of calm. She hated him so much.

The security guard turned to John. "You're the guardians?"

John nodded. "We are."

"You're sure you're okay to take her?" A flash of doubt crossed the guard's face, and a shot of panic raced up Anna's spine. Suddenly, being left in the Weatheralls' care didn't seem nearly as bad as having to stay with this guy. What if he grabbed her again? What if she couldn't get away? He might insist on dragging her to the police station to sort it out. They might actually lock her up until she was eighteen.

Or longer.

Oh God, she couldn't have the cops poking around.

But before Anna could panic, John reached out a hand and grasped the security guard's, giving it a firm shake. "Thank you so much for your help. My wife and I appreciate it. We can take it from here."

Coming from anyone else, it might not have had the same effect. But from a man like John—tall, distinguished, and used to getting exactly what he wanted—nobody was going to argue. Especially the security guard, who was favoring the leg where she'd kicked him. He was probably eager for Anna to be someone else's problem.

"Okay," the guard said, confirming Anna's suspicions by holding up his hands like this situation was a toxic spill and he wasn't going near it. "Good luck with her." He turned and headed back to the security booth.

"Honey."

Elizabeth's voice was gentle, but it had Anna's spine stiffening. People only spoke like that when they were about to tell someone something they didn't want to hear.

"It's clear you've figured out Gabe told us about your mother leaving and you living on your own."

Anna pressed her lips together and nodded, not trusting her voice.

"You can imagine we're very concerned." Elizabeth reached out and put her hand on Anna's arm. "Aside from the fact that you're a young girl living all alone, we also understand you've had some trouble with the landlord."

Anna snatched her arm away. "Gabe doesn't know anything about it. I had it all under control until he came along."

"Anna," Gabe growled back, leaning against the wall and crossing his arms over his chest. "Can you just *listen*?"

She shot him a hard look.

"You're a smart girl," John said in a low voice. "You know you can't continue with your current living situation."

"You're not my parents. You don't get to decide what happens to me."

"Well, it doesn't appear that your parents are available to make those kinds of decisions," John pointed out.

To Anna's mortification, her eyes filled with tears again.

"John," Elizabeth scolded, nudging him with her elbow. "This isn't helpful."

Gabe pushed away from the wall. "Can I have a minute with Anna," he barked. It wasn't really a question, and his dad's voice of authority had nothing on Gabe's.

She would have been impressed if she didn't hate him so much.

John and Elizabeth exchanged a glance, and then Elizabeth nodded. "We'll be right over here."

Gabe watched until they were settled in on a bench by the vending machine, and then he pointed to the closest vinyl chair. "Sit."

"Don't tell me what to do."

Gabe heaved a huge sigh, momentarily closing his eyes and running a hand through his hair. "Fine. *Please* sit."

"Fine." Anna dropped down in the chair, and he slid into the one next to her, so close she could have reached over and smacked him in that beautiful face.

Gabe shifted his legs so he was facing her. "Where did you think you were going?"

"It's none of your business."

"Right, okay," he said. And before she could stop him, Gabe leaned across her and snatched the bus ticket from the side pocket of her bag. He turned it over in his hands. "Chicago? What the hell is in Chicago?"

Anna made a grab for the ticket, but he held it out of reach. She didn't know why she'd bothered. There was no way she'd make it on that bus now. But that stupid piece of paper crumpled in Gabe's hands felt like her last hope. Her shoulders slumped. "I was going to look for my mom."

Gabe looked up in surprise. "Your mom is in Chicago? I thought she was in California."

"She is. I think. I don't know." Anna looked down at her hands. "I think she might be in San Francisco."

"So, you were going to hop on a bus to Chicago, and from there to San Francisco?"

She nodded.

"And then what? Did you plan to just wander the city looking for her?"

Anna's head jerked up. "What? No. I'm not an idiot. I have an address."

Gabe's eyebrows rose. "Really?"

Anna pulled her backpack into her lap and slid the worn scrap of paper from the pocket. "She used to call me. Back when she first left. The number came up on the cordless phone. I saved it and did a reverse phone number lookup. The calls came from a house in the Mission District in San Francisco."

Gabe reached over and gently took the paper, unfolding it and smoothing out the creases. "Capp Street."

Anna nodded. How many times had she googled that address and stared at the little dot on the map, wondering if it marked the spot where her mother lived. It was 2,576 miles from her apartment building in Pittsburgh to Capp Street in San Francisco.

"And what did you hope would happen if you found her?" Gabe asked, folding the paper and handing it back.

"I hoped I'd get some answers about where she's been and why she disappeared." Anna bit her lip. That sounded right. She did want answers. But she wanted so much more than that, too. "I hoped..."

*I hoped I could fix the mess I made and make it right.*

But Anna just shrugged. "I don't know. If she's still using, maybe I could help her. Convince her to come home."

Maybe she really was an idiot. The skepticism that passed over Gabe's face certainly implied that she was. He probably assumed what everyone else did—that her mom was a junkie who wasn't worth saving. But Gabe didn't know her like Anna did.

And he didn't know her mom never would have left if it weren't for Anna.

"Look, my mom went to California because she was chasing an opportunity that would give us a better life. I don't know what happened after that, but I have to believe she's still out there. That there's still a chance for me to get her back." She leaned her weight on the arm of the chair. "What if it were your mom who disappeared? What would *you* do?"

She knew he'd chase his mom to the ends of the earth.

"Okay." Gabe ran a hand through his hair. "But what if you couldn't find her when you got there? What would you have done then?"

"I—" Anna looked away.

"You didn't think that far, did you?"

Anna's face flushed because she *hadn't* thought that far. Or maybe she had, and she'd simply pushed the idea out of her mind that her mother might not be there. Because, for years, she'd been counting on that address, that house on Capp Street in San Francisco, exactly 2,576 miles away.

But she didn't owe Gabe, of all people, an explanation. He'd betrayed her and would do it again. Anna jumped to her feet. "If you'll excuse me, I really have to go to the bathroom."

Gabe actually had the nerve to laugh. "Nice try, kid." He caught her by the wrist and tugged her back into her seat. "I'm not letting you out of my sight just yet."

Anna pulled her hand from his grasp. "You can't keep me against my will forever."

"Anna, I'm not trying to keep you against your will." He turned in his seat to look at her. "I'm trying to tell you that you don't have to go to foster care. My parents want you to move in with them."

Anna's head jerked back, and her hands flew to the armrests of her chair because suddenly, she needed an anchor. "They... what?" she choked.

"They have plenty of room, and you can keep going to your university classes. Nothing would have to change except you'll be safe with them."

"They want me to move in with them," Anna repeated. Never in a million years would she have imagined this. "I—" She had no idea what to say, and the silence stretched across the narrow space between them.

Anna glanced across the room to Elizabeth and John and then back to Gabe. "Why would they want me to move in with them?" she finally managed to whisper.

Gabe's expression softened. "They care about you, kid. We all do." He gave her a wry smile. "Not that you're making it easy for anyone right now."

Anna tried to swallow down the lump in her throat. She never wanted to believe anything as much as she wanted to believe what Gabe was saying at that moment. It was what she'd spent so much time this past year secretly longing for. A family like Gabe's. A real home.

It should feel like she'd won the lottery.

Except it felt more like she was standing on the edge of a cliff.

Because the Weatheralls weren't really her family, and Anna knew better than to ever get caught up in that fantasy again. She'd survived by learning to never rely on anyone but herself, and when she'd stupidly let someone else in, look where it got her.

Anna shot a glance at Gabe. He thought he was protecting her. But as she pressed a hand to her aching shoulder, she could still feel the security guard pinning her to the concrete, trapping her beneath him like she was a wild animal. Anna rocked forward in her chair, trying to shove it from her mind. But it was burned there now, and she'd never forgive Gabe for it.

Her situation in that apartment was far from perfect, but it was hers. She'd earned the right to decide what happened to her. And Gabe had stolen that when he'd turned her in to his parents.

"Anna, move in with them." Gabe leaned in. "You don't always have to do everything on your own. I know you think you do, but you don't. You can trust them. And I know you're mad at me right now. But you can trust me, too."

Those silver eyes tunneled through her defenses, and she slid back in her chair to escape them. "Trust me" was so easy for him to say. He grew up with a loving family who adored him. But she was a stray who'd hung around long enough they'd felt bad and started to feed her.

They didn't really want her. And why would they? She'd driven her own mother away.

Gabe studied her with a silent intensity that left her feeling naked and exposed. She squirmed, shifting her gaze to the wall over his shoulder. Anna would never, ever trust him or his family. But if she didn't go with them, the social workers would show up and call the cops. What if they made the connection between her mom and that guy?

What if they figured out that Anna had been there that day?

She jumped when Gabe reached out and touched her arm. "This is your best option, kid."

Anna knew it was. She didn't have enough money to keep running, and stupidly, she'd told Gabe where to look for her if she did. The tears she'd been holding back spilled over. "I can't believe you sold me out like this," Anna hissed, swiping a palm across her wet cheeks. "I'll never forgive you for this, Gabe. *Never.*"

Gabe leaned forward, staring her right in the face. "I don't care if you forgive me. I care that you're safe."

And that was it. Game over.

He held out his palm. "Should we go talk to my parents? Make a plan to get your things?"

For the first time, the reality of moving in with John and Elizabeth sank in. Now that she wasn't going to make it to San Francisco—it might be *years* before she could make it to that house on Capp Street—her run-down apartment building was the only place that still connected her to her mom.

Anna shrank away from Gabe's outstretched hand. "What about my mom?"

Gabe cocked his head, searching her face. "Anna, you can't take a bus to San Francisco. You know that, right?"

He was pitying her. "Of course I know that. But..." Anna twisted the strap of her backpack in her hands. "But what if she comes back?" She hated the breathlessness in her voice, how it gave away that tiny bit of hope.

He looked at her sideways, and damn it, she knew what he was thinking. Her mom had been gone for two years. He didn't think she was ever coming back. *But he doesn't know for sure.*

Her mom had said she'd be back.

*I'm just going for a little while. I'll do this job and make enough money that nobody can ever hurt us again. Don't worry, baby. I'm going to take care of us.*

She was still out there somewhere. If she wasn't, Anna would know. She'd feel it.

"How will my mom ever find me? It's not like I can leave a forwarding address with the landlord."

"Well..." He dragged the word out, and she knew he was humoring her.

She felt her cheeks grow hot. His mother would never have had to leave him, so he didn't know what it was like to wait around for her to return. To agonize over what might've happened to her.

Gabe drummed his fingertips on the arm of the chair. "What about a neighbor in the building?"

"Mrs. Janiszewski. She lives upstairs."

"Okay, we'll leave my parents' number with Mrs. Janiszewski when we go over to pick up your things."

So that was it. Just like that, her whole life had been decided for her. For years, she'd been desperate to get out of that run-down apartment and away from the horrible landlord. But it should have been on her own terms. Not Gabe's. So little about her life had been in her control, and he'd taken this from her, too. If she didn't move in with Gabe's parents, they'd call child protective services. They'd shuffle her from place to place like a piece of luggage being tossed under the bus outside.

Anna knew if it came down to moving in with the Weatheralls or ending up in the system, she'd be stupid not to pick the Weatheralls. At least she could keep going to her classes, and a year from now, she'd be on her way to college and away from this place for good. And then maybe she really *could* make it to San Francisco, to find her mom and fix this mess she'd made.

She'd move in with the Weatheralls, but she'd never forgive Gabe or trust his family again. Because she was smart enough to know that allowing them in again could hurt her more than any shady landlord or foster home she might end up with.

# FIFTEEN

Gabe sat in a blue linen chair on one side of his parents' living room fireplace and pretended to be engrossed in whatever book he'd grabbed off his parents' shelf. In reality, he was watching Anna turn the pages of a fraying leather album while his grandmother pointed her wrinkled finger at a sepia-toned photograph, a smile deepening the lines around her mouth.

"Benjamin." Dorothy said, her voice hoarse from lack of use.

"I can tell by how you're grinning at him in the picture that he was your favorite brother." Anna smoothed down the curling photograph, and Gabe could just make out the image of a little girl in a sailor dress and knee socks standing next to a boy in a tweed suit and matching cap. He'd looked at that photo a dozen times over the years but had never thought to sit down and ask his grandmother about it. But Anna had. She'd asked Dorothy about every photo in the album and learned more about the older woman's story in a few months than he had in his entire life.

Gabe was still in awe that Anna had taken the time to learn how to draw his grandmother out like this. But if he were really honest about it, maybe it wasn't so much about the information she'd gleaned in a neuroscience textbook.

Maybe it was just Anna.

When she'd moved in with his parents a couple of months ago, Anna had dug up some old photo albums, and she and Dorothy were slowly working their way through them, piecing together the stories of Dorothy's childhood. Although his grandmother rarely recognized her family in the present, Anna had discovered that she had clear memories of people from her past. And though Dorothy didn't speak much, somehow, Anna managed to communicate with her just fine.

Dorothy began plucking at her skirt, a sign she was growing tired and would soon retreat inside her own world. Anna picked up on it right away, and she snapped the photo album shut. "Let's look at some more later, okay?"

Dorothy patted Anna on the leg, and the row of shiny diamond rings glinted on her weathered, sun-spotted hand. She'd been doing that a lot lately: patting Anna's leg, squeezing her hand, brushing her hair off her face. Dorothy was growing attached to Anna, even if she didn't know who Anna was. And it was clear from the yearning on Anna's face that she felt the same way.

Gabe went back to his book, surprised at the emotion in his chest. It was such a relief to see Anna looking comfortable and relaxed—happy even—instead of perpetually worn down like she'd been for so much of the time he'd known her. Since she'd moved in with his parents, she'd put on some weight, the dark circles under her eyes had disappeared, and her smile came much more readily.

Well, it came more readily for everyone but Gabe.

For Gabe, Anna offered a grab bag of silence, glares, and outright hostility. On some level, Gabe got it. He'd been the one to light the match and set fire to her old life. Despite clear evidence to the contrary, Anna still believed that she'd had all that shit with her landlord under control, and there was no reasoning with her. She'd vowed to never forgive Gabe, and she was really leaning into it. He'd been in the same room with her for the past ten minutes, and she hadn't even acknowledged him.

Still, he kept trying.

"Hey, kid, how's your summer class going?" he asked, tossing his book aside. He'd graduated from the university this past spring and was headed to grad school next month, but Anna was taking another class. Normally, she would have talked to him all about it, asked his advice on her midterm paper or something. But it had been crickets.

"What do you care?" Anna crossed her arms and glared at him.

With a grin he stood up and moved to her side of the room. "You know, you should watch those mean expressions. Your face could freeze like that. Then you'll be sorry."

Anna's lips quirked into a half smile, and Gabe felt a stab of triumph. It was by far the most promising reaction he'd managed to coax from her all summer. Her hand flew up to cover her mouth, but it was too late. He knew he'd chiseled a tiny crack. Gabe made a show of rolling his shoulders back and stretching, as if he'd just beat her at arm wrestling. "I knew you missed my jokes."

"Whatever." Anna rolled her eyes, and that wall immediately came back up.

Gabe eyed her for a moment and then dropped into the chair across the coffee table from her. "Anna, listen. I want to talk to you about something. I spoke to my new advisor at UC, and she suggested I attend the Hastings conference on economics and social justice this fall." Actually, his advisor had suggested he attend one of several options for conferences. He'd picked this one for a very specific reason.

Anna shrugged. "Okay." Her voice dripped with *Why are*

*you telling me this?* She really was an expert-level grudge-holder. He'd admire her for it if all that ire weren't directed at him. And if he didn't miss their old friendship.

"The conference is in San Francisco."

Anna's head jerked up. That got her attention. "Really?" she asked breathlessly.

"Yeah. So, I was thinking maybe you could give me that address you have for your mom. And I could go and check it out."

In a single moment, an entire rainbow of emotions crossed her face: shock, terror, and finally, hope. "Really? You're not kidding? You'd honestly do that for me?" Her shoulders slid up to her ears, and she grabbed one hand nervously with the other.

Why did she seem so surprised? Did Anna really believe that when he'd given up her secret, it was because he didn't care about her? Didn't she understand that he'd done it only because he cared about her? "Of course I would, Anna," he snapped. "What—do you think I'm just messing with you?"

Anna blinked. "No. I—" Her shoulders dropped. "I'm sorry. I know you wouldn't do that. I just can't believe it. I thought it would be years before I could get there to track her down."

Gabe rubbed the back of his neck. He had his reservations about this. For someone who was so insightful about other people, Anna seemed to have this huge blind spot when it came to her mom. From Gabe's perspective, the woman had bailed on her kid—full stop. Whatever she'd been chasing when she'd taken off for California, it wasn't a better life for Anna. Gabe had his doubts that this trip would turn up anything remotely like good news. But Anna was seventeen now, and she'd be graduating from high school in less than a year. Maybe it was better for her to learn the truth so she could move on with the rest of her life.

"I should be able to go on a break between sessions at the conference," he told her. "I'll call you as soon as I get there."

"Thank you, Gabe. Really. This means so much to me." And then she gave him the first real smile he'd seen from her in months.

Gabe rose from the plastic folding chairs lined up across the hotel conference room and checked his schedule. He had a two-hour break before the dinner program started at six, and the front desk concierge had told him it would be about a thirty-minute walk from downtown San Francisco to the Mission District. It looked like this was his window.

Why was he suddenly nervous about this? Maybe it was the look in Anna's eyes, full of anticipation and hope, when she'd handed over the address, neatly copied onto a note card along with the words *Deborah Campbell.* He'd already known her mother's name from his investigation at the nursing home that past spring. The last time around, he'd unearthed a ticking time bomb. Gabe hoped the results would be different today.

Thirty minutes later, he made his way down Mission Street, where the neighborhood seemed to be in the midst of gentrification. Modern condos and hip cafés lined the sidewalk, next to Mexican restaurants and vintage apparel stores that looked like they'd been there since the clothes inside were new. Did Anna's mother walk this same street, grabbing tacos from the place with the colorful murals and shopping for secondhand clothes at the store called Yesterday's News?

If he were honest, he didn't really expect to find Anna's mother in the house at the address in his pocket. But he hoped that whatever he discovered would at least help Anna get some closure. So, at the intersection of Mission and 19$^{th}$ Street, Gabe made a left and continued down the block until he came to a metal lamppost supporting a black-and-white street sign with the words *Capp St.*

Gabe checked the address and then glanced up at the buildings. On the same side of the block stood a small bodega with cut flowers and fruit displayed in pots along the sidewalk. The red awning over the store said *1906* in faded letters, so it looked like the address Anna had given him—*1908*—should be right around the corner.

He passed the bodega, turned onto Capp Street, and then stopped on the sidewalk. In front of him stood a temporary metal fence cordoning off a three-story gray house that looked to be abandoned. Gabe stepped closer, twining his fingers through the chain-link and gazing up at the building. The stucco outer walls of the Spanish-style house seemed in decent shape, but that was about the only thing that was. The door to the first-story garage sat at an angle as if it had been knocked off its track, plywood boards covered most of the upstairs windows, and a series of cracks ran through the concrete steps leading up to the splitting wood frame and faded front door.

And then that door swung open, and out strolled a fit-looking middle-aged man in a blue-checked button-up shirt tucked into tailored gray trousers. Gabe blinked. He didn't know what he'd been expecting, but it hadn't been this guy. The man locked the door and then headed down the stairs, carefully watching his footing.

"Excuse me," Gabe called out as the man approached the sidewalk.

The man looked up, focusing on Gabe. "Can I help you?"

"I hope so." Gabe cleared his throat. "Do you own this house? I was wondering if you could tell me anything about it. I'm looking for, uh, a friend, who I think might have lived here."

Now it was the man's turn to look surprised. "You had a friend who lived in this house? I find that hard to believe."

Gabe shoved his hand in the pockets of his own tailored trousers, remembering he was dressed for networking at an economics conference and not poking around abandoned buildings. He tried to think of a good explanation for what he was doing there and finally settled on the truth. "I'm actually looking for my friend's mom. She disappeared a couple of years ago. My friend thinks this place is her last known address. I was in town and told her I'd stop by."

"Ah." The man nodded like that made much more sense. He took a few steps to the left and swung open the gate attached to the fence. "Come on in." He waved Gabe through the opening onto the other side of the sidewalk and held out his palm. "I'm Cliff Desmond."

"Gabe Weatherall."

"I'm not the owner; I'm the real estate agent," Cliff explained. "This house is under contract, and the closing is tomorrow. I'm just here to do the final walk-through."

Gabe's gaze shifted back to the house. "How long has it been like this?"

"That I can't really answer." Cliff shrugged. "Clearly, nobody has been maintaining it or paying the bills for years. I got involved when my client bought it at auction from the city. She held on to it for about a year until real estate prices made it too tempting not to turn around and sell."

"So, who's buying it tomorrow?"

"They're a local development company."

"They're going to renovate it?"

"I believe they're planning to raze it and build lofts."

Gabe wasn't surprised. "I've heard there's a lot of that happening in San Francisco right now."

"Yep." Cliff flashed a set of straight white teeth. "Can't say I'm complaining. It's great for business."

"Is there any way to find out anything about the residents who were living here before the city took over?"

"My understanding is that there were squatters here. And it sure looks like it from the contents of the house."

"That's right," came a voice from behind them. "Squatters."

Gabe turned around to find a short, gray-haired man who'd

been sweeping the sidewalk in front of the bodega a moment ago. "Yeah? Can you tell us anything about them?"

The man leaned on his broom. "All I know is this place used to be a crack house."

Gabe's eyebrows shot up.

The shopkeeper shook his head, his face twisting with disgust. "Nothing but drugs and prostitutes coming in and out. Stealing from me and overdosing on the street." He waved a dismissive hand. "Good riddance."

"Based on the condition and contents of the house, I can pretty much confirm this," Cliff said more gently. "I'm sorry for what that might mean for your friend."

Unlike the shopkeeper, Cliff did look sorry. Gabe shot him a grateful look.

The shopkeeper banged his broom on the ground. "I'm not saying I'm going to love the noise and construction vehicles, but developers tearing down that house and building a brand-new loft will be the best thing to ever happen to the neighborhood. We've got young families, kids living around here. It wasn't safe."

"By any chance did you know any of the people who used to come in and out?" Gabe dug in his pocket and pulled out the photo Anna had given him. It had a faded, yellow sheen to it. The young woman in it wore an acid-washed denim jacket and had a 1980s perm. The picture had probably been taken before Anna was even born. Gabe knew it was unlikely that Deb Campbell still resembled the person in the photo after two decades and a very hard life, but it was all he had. "Her name's Deb."

The shopkeeper barely glanced at the photo. "I only paid attention to those people when they were being carried off in the back of a police car. Or in an ambulance on the way to the morgue."

Gabe sucked in a breath, but before he could respond, Cliff

cut in. "Thanks for your help." He gave the shopkeeper a thin smile and then turned his back to him. "Listen, young man, I don't know anything about this situation, but you seem like a good person to come down here looking for your friend's mom."

"Thanks." Gabe's shoulder slumped. "She was hoping to finally get some answers."

"Do you think this will give her any?"

"No." Gabe sighed. "I think this will only raise a lot more questions."

Cliff gestured toward the crumbling steps. "Well, if it might help, you're welcome to poke around in the house. There are some personal items that people left behind, and the developers definitely don't want them. They've already got a dumpster booked for the day after tomorrow."

"Really? It's safe to go in there?"

"Well..." Cliff held up a hand. "I'm warning you that it's pretty rough to look at. But structurally, it's perfectly safe. Come on."

The house was dark, the windows boarded up, with only a few small shards of light slanting through the cracks. A burned odor hung in the air, not cigarette smoke, something sharper. The shopkeeper had called it a crack house. Maybe that's what Gabe smelled. As he crept deeper inside, a sourness took over, like someone had spilled milk on the stained, drooping old couches in the living room and left it there for weeks—or maybe for years.

Gabe could see that once, the house had been beautiful, with the original hardwood floors and moldings around the doorways, but he'd probably been in elementary school when someone had last wiped down a surface.

Up a narrow staircase, Cliff showed Gabe three bedrooms, each with a couple of pieces of wooden furniture shoved up against the walls and mattresses on the floor covered in dingy bedding. Clothes spilled out of bureaus, and food wrappers, beer bottles, and other garbage littered the floors. He and Cliff entered the first bedroom, carefully steering clear of the bed, and Gabe made his way over to a desk under the window while Cliff headed for the bureau.

"What did you say your friend's mom's name was?" Cliff shuffled through a pile of papers that sat on top.

"Deborah Campbell."

Cliff tossed the papers aside. "There are some receipts here, old bills, but nothing with that name."

While Cliff flipped open the lid of a shoebox, Gabe poked through the desk drawers. There wasn't much there except for some more papers, a handful of dusty paper clips, and dried-out pens. All of this stuff could have been there for decades. He checked the date on a bill—*1990*. Long before Anna's mom would have been there.

He and Cliff moved on to the next bedroom where Cliff headed for the bureau again, and Gabe dug through the desk. It was more of the same. Just a bunch of junk that the developers would be happy to haul off in a dumpster. Still, Gabe kept looking, grabbing the handle of the bottom drawer and tugging it open. He jumped back with a gasp. "Jesus."

Cliff whirled around. "What is it?"

Gabe eyed the bent, blackened spoons, empty plastic bags, and uncapped needles lying on the bottom of the drawer. "It's—uh. I guess this is where someone liked to shoot up."

Cliff nodded. "Yeah, there's some of that in the bathroom, too."

Gabe's shoulders slumped. "I don't even know what I'm looking for here. I mean, it's not like a woman who abandoned her teenage daughter to live in a place like this was going to have held on to family photos or, I don't know, a diary or something." He slammed the desk drawer shut. "If Anna's mom *was* here, it was probably for drugs or..." Gabe's eyes shifted to the mattress on the floor. He didn't want to think about it. For Anna's sake.

They took a cursory look around the last bedroom but didn't find much more than the same old clothes, stained bedding, and garbage.

Back out on the street, Gabe held out his palm to Cliff. "Thank you so much for letting me look around. I really appreciate it."

Cliff shook his hand. "I'm sorry something didn't turn up."

Gabe shrugged. "Well, even nothing is more information than we had before this."

Cliff clapped a hand on his shoulder. "Your friend is lucky to have you."

Gabe headed back down 19th Street and around the corner to Mission Street, where he slumped back against a brick wall under the sign for a pawn shop. "Damn it," he muttered, running a hand through his hair. "What am I going to tell her?"

Anna had been so hopeful. But she must have known all along it was a long shot.

He fished his phone from his pocket and hit the button to dial Anna's new cell number. She picked up on the first ring. "Hello?"

His heart squeezed at the eagerness in her tone. Was she waiting by the phone for him to call? "Hey, kid. It's Gabe."

"Hi. How's it going?"

Gabe stuffed his free hand in his pocket as the wind picked up. "Someone forgot to tell San Francisco that it's still technically summer."

"Oh, poor you," she joked, and Gabe could picture Anna rolling her eyes. He grinned despite himself.

"How's the conference?" Anna asked.

"Anna." Gabe shifted from one foot to the other. "I went to Capp Street to look for your mom."

"And?" Her voice was practically a whisper.

Gabe took a deep breath, ready to tell her everything: the dilapidated house, the trash, the drug paraphernalia. But when he opened his mouth, he couldn't say the words. If Anna's mother *had* lived in that house, she'd likely been in deep with whatever illicit activity had been going on there. The shopkeeper had implied that many of the people living there had ended up in jail... or dead. But it was all speculation. There was really no evidence that Deb Campbell had ever been in that house, let alone this city. A Google search of a phone number wasn't an exact science.

Anna had been through so much, and this would only make not knowing what happened to her mother harder. She'd imagine the worst.

"I'm sorry, Anna," Gabe said gently. "The house has been sold to a developer. It's empty. Nobody lives there anymore."

"Oh..." She sounded so disappointed. "Okay."

"I'm sorry," he repeated.

"Well, was there...?" Anna trailed off, sighing. "Never mind."

"What were you going to ask?"

"Was there anyone you could have asked about her? Maybe a neighbor who knew her? Did you show anyone her photo?"

Gabe pushed off from the wall and paced down the sidewalk in front of the pawn shop and then back to the corner. "I talked to a guy at a local grocery store, but he didn't remember her." It wasn't exactly a lie. The shopkeeper *hadn't* remembered Anna's mother. "Apparently, the house has been empty for years." That wasn't a lie either.

Again, Gabe crossed in front of the display of other people's treasures in the pawn shop window: a couple of acoustic guitars, a mirrored tray full of watches, a bunch of old jewelry, all lined up under a flashing neon sign that read *Cash for Gold.* There wasn't a single thing in that house anyone would've wanted to save, let alone sell. It was better for the neighborhood that they knock it down and start over.

He paced down the sidewalk and back again. Anna was silent for so long that Gabe began to wonder if they'd gotten disconnected. "Anna? Are you there?"

Finally, she took a sharp breath. "We knew it was a long shot."

"We did. Still, I'm sorry."

A blue velvet tray in the pawn shop window caught his eye, glinting with gold jewelry.

"Thank you for going there, Gabe," Anna said.

"Don't thank me. I didn't do anything."

"You did. You have no idea how much this means to me." Her voice hitched at the end, and she cleared her throat.

And then suddenly, Gabe's heart jumped into his throat. Because there in the pawn shop window was a necklace that looked awfully familiar. He stepped closer. *Is it possible?* The pendant had the same half-moon shape with a similar pattern etched into the surface. But the window was too dirty to get a good look.

"Anna," Gabe said, trying to keep his voice even, "I should get back to the conference."

"Of course. Thanks again, Gabe."

As soon as they'd hung up, Gabe yanked open the door to the pawn shop and stepped inside.

A gray-haired older woman in a 49ers sweatshirt looked up. "Can I help you?"

"Yes, please." Gabe gestured at the window. "There's a necklace there that I'd like to see."

The woman pulled the velvet jewelry display from the window and set it on the counter. "Here you go. Which one are you interested in?"

Gabe reached over and gently lifted the small gold necklace. Heart pounding, he settled the pendant in his palm to get a better look. *It has to be.* There was no other explanation. It couldn't possibly be a coincidence that in a pawn shop, around the corner from where Anna's mother might have lived, was a mirror image of the necklace Anna wore everyday of her life.

"It's a pretty one, isn't it? Real gold," the woman pointed out.

Gabe ran a finger over the pendant. There was some sort of flower etched into the surface, and he was pretty sure the pattern would match up to the lines on the one Anna wore. Held together at the midpoint, the two pendants would form a circle.

"Do you know where it came from? Who sold it to you?"

The woman shook her head. "I don't ask questions."

How had this ended up in a pawn shop?

But Gabe had a feeling he already knew. He pictured the needles and other remnants of drug use in the desk drawer. People would do anything if they were desperate enough. Even sell their most precious piece of jewelry.

*The one that matches their daughter's.*

Gabe's fist closed around the necklace. "How much do you want for it?"

The woman eyed his neatly pressed conference clothes. "A hundred bucks."

"I'll give you fifty."

"Fine."

The fact that she took his lowball offer so readily somehow made it worse. How little had that necklace been worth to Anna's mother that she'd sold it for almost nothing?

The woman pulled out a receipt pad with the name of the shop on top, wrote out a few notes about the necklace and the price, and then tore it off. She tucked the receipt into the bottom of a small velvet box and laid the necklace on top.

A moment later, Gabe stood back outside on the sidewalk holding the cheap clamshell box. He should call Anna and tell her. But something held him back. How many times had he watched her grab that pendant and rub her thumb against the etched surface? It was usually when she was nervous or upset about something, and the necklace was obviously a comfort to her. It was her connection to her mother. The patterns fit together like a puzzle, and all this time, she'd been searching for the missing piece.

How could he call her and tell her that her mother had sold her half to a pawn shop? That it meant so little to Deb Campbell when it meant everything to Anna? He couldn't break that kind of news over the phone.

Gabe shoved the velvet box in his pocket and headed up Mission Street, back to his hotel. He'd started his graduate program at UC earlier that month and wouldn't be home again until winter break. But that was only a few months away. It would be better to bring the necklace home and give it to Anna in person. He could tell her everything he'd learned about her mom then.

# SIXTEEN

Anna tapped her pencil on her calculus book and stared at the clock. Gabe's plane from Chicago had landed that morning, and he'd be home for an entire week for winter break. One more period to go, and she'd see him for the first time since he left for grad school. She'd gotten a cell phone that fall, and they texted all the time, usually random observations about their day or stories to make each other laugh. Stuff they used to talk about when they were working on their project last year. It was almost like he was still there.

Almost.

Anna dug through her backpack, as if looking for a pencil, and clicked on her cell phone to read yesterday's text exchange.

*Anna*

*So, I've been helping your mother clean out your old bedroom in anticipation of your trip home. I found a pile of old* Victoria's Secret *catalogs and a half-full bottle of Jim Beam under the bed, left over from your depraved adolescence. You'll be glad to know I managed to throw them away before your mother saw them. You are still perfect in her eyes. You're welcome.*

*Gabe*

*Thanks for looking out for me, kid. You should have kept the Jim Beam though. Never know when you might need it.*

*Anna*

*Don't worry, I snagged plenty of treasures... like the 7th grade school picture I found in a drawer—the one where you had braces and a mullet—in case I ever need to blackmail you.*

*Gabe*

*Thank God you didn't find the photos from freshman year when I went through that overalls-with-no-shirt phase.*

*Anna*

*Oh, I found them. Matt and Rachel are locked in a bidding war.*

*Gabe*

*Damn. I'm gone for one semester, and you turn on me so quickly.*

Anna looked up to find her calculus teacher shooting her a grumpy look. Pressing her lips together to hide her grin, she shoved the phone to the bottom of her backpack and did her best to look like she was concentrating on the lecture.

When Gabe had first told his parents about her living alone, Anna had felt so betrayed, she'd sworn she'd never speak to him again. But she had to admit that moving in with John and Elizabeth had turned out to be pretty... okay. For the first time, she went to bed at night without worrying about how she would pay the rent or scrape together the money for the electric bill. She no longer listened for strange noises outside or got out of bed in the dark to double-check the locks. And she'd been able to cut back on her job at the grocery store to focus more on her schoolwork.

But the thing that had finally brought her around was that Gabe had gone to check out that house in San Francisco. She'd never forget his voice when he told her the house was empty and that they'd be tearing it down soon. For a second, she couldn't breathe, knowing that the address she'd been clinging to for years, her one hope to find her mom, had turned out to be a dead end. But then, Gabe's voice came through again, telling her he was sorry, like it meant something to him, too.

For the first time, she felt like someone else cared about what had happened to her mom. Like Anna wasn't alone in this.

It had meant everything. How could she possibly be mad at him after that?

And now he'd actually be there when she got home from school. Anna had about a million things she wanted to tell him, stories she'd been saving for when she saw him in person. Plus, she'd made a big decision about college next year, and if there was anyone she wanted to share that with, it was Gabe.

Her news probably wouldn't surprise him. Gabe's trip to the house on Capp Street had shown her that he understood why she needed to do this.

Finally, the bell rang, and she jumped up and headed for the door, not even bothering to pull on her coat.

Anna ran for the bus, her feet crunching across the frozen grass of the schoolyard while the first snowflakes of the year swirled around her.

When Anna arrived at the Weatheralls' house, the low rumble of Gabe's voice reverberated down the hall. Anna ran into the kitchen and slid to a stop, her heart thumping at the sight of him sitting with Elizabeth and Leah around the island.

Gabe looked up and spotted her. "Anna!" He jumped off his stool and headed for the doorway, throwing his arms around her. She hugged him back, relaxing as the last four months of missing him fell away.

"We've got a lot to catch up on, kid," he said, stepping back so he could look her in the eye.

She smiled. "I want to hear all about grad school."

He nodded. "Yeah, and I need an update on your college applications. But there's something else I want to talk to you about. It's important—"

The rest of his sentence was cut off by a voice out in the hall. "You can start the party. I have arrived." Rachel struck a pose in the doorway, a wide grin on her face. "Hey, big brother. Welcome home."

"You can start the party. *I* have arrived." Matt appeared in the doorway behind Rachel and gave her a playful bump with his shoulder.

Rachel retaliated by shoving an elbow into his side, and Matt reached out a hand that was obviously intended to mess up her hair. Rachel ducked out of the way and held up a palm. "Wait a minute! Why are we bullying each other when we could be bullying Gabe?"

Matt cocked his head and rubbed his chin in an exaggerated thinking motion. "Excellent point, sister."

Anna dove out of the way as Matt and Rachel surrounded Gabe, jokingly pummeling him with their fists.

"Agh! Help me, Anna! Leah!" He reached out a hand.

Anna shot a glance at Leah. "Should we?"

Leah sighed the sigh of an old woman who'd been dealing with this nonsense for fifty years. "I suppose so."

Anna and Leah each grabbed one of Gabe's hands to pull him to pretend-safety. In the jumble of arms and legs and siblings, he tripped over something and stumbled into Anna. His woodsy scent—the one that had grown so familiar over the past year, the one that still lingered on the old sweatshirt she'd pilfered from his childhood bedroom upstairs—enveloped her. For a moment, her legs wavered, and not from the force of being knocked sideways. Anna kept her head down but peered up at him through her lashes, noticing how the flush of exertion brightened his silver-blue eyes.

She'd always found Gabe beautiful. But unlike the rest of the female population, she was usually immune to it. He didn't care about impressing her the way he did girls his own age, so in the past year, he'd had no reason to hide his annoying habits from her. Like the maddening way he clicked his pen over and over when he was working through a problem. Or his painfully out-of-tune singing to the car radio. Gabe's physical appearance had ceased to be the first thing she noticed once she had laughed at the story of his embarrassing fifth-grade crush on his babysitter.

But every so often—when he smiled over at her from the driver's seat or stretched back in his chair, his muscles straining against his T-shirt—his beauty would knock her sideways.

Anna moved to the other side of the kitchen island. While more sibling chaos swirled around her, she focused on turning on the kettle and making a cup of tea, then carrying it to the breakfast nook where Dorothy liked to sit when the weather was too cold for the porch.

Dorothy smiled and patted her hand as Anna placed the tea in front of her. The older woman's calm energy always grounded Anna when she was feeling flustered. She'd never imagined herself making friends with an eighty-year-old woman. Anna had never known her grandmothers or spent any time with someone so much older than she was. She was fascinated by the entire life Dorothy had lived.

She looked up to find Gabe sliding into the booth across

from her. "Hi Grandma." He turned to Anna. "So, what's going on with college, kid?"

Across the room, Leah jumped up and down, clapping her hands. "Tell him, Anna!"

Gabe gave her hand a nudge. "Tell me, Anna."

"Well..." Anna looked down at the table. Dr. McGovern had written her an amazing recommendation letter, and the university had offered her a full scholarship to their joint pre-med-MD program. The letter had come earlier that week, and everyone had been so happy for her.

Of course, they'd assumed she'd take the offer and stay in Pittsburgh.

But Anna hadn't told them about the other letter.

The offer she actually planned to take.

They might be disappointed. Anna worried that John, especially, would be upset because he'd been so enthusiastic about her plan to do the accelerated program. Many of his colleagues at the hospital were professors there. The Weatheralls might not understand.

But Gabe would. He'd shown that when he'd gone to look for her mom. But she couldn't tell him now, in front of everyone.

"Uh." Anna studied the pattern on the table. "I got accepted to the university, and they offered me a full scholarship."

"*Damn*," Gabe said, his mouth curling into a smile. "That's amazing news. Their program is the best, right?"

Anna nodded weakly.

Rachel shoved her way into the booth next to Gabe. "They're giving her a stipend for books, plus free room and board in the honors dorm, too." She shot Anna a grin. "They *really* want her."

Elizabeth joined them, patting Anna's hand. "You know we'd love to have Anna stay here with us instead of in the dorms if she wanted."

Anna looked up. *They would?* Her gaze shifted around the table to everyone crammed into that little booth, smiling, laughing, jostling each other. And then it slid to Dorothy, whose hand rested on top of hers. What if she took Elizabeth up on that offer? What if she said yes and just... stayed here?

Gabe winked at her. "Anna has to live in the dorms; otherwise, how's she going to get drunk and stumble home from frat parties?"

Anna drifted back down to reality. Of course she couldn't stay with the Weatheralls. They'd already done too much for her. And besides, she had a plan to stick to.

"Yeah, I can't wait," Anna deadpanned. "I just love standing in dank basements drinking cheap, warm beer out of a plastic cup."

Gabe snorted out a laugh and shook his head. "Those frat boys better be classy enough to offer you a mixed drink." And then his face turned more serious. "Congratulations. You made it, kid."

Anna swallowed hard, remembering a time not long ago when getting into college seemed like a faraway dream. Now it was just around the corner. There were so many things she wanted to say to him about how much it meant to have had this past year and a half with him and his family.

Especially because she'd be leaving, and she didn't know when she'd be back.

# SEVENTEEN

The next morning, Anna woke to a quiet house and headed into the kitchen to start a pot of coffee. She pulled a mug from the cabinet and turned around as the back door opened and Gabe strolled in, looking like a sporting-goods poster boy in blue Adidas. Sweat had turned his hair into ebony waves around his temples, and when he pulled off his running jacket and tossed it on the bench by the door, his damp T-shirt clung to his chest in sweaty patches.

*God.*

Anna stepped behind the kitchen island to hide her drawstring pajama pants and the same paint-spattered T-shirt she'd been wearing the day she'd met him. But he seemed completely oblivious to her appearance as he flashed her a grin and grabbed his own coffee mug. Which, of course, he was oblivious. He didn't think of her like that.

"Out for a run?" she asked, stating the obvious.

"You have no idea how balmy Pittsburgh weather feels compared to Chicago."

Anna spotted her opening and grabbed it. "Yeah, I wouldn't know. I've never left Pittsburgh except once, for a school trip to

West Virginia." She didn't mention that the closest she'd ever come to leaving the city for real was during her failed escape to the West Coast this past spring. The one that he and a security guard who could moonlight as a Steelers defensive end had interrupted.

"You will." The trickle in the coffeepot came to a stop, and Gabe poured a cup, splashed in some milk, and handed it to Anna. "Do you still want to work for one of those international medical programs someday? The Red Cross or Doctors Without Borders or something?"

Anna took a sip from the mug. It was exactly how she liked it. He'd remembered from all their early morning meetings working on their project. "Definitely. But..." She hesitated. "Gabe, I'm going to have an opportunity to travel before then."

"Yeah?" Gabe took the other mug and filled it. "Is there a school trip?"

"No. But there's... college." Anna set her mug on the counter and looked him in the eye. "Gabe, I applied to UCSF. And I got in."

He slowly lowered his coffee to the counter. "U-C-S-F. As in... the University of California. In San Francisco."

"That's the one!" She said it in her best fake game-show-host voice, swinging her arm to point at him, but her joke fell completely flat.

"Why?"

"Why... what?"

"Why would you want to go there?"

If she didn't know him, she would have thought his face was impassive. But she did know him. And there was that little twitch in his jaw. This wasn't quite the reaction she'd been expecting. "Because it's a good opportunity, and they offered me a scholarship and room and board, too."

"But they're not an accelerated program, right? You'd have

to do the entire bachelor's degree and then get accepted to the MD."

"They're... yes." Anna's hands clenched around her mug. "But they're a good program. And I know I'll be able to get into the MD."

Gabe pushed away from the counter and crossed his arms. "So, you got into the best program, in a city where you have people who care about you, and you're going to a lesser program over two thousand miles away, one where you'll have to start over. Again, I ask you, why?"

"I wouldn't have to start over," Anna protested. "They'll take most of my transfer credits, so I'm not starting from scratch. And they're not lesser. They're just different." She wrapped her arms around her midsection. How could she have been so wrong about Gabe supporting her on this? *Was he just humoring me this fall when he helped me look for my mom?* "Maybe I want something different, to explore the world. Did you ever think about that? No, you didn't. You're too busy dictating what I should do with my life without consulting me first." Anna shot him a glare. "*Again.*"

Gabe stared at her, unblinking, for long enough to make her shift her feet uncomfortably. Finally, he shook his head and sighed. "Anna, your mother left you. You're not going to find her in San Francisco."

Anna's whole body went hot. "That's not why I'm picking UCSF—" But she was lying, and of course he knew it.

"Of course it's why." He slid onto the barstool across from her. "Look, I'm not trying to dictate what you should do with your life."

"Could have fooled me."

"I'm trying to keep you from making a mistake because you think you're going there to find something you're not." Gabe ran a hand through his sweaty hair. "Anna, I have something I need to tell you. I didn't give you the full story about what happened when I went to the address you gave me."

Anna's heart thudded in her chest.

"When I talked to that shopkeeper, he told me that before the house was abandoned, it was—" He broke off and looked away.

"What?" Anna's hands began to shake. "Tell me."

"It was a—he said it was basically a den for drug users and prostitutes. I went inside, Anna." A shadow passed over his face. "It was... rough."

"Why didn't you tell me?" Anna whispered.

"I didn't want to say anything over the phone. And we don't really know if your mom lived there. We don't know *anything* about what happened to her after she left, except that she called you from a number that may or may not have been connected to that"—he shuddered—"that house on Capp Street."

Anna grabbed the necklace at her throat. A reflex. "It's not a secret my mom was an addict."

Gabe's eyes drifted to her hand rubbing the etched gold pattern with her thumb. She dropped it to her lap.

"I know," he said. "And that's why this worries me. If she *was* living in that house... if she *wasn't* living in that house... Either way, I don't want you to throw away your best opportunity so you can chase something that maybe only exists in your head."

How could she explain it to him? This was his home; there'd never been a minute he hadn't belonged here. The Weatheralls had taken her in because she had nowhere else to go. Anna stared into the depths of her coffee cup. Her mom was out there, and after all these years of agonizing over what might have happened to her, Anna was finally in a place where she could find out. Where, just maybe, she could get her back.

"If my mom *was* living in that house, if she's in danger, if she's still using... well, that's all the more reason for me to go there," Anna murmured. "To help her."

Gabe looked at her sideways. "You'd have to find her first. How are you going to do that? And you know you can only help someone who wants to be helped."

Anna's head jerked up. "Maybe you should take your own advice."

"What is that supposed to mean?"

"It means... who asked for *your* help?"

Gabe flinched. "You didn't seem to have a problem with it when I was traipsing all over San Francisco looking in crack houses. But suddenly, you don't want my advice."

Anna's breath caught. *Crack houses.* Deep down, this was how he thought of her mom. She'd expected the kids at school to use horrible, disparaging terms like that. Never Gabe. But she should have known that a person like him, with a family like the Weatheralls, could never really understand. "I wanted your *support,* Gabe. But I was obviously wrong to hope for that."

"Well, if you had even one good reason to go to UCSF, you'd have my support."

As if her own mother wasn't a good enough reason. Not if she had the kind of sordid, tarnished life that Gabe seemed to think she did. Anna shook her head. "You know what? You sound just like your dad."

"What are you talking about?"

"It's not like *I'm* planning to move into a crack house, Gabe. I have a full ride to UCSF. It's a good program. But that's not enough. You can't imagine why I wouldn't want to follow the perfect path you've prescribed for me."

The flush from his earlier run drained from his face. "After everything I told you about my relationship with my dad, I can't believe you would say that to me."

"After everything I told you about my mom, I can't believe

you want me to write her off, like she doesn't deserve my care or concern."

"Damn it, Anna." Gabe's palm landed on the table, making her jump. "I don't want you to write her off. I want you to choose *you* and your future over this person who didn't give enough of a shit to even stick around."

Anna gasped. Gabe pushed away from the island, cursing under his breath. He opened his mouth to say something, but before he could, she lifted a shaking hand to stop him.

"Maybe this isn't really about my mom." Anna wrestled to keep her voice calm, pulling her palm into a fist against her chest. "Maybe I want a fresh start." She shoved her mug of coffee aside and slid off her stool. "Maybe I just want to get the hell out of here, and this is finally my chance." She pushed past him, but instead of letting her go, he reached out and took her by the arm.

"Anna, wait."

The familiar scent of him drifted across her, even more potent after his run, carving one more crack in her heart. She wrenched away from him before she could do something stupid like lean in. "Leave me alone, Gabe."

He backed up. "Okay, fine. We can talk more about this later—"

"No. I don't want to talk later." She took a breath. "I don't want to talk to you at all. *Ever.* This"—she waved a hand between them—"this is over."

With that, Anna turned and fled from the room.

This time, Gabe let her go, and she was grateful for that. Because he would never understand. And she could never tell him how it was all her fault.

How one decision Anna had made on one fateful day had driven her mother away.

Gabe thought she should move on. And as long as she

continued to let him into her life, he'd keep coming back around to this, over and over. It only proved she was making the right decision going to school in San Francisco. Because she didn't belong here.

And she never would.

# EIGHTEEN

Back in his childhood bedroom, Gabe flipped open his suitcase and fished out the velvet box with the necklace he'd bought in the pawn shop in San Francisco. He stared at the flower pattern etched into the gold. Since Anna had arrived home yesterday afternoon, he'd been discreetly trying to check out the one she wore. There was no question that the pendant in his hand was the mirror image of hers. Did she know that every time she talked about her mom, her hand automatically reached for it?

Gabe had planned to take Anna out for coffee later today and give her the second necklace. He'd promised himself he'd come clean about everything he'd learned on his San Francisco trip, from the search through the abandoned house to his discovery in the pawn shop. She'd be hurt, brokenhearted. But Gabe had hoped that she'd finally be able to move on and find some closure.

That notion seemed ridiculous now.

Anna wasn't any closer to finding closure than Gabe was to giving in to his dad's desire for him to be a doctor. He hadn't been able to believe it when she'd started talking about *moving* to San Francisco. For a moment, she'd tried to claim it had nothing to do with her mom, but it clearly had *everything* to do with her. Anna honestly believed she was going to find her mom and... he let out an incredulous laugh.

*And save her.*

The woman who'd abandoned her fourteen-year-old daughter, who'd left her behind without a second thought. This stupid necklace was only more evidence of Anna's mom's desertion and betrayal. She'd pawned Anna's love to get high.

But Anna wouldn't see it that way.

Gabe shook his head. He couldn't give this necklace to her. Maybe she was right, and he was trying to help someone who didn't want to be helped. But even if she hated him, even if she never spoke to him again, Gabe knew he was doing the right thing.

This necklace was solid evidence that her mother *had* been in that house in San Francisco, and Anna had been on the right track all along. If a googled phone number was enough to compel her to give up the best college program, to leave behind the people who actually cared about her, and to move all the way across the country... What would knowing about this necklace inspire her to do? How long would she keep chasing the ghost of her mother?

And what would she sacrifice along the way?

# PART II

# NINETEEN

## THREE YEARS LATER

"Anna, hey, wait up," a deep male voice called as Anna walked out the door of her advanced biology class.

Anna's lab partner and roommate, Sofia, looked over her shoulder and nudged Anna with her elbow. Anna turned around to find another one of her classmates, Sam Briggs, approaching. He stopped a few feet in front of her, and Anna had to tilt her head back to look him in the eye. Sam was tall—well over six feet, judging by how he towered over her—and broad-shouldered, with dark brown skin and eyes that matched.

"Nice work in there," Sam said with a grin, showing off a row of perfectly straight white teeth. Anna knew he was referring to the lab experiment she'd pulled off in class earlier.

"Thanks." She returned his smile with confidence. Now that she was in her last year of her undergrad program at UCSF and expecting her med school acceptance letters any day, Anna didn't bother with modesty. She and Sam frequently competed for the top spot in the classes they took together, and though their rivalry was friendly, she had to admit she enjoyed coming out ahead.

"So," Sam said, shifting his backpack from one arm to the

other, "any chance you're free this Saturday? I thought maybe we could hang out and talk about something *other* than cell division for once."

Sofia's elbow dug into Anna's side again.

"Um." Anna bit her lip. "I'll have to check my work schedule."

"Okay, cool. Text me," Sam said and then lifted his palm in a wave. "Catch you later."

As soon as he disappeared around the corner, Sofia turned to Anna. "I knew he liked you!" She raised her eyebrows. "Are you going to go out with him?"

Anna bit her lip. "Maybe."

"Well, do you like *him*?"

Anna hesitated, and then her lips quirked into a smile. "Maybe."

Sam was tall and muscular with perfectly chiseled features that made even their professors stop and blink when he answered a question correctly in class, which tended to be most of the time. He was obviously smart, and he'd applied to most of the same medical schools as Anna, so they had that in common. But it wasn't just her work schedule that held her back from going out with him. There was something about Sam—a self-assuredness that bordered on cocky—that reminded her of someone. Someone she'd spent the last three years trying to forget.

Anna followed Sofia out of the classroom building where they stopped at the intersection of two paths that crisscrossed the campus. It was the spot where they usually headed in different directions after advanced bio.

"I'll see you for dinner, right?" Sofia asked. "It's Taco Tuesday."

"Of course." San Francisco was famous for its Mexican food, and she and Sofia were on a mission to try as many Mexican restaurants in the city as possible. It had started when they were in their first biology class together, and Sofia had admitted during a lab experiment that she was homesick for her mother's cooking back in Texas. Over the past few years, they'd turned these dinners into a weekly ritual. "It's your turn to pick a spot," Anna reminded her.

"We'll go somewhere in the Mission." Sofia rolled her eyes, but her laugh showed she was joking. "Since that's your *favorite* neighborhood."

It was true that Anna usually chose the Mission neighborhood when it was her turn to pick a restaurant for dinner. They did have the best Mexican food in the city. And the best people-watching. Especially if you were watching for one person in particular.

But Sofia didn't know anything about that.

"Perfect," Anna confirmed. "I'll meet you at home at six."

Sofia took off down the path for her next class, and Anna moved in the direction of the library. Not ten seconds had gone by when she heard Sofia's voice call out, "Hey."

Anna spun around to look at her friend. "Yeah?"

"You should say yes to Sam. He's a real catch."

Anna laughed. With a noncommittal wave, she turned around and kept walking. Sofia was a good friend, but Anna didn't know how to explain why she was reluctant to go out with Sam. None of her university classmates knew about Gabe, or the Weatheralls. Anna had told everyone that her mom had passed away and a distant family member had raised her. It was easier than explaining the truth.

She kept walking, and about halfway to the library, her phone buzzed with a text message. She fished it out of her bag and looked at the screen. *Sam Briggs*, the name on the message read.

*You check your schedule for Saturday yet? How about I pick you up at seven?*

Anna smiled. What was that about Sam being self-assured? But she had to admit his interest in her was flattering. He *was* a catch, and she'd be dumb to turn him down just because he made her think of Gabe.

Even after all these years of silence.

Anna still kept in touch with the rest of the Weatheralls, and she knew Gabe was working on his PhD dissertation at the University of Chicago. But they hadn't talked since her senior year of high school. Not since he'd refused to support her choices to go to UCSF and look for her mom.

But Sam wasn't Gabe, and she wasn't a teenager with an unrequited crush anymore. *Sam won't treat you like a kid, or act like he knows what's best, or try to tell you what to do. He won't betray your trust.* And if he did, it wouldn't blindside her, because she'd never let herself get too attached. Anna had learned that lesson a long time ago.

Before she could overthink it, Anna began typing.

*Anna*

*Are you free for dinner tonight? How do you feel about Mexican food?*

*Sam*

*Love it. See you tonight.*

Anna smiled and shoved the phone back in her bag. She was looking forward to hanging out with him. And having Sofia along would be a good buffer.

But for now, she had a test to study for.

Anna was making her way up the steps toward the library when she felt her phone buzz again. This time, it wasn't just the short vibration of a text, but several long ones from a call coming in. Was Sam calling her? Maybe he wanted to get the address of the restaurant.

But when Anna glanced at the number on the screen, it wasn't Sam. She stopped abruptly on the steps and grabbed the handrail to steady herself. It was the last number she'd expected to see.

Though she'd intentionally deleted his name from her phone, she hadn't been able to bring herself to block him. And as much as she'd tried to forget it, she'd recognize that number anywhere. He'd texted for months after she'd stopped talking to him but had eventually given up when she hadn't responded. Now, he only sent her one text a year, on her birthday in June.

*I hope you have a wonderful birthday. I miss you. Still.*

But now, he was calling her on a random Tuesday in September.

Maybe it was a butt-dial. She should send him to voicemail and head to the library to study for her chemistry exam. Instead, she stood there, staring at that number lighting up her phone. Because the truth was, she missed him, too. The prospect of hearing his voice made her heart do a little flip.

Just as she was about to hit the button to answer, the phone stopped ringing. Anna dropped her hand with a sigh.

Part of her wished she'd answered the call, just so she could tell him how well she was doing and how wrong he'd been. She loved her program, had friends like Sofia, and great professors as mentors. She'd even been invited to participate in volunteer medical trips with some of the UCSF med school faculty and students over school breaks. They'd travel to parts of the world where medical care was desperately needed and set up temporary women's health clinics to offer exams and other basic healthcare services. It was an amazing opportunity to gain experience, and an honor to be invited as an undergraduate student.

Since UCSF had accepted Anna's credits from her high school program, she'd been able to skip a year of her bachelor's degree. So, she'd be starting medical school next year and wasn't even that far behind where she would have been if she'd gone to the accelerated program in Pittsburgh.

*San Francisco was the right choice*, she wanted to say. Even if she hadn't tracked down her mom yet. In San Francisco, nobody knew she was that kid who was one lucky break away from being homeless. Nobody knew anything other than what she wanted them to know.

Anna shook her head. What would be the point of telling Gabe any of that? Their friendship had ended a long time ago, and she'd put it behind her. Anna managed to convince herself all the way up the steps to the wide wooden entry doors of the library. And then, right before she went inside, her phone rang again.

She swiped to answer on the first ring. "Hello?" Anna asked cautiously.

"Hey, ki—" Gabe cleared his throat, cutting off the word before he could call her that old nickname. "Uh, I mean, Anna. It's Gabe."

"Hi." Did she sound as breathless as she felt?

"I'm surprised you answer calls from strangers."

"While you *are* very strange, I knew it was you."

His half laugh carried through the phone. "Okay, well, I'm surprised you didn't delete me from your contacts."

Anna pressed her lips together. She wasn't about to admit she had deleted him but still recognized his number. Or that his familiar chuckle was doing all kinds of things to her insides. She stood up straight. "Is there a reason you're calling?"

"Actually, yeah, there is." Across the distance, Anna heard him take a sharp breath. "Anna, it's my grandmother. I wanted to let you know she passed away early this morning."

"Oh." Anna's eyes filled. "Oh, Gabe. I'm so sorry." Dorothy had been declining for a long time, and over the past few years, she'd thoroughly retreated into her own world. Not even Anna's phone calls had been able to draw her out. The family had recently placed the older woman in hospice, so it wasn't like Anna hadn't known this was coming. But still, the reality of it nearly knocked her off her feet. She bit back a sob.

"The funeral is on Saturday," Gabe said. "I was hoping you could come."

Anna leaned against the brick wall, grateful for something so solid holding her up. She wanted to honor Dorothy and to be there to support Elizabeth and the rest of the family. But the emotions she felt about going back to Pittsburgh, back to the site of her old life, weren't so much mixed as they were puréed to a pulp. "Um." She stalled.

"Please? It would mean a lot to my mom." Gabe hesitated. "And me, too. I mean, not that you care about that last part."

Anna pushed away from the wall. "Of course I *care*, Gabe. I always cared. It was you who—" She snapped her mouth closed. Dorothy had just passed, and this wasn't the time to have this conversation. "Never mind."

"Listen, kid," he said, and damn it, she hated how much she liked hearing that stupid nickname come out of his mouth. "Leah got your old room ready. Come to my grandma's funeral, stay for the weekend, and you can tell me off in person. For old times' sake."

Anna swiped at her wet cheeks. "Well, when you put it like *that...*"

He chuckled again. "I'll see you soon, Anna."

Anna wasn't prepared for the emotions that welled up when she finally saw the Weatheralls. She arrived in a cab from the airport just in time for dinner on Friday night. When she walked into that old, familiar chaos in the kitchen, they gathered around her, making such a commotion that a stranger watching through the window might have thought she'd just returned from war. What had she been thinking, staying away for so long?

After Rachel hugged her, and Matt lifted her off her feet, John wanted to hear all about her med school applications, and Elizabeth ordered Rachel to bring Anna a drink and a plate of food. Then Leah, who was almost as tall as Anna now, moved in to tell her all about her upcoming homecoming dance.

Finally, Anna turned to face Gabe, who'd hung back by the stove where he'd been making dinner.

"Hey, kid." He wiped his hands on his mom's old apron, which was tied around his waist.

"Hi." Her eyes met his silver-blue ones, so much like the mist drifting in over the San Francisco Bay on her early morning runs. She'd switched to running in Golden Gate Park when the reminder of those eyes had hurt too much.

"I'm really glad you made it," he said.

Anna took a shaky breath. "I'm so sorry about your grandma." She looked over at the breakfast nook, where Dorothy used to sit. "She was the most amazing woman."

"She was." Gabe nodded sadly. "And she thought the same thing about you."

Anna pressed a hand to her mouth to hold back a sob, overwhelmed by the memories circling her in that kitchen. In three seconds, Gabe was in front of her, and in one more, she was in his arms, wrapped up in his familiar scent. She leaned in, pressing her cheek against his solid chest. And as much as she hated to admit it, as much as she didn't want it to be true, it felt like she was finally home.

Anna smoothed the skirt of her black crepe dress, making a half-hearted attempt to remove the creases it had collected between the funeral home, church, and gravesite in this unseasonably warm weather. It seemed only right for Dorothy's burial to fall on a beautiful autumn day with the birds chirping in the trees and the last of summer's flowers blooming in the garden. The weather was so perfectly like that late September day when she'd first met Dorothy that the smell of cut grass drifting over as Dorothy's casket was lowered into the ground had caused fresh tears to spring to Anna's eyes.

Now, back at the Weatheralls' house, she made her way through the funeral guests who'd gathered to celebrate the older woman's life, catching snippets about Dorothy's work as a volunteer for local political candidates and as a soprano in her church choir. Anna would have loved to stop and listen, but she was a stranger among Dorothy's family and friends. Did anyone even know about that kid the Weatheralls took in for a year when her own mother took off?

Under the pretense of clearing some wayward wineglasses, Anna escaped into the kitchen. She found Elizabeth there, looking poised and elegant in a black wool dress, her blond hair swept up into a French twist. A casual observer might have assumed the older woman was holding up just fine. But Anna spotted the run in her pantyhose and the missing hoop in her left ear. Her concern grew as Elizabeth stood with the refrigerator door open, staring blindly at the contents. Anna stepped up next to her, taking the refrigerator door from her grasp and gently pushing it shut.

Elizabeth blinked. "Oh, Anna, honey. I didn't even hear you come in."

"Can I get you anything? Maybe a plate of food?"

She shook her head. "I'm fine. Just a little tired."

"Of course you're tired." Anna put an arm around Elizabeth and steered her toward a stool at the kitchen island. "Why don't you rest for a bit?"

Elizabeth sank down and then patted the seat next to her. "Please sit with me. I'm so glad you could make it home."

Anna gave Elizabeth a sad smile. "Me, too. Dorothy was an amazing woman. I'm so grateful I was able to get to know her."

"She adored you."

And just like that, Anna's eyes burned again, and she quickly reached up to wipe them away. She'd read somewhere that when people experience a death, you should never lean in on the people closest to the loss, only outside the circle. As much as Anna wanted to fall apart, she existed outside the circle of people closest to Dorothy.

So Anna's heartbreak could wait until she escaped to her room, or better yet, until she boarded a plane back to San Francisco. Then, she could dwell on the loss of one of the only relationships in her life where she'd truly belonged. Where she'd felt... safe.

Dorothy hadn't known about Anna's past or cared where she came from. She'd trusted Anna with her memories, and she'd never tried to change her... or to save her. In some ways, those moments with Dorothy reminded her of the early days with her mom before she started using again. Before everything fell apart.

"I adored her, too," Anna managed to whisper.

Elizabeth gave her a sad smile, reaching out to push a lock of hair behind Anna's ear. *Just like Dorothy used to do.* Her heart nearly folded in on itself.

"I was going to do this later," Elizabeth said, sliding off her chair, "but since you're here now... I have something I'd like to give you." She opened a drawer in the cabinet across the room and pulled out a small velvet box. Then she sat back down next to Anna and placed it on the counter in front of her.

Anna couldn't even begin to imagine what was in that box. Or why Elizabeth would give it to her today, of all days. She reached forward and slowly lifted the lid.

Tucked neatly into the black velvet interior, a diamond ring caught the light overhead and glimmered. Anna recognized it right away. For as long as she'd known Dorothy, the older woman had worn that antique ring on her right hand. Through old photos, Anna had learned it had been a gift from Dorothy's husband on their first wedding anniversary.

Anna set the box on the counter, her eyes flying to Elizabeth's face. "I don't understand." Elizabeth had said she wanted to give her something. Surely she didn't mean this ring?

But Elizabeth waved her hand at the box. "She would have wanted you to have it."

Part of Anna wanted to pick up that beautiful antique, clutch it to her chest, and keep it forever. Instead, she shook her head. Anna didn't know anything about jewelry, but she could recognize the ring was valuable.

"Oh, Elizabeth. I couldn't possibly." She gave the box a nudge in Elizabeth's direction.

"Of course you can." Elizabeth picked up the box and held it out to Anna. "You have no idea how much it meant to me that you spent so much time with her, drawing her out when she seemed to be drifting further and further away." Her voice broke, and Anna felt the tears well up for about the hundredth time that day.

Anna picked up the ring, took a long look, and it all came back to her: the touch of a frail, age-spotted hand pressing down on hers, the smell of lilac drifting across the front porch, the voices of Frank Sinatra and Dean Martin. Those moments had meant everything to her.

But then Anna noticed the dark circles under Elizabeth's eyes and the lines of grief tugging at her mouth. Elizabeth had just lost her mother after a long illness. She was exhausted, vulnerable and, most importantly, not thinking straight. If Anna took that ring, she'd never be able to look at it without wondering if Elizabeth regretted giving it away.

"Thank you so much for thinking of me, but truly, I can't accept this."

"Take the ring, Anna." Gabe's voice resounded from across the room.

Anna jumped and spun on her stool to find him standing in the doorway with his arms crossed over his chest.

He hitched his chin at the box on the counter. "She really would have wanted you to have it."

Anna shook her head again. That ring was an expensive family heirloom, and she wasn't family. Her hand automatically flew to the gold pendant that always hung around her neck. This etched half-moon was her legacy. It might be more modest than an antique diamond, but the other half was somewhere out there. She hadn't given up on finding it—or her mom.

"Thank you, but I can't take it, Elizabeth. This is a special ring, and you should give it to one of your daughters."

Elizabeth opened her mouth to protest, but Anna snapped the box firmly shut. "Please. Give it to Leah or Rachel."

Elizabeth sighed and picked it up. "Maybe this wasn't the best time to discuss this. I'll keep it in the safe in case you change your mind."

"I won't."

"Anna." Gabe's voice was tinged with disapproval, and Anna shot him a hard look to let him know she wouldn't be arguing. He was always so sure he knew what was best for her. But just because he still thought of her as a child didn't mean she was anymore.

"Excuse me," she said, sliding off her stool and fleeing into the living room before Gabe could argue anymore.

Anna made her way around the coffee table, straightening the trays of appetizers, brushing crumbs into her hand, and doing her best to stay busy.

From the corner of her eye, Anna watched a woman of about Elizabeth's age greet a college-aged girl with similar hair color and facial features. The older woman was probably the girl's mother, or maybe an aunt. As the two embraced, it occurred to Anna that there was nobody in her life who looked like her or who remembered even one story from her childhood. Nobody who'd known her for more than a few years. Some part of her knew it was pointless to feel this sadness about her mom after all these years, but she couldn't help it.

Early that morning, before anyone else in the house was awake, Anna had rolled out of bed and pulled on leggings and sneakers. If any of the family had come downstairs to find her tiptoeing out the door, she would've said she was going for a walk. Instead, she'd hurried down to Forbes Avenue and caught a bus to Lawrenceville. She'd wandered the old neighborhood, partly curious and partly braced for the assault of memories. The old family pharmacy was a Rite Aid now, and the grocery store where she used to work had been sold to a hipster couple who'd put a smoothie bar in back.

Anna didn't know what she'd expected when she made her way to her old house, but she was surprised to find it had been boarded up, and the residents had moved on. Mrs. Janiszewski had been in her eighties when Anna knew her. Maybe she'd gone to a nursing home or had passed away. And Anna couldn't imagine where Don, the landlord, had ended up. Prison, if there was any justice in the world. But although she knew it was probably for the best that the house had been condemned—that place had been nothing but black mold, asbestos, and a fire hazard—it was just one more thread to her mom slowly unraveling. Anna knew the chances of ever finding her diminished with every passing year.

Three years in San Francisco hadn't turned up a single trace of her, although Anna had gone to the police station to put in a missing person report within the same hour her plane landed in the city. She'd tried everything, from knocking on doors on Capp Street to going to homeless shelters and handing out her mom's picture. How many times had she stared at strangers' faces on the street, looking for a resemblance? How many middle-aged women had she followed into stores?

"Hey." Gabe's voice pulled her from her thoughts, and she spun around to find him standing in front of her. "Can we talk?"

"Gabe, I'm not taking the ring."

He held up his hands as if to show they were empty. "I'm not here to badger you about the ring. I'm officially minding my own business."

"That's so unlike you," she scoffed.

Laughing under his breath, he took her elbow and tugged her to a quiet corner. "I want to talk about you and me."

Anna took a step back. "Maybe talking about the ring would be smarter."

"Anna." His face turned serious. "It's been three years since we talked. I want to say I'm sorry. And I was wrong, back then, about your choices. I heard from my dad that UCSF is a really good fit for you."

Anna nodded.

"I'm sorry I didn't support you going there or give you the space to decide what's best." His face darkened as he scrubbed a hand across his forehead. "I've regretted it so many times these past three years."

At the sadness on his face, Anna remembered his messages. *I miss you. Still.* Why hadn't she ever texted him back? Now that he was standing there in front of her, it all seemed so petty. "I'm sorry I never responded when you tried to reach out."

Gabe ducked his head to look at her. "I'd love to hear more about school. From you, this time."

Anna hadn't found anything like the friendship she'd had with Gabe during that time in high school, when it was just the two of them arguing and laughing over their project. Maybe she'd overreacted when she'd cut him out of her life. If she hadn't, would they have had these past three years as friends, instead of silence?

"I'd love to tell you about it."

"Yeah?" A smile lit up his face, making his silver eyes shine. "And your mom? Did you ever track down any information about her?"

Anna shook her head, her search that morning still fresh in her mind. That boarded-up house, those old streets. "No," she murmured. "I didn't."

"I'm sorry."

She'd been looking for three years and had nothing to show for it. And at twenty years old, she'd been on her own for six years, more or less. Her mom was gone. Why did she still care so much? Why couldn't she seem to let it go? She'd told her friends at school that her mom had died. And it was probably true. But until she knew what had happened for sure, she'd never really move on.

"Anna? You want to talk about it?"

Until she knew what had happened for sure, she'd always be the fourteen-year-old kid who'd driven her mother away.

Anna forced a smile. "Nope. It's all in the past. In fact, I think we should agree never to talk about my mom again."

His brow furrowed. For a moment he looked like he was going to say something and then thought better of it. "Okay. Minding my own business," Gabe finally answered, like he was trying to convince himself. "We don't have to talk about your mom, but we *are* talking again, right?" Gabe gave her that charming smile she'd never been able to resist.

Anna's heart squeezed. Was this the real reason she wasn't jumping at the chance to go out with Sam? "Yes," she finally answered. "We're talking again." But letting Gabe back into her life didn't mean she'd ever completely trust him. Not with her secrets. And—she took a shaky breath—never with her heart.

# TWENTY

## THREE YEARS LATER

When Gabe's cab pulled up, the house was lit up like Christmas and the party was in full swing. Cars lined the block and spilled from the driveway, so his cab had to drop him off several doors down from his parents' house.

His mom and dad had invited everyone who'd flown in early for Matt and Julia's wedding to stop by the house for cocktails, and it looked like most of the guests had taken them up on the offer.

As the best man for his brother's wedding, Gabe should've arrived earlier that day to help set up the party, but his flight from DC had been canceled. It grated that he was late for his own brother's big event. Part of the reason he'd taken the job as a senior research fellow at the Hastings Institute was to be closer to his family.

He'd been about to give up on a later flight and make the four-hour drive to Pittsburgh instead, when Anna had texted.

*Anna*

*Still in line at Reagan?*

*Gabe*

*Unfortunately, yes*

*Anna*

*No luck flirting with the gate agent to jump the line?*

*Gabe*

*He's sixty-two and apparently has four grandchildren*

*Anna*

*Haha. Well, I know you're unhappy about not being here to help, but Rachel and I have it under control. She's polishing silver, and I've volunteered to drive to that wine shop across town to pick up a case of your dad's favorite Cabernet.*

*Gabe*

*Would it kill him to serve a regular old Merlot?*

*Anna*

*I actually think it might.*

*Gabe*

*I'm glad you're there, kid*

*Anna*

*Chill out, get a drink from the airport bar, and we'll see you soon*

He'd shuffled forward in line, smiling at the sight of her words on his phone. Gabe could almost hear her voice saying them out loud in that wry, teasing tone. He'd meant what he'd said: he *was* glad she was at his parents' house, and not just because she was a calm presence in the midst of wedding chaos. It had been seven years since he and Anna had been thrown together on their class project, and he'd never had another friend quite like her. She was someone he could talk to, who made him laugh, who understood him and didn't let him get away with anything. She was almost like a sister to him. And that was a pretty high bar, given how close he was with Matt, Leah, and Rachel.

Still, with his new job in DC, and Anna in her third year of medical school at Stanford, he hadn't seen her in years. Their conversations were late-night ones, over the phone when he was headed to bed, and she was on a break from studying. He hadn't seen her in person since his grandma's funeral. She still volunteered on international medical trips during breaks and hadn't come back to Pittsburgh again. He'd briefly worried she might not make it home for the wedding.

Sometimes, Gabe wondered if Anna intentionally closed herself off from his family, if her volunteer work was partially an excuse to avoid holidays and family events. Maybe it was her childhood that still haunted her. Or maybe she just wanted to escape it. He wished it didn't mean she wanted to escape his family, too.

"That'll be forty dollars." The voice of the cab driver cut into his thoughts.

Gabe handed him a fifty and climbed out onto the sidewalk. As he headed up the driveway toward his childhood home, dusk settled over the yard and the streetlights flickered on. About halfway to the house, Gabe slowed his steps when he spotted someone sitting alone on the porch swing with their back against the armrest and body tilted toward the house. He paused in the driveway and squinted, trying to make out who it was in the fading light. It looked like a woman, maybe close to his age from what he could tell in the growing darkness, but unfamiliar to him.

She had one leg folded under her while the other dangled over the side of the swing as she pushed off from the floor with her bare foot. The gentle sway caused her dress to slide up her thigh, revealing long, trim legs. Then she shifted in her seat, and a curtain of thick, wavy hair tumbled over her shoulder.

He had the strangest urge to tangle his hands up in that hair.

Was she a friend of Julia's who'd come in for the wedding? Had they met at some other event before? He'd never felt so thrown off by a complete stranger, especially one he could barely see.

Gabe shook his head. *I'm probably just tired.* It had been a long day, and he still had hours of mingling with party guests ahead of him.

He straightened his tie and headed up the driveway. When he reached the porch steps, he stopped. "Hello?" he murmured.

The woman looked up as his voice cut through the silence. And an awareness of who she was hit him like a truck.

"Anna?" he managed to sputter.

She stood up, eyes widening. "Gabe!" Her face lit up with a radiant smile. "I wasn't sure if you'd make it until later tonight."

For a moment, all he could do was stare. Somehow, he felt like he was looking at Anna for the first time. How was she exactly the same and yet completely different? Back there in the yard, he'd had no idea she was the awkward kid he thought of like a sister. It highlighted the fact that she was no longer a kid, there was nothing awkward about her, and she was most definitely *not* his sister.

He tried to shove that thought back down to where it had come from.

"I, um, I managed to get a seat on an earlier flight. Anna, you look..." He trailed off.

Anna glanced down at her dress and smoothed a wrinkle from the skirt. "What?" She bit her lip, and something clenched in his stomach.

*You look... beautiful.* Gabe shook his head to clear it. Jesus. This was Anna. *Get it together.*

"You look nice," Gabe finished lamely. He couldn't tear his eyes away from her.

"Thanks." She smiled and pushed a lock of shiny hair behind her ear. For a second, he couldn't breathe.

Then Anna's grin widened. "You look hideous, as usual."

He bit back a laugh, and the world tilted back to normal. "Still waiting to grow into my looks," he said with an exaggerated shrug.

Anna leaned on the porch rail and shook her head with mock sorrow. "Yeah, well. I'd always hoped you'd develop a personality to make up for what you lack in appearance."

With a laugh, Gabe charged up the porch steps and crushed her in a hug. "It's great to see you, too, kid."

For the rest of the wedding weekend, Gabe snuck glances at Anna when she wasn't looking. At the rehearsal dinner the next evening, she was just as striking as she'd been at the cocktail party, this time in a rose-colored sundress and strappy sandals. But it wasn't just about the clothes. He was even distracted by her in a pair of plaid pajama pants and one of her ancient T-shirts in his parents' kitchen on the morning of the wedding. When he realized he was staring, he fled from the kitchen and went upstairs to take a shower.

By the time he went back downstairs, Anna and his sisters had already left for the wedding, and he didn't see them again before the ceremony. At that point, he was busy making sure his brother and the other groomsmen were in their places, and that the five-year-old ring bearer didn't accidentally drop the rings down the toilet.

Matt and Julia's wedding took place in an old stone barn with lofty post-and-beam ceilings, rustic pine floors, and enormous barn doors that let the early summer breeze blow in. The ceremony began, and Gabe swallowed a lump in his throat at Matt's expression when Julia walked down the aisle. Julia was beautiful in her wedding dress, with her long, dark hair tied up in an elaborate twist, but Matt smiled with such affection that Gabe suspected she could be wearing a paper bag and Matt wouldn't have noticed. Just as Julia approached, she grinned at Matt as if the two of them were in on some private joke.

This was the example that his older brother had set for him. One where his partner in life was also his best friend.

Gabe's gaze slid out to the wedding guests in the pews. He found Anna and, as if she sensed him looking, her eyes snapped to his. She stared back without blinking, and the breath whooshed from his lungs. A beat passed, and then another, and it was like a herd of horses slowly galloped across his chest.

Thankfully, the wedding officiant stepped forward to begin the ceremony, and they both looked away. Gabe sucked in a breath so forcefully, the groomsman to his left shot him an odd look.

For the rest of the ceremony, he kept his eyes on Matt and Julia as they said their vows and exchanged rings. After the photographs and dinner, Gabe danced with his mother and made the rounds with all the older ladies, who giggled and pressed their hands to their hearts when he led them out to the dance floor. Next, he cut in on Leah and one of Julia's teenage cousins. A teenager herself now, Leah acted like Gabe embarrassed her, even though he knew she secretly loved having him home.

Finally, he was able to sneak away and grab a beer and a minute to himself. He leaned his shoulder against a wooden post that held up the centuries-old roof. On the dance floor, Matt and Leah shimmied to an old eighties song, and over at the bar, Rachel and her new girlfriend—a woman from her law school class named Aaliyah—were doing flaming shots of something.

Then he spotted his mom and dad out on the dance floor, too, and he couldn't help chuckling. His mom kept stopping to bend over and clutch her chest with laughter at his dad's terrible dance moves. The more she laughed, the worse his dad's moves became until they were both laughing too hard to dance. It was rare to see his dad acting so unguarded and silly, but Gabe knew his mom was the one person who could bring it out in him.

It occurred to Gabe that his parents had always been another example of a solid, happy relationship. What did it mean that he'd made it to twenty-eight without coming close to finding something like that?

When the song ended, his dad came over and gave him a hearty slap on the back. "Great job on your toast."

A warm glow spread over Gabe. He'd practiced that toast for weeks and knew he'd nailed it, collecting a few laughs in the beginning before the tears during the sentimental part at the end. But sometimes he was still that kid who wanted his dad's approval. "Thanks. That means a lot."

"Your brother seems happy."

"He does." Gabe wondered what his dad thought about that. Over a decade after Matt had bailed on med school, it was hard to imagine him doing anything other than building houses. But did his dad still mourn what could have been? He seemed to have mellowed since Anna came along with her dream to be a doctor.

Gabe took another swig of his beer and searched the crowd until he found Anna sitting alone at a table a few feet from the dance floor. She'd slipped her feet out of her high-heeled shoes and now wiggled her toes as if they were finally free.

Damn it, she hadn't turned back into an awkward teenager

in the few hours he'd been looking in the other direction. He wished she had, because these feelings he was having for her were uncomfortable... and weird... and maybe a little intriguing.

"You ought to get back out there on the dance floor." His dad gave a nod in Anna's direction, and Gabe felt his face go hot. Did his dad suspect he was having these feelings toward Anna? Had he been that obvious about it?

*No,* Gabe told himself. His dad had always been protective of Anna, and he'd probably spotted her sitting alone. He would have done the same thing for Leah.

The last chords from the pop song faded, and the first notes of a slow ballad drifted across the room. His dad gave him another pat on the back and headed across the room to his wife.

Gabe's body moved in Anna's direction before his brain fully registered what he was doing. He'd only made it about twenty feet before he came to an abrupt stop in the aisle between two tables. Another one of Julia's cousins—Kyle or Cal or something like that—had stepped in front of Anna's chair and leaned down to say something that made her laugh. Then—*whatever his name is*—held out his hand. Anna took it, and Kyle-or-Cal led her onto the dance floor. He leaned in close to whisper something in her ear, and she laughed again.

Gabe had briefly met Julia's cousin at the cocktail party the other night. He supposed, objectively, the guy was good looking, if you were into that clean-cut, blond lacrosse-player type of look. Kyle-or-Cal had told Gabe he went to UCLA and was getting his MBA so he could eventually go to work in his father's company. Gabe tried to remember what kind of business it was—accounting maybe? The guy seemed a little boring for someone as interesting as Anna, but whatever.

Gabe stood stupidly in the aisle, wrestling with the feelings churning inside him. So maybe he was a little jealous. He'd never seen Anna with a guy before. Never even thought about her that way. She'd probably dated in college and med school, but it was a topic they never really talked about in their phone calls and text messages.

And on top of the jealousy, there was surprise, and maybe a little bit of relief. What had he been thinking, going over there to ask her to slow dance in front of his entire family? God, they would've been all over that. Just because he was having this moment of temporary insanity over Anna didn't mean it was a good idea to actually do anything about it.

At that moment, someone bumped into him from behind. He spun around to find a pretty dark-haired woman reaching out and grabbing his arm to steady herself. The woman introduced herself as Julia's friend Nadia from college and then leaned in a little closer to compliment him on the toast he'd given earlier.

Gabe glanced over at Anna. She still had her arms wrapped around what's-his-name as they danced. He dragged his gaze back to Nadia, taking in her dark eyes and full lips.

Gabe spent the rest of the reception dancing with Nadia and *not* watching Anna and Kyle-or-Cal talking together in a dark corner. Matt and Julia left for their honeymoon, and the guests began to trickle out to their cars. Gabe took Nadia's hand as they headed out the door, stopping briefly on the porch so she could dig through her purse for her car keys. At that moment, Anna pushed the door open and stepped outside.

"Gabe! Rachel and I were looking for you. Are you coming with us or riding with your parents?"

Had what's-his-name gotten Anna's number? He was an idiot if he hadn't. At that moment, Nadia found her keys and slid up next to him.

"I'm good." Gabe cleared his throat. "I've got a ride."

Anna's eyes skated from Gabe to Nadia and back again. "Oh. Right." Even in the dim light, Gabe could see Anna's cheeks turn a shade pinker. She flashed him a closemouthed smile. "Have fun." She nodded at Nadia and then headed down the lighted path toward the parking lot without another word.

He watched her for another moment before turning back to the woman at his side. It was better this way.

# TWENTY-ONE

## THREE YEARS LATER

When Anna descended the staircase from her second-floor apartment and swung open the front door, a jolt of electricity hit her right in the chest. Because there on the front step, looking effortlessly handsome in a pair of jeans and a button-up shirt with the sleeves rolled, stood Gabe.

He grinned down at her, and she forgot to watch her step. Anna stumbled over the welcome mat, losing her balance. He reached out to catch her, and in the next breath, she was pressed against his chest, enveloped in that familiar Gabe scent. She exhaled a shaky breath.

"Hey," he said with a grin. "I know it's been a while, but you don't have to throw yourself at my feet."

Three years. It had been almost three years since she'd seen Gabe at Matt and Julia's wedding. Not a thing about him had changed apparently. God, she'd missed him. She hadn't realized just how much until he was standing on her doorstep making his usual jokes.

It wasn't that they had intentionally gone so long without seeing each other. But he'd been steadily climbing the ladder as a research fellow at the Hastings Institute and was always flying somewhere to consult or present his research at conferences. And Anna had been working hundred-hour weeks as an OBGYN resident at UCSF. She'd barely had time to wash her hair, let alone schedule a visit to the East Coast.

But now that Gabe was standing in front of her with that familiar lopsided grin on his face, she couldn't think of a single reason why they'd waited so long. He'd suggested a few visits in the past, but she'd never been able to make them work. So when he'd called last week and offered to make the last-minute trip for her birthday, and Anna had realized that for once, she had a few days off in a row, she'd said yes.

And now... here he was.

Anna grabbed his arm and pulled him into the apartment building. "Come inside. Are you tired from your flight?"

"No, I'm fine. Used to traveling." He followed her up the stairs and into her apartment. "Cute place." Gabe said, turning in a slow circle to check out the shiny wood floors and twelve-foot-high ceilings. "This is all original, right?" He reached out to touch the molding around the door in appreciation.

"Yep. The house was built in 1880." As Anna tried to view the room through Gabe's eyes, she had a flash of memory from another time when he'd followed her up the stairs of an apartment building. Back then, she'd been so mortified for him to see where she lived.

It felt like a lifetime ago.

Now, Anna shared the sunny middle apartment of a three-story Victorian with another resident in her program. Given their erratic schedules, Anna didn't see her roommate very often outside of work, but they made a point to eat dinner together when they could, and Anna considered her a friend. Most of the apartment was furnished with hand-me-downs from the hospital residents who'd lived there before them, but Anna had filled the bay window with flowering plants that reminded her of Dorothy every morning when she sat there drinking her coffee.

There was nothing fancy about the apartment, but it was warm and inviting, and most importantly, it was a far cry from that run-down apartment in Lawrenceville where she'd felt so powerless and alone.

She watched Gabe as he set his travel bag on the floor by the couch. It was hard to believe he'd been in her life for ten years now. Even though she hadn't seen him in what felt like forever, they often talked on the phone while she was walking to the hospital for her overnight shift and—three hours later on the East Coast—he was heading off to bed. They'd open up about whatever was going on in their lives, and despite the distance, it felt like nothing between them had changed.

Gabe looked up from his suitcase, his storm-cloud eyes darkened with something she couldn't quite interpret, and that electricity jolted through her again.

*Well, almost nothing between us has changed.*

Sometimes during the most honest moments of their conversations, she wondered if they'd ever broach those long glances they'd exchanged at Matt and Julia's wedding.

Those long glances... sort of like the one they were exchanging now.

Gabe ran a hand through his hair, making it stick up in that familiar way, and Anna's heart lurched toward him. Though she'd dated other guys, nobody had ever inspired her insides to start up a gymnastics routine every time she was in his presence the way Gabe did.

But was she imagining that he felt it, too?

Maybe she was, because in the next moment, he'd turned his back to her and was pulling a jacket out of his bag. "Let's get some dinner? I hear the Mexican food is great."

Anna spun on her heel and grabbed her jacket from the

hook by the door. Gabe followed her out to the street, and Anna steered him down the block.

Her apartment was located just north of the Golden Gate Park Panhandle, in a nice residential neighborhood populated with young families and couples walking dogs through the narrow grassy area across the street. It was only about a mile and a half from the UCSF Medical Center, and she often walked to work.

Gabe knew that when she had an overnight shift, she usually left after dark, and that's when he'd call. He didn't say it, but she knew he worried about her walking alone. Ten years in, and Gabe was still worrying about her, though he'd gotten better about telling her what to do. Maybe he finally knew she wasn't a kid anymore.

Anna snuck a look at him, remembering those long glances and, with a jolt, realized just how much she hoped he knew she wasn't a kid anymore.

As they walked, Anna told him about the neighborhoods and pointed out attractions—the corner of Haight and Ashbury, the Castro Theater—and soon, they'd crossed Dolores Park and came out onto 19th Street. "It's the best place for Mexican food," Anna told him as she steered him toward the heart of the Mission.

They were almost at the restaurant Anna had picked out when Gabe came to an abrupt halt on the sidewalk. Anna slid to a stop next to him. "Everything okay?"

Gabe turned from the cafés and vintage shops lining the main drag to look down a perpendicular side street. His gaze landed on a sign marking an alley halfway down the block. Of course, Anna recognized it right away. *Capp Street.* That same bodega was still there on the corner, a brand-new awning waving gently in the breeze. Probably to mark the general upswing of the neighborhood since the "crack houses" had moved out and developers had moved in.

Anna had lived in the Bay Area for years now. She was unfazed by that corner, these streets, the gravity of this place. A modern chrome-and-glass loft stood where that old Capp Street house used to be. She'd been by a hundred times and didn't even think about it anymore.

But Gabe had been here before, too, a long time ago. And he obviously remembered it. For a second, he hesitated, and Anna thought he was going to turn and head down the side street. Instead, he gave her an overly bright smile followed by an exaggerated shrug. "Everything is fine."

They never talked about Anna's search to find her mom. She'd asked him not to bring it up, and he'd respected her wishes. But he was obviously thinking about it.

If only he knew how little there was to say.

They continued down Mission Street past a few more shops, and then Gabe stumbled again. This time, Anna turned around to find him staring into the window of a pawn shop. She examined the display but couldn't imagine what was drawing his attention. A couple of electric guitars? A line of gold watches? A velvet case displaying old jewelry? "What is it?"

He shook his head as if he were trying to clear it. "Nothing."

Anna studied Gabe's face. The tiny lines around his eyes had deepened, his jaw clenched. "Are you sure you're not too tired from your flight? Maybe we should've ordered takeout."

Gabe turned away from the pawn shop window. "I'm fine." He tucked her hand into the crook of his arm and gave her another one of his extra-bright smiles. "Can't wait to try those tacos you told me about."

# TWENTY-TWO

"So," Gabe said, as he settled at an outdoor table on Mission Steet, "I rented a car so we could pretend to be tourists and check out some of the sights." He kept his eyes on Anna so he wouldn't be tempted to stare at the pawn shop down the block. "Well, so you could pretend to be a tourist. I guess I really am one."

Anna laughed. "I think I might be a tourist, too. I'm embarrassed to say I haven't done as much exploring as I should have. You never actually visit the attractions until someone comes in from out of town to give you a nudge."

"Well, I'm always happy to nudge you."

"And maybe one of these days, I'll return the favor, and come and be a tourist in DC."

Gabe wondered if she really meant it. He knew she was busy. An OBGYN residency was no joke, even for someone as brilliant as Anna. But sometimes her excuses felt like, well, excuses. "You know you're always welcome."

She traced a finger along a gash in the beat-up café table, and almost like an acknowledgment, she murmured, "I really don't know why we keep going this long without seeing each other."

Didn't she? He'd offered to fly out here half a dozen times before she'd finally said yes. It always seemed to come back to that same old refrain. Every time he got too close to Anna, a barrier would come crashing down, like one of those rolling shutters to keep thieves out of a shop.

Like this embargo on talking about her mom. The subject was sitting there like a giant elephant at the table, and goddamn Capp Street was just around the corner. They should be talking about that. He wanted to know if she'd ever found any trace of her mom. He wanted to know how she felt about it. He wanted to wrap his arms around her against any heartbreak her mom might still be causing her.

He *hated* being shut out.

And he hated keeping secrets from her. That pawn shop necklace had been in the bottom of his sock drawer for close to a decade. But Anna had once quit speaking to him for three years, and it had been awful. If he told her about the necklace, would she ever speak to him again?

But if he *didn't* tell her, how much more would it hurt her if she finally found out? She deserved to know the truth, but if she wouldn't talk to him about her mom, how could he possibly know if she wanted the truth?

Gabe gazed across the table at the face that had left him feeling unsteady on his feet since the moment she'd opened her front door. It had nothing to do with how she'd stumbled and fallen into his arms. Somehow over these past few years, he'd convinced himself that his feelings for her at his brother's wedding had all been a figment of his imagination. But the moment he'd seen her again, he knew. And he knew she felt it, too.

A lock of dark, wavy hair slid across her cheek, and before he stopped to think, Gabe reached out his hand and tucked it behind her ear. She tilted her head up, her smile slowly fading. When their eyes met, that now-familiar spark crackled between them. Gabe quickly glanced away, busying himself with arranging the silverware beside his plate.

*Until I tell her the truth, I'm stuck here pretending this isn't happening.*

*And if I tell her, I'll lose her.*

Gabe cleared his throat. "Well, you'd better make that DC trip quickly, because I'm only going to be there for a few more months."

Anna's eyebrows rose. "Where are you going?"

"I got a job offer at the university in Pittsburgh. Tenure-track professor in the economics department."

"Gabe!" A grin spread across her face. "That's wonderful. Your parents must be so happy."

"I'm pretty happy, too. To be so close to my family..." He trailed off.

Back in college, when the other guys were sleeping off their Saturday-night-party hangovers, he was going over to his parents' house for Sunday dinner. And he wouldn't have had it any other way. He'd done a decade away to build his career, but now he could write his own ticket, and that was a one-way back home.

Anna leaned in. "They've always meant everything to you."

Of course, if anyone could understand, it would be Anna. She was part of that family, even if she didn't always seem to believe it.

Anna held up her water glass for a toast. "Congratulations on your new job, Dr. Weatherall. Now that you're working alongside Professor McGovern, maybe you'll finally get around to reading her boring book."

Gabe laughed at the memory of that conversation with Anna, back when they'd first started working on their project together. It didn't seem all that long ago. Anna had amazed him then, and she still did.

He chuckled. "Not a chance. You're going to have to summarize it for me."

"Oh Lord, I think I've blocked it out," Anna said, rolling her eyes. "But if *you* write a boring book, I promise to read the whole thing, and then I'll come and sit on your uncomfortable office couch and discuss it with you."

"It would be worth writing a book just to get you on my couch." Gabe sat back in his chair, realizing how that sounded. "Um. I didn't mean—" Okay, he *did* mean... but *Jesus*.

Anna didn't respond, and when Gabe finally got up the nerve to look at her, he realized she hadn't actually heard him anyway. Her eyes were glued to a spot over his shoulder, her smile fading. What was she looking at?

He swung around in his chair, but nothing appeared out of the ordinary. People strolled by, holding hands or looking at their phones, and beyond the sidewalk, cars stopped and started at the traffic light on the corner. Gabe turned back around and took in Anna's wide eyes. "Anna, what is it?"

"It's—I—" she stuttered. And before he knew what was happening, she jumped up from the table and took off down the sidewalk.

"Anna—wait!" Gabe called, but Anna kept moving, weaving around people as though she were trailing someone in particular. "Hey!" He stood to follow her, but at that moment, the server came by with their drink order. "Uh, sorry," he stammered, "I—we're not dining and dashing. We'll be right back." Gabe dug in his pocket for some cash as he strained to keep an eye on Anna. She was halfway down the block now, and she was—

What?

Anna was reaching out to touch the shoulder of a middle-aged woman with long salt-and-pepper hair.

*What is she doing? And who is that woman?*

Gabe looked down to toss the cash on the table, and when he looked up again, Anna and the woman were gone. Gabe took off down the sidewalk. At the end of the block, he slid to a stop in the spot where he'd seen them moments ago, spinning around to look for Anna.

"Hey," came a voice so low he almost didn't hear it. It was Anna, slumped against the brick wall of a bank building, the mystery woman nowhere in sight.

"Hey," he said, pausing to catch his breath. "Are you okay?"

She nodded.

"What was that about?"

Anna pushed away from the wall. "It was nothing. We should go back." She started walking in the direction of the restaurant. "Sorry to take off like that."

"Anna, wait." Gabe reached out and took her by the arm, turning her to face him. "Who was that woman?"

Her eyes darted over his shoulder again, but this time, instead of searching the crowd, they were dark, shuttered. "It turns out it was nobody."

"Well, who did you *think* it was?"

Anna took a deep, shaky breath and then blew it out slowly. "My mom."

*Her mom?* Gabe took a startled step backward. "Is your mom living here? Have you talked to her?"

"No. I have no idea where she is." Anna's mouth stretched tight. "I just thought..." She paused, kicking a piece of gravel on the sidewalk with the toe of her sneaker.

"Does this happen often? You chase someone down the street who looks like your mom?"

"No." Anna shook her head. "Never." But she still didn't meet his eyes.

"I wish I'd known you were still looking for her."

"I'm not."

He hitched his chin at the spot on the sidewalk where Anna had accosted the stranger. "You sure?"

"Yes, I'm sure."

Gabe slid his hands to her shoulders, wishing she'd look at him. "Anna, talk to me."

She turned away from him, but not before he saw the pain in her eyes. "Let it go, Gabe."

He shook his head. It had been over a decade since Anna's mom had abandoned her. He'd always imagined that Anna didn't want to talk about it because she'd given up. She'd put it behind her and bringing it up would only open old wounds. But those wounds had been bleeding all along.

*She hasn't moved on.*

As Gabe watched the darkness drift across her face, he had to acknowledge that maybe he wouldn't have either. What would it feel like to have no idea if your mother were alive or dead? To wonder if she were in trouble... or hurt... or if she'd simply cared so little that she'd moved on with her life. *What would that do to you, day in and day out?*

No wonder Anna was so closed off.

And with that realization, a heavy weight settled on Gabe's chest. If this was how she reacted to seeing a woman who looked like her mom on the street, what would finding out about that necklace do to her?

When they woke the next morning, Gabe didn't mention what had happened the day before, and Anna didn't bring it up either. It was Anna's birthday, and Gabe had made plans to take the rental car across the Golden Gate Bridge to explore Marin County. Anna had told him she'd only been there a handful of times, and as they wound their way up Highway 1, he loved seeing the kaleidoscope of excitement and awe move over her face at the sight of the redwood trees and the cliffs hanging over the Pacific Ocean.

After a hike through the centuries-old trees in Muir Woods, they headed farther north to Stinson Beach, where they wandered down to the water and sat on a piece of driftwood, digging their toes in the sand. It was an unusually warm night for Northern California, and a full moon shimmered across the water. Except for a couple strolling by with a dog pulling on its leash, they had the beach to themselves.

"So," Gabe drawled, "how come you're spending your birthday with me instead of with your new boyfriend?" He'd heard from Leah that Anna was dating another resident at the hospital. Not that Anna had mentioned him all day. But then, Gabe never mentioned the women he dated either. Over the years, they'd discussed just about everything, except that. Somehow, it was easier that way.

Anna picked up a handful of sand and watched it slide through her fingers. "He's not really my boyfriend. Just a guy I hang out with when we have time... which isn't very often."

Something stirred in his chest. "He didn't mind you giving up your rare days off for me?"

Anna shrugged, and Gabe had a feeling the guy did mind. "Best friend in the world trumps new sort-of boyfriend any day." She looked at him with a half smile. "I wouldn't have missed this. It's been a really great birthday."

"Happy birthday, kid." Gabe bumped her shoulder with his. "Twenty-six is a milestone, you know."

Anna wrinkled her forehead and looked at him sideways. "Maybe in some astrological sign, rising-moon kind of way. But I'm pretty sure in my ordinary calendar, twenty-six is a pretty run-of-the-mill birthday."

He laughed. "Do you really think I read horoscopes?"

"I always believed you had hidden depths." She shot him a

grin, and for about the hundredth time that day, he was struck by the effect Anna was having on him.

It was like someone had turned on a light in a dark room, and he could finally see her clearly. How had it taken him so many years to notice the way her huge dark eyes shined?

Gabe shook his head. "Twenty-six is a milestone because I met you when you were sixteen."

Anna smiled slowly, as if she were thinking back to those days. Did she remember that time working on their project as fondly as he did? Was she as grateful that it had brought them here to this moment?

"I hated being the younger one back then," Anna mused. "But look at us now." She breathed out a half laugh. "I'm still in my prime. And here *you* are"—her shoulders drooped dramatically—"an old man now."

He stood, tugging her up with him. "Oh, you're going to regret that."

"Yeah, what are you going to do to me?" she challenged.

He hitched his chin at the waves crashing on the shore. "Have you gone swimming since you've been in San Francisco?"

She slowly shook her head. "No."

Gently taking her by the elbows, he backed up, pulling her toward the water. "Don't you think it's about time?"

"Gabe," she said calmly, as if she were trying to reason with a toddler, "you do know this is the Pacific? In Northern California?"

"So?"

"So, we're talking fifty-five degrees if we're lucky."

Unfazed, he tugged her another few steps closer to the water. "We'll just jump in really quickly."

"We'll just get *hypothermia*."

Gabe's shoulders shook with laughter as a wave crashed

behind them, sending freezing water rushing in, swirling around their bare feet. Anna shrieked and shuffled backward, trying to pull them back to dry land, but Gabe held firm. When Anna seemed to realize she wasn't getting anywhere with that, she stopped struggling and looked up at him, head cocked and eyebrows raised in a silent challenge. The next thing he knew, she was lunging forward, aiming her shoulder right into his chest.

"Oof." Gabe's balance shifted, but he managed to turn his body to the left, narrowly avoiding the brunt of her weight knocking him backward into the water. Anna's shoulder slid past him, and *Oh shit*—at the last second, he realized she was about to topple into the waves instead. He reached out, snaking one arm around her to yank her back against his chest.

"Nice try, kid," he said, holding her there. But then the laughter died in his throat. Because she was pressed against him, her face inches away.

Anna stared up at him, eyes huge, and the air between them thickened. He could feel someone's heart pounding but had no idea if it was his, or hers, or both. She bit her bottom lip, and things stirred in all kinds of places he'd never felt before with Anna. In another second, with her pressed against him like that, she was going to feel it, too.

The warmth of her cut through the cool sea air, and Gabe tightened his grip, staring down into her beautiful face, reaching up with his other hand to brush his palm across her cheek. Their mouths drew closer.

And then it came back to him. That subject he'd been intentionally avoiding since yesterday on the street. Since almost a decade ago.

He couldn't do this. Not with this enormous secret between them.

He exhaled the breath he was holding and dropped his hand. "Anna," he said, wrestling his voice back to normal. "I can't—"

Eyes widening, she stumbled backward, away from him. Her cheeks flamed bright pink. "Oh my God. Of course you can't. This is—we aren't—"

Gabe closed the space between them. "Anna, wait. It's not you. It's not *us*. It's that I need to talk to you about something. About your mom." He raked a hand through his hair. "Yesterday on the street in the Mission..." *There's a pawn shop. There's a secret I never told you.*

She pressed a hand to her burning cheeks. "Please, whatever you're going to say, just... don't say it."

"Anna, I have to say it."

"No, you don't, Gabe." She wrapped her arms around her midsection, and he could see her shivering. Was it from the cool ocean air or this conversation? All he wanted to do was wrap his arms around her and promise her it would be okay. That they'd figure it out together. But he had no idea if that was the truth.

"I know how unhinged I must have seemed," she said. "Running after that poor woman on the street. Whatever you're going to tell me, I already know."

"I don't think you do."

"I know I've been chasing a ghost for all this time. My mom either died in a crack house, or she got her life together without ever bothering to contact me. Either way, I'm better off without that information." She looked past him at the waves crashing on the shore.

Gabe stared at her face, his heart twisting at the anguish he saw there. If this was truly how she felt, there was no way he could tell her about that necklace. It would only bring her more pain.

Anna headed back up the beach. He trailed after her.

"I know I need to get over it. I need to move on." Anna stopped at their driftwood seat, bending down to pick up her shoes from the sand, letting her hair fall around her face so he couldn't see her eyes. Gabe saw a flash of teenage Anna as she retreated from him. "And that's why I'm leaving."

"Leaving?" His heart stuttered. "What does that mean?"

"I'm moving, Gabe." She stood up straight and finally looked at him. "I've had an offer from one of my mentors to move to Jordan and work in the Syrian refugee camps there. As soon as my residency program is over next year, I'll be going."

"You're moving to"—he choked out the words—"the Middle East?"

Anna nodded. "It's time to get out of here and get on with my life."

"You can leave San Francisco and get on with your life without moving to the other side of the planet, you know." He moved closer, so he was standing in front of her. "Why not come home?"

"Because it will be the same there as it is here. It will be even worse. I'll always be looking over my shoulder."

"Anna. This isn't getting on with your life. This is running away." He reached out to take her hand, but she subtly shifted backward, avoiding his touch. His heart pitched sideways. "Please, can we talk about this?"

"There's nothing to talk about, Gabe. And this conversation is over." She looked at him straight on now, but her eyes were dark, distant, somewhere he knew he'd never reach.

And that's when he knew it really *was* over.

She was leaving. And all he could do was watch her go.

# TWENTY-THREE

## ONE YEAR LATER

Anna packed the last of her clothes in her travel backpack and checked her carry-on for her passport and airline information. She was in Pittsburgh for one more night, staying at the Weatheralls' before a 7:00 a.m. flight that would carry her to New York, then Paris, and finally Amman, Jordan. From there, it would be buses to Irbid, a small northern city where she'd meet up with the other physicians providing maternity care and childbirth assistance to Syrian refugees.

But for now, she was home. Whatever *home* meant.

She'd promised Gabe she'd save a long weekend before her flight to Jordan. This wasn't a volunteer medical trip over spring break. This was a move to the other side of the world, leaving everyone she cared about behind. Of course, they'd keep in touch, but phone and internet service would be sporadic, and it wouldn't be easy to come back if something happened.

For a few fleeting moments, she was tempted to take a job back in Pittsburgh, to come home to be close to everyone, just like Gabe had suggested. But Gabe had always been the smart, popular kid with a happy childhood and loving family. He had no idea what it was like to be in a place that constantly reminded him of a past he wanted to forget. He couldn't even imagine why a place where nobody knew anything about him would be appealing.

Anna checked her backpack one last time, then wandered downstairs, too wired to sleep. Gabe and the rest of the family had been over earlier for dinner, and they'd said their goodbyes already. Now, John and Elizabeth were asleep, and the house was dark except for the glow of one small light over the sink Elizabeth always left on in the kitchen. Anna made her way down the hall, still familiar with the contours of the walls and doorways from her teenage years.

The wave of melancholy she'd been fighting all evening finally surfaced as she stepped out the front door and into the cool spring night. The Weatheralls' porch always made her think of Dorothy, especially this time of year, with the garden blooming and a heavy floral scent hanging thick in the air. Anna closed her eyes and drifted back to that day when she'd connected with the older woman over Frank Sinatra. At the time, she had no idea her relationship with Dorothy and the rest of the family would change her life in such a profound way.

She sank down on the wicker loveseat and stared into the shadowy blackness of the front yard. The air tingled with the metallic charge of a spring storm, and in the distance, thunder rumbled. A pair of headlights cut through the darkness as a car glided down the quiet street. Anna sat up in her chair as it slowed in front of the house and swung into the driveway.

Who would be stopping by at midnight?

The driver turned off the ignition, plunging her into relative darkness. She blinked to let her eyes adjust, and her breath caught when she recognized the car.

*Gabe's.*

He got out and made his way up the path to the house. She couldn't help admiring the fluid way he moved in his jeans and T-shirt, completely comfortable in his own skin. She'd always thought he was beautiful, and that hadn't changed. Seeing him there, on the eve of her trip to the other side of the world, had her swallowing hard and fighting back tears. How was she going to get through the next chapter of her life without their constant text conversations, or the sound of his voice on the phone whenever she wanted to hear it?

"Hi," Anna said, her voice hoarse. "Did you forget something?"

Earlier today, when the whole family was over, she'd wished for a few minutes alone with him. Maybe he'd felt the same way.

"No, I didn't forget something." He stopped at the top of the steps. "I just thought maybe you'd still be awake."

She gave him a wry smile to hide her burning eyes. "Couldn't sleep. Want to sit?"

He sat down on the loveseat and looked at her for a long moment. Finally, he flashed her a crooked grin and leaned over to bump his shoulder into hers. "Dr. Anna Campbell, off to change the world. Who would have ever imagined it when you were that pain-in-the-ass high school kid who was barely scraping by in global econ until I came along to save you?"

She rolled her eyes. "Whatever, slacker. You'd still be trying to pass that class if it weren't for me. Good thing you're so pretty because you're as dumb as a rock."

Gabe laughed and shook his head.

They sat in silence, watching the lightning flash in the distance. After a moment, Gabe took her hand and squeezed it. An unexpected wave of heat worked its way up her arm and settled in her chest.

When he spoke, his voice had lost its playful tone. "I'm really proud of you, Anna."

He held on to her hand, and Anna ran her thumb across the calluses on his palm. Maybe it was because she was leaving and didn't know when she'd see him again, but she needed him to understand what he meant to her.

"Gabe, when we first met, you were just a kid, too. Most college guys wouldn't have paid any attention to some girl with an attitude, like me. But you did. You changed my whole life."

Gabe slowly shook his head. "I didn't do anything, Anna. I just cheered you on. You did this. You created this life for yourself."

Anna shook her head. Sometimes, just as she was falling asleep, she'd jolt awake, remembering that shitty apartment and sleazy landlord. What would have happened if Gabe hadn't found out about her? Would she have survived another year in that place, with Don stalking her for money and her electricity getting shut off in the dead of winter? Now that she wasn't a desperate kid anymore, it was clear what a dangerous situation she'd been in.

She felt Gabe's eyes on her but couldn't look back.

"Hey." Gabe put his hand on her cheek and gently turned her face toward him. "Hey. You are the strongest, most resilient person I've ever met. And I *know* that no matter what, you would've made it to where you are now."

She stared at him, gripped by those silver eyes. He breathed out as she breathed in, and the rest of the world faded away, the space between them the only place on Earth.

When she went over it later in her mind, which, of course she did a million times, she was never sure if he leaned in, or if she did.

But all of a sudden, they were kissing.

It was gentle at first, almost hesitant. And then Anna opened her mouth and pressed against him. He wrapped his arms around her and pulled her closer. Her hands slid around his neck and clutched the collar of his shirt as the kiss deepened. He was so familiar, the smell of him, the tenor of his voice. But at the same time, his arms pulling her closer, and the heat of his mouth against hers were new and foreign and thrilling.

They stayed like that, kissing each other for what could have been a minute, or an hour; she lost all sense of time and space. And then Gabe leaned back against the arm of the loveseat and pulled her on top of him.

She kissed him again, urgently, as she fumbled with the buttons of his shirt. He pulled off her cardigan and slid his hand under her T-shirt. She gasped as his palm made its way across her burning skin. Her lips moved from his mouth to his jaw and then to his neck. His head drifted back against the loveseat, and he murmured her name in the back of his throat.

The sound slammed Anna back to reality.

If they didn't stop *right now*, they weren't going to stop at all. She pulled away and scrambled to the opposite end of the loveseat, breathing hard. Closing her eyes, she turned away, as if that would keep her from having to face him. She pressed one hand to her mouth where, just moments ago, his mouth had been. The razor stubble on his face had left her cheeks flushed.

"Anna..." Gabe's voice was raw.

"Oh God. Please. Just don't say anything." She lurched off the loveseat and moved to the middle of the porch to put some space between them. Crossing her arms in front of her, she shivered, missing the heat from his arms around her.

*No. Stop it.*

She was leaving tomorrow. Moving more than halfway across the planet. How could she have let this happen?

Gabe sat at the edge of the loveseat with his elbows propped on his knees, and he dragged his hand through his hair. He glanced up, and she forced herself not to look away.

"I... should go to bed," she said in a shaky voice. She took a few steps toward the front door. "I have a car coming to take me to the airport at four in the morning."

Gabe stood up, and he was too close. Too appealing with his

rumpled hair and half-buttoned shirt. Anna took another step back.

"Let me come tomorrow and drive you," he said.

She shook her head. "It's already been arranged."

They stood there without saying anything, and it was awful. Unbearable. Gabe stuffed his hands in his back pockets as if he wasn't sure what else to do with them. She felt like someone had jammed a knife into her chest, slowly siphoning the air from her lungs. She had to get out of there before she wouldn't be able to leave at all.

No. This was goodbye. This had to be goodbye.

Anna threw herself at him, holding on tight. "Goodbye, Gabe," she whispered.

His arms closed around her. "Be safe," he murmured into her hair.

The tears choked the back of her throat, and she knew she wouldn't be able to speak again without crying.

Pulling away, Anna ran into the house and quietly shut the door behind her. She leaned her forehead on the frame and closed her eyes. Thunder rumbled again.

She pulled aside the window curtain and peeked out. As lightning flashed, she could see Gabe walking back to his car. He stopped and looked back at the house, then opened the car door and got in. His headlights gleamed through the front window, and the light slanted across the room as he backed out of the driveway. As his taillights disappeared down the street, rain started to fall.

# PART III

# TWENTY-FOUR

## FOUR YEARS LATER

Anna was already exhausted when she made her way through the open-air market to the front door of her building, and the narrow staircase leading four stories to her apartment seemed to mock her. Climbing those stairs was like descending into hell, only in reverse. The temperature rose at least five degrees with each flight, slowly choking her until she stumbled into her apartment, sweating and gasping.

She always left the door to the narrow balcony open, so while the apartment was still an oven, it was marginally cooler than out in the hall. Flipping on the overhead fan lowered the temperature another few degrees, and if she flung off her shirt and collapsed on the couch without moving at all, she could almost catch her breath.

She sat there, eyes closed, and tried to shut off her brain. At four stories up, the sounds of bleating goats, men arguing over games of backgammon, and women bargaining over everything from chickens to Persian rugs all blended into white noise that drifted in through the open door. The heavy scent of frying onions mixed with burning incense from the apartment next door was pungent but comforting after the past few weeks in the refugee camps, where access to proper sanitation was always a struggle.

Although she was based in a hospital in Irbid, Jordan that served refugees who'd fled into the country from Syria, the physicians all took turns traveling to the southern border where they worked in makeshift medical tents in the refugee camps. Those shifts were grueling, and at first, coming home to her stifling apartment had been a reprieve. But lately it only seemed to depress her.

Her job was to help bring babies into a world where she was constantly reminded that people could do the most terrible things to each other. Most of the time, she put her head down, kept working, and tried not to dwell on it. Her colleagues were confronted by the same daily tragedies as she was, so burdening them with her sadness wasn't going to do anyone any good.

She wished she could talk to Adrien. They'd been dating—if you could call a couple of nights a week of cooking dinner and sleeping together *dating*—for over a year. But Adrien was a surgeon who'd made a career out of working in war zones. Ten years in, he viewed people as a series of organs to repair and barely registered tragedy.

Gabe seemed to sense her exhaustion and had asked her about it in their last phone call. But she couldn't tell Gabe the kind of stuff she was dealing with when he was six thousand miles away. Couldn't talk about the women whose husbands were imprisoned or murdered, leaving them fleeing their homes with a slew of children and more babies on the way. Or the women who'd been kidnapped and raped by the terrorist groups before they managed to escape and make their way to the refugee camp. Or about all the mothers and babies she'd lost, the women and children who would have easily survived their complicated deliveries with medical interventions common in the US, who she couldn't save with the limited surgical and neonatal facilities available here.

She opened her eyes and stared at the fan spinning on the ceiling. So much for shutting off her brain. She sat up and blew out a heavy breath, then dragged herself off the couch and fished her phone from her bag. The Wi-Fi was actually working pretty well lately, and an alert immediately popped up. Three missed video calls from Gabe, all in a row. She switched over to her texts and clicked on the one at the top with his name on it. And then she stopped breathing.

*Anna, I'm so sorry to tell you this in a text. My dad had a heart attack. He was golfing with one of his old college friends, and he keeled over. Luckily his friend is a doctor, and he started chest compressions right away. The paramedics got there in about three minutes. He's in surgery right now. I'll let you know as soon as we hear anything.*

With shaking hands, Anna hit the button to call Gabe, but the signal must have fizzled out because the phone didn't ring. She stood up, paced the apartment, and then tried again. Still nothing.

Panic rose like she was the one having a heart attack. She was six thousand miles away. And the internet wasn't working. She shot off a text to Gabe, telling him to be in touch as soon as he knew anything, but the little blue bar across the top that showed the message sending seemed to be stuck at fifty percent. She wished she were there with him.

*She wished she were there with him.*

Anna paced the apartment again, obsessively checking her phone and trying not to crawl out of her skin. Nothing, nothing, nothing.

Maybe she'd call Adrien. There wasn't much he could do, except sit with her, but at least she wouldn't be alone. She was about to punch in his number when she stopped. Having to explain it all to him, who everyone was, why this mattered—it was too exhausting.

She'd told him about the Weatheralls, of course. But she'd had a feeling he wasn't really listening. If she called Adrien, he'd probably rattle off a list of questions about the heart attack. *Did John lose consciousness? What was the time frame between symptoms? Was it the left or right anterior descending?* Questions she didn't have answers for and that weren't helpful when all she wanted was someone to wrap their arms around her.

She couldn't talk to Adrien when all she wanted was Gabe.

Finally—*Thank God*—her phone buzzed with a text.

*We just talked to the doctor. He had a complete coronary artery blockage, and they did a balloon angioplasty. They said it'll be a long road, but he'll be okay. He's just waking up now and my mom's with him. I'll keep you updated.*

And then, right after the first, a second message appeared.

*I really miss you.*

Anna took a couple of deep, gasping breaths to slow the rapid thumping in her chest.

*I miss you, too.*

She shut off her phone and got ready for bed.

That night, she dreamed she was in Gabe's parents' kitchen, surrounded by the family. Dorothy sat next to her at the breakfast nook, and from across the room, Gabe looked over and gave her a smile.

When she woke up, Anna felt more rested than she had in months.

. . .

Several days later, Anna was making the same hot, sweaty trip up the stairs when her phone began buzzing insistently. Gabe had texted a few updates about John over the past few days, but her spotty cell reception had made it difficult to talk.

Anna pulled her phone from her pocket, expecting to see Gabe's name flashing on the screen, but instead, it was a number she didn't recognize.

A San Francisco number.

Anna took the last few steps at double speed and then stopped by her front door, swiping to answer the call.

"Hello?" she asked breathlessly.

"Hello," said an unfamiliar male voice. "I'm looking for Anna Campbell."

Anna's shoulders slumped. All these years later and a little part of her still expected to hear her mother's voice. Would she ever truly give up? "This is Anna," she said, only slightly curious. A 415 area code was probably someone from UCSF. She got fundraising emails from the alumni association every year. Maybe they were just following up on her donation.

"Ms. Campbell, this is Officer Deacon from the San Francisco Police Department."

Anna grabbed her apartment door handle for balance. It wasn't her mom. But was this the other call she'd been waiting her entire life for? "Yes?" she finally managed to choke out.

"You came in several years ago to put in a missing person report for a Deborah Campbell? I believe she's your mother?"

"Yes." Anna's vision blurred. "She is. Do you have news for me?"

"Well, I'm not quite sure if I have news or not." Officer Deacon took an audible breath. "I was looking through some old Jane Doe files, and I might have found something. We had a woman whose body was found in a park in the Tenderloin neighborhood years ago. No ID, but she fits the description in your missing person report. Same approximate age your mother would have been at the time, Caucasian descent, dark brown hair and eyes."

Anna pressed her back to the door and slid down to the floor.

"How would we know for sure?"

"You can submit a DNA sample for us to potentially ID her."

The smell of incense drifted in from the apartment next door, reminding her she was thousands of miles away. "I'm not currently in San Francisco. How would I go about doing that?"

"I can give you the information, there are labs across the country. They'll run the test and we'll compare it to the sample that was taken when the Jane Doe came through the morgue."

*The morgue.*

Had her mom been in the morgue? And where was she now? Probably in an unmarked grave somewhere.

"Ms. Campbell?" Officer Deacon's voice cut into her thoughts.

"I'm sorry. I'm not in the country right now." Anna pressed her hands to her temples. "I work abroad."

"Will you be back for a visit anytime soon? Vacation?"

Anna thought about John's heart attack. Her dream of Elizabeth and John's kitchen. Gabe's smile. Could she take a few weeks off?

"I'm going to have to figure this out."

"Okay, I have an email address for you here. I'll send you the information for the test, and you can let me know."

They said their goodbyes, but right before they were about to hang up, Anna pressed the phone back to her ear. "Wait."

"Yes?"

"How did she die? The woman in the park?"

Through the phone, Anna heard papers flipping. "It says here, uh, cardiac arrest."

Anna's spine straightened. "Not—not a drug overdose?"

"No. There was a small amount of an opiate in her system. The report says it's consistent with normal dosage for pain management. But that wasn't the cause of death."

"When did you find her? What was the date?"

The police officer flipped through his report for another moment. "Uh, let's see." And then he named a date.

It was only a couple of weeks after her mom had left. Right around the time her calls dropped off.

Anna's pulse pounded in her ear. If her mother had died of a heart attack, could that explain why she'd never come back? Maybe it had nothing to do with drugs or any of the other terrible things Anna had imagined over the years. Maybe her mom really *had* planned to do whatever job had taken her to San Francisco, and then come back to Anna. And in an awful twist of fate, she'd died in the park without any ID on her, and there'd been no way for Anna to know.

Maybe... maybe her mom never meant to stay away forever.

# TWENTY-FIVE

Anna opened her eyes and rolled over to look at the clock—8:00 a.m. She couldn't remember the last time she'd slept that late.

Every morning for four years she'd woken up right before sunrise to the sound of the *adhan*, or Islamic call to prayer, being broadcast through the loudspeakers of the local mosque. Soon after, the noises of the city coming to life would begin to drift in through her window: the woman next door clanging a pot as she made breakfast for her family, another neighbor beating a rug on the narrow apartment balcony, merchants setting up their wares in the market below.

Anna sat up in bed and listened, but other than the occasional car driving past the Weatheralls' house or bird chirping in a tree, all she heard was silence. Anna missed the commotion, especially the five-times daily call to prayer. She hadn't been raised with any sort of religious or spiritual tradition, but during the call to prayer, she found herself stopping whatever she was doing and sending up a silent thanks to God or Jesus or Allah, or whoever it was out there who might be looking out for her.

Anna sent up one of those little prayers right then, thankful she'd made it home safely, and grateful for the Weatheralls who'd welcomed her. After Gabe had surprised her at the airport, he'd taken her to his parents' house. Her old room had still looked the same as it had in high school.

And then, Anna sent up one more prayer, this time for her mom. Wherever she was, Anna hoped she knew her daughter had never forgotten her, had never given up on her. With one hand, she gripped the gold pendant around her neck. As heartbroken as Anna was to think her mom was truly gone, she'd found some comfort in it, too. The worst part had always been the wondering. The not knowing. And all the terrible scenarios she'd imagined.

Maybe she was finally on the brink of finding the answers she'd spent half her life chasing.

Anna rolled out of bed, brushed her teeth, and made her way downstairs. By the time Gabe had dropped her off from the airport last night, it was after two in the morning, and John and Elizabeth had been asleep. Elizabeth had left a note instructing her to wake them when she got home, but with John's heart attack only a couple of months earlier, Anna knew they needed their rest.

She paused in the kitchen doorway and took in the two of them lined up on barstools, heads bent together over the crossword puzzle in the newspaper. John had always been so strong and steady; it was hard to believe he'd almost died two months ago. After the heart attack, he'd bounced back in record time and still looked ten years younger than his sixty-five years. But the reality was that both he and Elizabeth were growing older and frailer. In addition to the heart attack, John had retired from performing surgery a year earlier because his eyesight wasn't what it used to be. And Elizabeth had fallen and broken her arm a few months before that. She still wore a brace on her left hand.

Anna's heart ached at the sight of them.

She was back in Pittsburgh to get a DNA test and some

answers about her mom. But if she were really honest about it, she was home for this, too. They meant so much to her—John and Elizabeth and the whole family—even after all this time and distance. The prospect of losing her mom—really, truly this time—had brought that into focus.

Anna swallowed hard as she stepped into the room. "Hi."

John tossed aside the newspaper, and Elizabeth lunged off her stool, hurrying across the room to throw her arms around Anna. "Oh, honey, thank God you're finally home," Elizabeth said, tucking Anna's hair behind her ear, cupping her cheeks in her hands, standing back to take her in. "Look at you. You're so thin. John, get Anna a cinnamon roll."

"She looks perfect," John said, wrapping a protective arm around Anna's shoulder. "At least let the girl sit down before you start fussing." He leaned in, whispering under his breath, "Elizabeth has become an expert fusser these past few months."

Anna laughed. "And aren't you lucky she has?"

John gave an exaggerated sigh. "I thought at least *you* would be on my side."

Anna's face turned serious. "I know we doctors are always the last ones to take care of ourselves. So you'd better be doing exactly what you're told."

He shook his head. "I knew I should have encouraged you to be an attorney."

"Oh stop." Elizabeth gave John a playful swat. "Don't listen to him. It means so much that you came home to check in after his heart attack. He just doesn't like to get sentimental about it."

Anna looked down at her hands. She hadn't told any of the Weatheralls about the other reason for her trip. Not even Gabe. They hadn't talked about her mom since that day on the beach all those years ago. And Anna never brought her up with the rest of the family either. She'd always been afraid of their questions... and what they might do if they ever learned the answers.

But over the past few months, her view of the past had

begun to shift. Maybe her mom had always loved her, and maybe these years apart had been due to nothing but a heart attack and a terrible tragedy.

Maybe she could finally begin to forgive herself for her part in her mom's disappearance and move on.

Elizabeth crossed the room to slide a cinnamon roll in front of her. "I'm sure you're still exhausted from your long flight. And you've been taking care of everyone over there nonstop for four years. You just relax and let me take care of you while you're here."

Anna felt something deep inside of her release: a tension she'd been holding for years. For decades maybe. She was tempted to fling herself into Elizabeth's arms and thank her for all the care the older woman had already given her.

At that moment, several pairs of footsteps clomped across the back deck. The back door opened, and Matt and Gabe walked through in old T-shirts and paint-spattered shorts.

"Ann-a-a-a-a-a-a," Matt intoned, wrapping her in his muscular arms. When he'd finally released her, Gabe leaned in to give her a slightly less bone-crushing squeeze.

"What are you guys doing here so early?" Anna asked. She took in their work clothes. "And looking like the June and July pages of a sexy-construction-worker calendar, too."

Gabe grinned as he poured a cup of coffee, splashed in just the right amount of milk, and handed it to her. Funny how he still remembered how she liked it, all these years later. "A branch fell from that old tree in the front yard during a big storm a few days ago. It did some damage to the roof. We're here to fix it."

"What are you up to today?" John asked her.

"I thought I'd go and see about a rental car that I can use for the next few weeks."

"Make sure you ask about extra insurance," Matt advised from across the kitchen island.

Gabe snorted, and Anna rolled her eyes. Matt had taught her how to drive when she'd lived with the Weatheralls during her senior year of high school. She was pretty sure he was never going to let anyone forget her close call with a chain-link fence.

John ignored his sons' chuckles to focus on Anna. "Who's going with you to the rental place? Rachel?"

"No, I think Rachel said she'll be in court today."

John's brows knitted together. "I'm not sure it's a good idea to go alone. You know how those car guys are, especially when they see a young woman all by herself. They're going to try to charge you an arm and a leg." He rubbed his chin. "Maybe I should go with you."

Before she could answer, Matt and Gabe began gesturing wildly behind John. Gabe's head bobbed as he mouthed, "Say yes."

She looked back at John. "Well, if you don't mind coming along, that would be great."

"I think that's probably smart," Matt interjected.

"Yeah, we don't want Anna to get scammed," Gabe added.

John turned to his sons. "You boys think you'll be okay on your own with the roof?"

Matt assumed a serious expression. "I think we can probably handle it," said the man who'd been building houses for almost twenty years.

Gabe gave an exaggerated shrug. "Yeah, we'll be okay."

John nodded. "Okay, I'll go change." He disappeared down the hall, and Anna turned to Matt and Gabe.

"He was planning to help you fix the roof?"

Matt grabbed a cinnamon roll off the tray on the counter and tore off a piece. "I know. The man had a heart attack two months ago."

Elizabeth sighed. "He was only allowed to supervise."

"Which might be even worse than him helping." Gabe shook his head. "Thanks for taking him along."

"Of course."

The truth was, she loved having John along. He was so earnest about helping her, Anna couldn't bring herself to remind him she wouldn't be committing to this car for the next decade, it was only a short-term lease. John insisted she test-drive every car on the lot, asked the salesperson a million questions about gas mileage, and then walked around kicking tires and looking under hoods.

It was exactly the sort of thing she imagined her father might have done if she'd ever known him. In the back of her mind, Anna had always told herself that, one day, her mom would give her more information about her father. But if her mom was really gone, Anna might have lost that chance, too. She might have lost every thread to who she was and where she came from.

Just like she'd felt with Elizabeth in the kitchen earlier, Anna was suddenly overcome with the urge to grab John by the hand and thank him for being there for her. She knew his interest wasn't really about finding a rental car. It was his way of showing he cared, and that meant everything.

"I think this is the one," John said, patting the roof of a reliable Honda sedan. "What do you think?"

Anna gave him an affectionate smile. "I think if you approve, then it's perfect."

John nodded at the salesperson. "We'll take it."

Anna tucked her arm into John's, and they headed inside to sign the papers.

When they pulled in the driveway later that afternoon, a ladder was propped against the house, and Gabe and Matt were on the roof. The July sun was high in the sky, and they'd pulled off their shirts and tossed them to the grass below.

Anna held her hand over her forehead to shield her eyes

from the glare as she craned her neck to check their progress. Both men were kneeling on the roof, the muscles in their arms and backs flexing and contracting as they hammered nails into the new shingles.

Did it just get about ten degrees hotter? She fanned herself with her rental car paperwork and grabbed her bag from the front seat of John's BMW. As she turned back around, Gabe hopped off the last two rungs of the ladder and landed in front of her.

"Hey," he said, shoving his hair off his forehead and leaving it standing up in sweaty spikes. "How'd it go?"

Anna kept her eyes trained on his face. "Good. They're dropping off my rental car tomorrow."

John came up beside her and told Gabe about the Honda she'd settled on, describing the fuel efficiency and other practical features. While they talked, Anna let her distracted gaze drift away from Gabe's face to trace the muscles stretched across his shoulders and down his arms. He was tan from working outside, and a smattering of brown hair dusted his chest and trailed down toward his navel. She appreciated the flat, solid abs of a man who stayed active and worked out, but not quite the carefully chiseled six-pack of someone who took it too seriously.

Her breath caught, and her body grew warm. After all these years, he could still knock her on her ass. She dragged her eyes from his torso back to his face, and then she grew even hotter.

Because Gabe was staring back at her like whatever this attraction she was feeling, he was feeling it, too.

Anna sat on a barstool in Gabe's parents' sunny kitchen, where the entire family had gathered to welcome her home, and a sense of peace came over her. She looked over as Gabe scooped up Matt's three-year-old son, Henry and jokingly threatened to dump him in the garbage can. Henry hung by his feet, squealing with laughter. Gabe glanced up, saw her watching, and winked. Then Matt galloped into the kitchen making horse noises while his two older sons clung to his back.

"Okay, it's time for this horsey to head out to pasture." Julia laughed as she unloaded the boys from Matt's back and settled them at the breakfast nook, where they dove into their pizza.

A glass of wine appeared in front of Anna, and she looked up as Rachel slid into the seat next to her. "Aaliyah wants to have dinner as soon as she gets back from London."

"That woman travels for work more than I do." Anna smiled. "Any movement on wedding plans?"

Rachel waved her hand as if she were shooing a fly. "Oh, you know... we'll get around to it."

Aaliyah had proposed when she and Rachel had graduated from law school, but it was the longest engagement in history. Rachel had made a name for herself as a divorce attorney who secured huge settlements for her clients—usually women. Anna suspected that her line of work had probably left her a little squeamish about the institution of marriage. She seemed happy enough being engaged.

Leah slid onto a barstool on the other side of Anna. "I wish Rachel would just go ahead and get married." Leah was twenty-six now and had married her high school sweetheart, Josh, last summer.

Anna had been in Jordan for Leah's wedding, and flying home for the weekend hadn't been practical. She'd sent a gift. But now the guilt gnawed at her. She and Leah had always been close, and Anna knew Leah looked up to her. She should have made it home.

"I'd love to plan another wedding," Leah said wistfully.

Anna eyed Leah's empire-waist sundress. "Pretty soon you're going to be too busy to plan anything. A baby takes up a lot of time."

Leah stared at Anna with her mouth open. Her hands fluttered to her abdomen. "But—I'm still barely showing! How did you know?"

"It's my job to know." She held out her hand to Leah's slightly rounded stomach. "Can I?"

Leah nodded, and Anna pressed on it gently a few times. "Twenty-seven weeks?"

"Twenty-six and a half!"

Josh joined them, and Anna reached up to give him a hug. This was Leah and Josh's first baby, and they radiated joy. Leah would be an amazing mother; she certainly had the best role model in Elizabeth.

Her heart clenched, thinking about her own maternal role model. Her mom had loved her once, a long time ago. But maybe her mom had loved her always. Anna wanted to believe it with her whole heart.

"We waited to tell you in person because we wanted to ask you something." Leah rubbed her belly. "We're so happy that you could take a few weeks off to come and see us..."

Anna nodded, and her thoughts drifted to the DNA test she'd be taking as soon as she could schedule it. She could have flown in weeks ago, gotten the swab, and turned around and left again. But when it came down to figuring out the logistics of her trip, she'd elected to stay longer in Jordan to arrange her schedule so she could visit for a few weeks in Pittsburgh. For about the hundredth time since she'd woken up in John and Elizabeth's house that morning, Anna was grateful for that decision.

"Well, is there any way you could stay even a little longer?" Leah bit her lip nervously. "Like maybe... a trimester or so?" She glanced at Josh. "We'd love for you to be here to deliver the baby."

"Oh, honey," Anna said, swallowing hard.

Leah held up a hand. "I know it's a lot to ask. I do. But

there's nobody else I'd rather have in the delivery room with me."

Josh made a show of clearing his throat.

Leah patted his leg. "Obviously, I meant other than you, sweetie. Although I'm still not a hundred percent convinced you're not going to pass out."

Matt wandered over and punched Josh on the arm. "Dude, you'll be fine. I suffered through childbirth three times."

"*You* suffered?" Julia screeched from across the room. "Keep talking like that, and I'll make sure you know about suffering."

Matt grinned. "The secret is to stay up by her head, and everything will be fine. Never go down by the... you know..." He waved his hand in the general area of his crotch.

"I'm sorry, the... what?" Anna said with a laugh. She saw a lot of squeamish husbands in her line of work.

Matt cleared his throat. "The doctor always encourages you to look when the baby is crowning, but never, ever do it." Matt glanced at Julia, who'd moved back to the breakfast nook with their three boys, and then muttered to Josh: "Trust me. I know from experience."

Josh rubbed his chin and nodded. "Got it. No looking."

Anna shook her head. "You know how many husbands swear they'll never look, and then when their baby's crowning, they end up staring in complete awe?"

"How many?"

"Pretty much all of them." She laughed at the stricken look on Josh's face.

Rachel walked over and smacked Matt in the arm. "Ew! Can you guys *please* stop talking about girl parts? If I have to hear my brothers discuss this for another minute, I'm seriously going to puke."

Matt grinned and rubbed his arm where she'd hit him. "Oh, come on, Rach. You like girl parts as much as we do."

Gabe laughed and reached over to high-five Matt.

Rachel looked back and forth between her brothers in horror. "Oh my God. Mom!" she called across the kitchen. "Gabe and Matt are being gross *again*!"

From across the room, Elizabeth smiled. "Stop fighting, children," she said in a singsong voice, not bothering to look up from the salad she was making.

Anna settled into her chair, strangely comforted by the familiar bickering. It had always been like this with the Weatheralls. Being surrounded by their warmth and laughter and good-natured arguments never failed to help her forget there was a world out there where bad things happened to people.

God, how she'd missed them all. Knowing that her mom might be gone made her want to hold on to this time with the people she cared about—the people who could still be here with her.

Anna considered Leah's request. Her supervisor had encouraged her to take a longer vacation when she'd put in for the time off. Burnout was common in her line of work, and Anna hadn't taken more than a long weekend in ages. And on the drive, John had mentioned that they were always looking for doctors to fill in at the hospital. Could she get a temporary position in labor and delivery, and stay long enough to deliver Leah's baby? Now that the police had some leads on her mom's disappearance, she could be close by if there were any new developments in the case, too.

Anna took another look around the kitchen. The truth was that if her mom really *had* died of a heart attack in that park in San Francisco all those years ago, she'd want to be here—surrounded by the Weatheralls—when she got the news. And she wanted to be with Gabe. He was the only person she'd want to hold her while she cried.

# TWENTY-SIX

Gabe watched Anna laughing with his family and felt a sense of calm settle in his chest that hadn't been there since she'd left for the Middle East. When he'd asked point-blank about how safe she was and what kind of risks she was taking, she said she was fine and changed the subject, which didn't surprise him even a little bit. She'd always insisted she could take care of herself. And he knew if anyone could, it was Anna. But still, some things weren't always in her control.

His obsessive reading of news about the war in Syria and aid work in the Middle East hadn't exactly reassured him she was out of harm's way. Just in the past few months, two hospitals had been bombed, and stories of missing aid workers, likely kidnapped by terrorists, had been coming through his newsfeed at an alarming frequency.

Last night had been the first in four years that he'd been able to sleep without a vague sense of dread camping out in his chest. When Anna was gone, there were so many nights he gave up on sleep entirely, wandering out to his balcony to stare up at the night sky, wondering if she could see the same stars from where she was on the other side of the world.

He watched Anna grab a slice of pizza and slide into the breakfast nook with Julia and the boys. "Hey, Henry." He heard her voice carry from across the kitchen. "Knock, knock."

"Who's there?" came Henry's little-boy voice.

"Interrupting cow."

"Interrupting co—"

"MOO!"

Gabe snickered, but Henry laughed so hard he fell out of his chair and spilled his juice down Julia's arm.

"Henry!" Julia jumped up and grabbed at the napkins in the middle of the table.

Anna made an exaggerated cringe face. "Sorry."

Gabe laughed again.

"You want one?"

Gabe looked up to find his dad standing above him, holding two beers. "Sure. Thanks."

Gabe took one, and his dad sat down on the next barstool and tipped back the other bottle.

"You supposed to be drinking that?" Gabe gestured at the beer.

"I feel better than I did before the heart attack. Your mother won't let me eat anything good anymore. Don't try to take away my beer, too." He took another swig and then nodded in the direction of the breakfast nook. "It's good to have the whole family together again."

Gabe glanced at Anna and then back at his dad. "Yeah, it is."

"I'm really proud of her."

Gabe nodded. "You got your doctor in the family after all." The words were out of his mouth before he thought about what he was saying. It was a subject that hadn't come up for a long time, and one he didn't spend a lot of time dwelling on. The truth was, that ship had sailed a long time ago. Gabe was a few years away from tenure at the university, he had invitations to lecture all over the country, and he'd published his research in all the major journals. But apparently, he still harbored a little bit of... maybe not bitterness. More like annoyance about the pressure to be a doctor when he was younger.

His dad looked at him for a long moment. "I'm glad we have Anna in the family. But you know, it wouldn't have been the end of the world if we never got a doctor."

Gabe's eyebrows shot up. His dad must have hit his head during the heart attack because that mellow attitude wasn't quite how Gabe remembered it.

His dad cleared his throat. "I know I don't say it much, but I couldn't be prouder of you. I'm sorry if I didn't make that clear when you were younger." He paused and squeezed the back of his neck as if his words were making him ache physically. "My family didn't have much money when I was growing up, and my mom struggled. After my dad died, we weren't just working class. We were poor. My mom worked three jobs, sometimes there wasn't enough food in the house, and we went to bed hungry. I wanted you kids to go into professions where I knew you wouldn't struggle. But I may have let it get out of hand."

Gabe rocked back in his seat. He knew his grandfather had been a steelworker, and he'd died young. But he'd never really thought about what it must have been like for his dad to grow up with a single mother who had few job skills. He never talked about it. By the time Gabe knew her, his grandmother had always seemed comfortable.

It occurred to Gabe how hard she must have had to work for that success.

His dad's voice broke into his thoughts. "I know I was hard on you, and even more on Matt. I told him this, and now I'm telling you. I'm sorry."

Gabe scrubbed his hand over his forehead, trying to catch his brain up to this shift in perspective. "You don't need to be sorry. I wouldn't be where I am if you hadn't pushed me."

His dad cocked his head. "Well, then I hope you'll forgive a guy who recently saw his life flash before his eyes for giving you one more push." He hitched his chin in Anna's direction. "She's not going to stick around for long."

Gabe's heart thudded. His eyes were drawn back to Anna, and as if she sensed him watching, she looked up and gave him that smile that lit up her face. From somewhere far away, he heard his dad say, "Unless someone gives her a good reason to."

Gabe's head jerked back around.

His dad met his gaze head-on. "Take it from me. Life can change in a second. Don't miss your chance."

Gabe opened his mouth and then closed it. And then, he couldn't help it. He laughed. As usual, there his dad went, thinking he knew what was best. Giving one of his kids a subtle, or not-so-subtle, nudge in the direction he thought they should go.

But this time, Gabe couldn't be mad about it. Because this time, he suspected that his dad was right. "Thanks for the advice."

His dad squeezed his shoulder and then hopped off the barstool. Gabe watched him cross the kitchen and sidle up next to his mom at the stove, reaching across her to grab a mushroom from one of the pizzas. His mom slapped his hand, and his dad laughed and slid his arm around her, kissing her on the cheek.

Gabe took a healthy swig of beer as the chaos of his family swirled around him: his nephews giggling at a joke, Leah and Julia discussing baby names, his dad's low chuckle as he flirted with his mom.

How had he grown up where family was everything and never found someone to share it all with? Gabe's gaze stopped on Anna. Maybe because he'd spent most of his adult life comparing every woman he met to one person.

# TWENTY-SEVEN

Gabe had been staring at the data from his latest research for so long, his eyes were starting to cross. So, when his phone buzzed across his desk, he was grateful for the distraction. He turned his attention away from housing prices and income levels and looked up to find a text from Rachel.

*Anna and I are meeting at Tram's at 8. Want to have dinner with us?*

Gabe looked at the clock on his computer—seven thirty. He glanced at his spreadsheet and back at his phone.

It was really no contest.

Twenty minutes later, Gabe drove through Lawrenceville, Anna's neighborhood from the old days. Stopping at a red light on Butler Street, he spotted a group of twentysomethings flipping through their iPhones as they waited outside a packed Mexican restaurant. Two doors down, kids lined up with their parents to get ice cream at a local shop.

He'd been to Lawrenceville dozens of times over the past few years, but for the first time in a while, he considered how the place had transformed in the years since Anna lived there. First, the artists had moved in, drawn by rock-bottom housing prices and empty storefronts they converted into gallery spaces. Next came the boutiques, bars, and trendy restaurants owned by up-and-coming chefs who could never have afforded their own places in bigger, more expensive cities. Finally, the young families took notice and started buying up the developers' flips faster than they could churn them out. His brother had an office in Lawrenceville, and his development company was famous for some of the neighborhood's higher quality renovations.

Gabe turned his car up Main Street and parked at the top of the hill. To his left, the clouds morphed into slashes of pink and orange behind the city skyline, and to his right, the setting sun reflected off the shiny new windows of the brick row houses.

What would Anna think when she passed by her old haunts, now cleaned up and covered with fresh paint? Her childhood wasn't the kind that after a while faded into a rosy haze of memories the way Gabe's childhood had. It was the kind that lingered like the acrid smell of cigarette smoke trapped in a shirt that won't come clean, no matter how many times it goes through the wash.

Would the same sunset that people paid hundreds of thousands of dollars to view from their brand-new rooftop decks remind Anna of the dread she used to feel when darkness descended, and she had to watch her back on her way home? Would she pass those streets that bustled with trendy kids and young families and still flinch at the intersections where drug dealers used to harass her?

Gabe had no idea what had happened to Anna's old house —if it was still a ramshackle apartment building run by the same drunken slumlord, or if some developer had renovated it back into a single-family home and sold it for a million dollars. Anna probably avoided that particular part of the neighborhood the same way she avoided talking about her mom. Had Anna's move to the other side of the world helped her to finally come to terms with her childhood? Or did she still scan the crowd for women with familiar features?

Gabe knew that time was running out on staying silent about her mom's necklace. Even if she didn't want to talk about her mom, even if she didn't want to know about the necklace, he had to tell her the truth. He couldn't ask her to stay with this secret hanging over them. Even if it meant that she might turn around and leave.

Gabe shifted away from the view and walked the half block to Tram's, a Vietnamese restaurant that, despite the substantial upswing of the neighborhood, had kept its original character.

The place was packed when Gabe pulled the door open and stepped inside. Anna sat alone at a table, studying the menu. Her head jerked up when he slid into a chair across from her. "Gabe! Hey! I didn't know you were coming."

"Rach didn't think you'd mind."

"Of course I don't mind."

Gabe settled into his chair and regarded her across the table. "It means a lot to my family that you came home after my dad's heart attack." It meant a lot to him, too.

Gabe had been more than a little surprised when he'd gotten her text saying she'd finally planned to come. He'd almost given up on the idea when her time in the Middle East had stretched to three years, and then four. Apparently, she'd started dating some surgeon, Adrien or something. One Sunday at dinner, he'd had to listen to Leah chattering about meeting the guy over a Zoom call.

But now Anna was here, and this surgeon guy was over there.

Now, all he had to do was get her to stay.

"It's really nice to be home for a visit," Anna admitted, pouring wine into their glasses from the bottle on the table.

*A visit.*

"You've been over there for four years. That's a long time. Do you ever think about settling down?"

"What does 'settling down' mean?" She squinted at him. "Like moving back to the US?"

"Like moving back *home*. To Pittsburgh." He leaned forward in his chair. "And like marriage, kids, all that stuff."

Anna sat straighter in her chair. "I don't know. I didn't grow up playing with dolls or dreaming about my wedding. My dreams were always about becoming a doctor, having a life away from... Well, away from this neighborhood actually."

"Yeah, but you made it. A long time ago. What about new dreams?"

"I'm not sure I had the best role models when it came to marriage and parenting." She picked up her silverware and arranged and rearranged it on her napkin.

This was the closest she'd come to talking about her mom in years. Gabe pressed his lips together, hoping his silence would prompt her to keep talking.

Finally, Anna shrugged. "It doesn't really bode well for me to make a relationship work, or to care for small human beings."

He stared at her. Was she serious? How could she think that?

"You're a great doctor, and it's not just because you're smart. It's because of who you are—your patience, your concern for people. Like my grandmother, back when you used to spend hours poring over photo albums with her. Or Leah, who always looked up to you so much. You know she cried when she found out she was pregnant because she thought you wouldn't be there to deliver the baby."

Anna's face creased with sadness.

Gabe took a deep breath. "And then there's me."

"What about you?"

"You're the best friend I ever had. I can't imagine my life

without you." He leaned in with a sudden intensity. "Anna, consider staying in Pittsburgh."

Anna twisted her spoon in her hands. "Gabe, I have a whole life there—"

"*You have a whole life here—*" He stopped and took a deep breath. "At least stay long enough to deliver Leah's baby." He was overwhelmed by how much he wanted her to say yes. "And after that..." He reached over and put his hand on Anna's to still her nervous motion. Her head jerked up at the gentle pressure, and their eyes met. "After that, consider staying for me."

She didn't reply, but she didn't look away either. The air grew heavy as they stared at each other across the table, but before he could say anything else, a voice cut in.

"Sorry I'm late."

Faster than Gabe could blink, Anna snatched her hand out from under his.

Rachel stood above them in a conservative gray suit and black heels. Then she pulled off her jacket and flung it over a chair, revealing a sleeveless blouse that showed off the six or seven tattoos scattered up and down her arms. She plopped down into the chair next to Anna and sloshed some wine in her glass. "Traffic on 28 is the worst."

But Gabe barely heard her, because his heart was doing backflips at the tiny, hopeful smile tugging on Anna's lips.

# TWENTY-EIGHT

"Dr. Campbell?" came a voice from behind Anna as she made her way down the powder-blue hallway of the hospital birth center. She turned around to find Constance, one of the labor and delivery nurses, approaching. "Room 321 has settled in. Contractions three minutes apart."

"Thanks." Anna gave her new colleague a smile. "Call me Anna." She was used to a more casual way of interacting with people from her work in the refugee camps. It would take some time to readjust to the formalities and policies of a large modern hospital.

Anna's extended stay in Pittsburgh had all come together perfectly. John had connected her with the head of obstetrics at the hospital, and they were more than happy to offer her a temporary position in their birth center. And Rachel had helped her find a tiny furnished carriage house over a detached garage in a quiet neighborhood nearby. The owner, a college professor friend of Rachel's, had gone overseas for a sabbatical and offered Anna a six-month lease.

It was perfect timing for Anna to deliver Leah's baby and

get the results of the DNA test she'd taken last week. And after that...

Well, after that, she'd just have to see.

Gabe wanted her to stay. *For him.* Though he hadn't brought it up again, that possibility was always in the periphery. It wasn't new, that low hum that started every time they were in a room together, as if the two of them were on a slightly different frequency than everyone else. But for the first time, Anna was open to possibility. That Gabe could love her. And that she deserved his love. For the first time, Anna was open to telling him everything: about her past, and her mom, and why she'd left.

Ever since she'd answered that phone call from the police officer in San Francisco, it was like someone had turned a valve to shut off the pressure that had been filling her chest. Anna had been preparing for the worst for half her life. If her mom really had died of a heart attack in that park, there would be some comfort in knowing that she'd gone peacefully. She hadn't suffered. And she hadn't meant to stay away forever.

Maybe her mom had always planned to come back.

And maybe Anna wasn't to blame.

And if all that were true, maybe Anna *could* have all those things she and Gabe talked about a few weeks ago. Marriage, kids. A family.

And maybe she could have them with Gabe.

"Anna?" Constance's voice cut into her thoughts. "There's a patient in 316 I think you should see right away. A woman at about twenty-five weeks." Concern creased the nurse's face. "She says she fell down the stairs, but her injuries aren't consistent with a fall. I suspect domestic abuse, but she's not talking. She doesn't have an obstetrician yet, and she's uninsured."

"I'll go right now." Anna hurried down the hall, and Constance showed her to the room of a young pregnant woman in her early twenties.

"Hi," Anna said. "I'm Dr. Campbell, but you can call me Anna. I'm an obstetrician, so they asked me to come and examine you. Is that okay?"

The young woman studied her from under about five layers of black eyeliner and finally nodded. "I'm Hayleigh."

Anna quickly skimmed Hayleigh's chart and then glanced at the purple bruise forming around her eye and the gash across her cheek bleeding through a gauze bandage. "The nurse is going to come in a minute to stitch up that cut on your cheek, but first, we need to check on your baby, okay?"

Anna asked Hayleigh to lie back so she could check the baby's heart rate. Hayleigh winced and pressed on her rib cage as she shifted on the exam table, and the areas of her upper arms that slid out from beneath her T-shirt showed finger-shaped bruises.

As Anna reached for Hayleigh, the acrid odor of cigarette smoke rose, and Anna was hit by a vivid memory. Her hand stilled as the stale tobacco scent swirled around her, the same as the one that used to envelope her when her mom would slide onto the couch next to her or lean over to give her a hug. Despite the burned sharpness, Anna was oddly comforted by it. The smell of her childhood. Her mom. Being here in Pittsburgh again seemed to bring the memories back stronger.

Anna's hands shook as she gently pulled Hayleigh's T-shirt up and over her rounded belly.

"Is that going to hurt?" Hayleigh asked, eyeing the machine in Anna's hand.

"This?" Anna held up the Doppler monitor. "No, not at all. We just hold it on your belly to hear the heartbeat. Is that okay?"

Hayleigh shrugged. "I guess so."

"If you feel any discomfort, just let me know."

Anna pressed on Hayleigh's stomach a few times, first with

her hands and then with the Doppler. After a moment, a loud, steady beat, like a train chugging by, filled the room.

Anna smiled. "That's your baby's heartbeat—135 beats per minute, which is perfect."

Hayleigh winced as she struggled to prop herself up on her elbows. "Really? That's a heartbeat?"

Anna nodded. "Yes. Is this the first time you're hearing it?"

Hayleigh nodded and looked away. "Um. Yeah."

"Have you seen a doctor yet with this pregnancy?"

Hayleigh shook her head. "I didn't even know I was pregnant for a while, and then... I was going to find one soon."

Hayleigh was pretty far along, but Anna knew she had to tread carefully. Berating her for not seeking prenatal care would only discourage her from coming back. "It's okay. From the estimate of your last period, it looks like you're about twenty-five weeks, so it's a good time to start seeing someone regularly."

She helped Hayleigh into a seated position and told her about the care she could expect at the birth center. Then she pulled her stool up close so she could look the younger woman in the eye. "The baby's heartbeat sounds good, but I'd like to send you for an ultrasound, just to be sure everything is okay, and so we can get a more accurate estimate of your due date."

Hayleigh nodded.

"Can you tell me how this happened?" Anna asked gently.

Hayleigh stared at her faux Uggs. "I fell down the stairs," she mumbled.

Anna's stomach clenched, and another memory came rushing back.

A rickety staircase leading to a dark basement. Except nobody had fallen. Not exactly.

Anna shook it off and focused on her patient. She placed a gentle hand on Hayleigh's arm. "When I was a kid, my mom got into a lot of fights with her boyfriends. Sometimes they got physical, and her injuries looked a lot like yours." Hayleigh's head jerked up and Anna continued. "Did someone do this to you?"

Hayleigh narrowed her kohl-rimmed eyes. "If you tell anyone, I'll deny it."

Anna nodded. "Okay. I promise." If Hayleigh didn't trust her, Anna would never see her again. And then what would happen to Hayleigh? To her baby?

Hayleigh sighed and stared down at the floor, her face looking younger than her twentysomething years. "I can't leave him, so don't even suggest it. He'll never let me go, especially with the baby coming."

"If you tell the police what happened and press charges—"

"I can't." Hayleigh's head whipped back and forth. "That would ruin his life. He doesn't mean to; it's because his dad used to slap him around; he doesn't know any other way. He's sorry. I know he is. And I know, deep down, he loves me."

Anna leaned back on the stool as a familiar voice echoed. *He's tired. He's high. He's sorry.* He was always tired. He was always sorry. Until he did it again.

Would appealing to Hayleigh about the safety of her child work instead? Had it ever worked? Anna didn't have very many other options. "I'm worried he could hurt the baby."

Hayleigh's eyes widened. "He'd never hurt the baby! It's just sometimes I can be annoying, and I do stupid shit to piss him off."

Anna held Haleigh's gaze. "Babies can be pretty annoying, especially with all the mess and crying."

"Look." Hayleigh said sharply. "You have no idea what it's like. If there was a way I could support this baby on my own, I would. But how am I going to do that? I don't have shit. And nobody wants to help a person like me."

How could Anna argue with that when she'd lived through her own version of this story? There had to be another way. There had to be something she could do.

Anna pulled one of her cards from the front pocket of her scrubs. She scrawled a name and phone number on the back and handed it to Hayleigh. "This is my friend Rachel's number. She's a lawyer who has a lot of experience with situations like yours, and sometimes she takes on cases for free. If you want help, or even to just discuss your options, you can talk to Rachel."

Hayleigh took the card and stared at it for a moment. Then she nodded and tucked it into her purse. "Thanks."

Anna got to work ordering an ultrasound and calling for the nurse to stitch up Hayleigh's cheek, but the whole time her heart was breaking. Hayleigh believed she deserved a trip to the emergency room for being annoying, and in a few months, her baby would be born into that same situation. But none of it was Hayleigh's fault. Anna knew that.

When the nursing assistant came to take Hayleigh for her ultrasound, Anna hung back, shivering despite the warm air blowing in through the vents. If she could view Hayleigh's situation so clearly, why was looking back on her own life like peering through a fog? Would she ever give herself the same grace and forgive herself for what she'd done? Or would it hang over her forever, like that smell of cigarette smoke that still lingered in her memories?

# TWENTY-NINE

Gabe got home from a run along the North Shore trail and stepped into his loft just as rain started to fall outside. It was a rare Sunday without dinner at his parents' house because they'd gone to Connecticut for his dad's college reunion. Matt and Julia had taken the kids to visit Julia's family, and Leah's husband, Josh, had left that afternoon on a business trip to New York.

The evening stretched in front of him. Maybe he'd text Anna, see if she wanted to have dinner. She'd been so busy with her new job lately that the only time he'd seen her was at his parents' house for dinner on Sundays. Not exactly a situation that was conducive to exploring their future. The last time they'd talked, he'd gotten the feeling she might be open to exploring it.

He just needed to find the right moment to tell her about the necklace. Because until he came clean, he'd never have a real future with Anna.

There was a knock at the door. As if he'd summoned her, Anna stood on his welcome mat with a bag of takeout Chinese food in her hand. Gabe took in her flushed cheeks, lips curving into a grin, and dark hair falling down her back in waves. He was ridiculously happy to see her.

Anna brushed past him into the loft, and Gabe watched her back as she headed for the kitchen. He turned to close the door and found Rachel standing there, holding a bottle of wine. Damn it. Anna hadn't come alone.

"Oh, hey, no need to call first," he muttered, grumpier to see his sister than he should have been.

Rachel shoved the wine at him. "Sundays are family time."

Gabe grabbed the bottle. "Don't you have a fiancée you should be hanging out with?"

"Aaliyah's traveling." Rachel shrugged. "London."

Gabe turned back to the door just as eight-months-pregnant Leah waddled in. "Hi. We're here, too," she said, rubbing her belly.

Unlike Rachel, his baby sister never annoyed him. He grinned and gave her a hug around her enormous stomach. "How are you feeling? How's the parasite?"

"She's good. Three and a half more weeks to cook."

Gabe followed Anna and his sisters into the kitchen, dumped the wine on the counter, and headed for the shower to wash off his run.

When he came out, the three women were sitting around the kitchen island eating egg rolls and talking in low voices.

"How far along was she?" Leah asked, pressing her hand to her belly with a look of horror on her face.

"About twenty-five weeks."

"How far along was who?" Gabe asked, grabbing a beer from the fridge.

"Anna's patient whose boyfriend beat her up," Rachel muttered, her voice grim.

Gabe put the beer down. "Shit. Is the baby okay?"

Anna nodded. "Yeah, this time. Hopefully, there won't be a next time. Rachel, I gave her your number. I hope that's okay. Short term, she needs a protection-from-abuse order. But once the baby is born, there will be custody stuff to deal with."

"Yeah, of course. I'd love to do what I can to keep that asshole away from both her and the baby."

Gabe flashed his sister an affectionate smile. For all the wealthy women with cheating husbands Rachel helped to win multimillion-dollar settlements, she took on a similar number of pro-bono cases for women at a domestic violence shelter, and she also handled foster care adoptions.

"Thanks, Rach," Anna said. "I hope she'll call you this week. It seems like it's one of those situations where she just keeps making excuses for him and going back." Darkness crossed her features, and Gabe wondered if she was thinking about her mom. He'd never forget Anna telling him about the violent men who used to hang around the apartment when she was young.

"Well, maybe the baby will be the catalyst she needs to finally leave him for good," Rachel said. "I'm happy to do whatever I can."

"Thanks." Anna reached out and gave Rachel's hand a squeeze.

Gabe moved a stack of mail out of the way and took a plate, piling it with food. Rachel grabbed a heavy, cream-colored envelope off the top of the mail and flipped it open, pulling out a wedding invitation.

"Who are Chad and Katie?" she asked.

Gabe glared at her over his lo mein. "You know it's illegal to open other people's mail, right?"

"Yeah, yeah. Sue me," Rachel said, examining the invitation. "Ooh, it's in a fancy Chicago hotel. Who are you bringing as your plus-one?"

Gabe shrugged. "I hadn't thought about it." He was a big fat liar. As soon as the invitation arrived from his grad school friends, he'd thought about inviting Anna.

"Everyone knows you can't go to a wedding without a date. If there are any single bridesmaids or gay cousins, you'll be like a piece of meat dangling in front of a starving lion."

Gabe rolled his eyes. "That's great, Rachel. You're such a feminist."

"I'm just telling the truth—" Rachel muttered, but her next words were cut off by Leah sliding off her barstool, clutching her rounded midsection.

"You guys, I'm not sure I should have eaten that egg roll."

Gabe took in his sister's pained expression. "Hey, Leah, are you okay?"

"I'm just going to run to the bathroom—oh no," Leah gasped, staring down at her feet. A flush crept up her cheeks as liquid pooled around the legs of his chrome barstools. "This is so embarrassing. Gabe, I think I just peed on your floor. I can't believe nobody tells you about stuff like this. I've been sneezing and peeing myself for this entire pregnancy."

"And with that information, I am officially never having children," Rachel interjected, holding her stomach.

It was a rare moment when Gabe was on the same page as Rachel. With two sisters, he'd spent his entire life learning about way more female problems than he ever wanted to know about. But this was definitely a new low.

Then Anna spoke, and it got worse. "Sweetie, I don't think you just peed. That was your water breaking."

Gabe's hands were shaking by the time the sign for the hospital finally appeared. With rain pelting on the windshield, Leah gasping and writhing through her contractions, and Rachel backseat-driving from the front seat, he'd never been so happy to see the word Emergency lit up in bright red in his entire life.

"Josh! I need Josh!" Leah's panic-stricken eyes swung back and forth between Gabe and Anna as they helped her from the car and put her in a wheelchair. They'd called Leah's husband from Gabe's apartment. Josh's plane had landed in New York City an hour earlier, and he was doing his best to get on a flight home.

"He'll be here as soon as he can," Gabe reassured her for the fifteenth time.

Anna rubbed Leah's arm. "First babies usually take a while. If Josh can turn around and come right back, he should be able to make it in plenty of time."

"It's too early for the baby to come." There was a tinge of fear in Leah's voice that echoed Gabe's own thoughts. She'd said she had three more weeks. That couldn't be good, right?

When Anna spoke, her voice was low and soothing. "You're almost thirty-seven weeks, which is full term. It's a little earlier than we were planning, but the baby will be fine."

Anna stood and turned to Rachel and Gabe. "Josh won't be here for hours, and your mom is out of town." She looked back and forth between them. "Somebody needs to come in the birthing room and coach Leah through her contractions."

Gabe stumbled backward. "Don't look at me."

Anna turned to Rachel. "Rach? Can you handle this?"

Rachel squeezed her eyes shut. "Yes. Of course. She's my baby sister. I can do this. Of course I can." She sounded like she was trying to convince herself, but Gabe didn't have time to worry about it.

Soon, they had Leah in an elevator and on her way to the second floor. Gabe made sure his sister was settled in a birthing room and then turned to escape to the waiting area. He'd almost made it out the door when Anna called his name. He spun around to find her inclining her head toward Rachel.

*Oh shit.*

Rachel stood in the middle of the room, clutching the back of Leah's wheelchair. Her face was as white as the sheets on the hospital bed as she stared blindly at the wall in front of her. Leah let out a low moan as another contraction hit, and Rachel swayed, moaning in harmony.

Swiftly, Gabe recrossed the room and grabbed Rachel by the shoulders, shoving her into a chair before she could do something stupid, like pass out. She bent forward and put her head between her knees, taking loud, gasping breaths.

Suddenly, he remembered why Rachel was never going to be the doctor in the family. Not even his dad had seriously entertained the idea after she'd fallen off her bike in fourth grade and thrown up at the sight of her own scraped knee.

He turned back to Leah and crouched next to her. "Um... just breathe." That was what he was supposed to say, right? He had a feeling the movies about women giving birth weren't exactly accurate, but he didn't have a lot of other references to draw from.

Leah's contraction passed, and she slumped back in the wheelchair to catch her breath. Anna leaned forward and whispered in his ear, "Take Rachel to the waiting room. I don't need two patients in here."

The waiting room was a great idea. He couldn't wait to get there. But before he could escape, Anna grabbed his arm. "You have to come back though."

"What?" he hissed.

"Leah needs you. She needs someone here with her."

Gabe glanced at Leah, who had her eyes closed and was panting loudly. "She has *you* here with her."

"I'm not her friend right now. I'm her doctor."

"Isn't there a nurse?"

"Constance has a couple of patients she'll need to check in

on. Leah needs someone who can hold her hand the whole time. She needs *you*."

Damn his mom and Josh for having the nerve to go out of town when Leah was pregnant. His mom, especially, should've known how volatile pregnant women were. Apparently, this whole due-date thing was just a suggestion, and they could actually blow at any moment.

He grabbed Rachel's arm and pulled her down the hall toward the waiting room. Rachel shuffled along next to him, still pale and shaky.

"Gabe," she muttered, "I think I might puke."

"Rachel, if you puke right now, I'll kill you."

Rachel flopped on a couch, and with one last look of longing around the waiting room, Gabe headed back to Leah.

While he'd been gone, Anna had changed into scrubs and gotten Leah into a hospital gown and on the bed. Another contraction hit his sister, and he hovered by the door as Anna held Leah's hand and murmured to her. When it was over, and Leah had flopped back down to rest, Anna motioned him over, indicating he should take her place. He didn't have much choice, so he moved into the chair next to Leah and took her hand.

"Shouldn't I be wearing scrubs, or something sterile or something?" In movies, everyone wore those surgical gowns and gloves and strange bonnet-like hats.

"Why?" Anna looked at his jeans and faded gray T-shirt. "Are you planning to get messy?"

He recoiled. "God no!"

Anna's mouth hinted at a grin. "You're fine."

Gabe had a feeling she was enjoying seeing him so flustered. Which was fine. He could admit he was out of his element. This was not something he ever wanted to excel at.

For the next few hours, he basically made it up as he went along: holding Leah's hand, telling her she was doing great, and reminding her to breathe. Eventually, he settled into his role of birthing coach, wiping Leah's forehead with a cold washcloth, fetching her cups of ice water, and helping her get out of bed to shuffle down the hall when Anna suggested that it might help move her labor along.

Anna monitored Leah's and the baby's heart rate, checked for dilation—while Gabe pretended he really needed to pee and fled the room—and assured him and Leah they were doing great.

Gabe didn't know if that was really true because hours later, Leah was still laboring, and he was a mess. His clothes were wrinkled and sweaty and his voice was hoarse from shouting encouragement over the contractions. Leah's contractions became increasingly intense and close together, and Gabe watched helplessly as she writhed around on the bed, moaning that she was going to die. His panicked gaze swung to Anna, who sat by the bed adjusting a fetal heart rate monitor on Leah's stomach. Her hair wasn't even messed up.

Anna lifted the sheet to check Leah again, but by this point, Gabe was too worried to leave the room. He leaned down to his sister and told her it would be over soon, praying that he was telling the truth. Anna looked up and nodded.

She adjusted the sheets over Leah's legs so she could have access to... whatever she needed... thankfully hiding everything.

"Sweetie, you're ten centimeters," Anna murmured. "When the next contraction hits, I want you to squeeze Gabe's hand and push as hard as you can. I don't know about you, but I'm ready to meet this baby."

Gabe had never been more ready for anything in his life. But Leah shocked him by curling up in a fetal position and shouting, "No!"

Both Anna and Gabe turned to stare at her. Leah forced the words out between gasps. "I'm not having this baby until Josh gets here! Anna, I can't. He needs to be here. Don't make me!"

Gabe had been on the phone with Josh about every twenty minutes for the last six hours. With downpours all over the East Coast, flights from New York had been canceled, but Josh had managed to rent a car and was doing his best to get there as fast as he could. The last Gabe heard, Josh was somewhere on the turnpike, about forty miles from Monroeville. It wasn't that far away, but with the storms, they had no idea how long it could take.

Anna reached over to brush the sweaty hair from Leah's forehead. "It's not up to me, sweetie. The baby's going to come when it's ready. The safest thing for both you and the baby is not to fight it and to help her along."

Another contraction hit, and Leah curled in a ball and moaned. When it was over, she gasped, "I am not... pushing until Josh... gets here!"

The monitor on the wall let out a long, shrill beep.

Gabe jumped and looked to Anna in alarm.

Anna punched some buttons on the monitor. "Leah, your heart rate is going up. It's really important you listen to me right now. You need to take some deep breaths and calm down. Can you do that?"

How was Anna so serene? This was literally the most terrifying moment of his life. But it wasn't about him. He did his best to channel some of Anna's calmness and focus on his sister. "Listen, Leah. Josh is coming as fast as he can. But he would never, ever want you to do anything that might harm you or the baby. You know I'm right, don't you?"

Leah hesitated, and Gabe held his breath.

Finally, she nodded. "Okay."

Anna flashed Gabe a smile and then moved back down to the bottom of the bed. A minute later, another contraction hit, and Anna lifted the sheet and said, "Okay, here we go. I want you to push as hard as you can. You can do it, sweetie."

Leah clutched Gabe's hand so tightly that he was pretty

sure she crushed a few fingers, but he didn't care. Anna was busy doing mysterious things under the sheet, but Gabe didn't care about that either. He was completely focused on helping his sister and her baby. He leaned in and encouraged her, telling her she was amazing, she was doing great, he was so proud of her.

She pushed for over an hour, definitely something that didn't happen in the movies. By the time Anna told them the baby was crowning, sweat drenched Leah's hospital gown and his arms were aching and bruised from Leah grabbing at him.

"Okay, Leah," Anna said. "A few more pushes and you're there. You can do it."

Leah braced to push again just as the door burst open, and Josh stumbled into the room. He looked around, wild-eyed, and then ran to his wife.

"You made it!" Leah exclaimed, clutching him with tears streaming down her face.

Anna grinned at him. "Welcome, Dad. Ready to meet your baby?"

Josh nodded and leaned over Leah, smoothing her hair back and murmuring something Gabe couldn't hear.

Anna lifted the sheet again. "Next contraction, one more big push, okay?"

Leah nodded, and Josh took her hand. Gabe took a step back to give them some space, but Leah's other hand shot out, and she groped blindly for him. "Gabe! I need you here too!"

Gabe blinked away the burning in his eyes. Anna looked up and smiled. He took Leah's other hand, and together they all cheered her on as the next contraction hit, and she pushed as hard as she could. A moment later, she flopped back on the bed, letting out a huge gasp as Anna pulled a bloody, wet, wiggling baby out from under the sheet and placed her in Leah's arms.

"Congratulations, Mama," Anna said, smiling and crying at the same time. "You have a baby girl."

Leah and Josh huddled around the baby with tears pouring down their faces. Anna got to work checking the baby and back under Leah's sheet, and then she bustled around the room doing whatever it is doctors did after babies were born.

Gabe backed up against the wall and stared at the baby. That slimy, disgusting, wailing creature was the most amazing thing he'd ever seen. He couldn't believe he'd helped her into the world. Anna's job as a doctor had always impressed him, but he'd had no idea how incredible it was that she did this every day.

A minute later, Anna slid up next to him. "Congratulations, Uncle Gabe."

Gabe tore his gaze away from the baby and turned his exhausted eyes to Anna. "Thanks," he murmured, his voice hoarse.

"I'm done here, and Leah is in good hands with Constance." Anna gestured at the little family all piled on the bed with their heads pressed together. "Maybe we should give them some time alone?"

Gabe nodded, still dazed, and followed Anna into the dim hallway. He glanced at his watch—three in the morning. Anna headed toward the waiting room, but Gabe stopped and took her arm, tugging her back toward him.

"Anna. That... that was amazing. You were amazing."

Anna smiled. "All I did was catch the baby. You and Leah did the hard work." She reached down and squeezed his hand. "You were really great, Gabe. Really," she whispered.

Gabe tightened his grip. He had to tell her the truth. He had to come clean about the necklace.

And then he had to beg her to stay.

Thankfully, a door down the hall opened, saving him from spilling all his secrets right there in a hospital hallway at three in the morning. This wasn't the right time. But he needed to do it soon.

Anna tugged him toward the waiting room. "Come on. Let's go tell Rachel she's an aunt again."

"Wait." He turned to face her. "Anna, come to that wedding in Chicago with me. Be my date." He held his breath.

And then her lips curved into a smile. "I'd love to go."

Gabe's shoulders relaxed. With two days alone in Chicago, they could finally talk. Really talk.

And they could finally put their secrets behind them.

# THIRTY

Anna dropped her suitcase next to the hotel bed and checked out the room. Gabe had booked a suite in the same hotel as the wedding. It had a bedroom with a king bed and a small sitting room with a pull-out couch bed.

They hadn't discussed sleeping arrangements.

"Bundle up, buttercup," Gabe said from the other room, leaving his suitcase next to the couch. "It's Chicago in January, and we're being tourists today. The wedding isn't until six tonight, so we've got all day."

Gabe took her to his favorite brunch spot, and after breakfast they headed out into the snow, stopping on the sidewalk so Gabe could wrap his scarf around her neck. Then he tucked her gloved hand into the crook of his arm and led her down the street to Millennium Park. They wandered through the Frank Gehry-designed music pavilion and took selfies in front of the famous silver bean sculpture. Then, to escape the crowds of tourists heading to the ice-skating rink, they strolled over to Lurie Garden, a four-season perennial garden situated against the dramatic backdrop of the Chicago skyline.

Snow fell around them, blanketing the path with a layer of

powder that muted their footsteps as they wandered among the clusters of weathered seedpods and dormant grasses. A stillness fell over the landscape, secluding them from the buzz of the city around them. Even their breath was hushed, turning into puffs of ice as it drifted off into the frozen air.

As they turned the corner down another deserted path, Gabe stopped walking and took her by the shoulders. "Anna, I'm really glad you're here with me."

She smiled at his earnest expression. "So am I." These had always been their best moments, just the two of them falling back into their easy friendship, never running out of things to say to each other but comfortable with the silence, too. Over the years, this connection between them had stretched like a rubber band, and the greater the force that sent them pulling away from each other, the harder they eventually snapped back together.

Gabe, as usual, knew exactly what she was thinking. "It's been a long road for you and me, hasn't it?" He leaned in. "I know maybe I haven't always let you know how important you are to me. I want that to change, starting today."

She stared back at him, unable to tear her eyes away. He took another step toward her, and she could feel his warm breath graze her frozen cheeks.

A sudden gust of wind blew across the meadow, bending the ice-coated plants with its force. Anna clamped her hand to her head to keep her hat from blowing away, and Gabe turned his back against the gale, protecting her with his body. She leaned into him, and he wrapped his arms around her, pulling her against him for warmth.

She shivered, but it wasn't from the cold.

Later that afternoon, they headed back to the hotel to get ready for the wedding. Anna closed the door to the bedroom while

Gabe showered and then dressed in the sitting room. Anna could usually be ready for anything in twenty minutes, but it took her over an hour because she kept stopping to stare off into space while Gabe's words from earlier swirled through her head.

*I want that to change, starting today.*

For the first time in a long time, Anna felt hopeful. She was proud of the work she was doing at the hospital with patients like Hayleigh, who Anna had been thrilled to see back for a prenatal checkup a few weeks ago. Her mom's DNA test results were expected any day, after a backlog at the lab and months of waiting. Soon Anna might have the answer she'd been longing for. And having spent the past few months coming to terms with the fact that her mom might be gone had helped her to appreciate the people who were still there. Especially the Weatheralls.

And Gabe.

Her whole body buzzed as if she'd overdosed on caffeine, except the only stimulant in her system was the man in the other room. She wasn't the poor, desperate high school kid anymore, crushing on the popular frat boy. She was the kind of woman Gabe would be lucky to attract. Maybe it was time to start acting like it, time to go after what she wanted.

Anna pulled on her little black dress, took one last look in the mirror, and then opened the door to the sitting room. Gabe sat on the couch drinking a bottle of water from the minibar and flipping through a magazine. In his perfectly tailored suit, vest, and tie, with one foot propped on his opposite knee, he looked like someone had just snapped his photo for a fashion spread in an upscale men's magazine.

Gabe looked up and then stopped short, his water partway to his lips. "Jesus," he muttered. His gaze slowly drifted from her face, all the way down to her feet, and then back up. "You look gorgeous."

"You look great, too." She grinned. "We make a pretty good-looking couple."

"We sure do."

"So, then Gabe looked down at the assignment and realized he'd been arguing his point for twenty minutes, and *he'd read the wrong book.* Anyone else would have admitted their mistake, but Gabe didn't even flinch. He just kept arguing until the professor was so confused, she gave up and dismissed the class early."

Anna laughed at Gabe's friend's account of his grad school class, remembering her days of working with him on their global economics project. "That sounds just like the Gabe I know. He always has to be right, even when he's wrong."

"Hey!" Gabe protested in mock outrage, returning from the bar with two drinks in his hand. He plunked one in front of Anna and then slid onto the chair next to her, gazing around the table at his slightly inebriated ex-classmates. "Can we be done with the embarrassing Gabe stories now, please?"

Gabe's friend Jess, a Harvard professor of economics, laughed. "Oh, come on. Your girlfriend needs to know what she's getting into."

Gabe turned to Anna, flashing her a crooked smile. "Oh, Anna knows what she's getting into." He rose to his feet, giving her hand a tug. "Come dance with me?"

Anna headed across the ballroom with Gabe, and most of his friends got up to follow them. They all piled on the dance floor as the DJ played Beyoncé and Prince and requests from the wedding guests.

And then there was a break in the dance music, and the DJ put on a slow song by Adele. Gabe reached out and took Anna by the hand, pulling her against him. She leaned in, his familiar woodsy scent encircling her. Gabe rubbed his chin on her hair and tightened his arm around her, sliding his palm up her back. His fingers grazed the skin at the nape of her neck, sending a shiver down her spine.

They didn't speak. They just held on to each other and swayed as the music swirled around them. Anna closed her eyes, and as his heart beat against her, she forgot everything else. The last strains of the song played, and they stopped dancing but didn't move apart.

In a hoarse voice, Gabe murmured, "You want to get out of here?"

Anna's heart hammered against her ribs. It was such a simple question, but there was so much meaning behind it. She was so tired of wrestling with these feelings for him. Tired of denying what she wanted so badly.

"Yes. Let's get out of here."

A slow smile spread across his face. He took her hand and, without stopping to say goodbye to anyone, they headed out the French doors of the ballroom into the hotel lobby.

They hurried into the elevator, and Anna pushed the "door close" button before someone else could come along. If she had to make small talk with some hotel guest, she might come crashing back to the real world. And for once in her life, that was the last place she wanted to be. Especially when Gabe was staring at her with those storm-cloud eyes darkened with desire.

The elevator door slid shut, and they were alone.

Gabe plunged his hands into her hair, pushing her back against the wall and capturing her mouth with his. She grabbed him by the shirt and kissed him back, pulling him hard against her.

They stayed like that, kissing each other with more than a decade of desire burning between them. The elevator door opened with a ding, and they stumbled out onto their floor. Anna pulled his mouth back to hers, and Gabe backed her down the hall until she bumped up against the door of their suite. Her whole body hummed, and she didn't care at all that someone might come out of their hotel room to catch her yanking his shirt from his pants to run her hands up his hard chest.

Gabe pulled the key card from his pocket and reached behind her back to slide it into the door. He half laughed, half swore under his breath as he fumbled and dropped it on the floor.

After a few tries, they finally managed to get the door open and fall into the suite. Gabe's tie came off and landed on the floor, followed by his shirt. In another minute, her dress was in a puddle at her feet.

And then Gabe stepped back to stare at her. "My God, you're beautiful. I could look at you all day."

They came back together, lips colliding, breath hitching. Gabe's arms snaked around her back, one hand pulling her against the hard planes of his chest, the other reaching up to unclasp her bra. A strap slid off her arm, and he followed it with his mouth, planting hot kisses from her neck to her shoulder, and then to the tops of her breasts.

Anna slid her hands into his hair, showing her appreciation with a low moan that reverberated from her chest. Gabe took his time exploring, and Anna's head fell back as sparks ignited from every place his mouth and hands caressed, gathering hot and urgent at her core. And then he found that place, too, backing her up against the door to the bedroom. She grasped the wooden frame, grateful for the support when Gabe's hand moved lower and her legs wavered, threatening to give out.

Anna gave in to the sensation, her mind a blur, her body arching toward Gabe as he found all the right places to send her to the peak.

When she finally came down, Gabe leaned back to look in her eyes, brushing a sweaty lock of hair from her forehead. "This is all I've been able to think about since you came back home," he murmured. "Touching you. Feeling your body against mine."

Anna's vision came back into focus, tracing the lines of Gabe's muscled chest, his flat stomach, the silver belt buckle sitting just above the evidence that she was turning him on as much as he'd done to her. This was the only part of him that she didn't know, the only part she'd never seen, aside from in her dreams. Dreams where she'd wake up hot, sweaty, and longing to close her eyes and sink back into each excruciating, imagined moment with him.

She reached out, sliding his belt strap through the buckle, and unclasping the button beneath. Gabe quickly rid himself of the rest of his clothes, and Anna took him in her hand.

It was her turn now to explore, caress. He inhaled a heavy breath, and her heart jolted because there was nothing imaginary about this moment, or the emotion on Gabe's face that told her this was about so much more than physical pleasure.

Their mouths came back together as they made their way through the doorway into the bedroom. Anna's legs hit the bed, and she tumbled backward, pulling him down on top of her.

For the first time in her life, she understood what it meant to be swept away. She couldn't focus, couldn't think at all. All she could do was ride the wave that was Gabe. His mouth and hands hot on her skin, his beautiful, hard body inside her, and his eyes—*those eyes*—staring down at her.

Swept away didn't even begin to describe it.

# THIRTY-ONE

By the time midnight rolled around, Anna had worked up quite an appetite. Thanks to all her nervous energy, she hadn't eaten much at the wedding, and then the past hour with Gabe had left her positively starving.

She sat up in the bed and pulled on Gabe's dress shirt. After all the things they'd just done to each other, it was a little late for modesty. But still, this was *Gabe.* She was having trouble wrapping her mind around the fact that he was here, and he was hers.

She peeked at him over the room service menu as he called in their order. He'd stretched diagonally across the bed, his tall frame covered by nothing but a thin sheet riding low on his hips. Her body started that hum again. Could he possibly do it again? Because she was pretty sure she'd never get enough of him.

Gabe hung up the phone. "Food will be here in half an hour." He rolled toward her, propping himself on one elbow. "How did I not know until right now that you like to eat pancakes at midnight?"

"Babies don't always show up during a nine-to-five schedule. Sometimes breakfast rolls around at midnight."

"What else don't I know about you?" Gabe sat up, tugging on her collar and trying to peek over her shoulder. "Besides the fact that you have a *tattoo* you never told me about?"

Anna gave him a sheepish shrug. He was referring to the botanical design that curved from the spot under the back of her neck to her left shoulder. "A couple of colleagues and I took a trip to Paris last year for a break from work. We drank way too much champagne and stumbled into a tattoo parlor at one in the morning." She wrinkled her nose at him. "I'm a total cliché."

Anna didn't mention that the design was loosely based on the etching on the necklace her mom had given her. She leaned back against the pillows before he could notice.

Gabe shook his head in amusement. "You're just full of secrets. What else are you keeping from me?"

Anna's smile faltered. There were some things she'd never told anyone. Things, until that moment, she'd believed she never *would* tell anyone. But until that moment, she'd never felt this safe either.

For the first time in her life, maybe she was ready. Not just to keep moving forward, as she'd always done. But to put the past behind her and move on.

"I want to tell you everything, Gabe. But some things might take me a little bit longer."

Gabe's face grew serious, mirroring her own mixed emotions. They hadn't talked about her mom in years. Was he upset that she'd kept that part of her life from him for so long? He took a shaky breath, looking almost nervous about whatever it was he was about to reply.

Before things could take another serious turn, Anna dropped a hand on his chest, pulling her mouth into a smile. "I think it's your turn to tell me a secret. I want to hear your most embarrassing one."

For a moment, Gabe looked almost relieved, and then he seemed to get into the spirit of things, tilting his head and rubbing his chin as if he were debating whether to reveal something deep and dark. "Okay. I may be just a little bit addicted to"—he paused, taking a deep breath—"binge-watching cheesy teenage TV dramas. You know, like *Gossip Girl* and *Pretty Little Liars*. I guess it's something you should know about me."

"*No.*" Anna pressed her hand to her mouth, her shoulders shaking with silent laughter.

Gabe turned just the slightest bit red, which made her laugh even harder. "It's not my fault. Leah made me watch them with her when she was a kid, and then I got hooked."

Anna made air quotes with her fingers. "'Made' you watch."

"She forced me."

Anna collapsed back against the pillow, wrapping her arms around herself in a fit of giggles. When she finally got a hold of herself, she found Gabe looking at her with a lopsided grin on his face.

He reached out and tugged on a lock of her hair. "Can you imagine if someone had told us that first day in global econ, when we were glaring at each other across the room, that we'd end up like this?"

"What? Sharing our embarrassing secrets? If I'd known you were locking yourself in the frat-house bathroom to watch *Veronica Mars* back then..."

"No. I mean like *this*." He inched toward her, running his hand up her bare leg. "You and me together."

Anna thought back to that skinny kid in her too-large T-shirt, terrified to find out who she'd be stuck working with on their project. And then to that cocky frat boy surrounded by his beautiful friends. She wouldn't have believed it. And Gabe? "You would've been horrified."

"No." Gabe squinted at her. "Horrified? Well, you were

younger than me, so I might've been creeped out thinking of you like that. But no. I would've been... intrigued."

She shot him a disbelieving look. "Oh, come on. We hated each other in the beginning."

"That's why I would've been intrigued. Nobody ever argued with me like that, except for you. And my family." He chuckled, shaking his head. "I should've known." He reached up to brush her hair off her cheek, and his smile faded. "I'm an idiot for letting so much time go by."

Anna's lungs felt heavy in her chest. She'd spent so much of her life looking for her mom, dwelling in the past. Maybe it was time to finally start focusing on her present—and her future. But sometimes it wasn't so easy. The present was this beautiful day she'd spent with Gabe. It was their friendship, still one of the most essential parts of her life, even after so much distance and time. And it was Gabe in her bed, gazing across the rumpled sheets like he couldn't believe how lucky he was.

Could she let go of all the past heartache, all the mistakes she'd made, to open herself up to a future with him?

Could she take the risk?

Gabe tugged her down to the bed until she was lying on her back, looking up at him. He rolled on top of her, his body pressing her into the mattress as he propped his elbows on either side of her head. He kissed her forehead, one cheek, the other. Then he pulled away to look her in the eyes, his mouth hovering only inches from hers. "I've wanted you like this for so long. For longer than I even knew myself."

She reached up and pushed back the thick, dark lock of hair that flopped over his forehead, the one she'd been watching him run his hands through for years, and then she let her fingers trail down his cheek. "I know just how you felt."

. . .

The next morning, Anna threw her hair into a messy ponytail and dug around in her suitcase for a pair of jeans. Gabe was still in bed—he'd barely stirred since he'd fallen asleep—but she'd woken up wrapped up in the warm haze of their beautiful day yesterday. And last night.

Her breath caught, and she was tempted to crawl back under the covers and cuddle up against his warm back. But the coffee shop downstairs was calling to her. She was desperate for caffeine, and while she was at it, maybe some extra-strength Tylenol. In retrospect, three glasses of wine on an almost empty stomach were not her best moment, but she'd had so much fun dancing with Gabe at the wedding that she didn't regret a thing.

Anna bent down to tie her shoes, and when she stood up, the pounding in her temples nearly knocked her over. Okay, maybe she regretted the wine part a teeny, tiny bit.

Keeping her head as steady as possible, she dug through her bag for something to take the edge off, but she didn't usually get headaches, so she'd forgotten to pack anything.

Gabe's suitcase sat next to hers, his toiletry kit right on top. She reached into it, past his travel-sized toothpaste and shaving cream, looking for a container that might hold over-the-counter pain medicine. Her hand brushed a small velvet jewelry box, and she pulled it out of the bag.

It was definitely a strange thing for Gabe to have tucked in his suitcase on a trip to Chicago. But it was small and fit neatly into his toiletry bag. When she shook it, something rattled around inside. Maybe he'd taken some medications out of their larger containers and used this instead.

Anna flipped the lid open. And then she froze.

Tucked into the box sat an etched gold half-moon necklace. Her hand automatically flew to her own neck and closed around the pendant that rested there. The one she'd worn for two decades. Where did Gabe get the exact replica of the necklace her mom had given her?

And then she ran her fingers across the flower pattern, and it occurred to her that this necklace wasn't a match. It was a mirror image. It was the match to the necklace her mom used to wear. The one that fit together like a puzzle piece with her own pendant.

Where could Gabe have found this? Her mom had bought the necklaces in a gift shop in Lawrenceville when Anna was a little kid. It was possible the jewelry designer had made more than one of each design. But that was two decades ago, and that store was long gone. What were the odds that Gabe would have stumbled on a copy of her mother's half?

Had he somehow researched it and tracked down the designer? Anna flipped the box over in her hand, looking for some sort of logo, and then she lifted the velvet square where the necklace rested and peered underneath.

Folded in the bottom of the box was a handwritten receipt. Anna pulled it out, smoothing it flat on her leg. At the top of the page, the name and address of the shop were professionally printed, and underneath, the store clerk had scrawled a short description of the necklace and the price.

Gabe had bought the necklace for fifty dollars in a place called the Gold Rush Pawn Shop. Something about that name was familiar.

And then Anna's heart slammed into her chest. Because underneath the name of the shop was the address—*1989 Mission Street. San Francisco, California.*

Gabe had bought this necklace in a pawn shop around the corner from the house on Capp Street. Her breath caught, and her vision blurred so that she could barely read the words on the page. But she managed to scan past the address to a date written on the top of the page.

Fourteen years ago.

*Was it possible?*

This wasn't a replica of her mom's necklace. This had to be

the real thing. And if Gabe had found it in a pawn shop, her mom must have sold it when she lived around the corner.

By this point in her life, Anna was rarely blindsided. Nothing about her resembled the lonely teenager struggling to survive after her mom left. But holding that necklace and realizing all the betrayals it represented—her mom's, Gabe's—Anna was right back there, huddled in a shabby apartment hiding from her landlord. Walking the halls of her high school while kids threw gum in her hair. Staring down a set of dark basement steps. Watching her mom pack a bag and walk out of her life.

Anna ran into the bathroom and threw up.

And then she silently packed up her things and walked out.

# THIRTY-TWO

Gabe woke to the sun streaming through the windows, hitting him right in the face. He squinted and stretched, pleasantly sore from the dancing and other... exercise... he'd gotten the night before. All at once the memories came rushing back.

*Anna.*

It wasn't a shock that it happened; it had been building between them for a long time. And it wasn't a shock that it was even better than he'd imagined. No, the shock came from how calm and clear-headed he felt. Never once had he felt so sure about anything the way he felt sure right at that moment.

A burst of happiness flared in his chest. Anna was everything he ever wanted. She was more beautiful in an old T-shirt with her hair sliding out of a ponytail than any woman he'd ever met. She could challenge him in any argument about economics, politics, or the state of the world, but at the same time, she wasn't above laughing her head off at a dirty joke. She called him on his shit and didn't let him get away with anything. She was brilliant and compassionate and sexy as hell.

He wanted every day to be like yesterday. He wanted to fall asleep next to her and wake up knowing she was his. He wanted to make her happy, to make her laugh, to make her gasp with pleasure and let go of her careful control the way she had over and over the night before.

He was sure she was feeling it, too. Despite the walls Anna put up to protect herself, he'd been the one person who always managed to chip away at them. Their connection had defied all the barriers that should've come between them. And now that was in the past, and it was finally time to grab what had been right in front of them all along.

Gabe rolled over, eager to be close to her, to touch her, to watch her sleeping next to him with her dark hair fanned out on the pillow. But except for a crumpled hotel sheet, Anna's side of the bed was empty.

He hadn't expected her to be awake already, especially after so little sleep the night before. Tilting his head toward the bathroom, he listened for the sound of running water, but all he heard was silence. Their flight wasn't until that afternoon, and they didn't have to check out of the hotel for a couple of hours. He rolled out of bed and headed for the sitting room. Plenty of time to coax her back to bed.

Except the sitting room was empty.

Anna had probably run down to the coffee shop in the lobby. He grabbed his phone to send her a text when his eyes settled on his suitcase.

*Oh. Shit.*

Sitting right on top, next to his toiletries, was the cheap velvet box from the pawn shop. Its lid was open, and the contents spilled out.

The necklace.

Anna had found the necklace.

He'd brought it with him, hoping to find the right time to give it to her. Heart hammering, he swung around to look through the door to the bedroom.

All of Anna's stuff was gone.

Gabe hit the call button next to her name. It rang twice and then a recording picked up. She'd declined his call and sent him to voicemail. Okay, so this was bad. This was really bad. He was an idiot. He should have told her about the necklace last night.

Hell, he should have told her years ago.

Gabe fired off a text.

*We need to talk. Just stay where you are, and I'll come right now.*

A little gray bubble with an ellipsis popped up under his sent message, indicating she'd read it and was responding. He stared at his phone, shifting his weight back and forth as he waited. The ellipsis disappeared, but no message came through. A minute passed and nothing. She wasn't going to respond. He sent another text.

*Anna, I screwed up. Please just talk to me.*

Still nothing.

The gray bubble with the ellipsis appeared again, and finally, a response popped up.

*There is literally nothing you can say. I'm shutting off my phone and getting on a flight. Just leave me alone.*

Gabe slammed the phone down on the table. He needed to get to the airport before her flight took off. Grabbing a pair of jeans and a T-shirt, he pulled them on as he moved around the suite picking up his things and throwing them in his overnight bag.

A moment later, he was out the door.

The elevator took an eternity, and Gabe tapped his foot as it slowly drifted to the lobby. He tossed the room key and his credit card at the desk clerk and fidgeted as the clerk took what had to be a year to check the computer, print some documents, and hand them over to sign. Gabe scrawled his signature and then used his phone to request a Lyft to pick him up.

By the time Gabe got through security at the airport, the flight he suspected Anna was on had already boarded, and the doors were closed. Although he tried, Gabe couldn't charm the gate agent into opening them back up for him. And it was no wonder, he realized, as he stared at himself in the airport bathroom mirror. Less than four hours of sleep had left him pale and wild-eyed. And in his rush to leave the hotel room, he hadn't noticed he'd put his shirt on inside out.

To make matters worse, while he waited for his plane to board, a heavy snow began to fall, and his flight was delayed until after midnight. By the time he finally boarded, he was jittery from lack of sleep combined with about six cups of airport coffee, and he was worried that Anna still wasn't answering his calls.

And terrified that she never would.

# THIRTY-THREE

Hayleigh was back in the ER with a broken arm and another black eye. Anna got the call on Monday morning as she arrived for her early shift at the hospital. She rushed down to examine the younger woman, and by some miracle, the baby was okay again.

After avoiding Anna's eyes and trying to change the subject, Hayleigh finally admitted she'd never called Rachel about helping her leave her boyfriend. It wasn't Anna's place to push, but the baby was due in a couple of weeks. In the end, all she could do was give Hayleigh another card with Rachel's number on it. And then she shoved her hands into her pockets to force herself not to dial the phone herself and hand it over.

Anna went straight from Hayleigh's room to a patient who was in labor two months early, and then to another who had preeclampsia and needed an emergency C-section. But not even running from one end of the birth center to the other could distract her from the shock of the past weekend.

The wonderful, terrible weekend.

Late that afternoon, Anna was finally able to grab a granola bar from the vending machine and head for the doctors' lounge for a short break. She almost regretted that there wasn't some other emergency for her to deal with, because as soon as she turned on her phone, five texts from Gabe popped up, all begging her to talk to him.

Anna couldn't begin to imagine what he could have to say. Gabe had been carrying around that necklace for years. For *over a decade*. He'd let her go on thinking she was crazy for moving to San Francisco, for searching the crowd for women with her mom's features. And all the while, he'd known Anna's mom had lived in that house in Capp Street after all. What if she'd told him about the woman in the park and the DNA test? Would he have kept on lying and letting her believe that maybe her mom hadn't meant to leave her forever?

Anna was about to shut her phone off when it buzzed with a phone call. No doubt it was Gabe again. Sighing, Anna flipped it over in her hand. But no. The number was one she only vaguely recognized. A number with a San Francisco area code.

With her hands shaking, she swiped to answer.

"Ms. Campbell, Officer Deacon here," came the voice through the phone.

Anna slowly sank down on the couch, grateful the lounge was empty. "Yes? Do you have any news for me?"

"I do." Officer Deacon hesitated, and Anna could hear her heart beating. This was the moment she'd been longing for and dreading in equal measure. And then he spoke again. "I'm happy to report that the DNA tests weren't a match."

"Oh." The breath whooshed from Anna's lungs.

"The woman we found in the park wasn't your mother."

"That's—" Anna's voice shook. "Great. I'm—that's great." So why did she feel dangerously close to crying?

"Obviously, we'll keep your missing person report open, and we'll reach out if we have any other leads," the officer continued. "Now that we have your DNA, we'll be able to investigate any other Jane Doe matches more quickly."

Dazed, Anna nodded.

"Ms. Campbell?" the officer prodded.

"Yes, I'm here. Sorry. Yes. Please call me if you have other leads." Anna hung up the phone and stared across the lounge. If that woman wasn't her mom...

Then her mom might still be out there somewhere. Still living her life.

*Without me.*

It wasn't that Anna had wanted to learn her mom had died... It was that she'd clung so desperately to the possibility that her mother had never really intended to leave her. But now... now she was back to square one. Still unknowing if her mother was out there somewhere. Unknowing if she could have come back. And she just hadn't wanted to.

Anna closed her eyes, picturing that cheap velvet box with her mom's necklace. The Gold Rush Pawn Shop. Had her mom pawned the necklace to pay her dealer? To buy drugs? To continue living her life on the other side of the country, while her teenaged daughter struggled to survive? Anna wasn't sure which betrayal was worse.

That her mother had so easily discarded her. Or that Gabe had kept it from her for so long.

When Anna heard a knock on her door later that evening, she knew exactly who it was. She'd expected to feel something when he finally showed up on her doorstep—rage, sadness—but it was a relief to find she'd worn out all her emotions and had settled on blessed numbness.

Taking a deep breath, she swung the door open. Gabe stood on her welcome mat, his arms braced on either side of the door-frame as if he was trying to prevent her escape. Which, come to think of it, maybe he was. He wore jeans and an ice-blue hoodie that exactly matched his eyes. His dark hair was sticking up on one side, and he hadn't shaved in a couple of days, but even disheveled looked so, so good on him.

He leaned in, and her heart flipped. Okay, so maybe she wasn't totally numb.

"Anna, please talk to me."

She avoided looking at him and escaped into the house, leaving the door open as his only invitation to come in. He followed her into the kitchen where she turned on the tea kettle, mostly to have something to do with her hands.

"Anna," he said from the doorway. "I don't blame you if you hate me."

Anna took a mug from the cabinet and banged it on the counter. "Really? After all these years, you're finally going to allow me the privilege of deciding my own feelings?"

From behind her, she heard him suck in a breath. "I should have told you right from the beginning."

She flung in a tea bag. "What were you *thinking*, keeping this from me?"

He came up behind her, and she turned around, crashing into his chest. He reached out and took her arm, and *damn it,* her heart flipped again.

"I thought I was protecting you. When I first found the necklace, you were seventeen years old, and the ground had dropped out of your life. I didn't know how to tell you that your mom had probably pawned the necklace, on top of everything else."

"You just open your mouth and say it." She wrenched away from him, burning with mortification and a deep, impenetrable sadness. Every time she thought she hit the bottom of her sordid childhood, she managed to plunge a little lower. Gabe had known, but he left her to find out this way. "Were you ever going to tell me?"

"I did try." His eyes searched hers. "That time on Stinson Beach, I tried to tell you, and you told me you didn't want to hear it."

Anna bit her lip, remembering that almost-kiss on the beach, and how he'd backed away and said they needed to talk. She'd cut him off and told him she was leaving.

"I had the necklace in Chicago because I promised myself that I'd tell you before the end of the weekend. I should have told you before we—" He cocked his head. "But it was such a perfect day, and then..." His voice lowered. "It was an amazing night. And I didn't want to ruin it. Or send you running."

"That should have been my decision."

"You're right." He stuffed his hands in his back pockets. "I completely fucked this up. And I don't blame you if you never forgive me. But I hope you'll give me another chance."

"How could I ever trust you again?"

"Anna. I made a mistake. But you know me. And you know how much you mean to me. And you know you and I are never going to find anything as good as what we have together." Something flashed across his face, a vulnerability she'd never seen before.

She tried to take a step back, but the counter pressed into her back, and there was no place else to go. She turned her head away from him and closed her eyes. It was too much. She needed him to be difficult and sarcastic and to argue with her. Because there were about a million reasons why this was a terrible idea. But when he looked at her like that, it was hard to think of one.

Gabe's hand slid across her cheek, gently turning her face back toward him. "Anna." It was practically a whisper. He was so close she could feel his breath brush her ear. "Look at me. Please."

Her eyes fluttered open and found his. Years of longing slammed into her like a runaway train. The force of it pushed the air from her lungs. She grabbed the counter behind her, not sure if her legs would hold her. Before her knees could buckle, Gabe's arm snaked around her waist, pinning her against him. His hand tangled in her hair, and his mouth found hers, rough and hot and urgent.

The counter dug into her back, and his unshaven face grazed her cheek. Her hands roamed his back, clutching his straining muscles. In a swift move, he had her scrub bottoms untied and on the floor. She kicked them away, and as he lifted her onto the counter and pressed his hips between her legs, the rough denim of his jeans scraped her thighs. She jerked his sweatshirt off his shoulders and tossed it to the floor. Dragging his T-shirt out of the way, she groped for the waistband of his jeans as he left a trail of hot kisses down her neck.

His hands were everywhere, sliding under her T-shirt and searing her skin. She fumbled with his belt buckle, and he let her go just long enough to yank the zipper of his jeans down and shove his boxers aside. She wrapped her legs around him and gasped against his mouth as he moved inside her, the rhythm so intense the house could have burned down around them and it wouldn't have matched the heat from their bodies. She clung to him as his palms grasped her hips, pushing himself deeper into her until they tumbled over the edge together.

Moments later, Anna leaned against Gabe's chest, her body vibrating to the beat of his heart. He held her there, one hand still tangled in her hair and the other wrapped around her back. She closed her eyes and, still half-dazed, got lost in the feel of him. They stayed like that, not saying anything until their breathing slowed.

Gabe leaned back, taking his heat with him. Anna opened her eyes, willing the world to go away for just a little longer. But the setting sun chose that moment to drop just beneath the window frame, hitting her straight in the face and dragging her back to reality. *Oh God.* What had they done?

"Anna," Gabe murmured in a low voice. "I think we should talk. Really talk. I want us to be completely open with each other."

Anna leaned back against the counter, away from him. *Open.* Gabe wanted them to be open. What did that even mean?

Their entire relationship had been based on nothing but a giant, cracking pillar of lies and secrets, starting from the moment they'd met. And Gabe didn't even know the half of it. He thought her mom selling her necklace in a pawn shop was so dark and sordid, he couldn't even be honest with her about it. He didn't know what dark and sordid was.

Thank God she hadn't spilled everything the other night in Chicago. How could she ever think she was safe with him, that she could trust him?

Feeling vulnerable and exposed, Anna made a futile attempt to yank her T-shirt down over her legs. Sensing her discomfort, Gabe took a step back and picked up her scrubs from the floor, laying them on her lap.

He turned his back to fix his jeans. "I'll meet you in the living room, okay? We have a lot to talk about."

The moment he was out of the room, Anna jumped off the counter and fled from the kitchen. In the bathroom, she pulled on her clothes and splashed water on her face. When she pulled the towel away from her eyes, her reflection stared back at her in the mirror.

When was she going to learn she could only trust herself?

Anna found Gabe standing in the middle of her living room, staring at the boxes sitting on her couch. In the months that she'd lived in the carriage house, she'd accumulated more than she'd expected: a row of novels lined up on the shelves, a set of candles in her favorite scent, a pair of handmade bowls she'd picked up at a craft fair just because they were too pretty to pass up. She'd stuffed them all in those boxes when she'd gotten home from the hospital earlier today and had planned to drop them off at the Goodwill tomorrow morning.

"What's all this?" Gabe asked, his voice measured. "Are you —packing?"

"My lease is up soon."

"Rachel's friend doesn't get back until after the spring semester. I'm sure she'd extend the lease." He paused, regarding her across the small living room. "If you wanted her to."

Anna didn't meet his eyes.

Gabe took a step toward her. "Anna? What's going on here?"

"You always knew I was going back."

His head jerked up. "Back? To the Middle East?"

Anna nodded.

"What about this?" He waved a hand between them. "What about us?"

She reached for the pendant around her neck, fumbling to rub the etched pattern with her thumb, searching for the comfort it had given her for almost two decades. But her hand grasped at the air.

She'd ripped the necklace off and tossed it in one of those boxes on the couch. Her mom was gone, she'd left, and pawned any evidence of her only child. And if Gabe ever knew what Anna had done, he'd want to run, too. And pawn all the evidence she'd existed.

"There's no *us*, Gabe. It was a mistake to come home and an even bigger mistake to stick around this long."

Gabe raked a hand through his hair. "You don't really believe that, do you? You don't regret being here after my dad's heart attack or delivering Leah's baby. Spending time with Rachel and my mom, or Matt's kids." Gabe crossed the room in three strides and took her by the shoulders. "And I sure as hell know you don't regret being with me."

Anna looked away. She couldn't lie to him, not about that. "It doesn't matter. I don't belong here. I never belonged here."

Gabe turned away, shaking his head in frustration. He paced across the living room and then spun abruptly on his heel to look at her. "*I'm not the one who left you.*" He raked a hand through his hair as his voice rose with each word. "I'm right here, Anna. *I'm right here.*" And with that, his voice broke, and he seemed to lose steam. "I've always been here." His shoulders drooped, and when she met his eyes, they were red-rimmed. "Anna, I know you've been through a lot, and you've been hurt. But when are you going to find a way to let go of your past and allow yourself to be happy?"

He stood with his arms crossed in front of him, biceps flexed beneath the T-shirt she'd been clinging to just minutes earlier. His hair stood up where he'd run his hand through it, and his silver eyes flashed. She hated that, even now, her attraction to him was so strong it felt like a physical presence in the room. So she did the only thing she could do.

She lashed out.

"Are you assuming you would make me happy?"

Gabe flinched like she'd slapped him. "Yeah. Okay." That flash of pain was a knife right to her heart. "You're right. I'm an idiot to think you'd ever let yourself be happy with me."

Anna turned away, staring out the window. But she could still feel him standing in the middle of the living room, watching her. She silently cursed her weakness. They should never have started any of this.

And then Anna heard his footsteps thump across the floor. A moment later, the front door opened and then slammed shut again.

The ache in her heart was as familiar as breathing. If she were really honest about it, she'd been slowly trying to fill this Gabe-sized hole there for close to half her life. When she'd lived thousands of miles away, she'd been able to keep these feelings carefully tucked away in the back of her consciousness, like a late-night dream that, in the light of day, seemed hazy and vague. She'd spent a decade and a half doing everything she could to keep him at arm's length. Because if she loved him, she'd lose him.

Just like everyone she'd ever loved.

# THIRTY-FOUR

Anna was back in the doctors' lounge taking a break between patients when the on-call phone clipped to her scrubs began to buzz. "Hello, this is Dr. Campbell."

"Hey, Doc," came the voice of Constance.

"Helen in 315 can't be ready to push yet." Anna had left her patient comfortably watching *The Bachelor* once her epidural had kicked in an hour ago. Constance had told her she'd call when the patient had progressed.

"Nope. Contractions are four minutes apart, and she's doing fine. But Sue Ellen didn't get a rose from the bachelor, so she's in for a rough night."

Anna smiled. She'd enjoyed this job and would miss her coworkers when it ended in a couple of weeks. She'd given her notice on Tuesday, the morning after Gabe had walked out, and it had been harder than she'd expected.

"A call came in through the main switchboard for you," Constance said. "I'm going to patch it through."

Anna crossed the room and pulled open the refrigerator door where she'd stashed her lunch. She should probably eat now, before Helen's contractions intensified. And this call was probably another patient in labor. Sometimes they panicked and called the hospital directly, rather than her on-call line.

"Hello?" Anna said, propping the phone between her cheek and shoulder to push aside someone's sandwich and reach for her salad behind it.

"Hello?" a voice rasped in a thick Pittsburgh accent. It sounded like it belonged to an old woman with more than a few decades of heavy smoking in her past. Definitely not the urgent tone of a patient in labor. "Is this—?" the woman continued. "I'm trying to reach Anna. Anna Campbell."

"This is Anna Campbell," Anna said, her brows knitting together. There was something familiar about that voice. "Who is this?"

"Oh, good. I, um... Well"—the woman stumbled over her words—"I... Anna, this is your mother."

Anna stopped breathing. The phone slipped from its cradle between her shoulder and ear, and she grabbed it right before it hit the floor. Slamming the refrigerator door shut, she clutched the phone in one sweaty hand and circled back to the table, grasping blindly for a chair with the other hand.

Sinking down, Anna sucked in a shallow breath. "Is this a joke? Who is this?"

There was a pause, and then finally, "It's—I'm your mom."

Her mom was dead.

Well, of course Anna didn't actually know that. But she'd spent the last six months convincing herself that her mom had died of a heart attack in the park, and it had become real in her mind. Once she'd gotten the DNA results and learned about the pawned necklace, Anna had decided that she was better off keeping up the pretense. Wherever her mom had ended up, she didn't care to have Anna in her life. And it was time for Anna to move on, once and for all.

"What's your name?" Anna demanded.

"It's Deb. Deb Campbell. Anna, it's me."

Anna braced her free hand on the arm of her chair to stop it from shaking. That voice. That voice was so familiar. She closed her eyes to shut out the roll of vertigo. "What do you want?" she managed to choke out.

"I thought maybe we could get together to talk."

Anna's eyes flew open. "Get together? Where are you?"

"I'm in Pittsburgh. I just—" Her mom broke off in a hacking cough that lasted for almost a full minute. Finally, she got a hold of herself. "Sorry."

"You're in Pittsburgh?" Anna asked, hearing the tinge of hysteria in her voice. "Since when?"

"Oh, it's been years."

*Years.* Her mom had been here, in Pittsburgh, *for years.* Had she even tried to reach her only child? Gone to the old neighborhood and asked around? It wouldn't have been hard to find Anna if she'd wanted to.

*Which means she didn't want to.*

"Uh-huh." Anna's voice was miraculously calm, given the way her stomach churned and her whole body trembled. "And now you want to get together? Why now?"

But suddenly, Anna knew *why now*. It was the same reason she'd pawned the necklace all those years ago.

Her mom cleared her throat. "Well, I—thought we could talk about that in person."

And there it was.

"Right. Because I can't give you money over the phone. Or —no. That's right, you called me at work. You know I'm a doctor. Were you hoping for drugs?"

"Well, actually, I'm—" Her mom began coughing again.

Anna sat there listening to that horrible hacking, and her shock slowly ignited into anger. It was such a relief because she could handle anger. She was a successful adult, not a scared kid trying desperately to survive. And she didn't need to give this woman one more second of her energy.

"Listen, you're not getting money or drugs from me. Don't ever call me again." She hit the button to hang up and then flung the phone on the table in front of her.

Anna shrank away from it, shoving her chair back until it hit the wall behind her.

Who knew if that was even her mom? Anna hadn't heard from her in almost twenty years, and suddenly she was calling out of the blue? If it *was* her mom, the only explanation was she'd done some googling, figured out her kid was a doctor and back in Pittsburgh, and saw an easy payday. Well, that was never going to happen.

But as Anna sat there, hands still shaking, the doubts crept in. Maybe she shouldn't have acted so rashly and hung up like that. The call had come through the massive hospital phone system. Was there any way to trace it? If Anna ever wanted answers about where her mom had been since she was a teenager, had she lost the chance when she slammed down the phone?

She took a shuddering breath. Did answers even matter? Maybe the only nice thing her mom had ever done for her was to take off in the first place.

She jumped out of her chair and paced the small room, but before she could decide what to do, the door to the lounge flew open. Constance stood there, breathing hard, her hair tumbling out of the neat bun she usually wore on the top of her head.

"Anna," she gasped, pressing a hand to her chest. "We need you right now."

Anna took an unsteady step toward her coworker. "Is it Helen?" She rubbed her temples, trying to catch her brain up to the present moment. Her patients needed her.

"No." Constance sucked in another breath. "It's another patient. A girl named Hayleigh."

*Hayleigh.* "Is she in labor?" *Please don't say her boyfriend beat her up again.*

"No." Constance shook her head. "No, she's not in labor." The lines around her eyes deepened, and for a moment, she looked dangerously close to crying.

Anna's heart began to pound. Constance had worked in labor and delivery for thirty years, and she'd seen it all. This couldn't be good. "What happened?"

"Her boyfriend... He—" The nurse's shoulders slumped beneath her scrub shirt. "He shot her. She's not going to make it. We need you to do a C-section to deliver the baby."

# THIRTY-FIVE

Gabe was in the middle of a lecture about the dynamics of income and poverty traps when his messenger bag buzzed for about the tenth time in five minutes. He always turned his phone to vibrate and left it in his bag when he was teaching. Usually, he didn't notice if he received an occasional call or text. But this was so distracting that even a couple of girls sitting in the front row started giggling when it buzzed again. One of them raised her hand.

"Dr. Weatherall?"

"Yes, Amelia?"

"Um. I think someone is trying to get a hold of you."

Amelia's friends burst into a fresh round of laughter.

Gabe sighed. "It seems that way, doesn't it? Okay, let's take a ten-minute break, and when we come back, we'll discuss the midterm paper."

The students got up from their chairs and clamored out of the lecture hall as he fished his phone out of his bag.

Six missed calls from Anna, plus a voicemail.

His heart thudded, and he quickly hit the button to listen to the message.

"Hi, it's me. I, uh..." It was Anna's voice, but it was so strangled—as if she was trying not to cry—that he could barely make out her next words, but it sounded like "I need you."

His vision turned bright white, as if someone had flashed a spotlight right in his face. Gabe grabbed onto the desk in front of him as blood pounded in his ears.

"I know I don't have any right to ask you this, but—" And then she said something else, but he couldn't decipher it.

Gabe stuffed his papers and laptop into his bag and gestured at his teaching assistant. "I have to leave right now. Can you finish up? Give everyone the midterm assignment." He didn't even bother to wait for her to nod before heading for the door.

Ignoring the stares of his students, Gabe pushed past them and took off down the hall, dialing the phone as he ran.

*Damn it.* Straight to voicemail. Maybe she was calling *him* again, or maybe she'd tried Rachel or someone else.

Gabe burst out the doors of the building and rounded the corner to the parking lot, clicking the button to unlock the door as he ran to his car. He tried Anna's number again, without success, and then tossed the phone on the seat next to him.

He sped out of the parking lot, yanking the steering wheel in the direction of Anna's house.

# THIRTY-SIX

As soon as Anna got to her carriage house, she regretted rushing home. At the hospital, she'd longed to put it behind her: the stream of police officers, the coroner taking Hayleigh's body away, the social worker questioning Anna about Hayleigh's emergency contacts and the baby's next of kin.

And then there was that phone call.

All she'd wanted was to go home, fall into bed, and escape it all. But when she'd gotten there, her body ached too much to get comfortable, and she felt too wired to sleep. The police had said Hayleigh's attacker was in jail, but that didn't stop her from jumping every time the wind rattled the windows and shook the front door. She checked that all the locks were secure and then, just to be sure, checked again. It was irrational; he wouldn't be coming for her, but that didn't stop the terror anyway.

Or the echo of that voice on the other end of the line.

Rachel would offer to come over if she called her, but Anna couldn't ask her to. It was late, and the snow was really coming down now. She paced another loop around her tiny apartment, checking the door and window locks again. Then she sank down on the couch.

Anna longed for Gabe with an ache greater than any physical pain she'd ever felt, but he wasn't answering his phone. Maybe it was better. They hadn't talked since he'd walked out on her, and her heart couldn't bear any coldness and distance in his eyes tonight.

At that moment, a knock rattled the door. Heart pounding, she jumped up from the couch and stood frozen in the middle of her living room.

*Hayleigh's attacker is in jail,* she told herself.

But that wasn't really the monster she feared. The one who stalked her dreams.

Another knock.

All she had to do was walk over and peek out the window, except her legs didn't seem to be working. Suddenly, her phone vibrated in her hand, and she read the text with shaking hands.

*Hey, are you home? I'm outside.*

Anna hurried to the door.

Gabe stood in the porch light with his hands shoved in his pockets and his shoulders hunched from the cold. Snowflakes clung to his shirt and shimmered on his dark hair. She'd never been so happy to see anyone in her entire life. She wanted to throw herself into his arms, but the memory of their last encounter hit her like the frigid wind that blew into the house. So she held back, pulling her cardigan around her.

"Hi," she mumbled.

Gabe's frantic gaze skated down her body and back to her face. "Are you hurt? What happened?"

"No, nothing like that," she murmured. "I'm okay. It's—I lost a patient tonight. The woman I told you about whose boyfriend beat her up. This time, she didn't make it."

"Oh, Anna." He took a step toward her and put a hand on her cheek. "I'm so sorry," he breathed.

Anna wrapped her arms around herself. "Thank you for coming."

She turned as he eased past her into the house, stopping to kick off his boots before continuing into the living room. Her heart clenched at the sight of him standing there. He was so tall and solid, he seemed to fill up her whole apartment. His dark hair stuck up on top, as usual, and she fought off the urge to reach over, smooth it down, and brush the snowflakes off his shoulders.

"Where's your coat?" she asked.

Gabe shrugged as he glanced down at his trousers and oxford shirt. "I don't know. In my office, I guess. I ran out in the middle of a lecture."

Anna looked at her feet. "I'm sorry."

Gabe took a step toward her and then stopped short, pulling his hands into fists as if he was trying to keep from reaching for her. He stuffed them into his pockets and said in a low voice, "Anna, no matter what, I'm your best friend. You can always call me. I'll *always* come."

She was dangerously close to crying. The silence stretched between them as she hovered by the front door, unsure of what to say now that he was there. They'd always had such an easy way with each other, and now awkwardness gripped her. The ache in her heart doubled in size, and her eyes burned. She needed to get it together.

"I'm going to change out of these scrubs." Before he could answer, she fled to her bedroom, leaving him standing alone in the middle of the living room.

In the safety of her bedroom, Anna's tears spilled over. She scrubbed her palm across her wet cheeks and opened her closet door, digging around for something to wear. She'd changed into clean scrubs after the delivery. The ones she'd been wearing were covered in Hayleigh's blood, not from the C-section, but as a result of the bullet wound that the ER docs had tried to stave off long enough to allow her to bring a motherless child into the world.

Anna shuddered as the reality of those words hit her.

*Another motherless child.*

Anna yanked some clothes from the closet, but instead of pulling them on, she slumped down on the bed. The more she tried to stop the tears, the more they dripped down her cheeks. She didn't know how long she sat on the bed, her eyes slowly leaking, until her bedroom door creaked open, and she looked up. Gabe leaned against the doorframe, arms crossed in front of him and a worried look on his face.

"Hey." His voice was gentle, which put one more crack in her heart. "You okay?"

Anna nodded and swiped at her wet cheeks with the palm of her hand.

"Do you need anything?"

She shook her head as more tears spilled over.

He walked into the room and sank down on the bed next to her. "You sure?"

"Yes... no."

It was all too much. She turned her face away from him, her shoulders shaking with silent sobs.

"Hey," Gabe whispered, tugging on her shoulder, and turning her toward him. He didn't say anything else, just wrapped his arms around her and pulled her against his chest.

Once she started sobbing, she couldn't stop. It was like the sky had opened up after years of drought and all at once dumped a monsoon. She cried for the newborn baby whose violent father was in prison and mother was gone. She cried for the child she'd been, for the violence in her own young life, and the adults who'd never tried to protect her. And then she cried for Gabe, for the one person who'd always, *always* been there for her, and for the anguish of almost losing him.

Gabe tightened his arms around her and pressed his cheek

to the top of her head. She clung to him, twisting her fist into his shirt and sobbing into his chest. Gabe just held her and let her cry.

After a long time, her sobs waned into quiet gasps, but she stayed in Gabe's arms with her head on his chest and his heart beating against her. The rhythm soothed her. Finally, she took a deep, shuddering breath and sat up.

He took her face in his hands and pushed her tear-soaked hair off her cheek. "You must be exhausted. Do you want to go to sleep?"

Anna shook her head. "I'm not sure if I can."

"When was the last time you ate something?"

She had no idea. The day was ten years long. "Breakfast, I guess."

"You need to eat. Why don't you get changed first?"

Five minutes later, Anna found Gabe bustling around the kitchen. When she walked in, he poured her a glass of water, then giving her the side-eye when he saw the contents—or lack of contents—of her refrigerator, he called the Thai place around the corner for takeout.

They sat with their backs against opposite arms of the couch, feet tangled in the middle, and ate out of the cartons. They didn't talk, but the silence was comfortable instead of awkward, which calmed her a little more. After a few minutes, she shoved her chopsticks into her pad Thai and looked over at Gabe. His hair still stuck up on one side, his shirt was wrinkled where she'd cried all over him, and his silver eyes seemed paler in the dim light. A dull ache of longing gnawed somewhere deep.

She took a deep breath. And then she took a chance.

"Gabe, there's something I never told you."

Gabe's head rose to look at her, but he stayed silent.

She studied her food, stabbing her chopsticks into the

carton over and over. "Something—" Her breath caught. "Something that happened... a long time ago."

Gabe slid across the couch cushions so he was sitting next to her. He took the food and put it on the coffee table, and then he reached for her hand.

Anna forced her voice to sound even, as if she were rattling off the vitals of one of her patients instead of telling him about the horrors of her childhood. "When my mom lost her job, she started bringing men home."

Gabe nodded.

"I told you this already. But I didn't tell you all of it. The men gave her money and drugs. She couldn't find another job, and they took care of us. But..." She paused and peeked at Gabe. He knew more than anyone else about her past, but this...

She'd never told *anyone* this.

"Most of them weren't very nice to her." There had been a lot of fights, a lot of screaming arguments where Anna would hide out in the bedroom closet and hope it would be over soon. Or she'd slip down the fire escape to wait it out in the library a few blocks away. "When I was thirteen, she brought this guy home, and he—he was even worse than the others." Gabe sat so close she could feel the muscles in his arm bunch with tension, but she stared ahead and couldn't look at him. "She'd do one little thing wrong—burn a pan of food or bring him the wrong beer—and he'd reach out and smack her across the face."

Her mother had kept making excuses. *He's tired. He's high. He's sorry.*

"He was *always* sorry, according to her. Except he didn't ever seem that way. He seemed to be getting worse." Soon it wasn't a backhand over burned food—he was using his fists. Her mom ended up in the hospital with a dislocated shoulder, and the next time, two broken ribs. "But she just stayed. She said we needed him. He took care of us." Anna looked down at her hands. "I got a job at the grocery store, hoping if I brought home enough money, maybe we wouldn't need him anymore. But it wasn't enough. It was never enough."

Her paltry grocery-store salary was never going to cut it. "One day at school, I had a fever, and the school said my mom had to come and get me. When I got to the parking lot, her boyfriend was there with her, and he was pissed that I'd interrupted his day. He said they had things to do. My mom told him just to drop me off at home, but it was out of the way, and we had to stop at his place first."

Anna could still remember the sharp pain of her sore throat, the fever chills, the slam of the door when they told her to wait in the back seat of the pickup truck.

Even now, decades later, she still went over and over it in her head. Maybe if she'd gone in with them, it wouldn't have played out the way it had. Maybe if she'd been able to hide how sick she was, he wouldn't have had to pick her up, and none of it would have ever happened.

"I think I fell asleep because it was getting dark when I woke up. So, I went in to look for them. They were in his kitchen fighting. It was... bad. I don't know what set him off. It could have been anything. But my mom was on the ground, bleeding, and he was—" Anna closed her eyes. "I thought he was going to kill her. I ran in and tried to pull him off her. But he grabbed me and wrestled me to the ground."

Gabe sucked in an audible breath and tightened his hand around hers.

That was when the panic had set in. He was so big, so heavy, and she could barely breathe—how could she get him off her? If only she could get out from under him, she could find something, anything to use as a weapon.

"And then I looked up, and my mom was there, yanking on his arm, screaming at him to leave me alone. He stood up, to go after her, and that's when I—"

Anna stopped talking. This was it.

"That's when I pushed him."

The worst thing she'd ever done.

"His shoulder hit the frame of the basement door, and then he stumbled... and fell down the stairs. And he just lay there, bleeding, his body bent at a weird angle. And I knew. I just knew." Anna took a ragged breath. "I killed him."

Anna stopped talking, and Gabe leaned back against the couch cushions and scrubbed his hand across his forehead as if he was trying to erase the terrible image she'd left in his mind.

*Of course he wants to erase it.*

This wasn't normal. Normal people didn't kill their mom's boyfriends. Normal people didn't have terrible, sordid histories that kept getting more terrible and sordid by the minute. *Of course he wants to be as far away from me as possible.*

Except that when she finally turned and looked at him, he didn't get up and walk away. He reached out, sliding his arm around her and pulling her into his chest.

It was so, so good to be back there again.

"My mom and I ran," she continued. "Just took off before anyone knew we were there."

When he spoke, his voice was raw. "Anna, I'm so sorry." He shook his head. "It sounds so inadequate to say that. But I *am* sorry that happened to you. And so angry, and I hope you know that *none* of this was your fault."

"She left, Gabe," Anna murmured into the cotton of his shirt. "The next day, she packed a bag and she left."

"And you blamed yourself."

"She owed some people money, and with the boyfriend"—Anna flinched—"*gone*, she didn't have any way to pay it. They were going to come looking for her if she didn't figure something out. So, she made some calls and found out about a job opportunity in California. And she took it. I'm sure it was something shady and illegal. But she was desperate. After that, she called a couple of times from that number on Capp Street. And then she disappeared."

"And you've been looking for answers ever since." Gabe loosened his arms, sliding back so he could look her in the face. "Do you still blame yourself?"

Anna closed her eyes, remembering the pawned necklace, the familiar voice over the phone, asking to meet. *Did* she still blame herself? Or was she finally realizing that Deb Campbell had always put her addiction ahead of her daughter, and Anna just hadn't seen it?

"I'm not sure how I feel. I know rationally that it's not my fault any more than what happened today is Hayleigh's baby's fault. I know *none* of it is my fault. But the shame is like a groove worn in a rock from two decades of water running through it. Everything I've ever done has flowed from that direction."

"So, we need to divert the river."

Could she? Could she finally face her terrible childhood head-on and learn to carve new pathways? It would be the hardest thing she'd ever done.

She looked at Gabe across the narrow space. He'd said "we." Could he possibly be up for this? Could she trust that he'd stick with her when it got horribly messy?

But maybe that was the point. She'd never know if she kept running. If she kept doing what she'd always done.

They finished their Thai food and put on a mindless comedy on Netflix. Before the opening credits were even over, she felt her body growing heavy. The next thing Anna knew, she was in her bed, alone. She sensed movement in the corner of the room and struggled to sit up.

Gabe sat in an armchair in the semidarkness, a book

propped against his crossed leg and her small reading light casting shadows across his face.

"Gabe," she breathed. "What time is it?" She had no memory of going to bed. Had Gabe carried her there when she was asleep?

Gabe glanced at his watch. "About two in the morning."

"You're still here."

"I didn't want you to wake up alone."

"Oh," she said, her heart rattling. Even after everything she'd told him...

*He didn't want me to wake up alone.*

Gabe yawned and leaned back, stretching his long legs in front of him. "I was just contemplating crashing on your couch."

Anna pictured that little couch in her living room. She was pretty sure it came from a line of extra-small furniture made for tiny apartments like hers. She couldn't imagine Gabe squeezing his tall frame on that thing and getting any sleep at all. She should tell him she was fine and encourage him to go home. Except she couldn't quite make her mouth form the words.

Instead, she gestured at the spot next to her in the queen-sized bed. "You could sleep here."

Gabe looked at her sideways. "You sure?"

She nodded.

He stood and made his way over to the bed. Anna looked away as he pulled off his wrinkled oxford shirt and belt, but he left his trousers and T-shirt on. The bed sank under his weight as he climbed in next to her. Gingerly, she lay back down on her side, so she was facing him.

Closing her eyes, she tried to drift off, but Gabe consumed all her other senses. The bed was suddenly ten degrees warmer, and his familiar woodsy scent drifted across the pillows. She could hear him lightly breathing and feel the gentle rise and fall of his chest.

After a few minutes of pretending to sleep, she opened her

eyes and peeked at him. At that exact moment, he turned his head toward her, and their eyes met. She blinked but didn't look away, and her heart did a slow roll in her chest.

Gabe's arm slid out, tugging her against his side. She settled in, feeling his heartbeat under her cheek and the warm pressure on her hip where his hand rested. A minute later, she was asleep.

# THIRTY-SEVEN

Anna woke up alone. It was morning, and the sun streamed through her window, slanting across her pillow. She squinted and rolled over. There was no evidence Gabe had been in the spot next to her. Had she dreamed that he'd come over last night? No, it was too real to be a dream, and she could still smell him on her pillow. She hugged it to her chest.

Her phone vibrated, and she grabbed it from the side table.

*Gabe*

*Hey, sorry I had to go. I had a meeting I couldn't miss. I should warn you that you won't be alone for long. The Weatheralls are descending. See you soon.*

At that moment, there was a knock at the door. Braver than she'd been the night before, Anna rolled out of bed and limped to the front window to peek out. Elizabeth, John, and Leah stood on the front porch, laden with the baby bundled in a car seat, a cardboard coffee carrier, and a bag from a local bakery.

Elizabeth and Leah clamored into the house, fussing over Anna, and growing teary as they asked about Hayleigh's baby.

John didn't say anything, but he hugged her for a long time, and she pressed her forehead into his chest to hide her burning eyes.

They stayed for breakfast, all crowding around her small dining table and passing around croissants and the sleeping baby.

Rachel showed up a few hours later, just as the others pulled out of the driveway. She burst through the front door and nearly knocked Anna over with her hug. "God, Anna. I'm so sorry. This situation is so freaking terrible."

Anna couldn't help but smile. Leave it to Rachel to tell it like it was. "Freaking terrible pretty much sums it up."

Rachel took Anna's hand and tugged her down on the couch. "Tell me what I can do. Can I help the baby in any way?"

"They're looking for next of kin, but I'm not hopeful. I don't think Hayleigh had much support from family. If any."

Rachel's silver-blue eyes filled with tears. "Shit," she murmured, swiping at them with her palm. "I'm just so sorry I couldn't do anything to help her."

"It's not your fault. I know Hayleigh never called you." Anna reached over and gave Rachel's hand a squeeze. "I think I'm finally learning that you can't save someone who doesn't want to be saved."

Rachel regarded her across the couch cushions. "Are you thinking about your mom? I hope it's okay that Gabe shared a little bit about how you were looking for her. He thought maybe I'd have some resources to help."

Anna blinked. "Do you?"

"Well, I do work with a private investigator on occasion." Rachel gave her a sideways smile. "Catching cheating spouses in the act is my bread and butter, you know."

"She called me, Rach."

Rachel's eyes widened. "Your mom did?"

Anna hadn't even told Gabe about the phone call. After

everything that had happened last night, she hadn't wanted to give it any more energy. But now, she couldn't help remembering her mom's voice, deep and rough from decades of smoking. "I think it was her. She called through the birth center's line, and it sounded like her. But it's been so long, I don't know. And then I hung up before I could really get any information."

That was the most confusing part. She'd been so close to finally getting answers about where her mom had been all this time. So why *had* she hung up the phone?

"Well, if you want my help, just say the word."

Anna gave Rachel a grateful smile. "Thanks." But something held her back. "Is it okay if I let you know?"

"Of course."

A few minutes after Rachel headed to work, Julia stopped by on her way to pick up the boys from school and stuffed Anna's freezer full of homemade meals. Anna began to suspect the Weatheralls had carefully coordinated their visits so she wouldn't be alone, because a few minutes after Julia left, Matt showed up with his toolbox and a set of heavy-duty dead bolts. "I know you're totally safe here, but I thought you might feel better with a little extra security." He shot a glance at the moving boxes in the corner. "Just in case you decided you wanted to stay here in Pittsburgh a little longer."

Anna was saved from having to answer by the whir of the drill.

Matt gave her a hug and left just as it was beginning to grow dark. Anna circled her apartment, checking the doors and windows, grateful for the extra lock. A few minutes later, she heard another knock on her door and peeked out the window.

*Gabe.*

"What's all this?" Anna asked, following him into the kitchen where he piled grocery bags on her counter.

"I saw the contents of your refrigerator, kid."

Having grown up on canned vegetables and peanut-butter sandwiches, Anna had never learned how to cook as a child. By the time she was an adult with enough money to afford real food, she was too busy with medical school and then with her erratic on-call schedule to do more than grab a sandwich at the hospital or a bowl of cereal before bed.

"I have a freezer full of homemade meals," she protested.

"And if Julia hadn't brought those over, what would you have eaten tonight?"

"Um," she mumbled.

"Uh-huh," Gabe said. "I'm cooking."

Of course, Gabe was a great cook. His mother had made sure all her children could prepare a whole menu of gourmet dishes before they left for college. Anna imagined Gabe mostly used his skill to impress women. She settled at the dining table and watched him chop an onion with the proficiency of a *Top Chef* contestant.

Fine. She was impressed.

Gabe plunked a glass of wine in front of her, and soon the smell of caramelized onions filled the kitchen. They chatted about Gabe's meeting that morning while he moved around the room, cracking eggs into a bowl and sprinkling them with freshly chopped herbs. Thirty minutes later, he put two plates on the table, each topped with a decadent slice of caramelized onion and Gruyère frittata, and a salad made from crisp butter lettuce and pears.

Anna ate every bite and then dug into the seconds Gabe slid onto her plate. She finally looked up to find him watching her, a smile stretched across his face.

"What?"

"You know, it's okay to let someone take care of you once in a while."

Anna leaned back in her chair. At some point over the last

hour, the tension had left her body, and the throb in her shoulders had subsided. She couldn't think of why she'd argued with him about cooking for her, or about anything really.

Gabe slid into the chair across from her. "Speaking of taking care of you... how are you doing with everything that happened yesterday?"

Anna set her fork next to her plate. Gabe still didn't know about her mom reaching out yesterday. She'd been too overwhelmed to bring it up last night, but after her conversation with Rachel, the call had been playing on repeat in her head. "Gabe, my mom called me."

"What?" Gabe's eyes widened, and he slowly sank back against his chair. "Wow."

"I know."

"How—?" His face looked like hers must have when she'd answered the phone. Gabe knew what this meant, how much she'd been through, looking for her mom. He sat up abruptly and took her hand. "How are you? Are you okay?"

"Yeah, I think so," Anna said, remembering the sweat dripping down her back, the roll of vertigo when the call had come through. "She said she's in town and asked me to meet."

Gabe blinked. "Did you agree to?"

"No. I accused her of calling me for drug money and hung up on her. I can't quite figure out why." Anna stared down at her hands. "I spent so much time chasing her, and when I had the chance to finally find out where she's been all my life, I blew it."

Gabe leaned an elbow on the table, letting the silence settle around them, giving her the space to process it. She kept coming back to this. Why *hadn't* she agreed to meet when her mom had asked? Why had her first reaction been denial?

Anna reached for the place where her necklace used to be, and her hand landed on the collar of her shirt instead. Maybe she hadn't wanted answers from her mom because, deep down, she already knew everything she needed to know. Maybe she was finally choosing her future over the pain and heartache of her past.

Maybe she was finally ready to forgive herself and move on.

Her gaze flew to Gabe's. "Or maybe I didn't blow it."

"Maybe you didn't." Gabe leaned in. "Maybe you made a choice," he said, proving for about the thousandth time since the day they'd met that he knew her better than anyone.

After dinner, they carried their glasses into the living room. Anna stopped in the doorway and watched Gabe walk over to the couch. The streetlights slanted in through the window, casting the room in a low, warm glow. He pulled off his sweatshirt and tossed it over a chair. Even in jeans and an old T-shirt from his college days, he was beautiful. The T-shirt was so faded she could barely make out the Greek letters of his fraternity on the front. In some ways, he still reminded her of that college kid from a lifetime ago—handsome, cocky, smart—but there was so much more to him. He'd been her constant, her anchor, for the past decade and a half, always there, always showing up.

Gabe turned and squinted at her. "You okay?"

She gave a start, realizing she was still hovering in the doorway. "Yeah. I was just thinking how nice it was to have you stay over last night." She forced a small laugh. "Even if you do hog the bed."

Gabe didn't even crack a smile. He just stared at her for a moment, his face cast in shadows so she couldn't read his expression. Then he shoved his hands into his back pockets and said in a low voice, "Anna, I'd stay forever if you'd let me."

Anna's heart hammered in her chest, and before she could plan her next move, she was walking across the room. She stopped in front of him, so close that even in the dim light she could see every detail of his ice-blue eyes. He blinked, and astonishment flashed across his face in the moment right before she slid her hand behind his neck and pressed her mouth against his.

Gabe's arms closed around her. He twisted his hands into the back of her shirt to pull her closer, kissing her with an intensity that left her breathless. She held on to him, all the hurt and pain of the past few days falling away. He slowly backed up until his legs hit the couch, and tumbling backward, he pulled her down on top of him. She grasped his T-shirt, tugging on the hem to pull it over his head.

Gabe stilled.

"Is something wrong?" Her voice shook at the end.

His hands slid into her hair, and he tilted her head to look at him. "Anna, is this okay?"

She nodded, but he held on, his eyes piercing hers. "Are you sure? You've been through a lot. We can stop if you're not ready for this."

She looked into that beautiful face, the one she'd loved for close to half her life. The one that reflected the same hope and wonder she could barely contain.

"Gabe," she whispered. "I'm ready for this."

# THIRTY-EIGHT

That Sunday, Anna got home late from her shift at the hospital and ran into her house to change out of her scrubs. She was supposed to have been at Elizabeth and John's house for dinner over an hour ago, but she'd been delayed by an emergency C-section. Anna had texted Gabe from the hospital and told him she'd be over in forty-five minutes.

On her way out of the bedroom, she tripped over the moving boxes. Gabe hadn't asked about them again, and she knew he was trying to give her space to figure out what she wanted. Anna glanced at the clock. She was already late, so what were a few more minutes?

It took about five to line her books back on the shelf, put the candles on a side table, and slide the photos on the mantel. At the sight of her things back where they belonged, a weight lifted.

She was about to text Gabe and tell him she was *really* on her way this time when there was a knock on the door. Maybe he'd come looking for her. She smiled and hurried into the living room, swinging the door open.

And then she froze.

It wasn't Gabe.

On her doorstep stood an old woman with posture so stooped that her shoulders seemed to fold in on themselves. She was skinny, verging on skeletal, with sunken cheekbones and bruised half-moons under her eyes. Her long, lank hair was streaked with gray, and her plaid flannel shirt and stained jeans practically swallowed up her bony frame.

Anna stumbled backward, clutching the door handle for balance, unable to tear her eyes away. She opened her mouth, but nothing came out.

Finally, she managed to whisper, "Mom."

"Hi, baby. Can I come in?"

# THIRTY-NINE

Anna stood shaking in the doorway and stared at her mom. Deb Campbell was only fifty-five years old, but she had the gaunt, careworn look of a woman at least twenty years older. The acrid smell of cigarette smoke hung around her like a fog, and those had to be track marks peeking out from underneath her rolled-up sleeves.

Behind her, a car idled in the driveway with a middle-aged woman in the driver's seat. Anna had no idea if she was annoyed or relieved her mom planned for this to be such a short visit that she didn't even bother to tell her friend to turn off the engine.

Anna didn't say anything, just held the door open wider and allowed her mom to walk through it.

Her mom limped into the living room and looked around. "Nice place you got here."

"Thanks."

"You own this?"

"No, I'm just renting." Were they really making small talk right now?

"Huh. Successful doctor like you, I would've thought you'd own a big fancy house or something."

Ah, okay. So, there it was. Anna crossed her arms in front of her. "I see you googled me."

"Well, you *are* my kid after all. I did check up on you once in a while."

"I wouldn't say that."

"What, that I checked up on you? I know I didn't call or anything, but—"

"No," Anna interrupted. "I wouldn't say that I'm your kid."

Anna's mom stared down at her hands and then shrugged. "I know I wasn't the best parent"—perhaps the greatest understatement Anna had ever heard—"but I did think about you. And, you know..." Another shrug. "You were probably better off without me."

This, at least, was the truth.

"How did you even find out where I live?"

"My old friend Barbara from high school—you remember her, the one who got me the job at the nursing home when you were a kid? Anyway, she works at the same hospital as your practice and did some digging." She shuffled over to the couch and sank down onto the cushions. Her head flopped back, and loud pants came from the back of her throat. "Can I get a glass of water or something?"

Anna stood there, arms crossed. Even that tiny bit of hospitality felt like too much for her to manage right now. She was frozen to the spot. "Why are you here?" she demanded. "I assume you need money. Or, no. It was drugs, right?"

Her mom didn't answer right away. She just lifted her head and slowly gazed around the room. Finally, she looked at Anna straight on. "I'm dying. I got cancer."

Anna blinked, waiting for shock, or anger, or *something*, but there was... nothing. She whirled around and fled to the kitchen, leaning against the counter while she tried to get it together.

Her mom was there. And she was dying.

Her brain seemed to be flitting around the room like a fruit fly.

She needed something to do with her hands, so she filled a glass with water and carried it back to the living room. After she set it on the coffee table in front of her mom, Anna sat in a chair on the other side of the room.

"What kind of cancer?"

Her mom broke into a fit of coughing. She grabbed the glass, took a gulp, and then pounded on her chest a few times. "Colon cancer," she croaked when she'd recovered. "One day I just started shitting blood. I finally saw some doctors, and they said by then it had spread to my liver and lungs. There was nothing they could do for me."

Anna nodded, still numb. "How long?"

"They said I got a couple of months."

"Where are you staying?"

"Barbara got me into some hospice thing. I got my own room, and it's all paid for by Medicaid. The craziest part is after spending more than half my life hustling for dope, now the doctors are practically throwing morphine at me." She started chuckling but broke off into another fit of coughing.

Anna sat in her chair, arms crossed in front of her and face expressionless. She understood the irony, but it was pretty hard to see the humor. She waited for her mom to take another gulp of the water and pound on her chest.

Her mom got her coughing under control and looked around the room again, picking up a framed photo of Anna and Gabe from the side table. They had their arms around each other, grinning at the camera. "Well, here's a good-looking guy. This your boyfriend?"

Anna hesitated, focusing on that photo. Gabe smiled back

at her, and somehow that seemed to kick-start her frozen heart. "Yes."

Her mom set the photo back on the table. "You got any kids or anything?"

"No."

"Well, I bet when you do, you won't screw it up like I did."

Was that Anna's cue to say, "Oh, you weren't so bad," or something similarly magnanimous? Her mom fidgeted in her seat and plucked at a stray thread on her shirt as the silence stretched between them.

"So, anyway," her mom finally said, "I just wanted to let you know about... you know."

Anna nodded. Her mom was dying, and all she could muster up was a vague sense of pity. What was the matter with her? She felt more compassion for her patients than she did for her own mother. But Anna had relationships with her patients. She knew about their lives, their families, their hopes, and fears. While this woman was a stranger.

Her mom grabbed the arm of the couch with both hands and struggled to heave herself up. "Well, I should be going. That's Barbara out in the car."

Anna jumped out of her chair. "Here, I'll help you."

"No, no. I got it." Her mom stood and then bent over, panting. After a few deep breaths, she turned and limped back toward the front door. Anna opened it for her, and she staggered onto the porch. When Barbara saw the door open, she got out of the car and ran up to the porch to help. Barbara nodded hello to Anna and then took her mom's arm and helped her down the steps.

Anna stood on the porch and watched them shuffle across the driveway.

When they got to the car, Barbara opened the passenger door. Her mom leaned down to get in, and a weird sort of panic hit Anna. Her mom was leaving. And Anna was glad. She didn't want her there, looking at the photos and objects from the life she'd worked so hard for. Didn't want her cough and her smoke smell and that voice that brought back nothing but the most painful memories.

But still, this would be it. Her mom was dying. In a few more months, it would be too late.

"Hey." The word was out of Anna's mouth before she could change her mind.

Her mom looked up. "Yeah?"

Anna hesitated. And then finally, "What nursing home is it? Where you're staying?"

"Canterbury Place, over in Lawrenceville. I'm back in the old neighborhood." She laughed and then broke off coughing again. Barbara took her arm to help her into the car, but her mom stopped and turned back to Anna. "Stop by sometime. I mean... if you want to. Bring your boyfriend."

"I'll..." Anna had no idea if she would. It was too much to think about now. "I'll try."

Her mom nodded and got into the car.

Anna turned and went back into the house. She stopped in the living room, and suddenly, she was shivering uncontrollably. A wave of nausea rolled over her. Maybe she was in shock. Maybe she should lie down, just for a minute.

Anna pulled a blanket off the back of a chair and wrapped it around her as she made her way to the bedroom. Then she curled up on the bed and immediately fell asleep.

When Anna woke, exhausted and disoriented, the sun was just starting to set. She had no idea what day it was. Had she been up all night delivering a baby? Was that why she felt like she'd been hit by a truck?

She staggered into the living room looking for her phone and was overwhelmed by the scent of cigarette smoke.

Oh my God.

*My mom was here.*

Anna sank down in a chair. *My mom is dying.*

She had no idea what to do with that information. After searching for her, waiting for her to come back for years, believing she was dead, learning she wasn't—Deb had finally appeared. And with only a couple of months left to live. Anna ransacked her heart for something, some feeling of sadness, or loss, or... anything. But all she felt was numb.

She still had no idea where her mom had been all this time. Anna had always assumed it would be the first question she asked if she ever had the chance. But now, well, it didn't seem to matter that much. What mattered was where she *hadn't* been.

With her own daughter.

The cigarette smell drifted over to Anna from across the room. Her heart began to race, and her hands started shaking. And just like that, she was back in that old apartment with the dingy brown rug and yellowing stains on the wall, huddled in the bedroom while her mom and some guy—both clearly high—screamed at each other in the living room.

And just as that memory began to pull her under, the phone rang.

Anna lunged out of the chair and ran from the room—and from that terrible smell—into the kitchen where her phone sat on a table. Gabe's name was flashing on the screen, and she swiped to answer it. "Hello?" she managed to whisper.

"Anna, thank God. I was really worried. Is everything okay?"

"Yeah..." Anna suddenly remembered she was supposed to be at Sunday dinner hours ago. She checked the day and time on her phone. She'd slept for an hour. "I, uh, I think I fell asleep."

Through the phone, she heard Gabe chuckle. "Sounds like maybe you're still half-asleep."

"Yeah." She sighed, sinking down in a dining chair. Just hearing his voice soothed her. She wanted him to keep talking. "Did I miss dinner?"

"We saved you a plate."

Anna rubbed her temples as if that would erase the painful memories of her mom. She needed to get out of there. "I'll be there soon."

"You sure you're okay? You sound a little out of it. I can come there."

"No. I'm fine. Just waking up. I'll be there in ten minutes."

"Hurry, okay? You know how my mom convinces herself we've died in a fiery crash whenever one of us is running late."

Anna smiled because it was true. When it came to family, there was nobody more protective than Elizabeth.

And with that thought, the fog lifted.

Her mother wasn't dying. A woman named Deborah Campbell who had given birth to a baby years ago—a woman who was tragically inadequate at being a mother—was dying. Maybe her mother had loved her once, before her addiction had taken over, or maybe Anna had just wanted to believe it. But that woman was not her mother, not her family.

Anna closed her eyes, picturing the Weatheralls all sitting around John and Elizabeth's enormous dining table, laughing and bickering like they always did. And then slowly, the images kept coming, rolling faster and faster until they eclipsed any lingering memories of her childhood: Elizabeth stopping by Anna's bedroom to chat about school, making her favorite meal on the night before a big test, framing the school newspaper article announcing she'd been named valedictorian of her class. And John solemnly tucking a hundred-dollar bill into her pocket when she left for college, "for emergencies," and calling her every evening for a week to help her prepare for medical school interviews; Matt taking her to a school parking lot to teach her how to drive, flinching when she almost sideswiped a chain-link fence with his brand-new pickup truck, but telling her she was doing great; Leah and Julia sending care packages of baby clothes and blankets for the refugees in Syria.

And Rachel. Loyal, steadfast Rachel, whose law firm quietly made donations to the nonprofit health clinic where Anna used to work. Rachel, who'd cried with her over Hayleigh.

And then there was Gabe.

There were so many cracks she'd fallen through in her life. So many ways people should have known better—done better.

Not once did a neighbor stop her to ask if she was okay after the screaming, violent fights between her mom and her drug-dealer boyfriends had echoed through the halls of their apartment building. Not once did a teacher intervene when her mom showed up stoned for parent-teacher meetings, or when she stopped showing up at all. And not once did a cafeteria worker notice that Anna hung around after the bell rang to grab the food from the trash that the other kids threw away without a second thought.

Only one person had ever paid attention.

*Gabe.*

Back then, it was Gabe who used to come to their project meetings with extra sandwiches and insist she eat them. It was Gabe who'd found her at the library late at night—where she went to study when the electricity was shut off in her apartment —and offered to drive her home. It was Gabe who'd made sure she was safe, really safe, for the first time in her life.

And it was Gabe who'd made her a part of the only family she'd ever known.

Anna grabbed her car keys off the kitchen counter and headed for the door. "I'm on my way."

# FORTY

Gabe stood at his parents' kitchen sink washing a set of wineglasses and gazing around the kitchen. The whole family had managed to make it for Sunday dinner today. Leah, Josh, and the baby had already been there when he arrived, and Matt had shown up with Julia and the kids a few minutes later. Rachel had rolled in a few minutes after that, with Aaliyah, who had a rare week off from traveling.

The only person missing was Anna.

She'd texted when she was leaving the hospital, but that was hours ago. And then... crickets. He'd finally gotten her on the phone about fifteen minutes ago, but she'd sounded distant. Out of it.

She'd said she was on her way, but he couldn't help but wonder. Had she changed her mind? Was she running away again?

Gabe took a deep breath to calm his nerves. Their last few days together had been amazing, and Anna had seemed fine when she'd left his place to go to work early this morning. But that didn't mean she *was* fine. It had taken him fifteen years to understand that nothing about healing from trauma like Anna's was going to be easy or straightforward. And just because his family had shown up in her life like some TV sitcom family, it didn't magically erase everything she'd been through.

All he could do was let her know she could count on him and keep letting her know until she believed it. He reached into his pocket, and his hand closed around the small velvet box he'd tucked there earlier. Would this help convince her?

Gabe dried off a wineglass and filled it from the bottle in the fridge. Then he paced across the kitchen and back again.

On his third lap, Rachel looked at him with narrowed eyes. "You're acting weird. Are you okay?"

Gabe glanced into the bottom of his empty glass and rubbed his forehead, too tired to come up with a snarky reply. "Not really."

Rachel's face flashed with the ferocity that she usually reserved for fighting for her clients at the women's shelter. "What happened? What's the matter?"

"I don't know where Anna is."

"Didn't she text from work?"

"Yeah, but that was hours ago."

"So call her."

"I did. She says she's coming."

Rachel cocked her head, looking at him sideways. "But you think she won't?"

"I don't know." Gabe took a shaky breath. "Rach, I'm crazy in love with her."

Rachel pressed her lips together, clearly trying to suppress a smile.

"What?" Gabe demanded.

She raised her hand to her lips. "Nothing. It's just..." She was definitely grinning. "Maybe you're not as dumb as I thought you were."

Gabe ran his hand through his hair and then glanced at his sister. "We haven't talked about whether she's staying or not."

Rachel's gaze drifted over his shoulder. "Well, you can ask her right now."

Gabe turned to find Anna standing in the doorway. She wore an ordinary T-shirt and jeans, with no makeup and her hair pulled into a messy bun, and he'd never seen anyone more beautiful. His heart slid into his throat.

Anna's gaze slid to his. "Ask me what?"

The activity in the kitchen swirled around them. From somewhere far away, he vaguely registered Rachel walking away from him, across the room to Aaliyah. His mom and Julia had taken over washing and drying dishes. Matt brought a broom to sweep up some crumbs the kids had dropped, and Leah bustled in and out carrying dishes from the dining room. The kids ran in yelling something about a storm trooper and ran out again.

Gabe's eyes stayed locked on Anna's, and he slowly made his way across the room. Leaning in, he gently pressed a hand to her cheek. "Will you marry me, Anna?"

# FORTY-ONE

Anna couldn't possibly have heard him over all the noise in the kitchen. For a moment, she was speechless, and finally, she managed to gasp, "What?"

Gabe's mouth curved into a smile, and this time, he spoke in a loud, clear voice that carried over the din of his family laughing and talking around them. "Anna, will you marry me?"

The conversations trailed off as everyone turned to look at them.

"Whoa," Matt muttered, and Julia shushed him.

A whispered, "Oh my God!" sounded like it came from Leah, and someone else gasped. Then the room went silent.

Gabe didn't look up or acknowledge their audience. Instead, he reached into his pocket, pulled out a velvet box, and placed it in her hand. Startled, she opened the lid and looked down, recognizing the familiar piece of jewelry.

His grandmother's beautiful, antique anniversary ring, the one Anna had refused to take when Elizabeth tried to give it to her years ago.

He'd had it in his pocket. He must have planned this. Her

eyes flew back up to Gabe's face. She was having trouble breathing.

He held her gaze. "There is nobody else in the world who I want to talk to about everything. Or who makes me laugh like you do. Or who makes me completely crazy." He paused and flashed her a crooked smile. "Or who I'll ever love the way I love you."

The tears that had been welling up spilled over.

He leaned in and took her face in his hand, brushing the tears away with his thumb. "And, you know, I'm not the only one who loves you. Look around you, kid."

He gestured around the room at his family, who Anna sensed were all staring at them, completely riveted, but she wasn't sure because she couldn't tear her eyes away from Gabe.

"Anna, you're as much a part of this family as I am. So marry me, and let's make it official."

The tears flowed freely now, pooling under her chin and dripping on her shirt. She looked up at the Weatherall family lined up against the kitchen island. Her gaze drifted from Elizabeth, who had tears streaming down her face, to John, who put an arm around his wife and gave Anna an affectionate smile. Leah clutched Josh's hand as her shoulders shook with silent sobs, and Rachel looked a little weepy through her smile. Matt flashed her a happy grin, and Aaliyah and Julia nodded as if they agreed with everything Gabe said.

Anna turned back to Gabe, who stood with his hands balled into fists and his shoulders tense. On his face was a look of vulnerability, and hope, and she'd never loved him more than she did right at that moment. They stared at each other, unblinkingly, as his family stood as still as statues across the room.

And then a wave of happiness crashed over her, and she couldn't keep the smile off her face. Before she could speak, Gabe took her by the shoulders and kissed her. From far away, a loud cheer went up in the room, but all she could think about was Gabe. She slid her hand behind his head and kissed him back, holding on with fifteen years of longing and heartbreak and love.

When they pulled apart, Gabe leaned his forehead against hers and murmured, "Is that a yes? That'd better be a yes."

"*Yes!*" She was laughing and crying at the same time.

Gabe took Dorothy's ring and slid it on her finger, and then he kissed her again.

Suddenly, the family surrounded them. Matt and Julia's boys flung themselves against her hip as John pulled her into his arms for a hug. She let go and bumped into Leah, who was jumping up and down. Matt hugged Gabe, pounding him on the back, and then he turned and picked her up off her feet. Julia shoved her way in to grab her hand and gasp over the ring, and then Rachel displaced Julia and flung her arms around Anna.

When they broke apart, Rachel regarded her solemnly. "You know he's my big brother and I love him more than just about anyone."

Anna nodded.

Rachel smiled. "I don't think I could have let him end up with anyone except for you."

Anna hugged Rachel again, and then Elizabeth appeared. She took Anna's hand and rubbed her thumb over the ring.

"My mother's ring looks great on you," Elizabeth said.

"Thank you for giving it to me," Anna said, her voice hoarse.

Elizabeth pressed her hand to Anna's cheek. "You know, when you told me to give it to one of my daughters, the thing you didn't understand was that I *was* giving it to one of my daughters."

And then Anna was crying again, and Gabe's arm came around her, pulling her close.

And briefly, fleetingly, Anna thought of Deb Campbell.

In the end, her mom leaving had been a gift. One that had brought her to this. Anna leaned back to look into Gabe's eyes. "Do you still have that necklace? The one that was my mom's?"

He tilted his head in a questioning gesture. "Of course I still have it."

"I think I should return it to her," Anna said. Her mom only had a few months left, and she was all alone. Maybe it would be a comfort to her.

His eyebrows shot up. "Did you—?" *Did you talk to her again?*

Anna nodded.

Gabe took her face in his hands as if he were checking her over to make sure she was okay. She smiled to reassure him. "I'll tell you all about it later. But do you think you could come with me if I go?"

"I'll come anywhere with you," he said, and then he pressed his lips to hers. Anna slid an arm around his neck and kissed him back.

From somewhere far away, Rachel's voice cut in. "Get a room, you two."

Anna laughed, pulling back, and stopping right in the middle of all the chaos to look around at Gabe's huge, loud, sweet, loving family.

*Nope,* she corrected. *They're not Gabe's huge, loud, sweet, loving family.*

*They're my family.*

And then she smiled and jumped right back in.

# EPILOGUE

## ONE MONTH LATER

Anna watched her fiancé swing her car door open. An appreciative smile tugged at her lips as she took in his tall, lean frame clad in a dark suit and crisp white shirt. A gust of early-spring wind teased his black hair, blowing a lock across his forehead. She paused, reaching to brush it back. Gabe caught her hand and pressed a kiss to her knuckles in the spot right next to his grandmother's diamond ring.

Her heart gave a familiar squeeze, just as it always did when he was near. Anna marveled every day when she came home and found Gabe waiting for her. He often had dinner on the stove, a glass of wine on the counter, and a smile on his face like he couldn't quite believe she was real. After loving him for almost half her life, she couldn't quite believe he was, either.

And in a matter of hours, he'd be her husband.

Anna smoothed the folds of her knee-length cream-colored chiffon skirt and slid into the car. Gabe reached over to make sure the delicate fabric of her wedding dress wasn't caught in the door before he closed it after her and rounded the car.

Leah had objected when she heard that Anna and Gabe were planning to spend the night before their wedding together.

"It's bad luck for the groom to see the bride in her wedding dress!" She'd gazed around the Weatheralls' dinner table for support, but all she'd gotten was an eyeroll from Rachel.

"Nothing about this wedding could go wrong as long as we end up married by the end of the day," Gabe had said.

Anna had wholeheartedly agreed. Gabe had been with her through everything important in her life—the good and bad, the incredibly painful, and now—the joy. It only made sense that they be together for every moment of this beautiful day. The day they'd finally become a family in every sense of the word.

Anna didn't care about traditions. All she cared was that by tonight, she'd officially be a Weatherall. It was why they'd decided on a small city hall ceremony. They'd lost so much time together already, and they didn't want to wait another day. Besides, Anna didn't have any interest in a big splashy wedding with a lot of guests, either. As long as their family was there, it would be perfect.

With that thought, Anna's shoulders tensed, and her breath caught. There was one member of her family who wouldn't be in attendance. Deb Campbell. Anna hadn't invited her to the wedding. It was the right choice, but the part of Anna that had searched for her mother for decades had hesitated—briefly—at that decision.

Gabe had recognized Anna's uncertainty and gently suggested they stop by the nursing home on the way to the ceremony. It had seemed like a good idea when they'd talked about it. But now the reality of coming face-to-face with her mother again had Anna's nerves rattling.

Gabe knew her better than anyone, and she could tell he'd picked up on her change in mood as soon as he'd slid into the driver's seat. Stopping with his hand on the ignition, he turned in her direction. "Are you sure you still want to do this today?" He gave her a crooked smile, his silver-blue eyes crinkling at the corners. "We can just stay here in the car and make out instead."

Anna laughed, her shoulders relaxing. With Gabe beside her, everything would be okay. No matter what happened.

When they arrived at the nursing home, the woman at the front desk directed them to Deb's room. As they walked down the hall, Anna's high heels tapping on the tile floor, Gabe reached over to weave his fingers through hers. She leaned in, her shoulder brushing his arm, the warmth and solidness of him driving away any last-minute apprehension.

At Deb's door, they peeked into the small, white-walled room with a standard hospital bed on one end and a vinyl recliner on the other. Deb sat in the recliner, her thin frame swallowed up by a pair of hospital-issue pajamas, her head tilted up at a TV secured to the opposite wall. She looked only mildly interested in the two women on the screen moving furniture around a living room that looked recently renovated. And though it was well past lunchtime, a sandwich and cup of applesauce sat on the tray beside her. Anna wasn't sure if it was the doctor part of her, or daughter, who worried at seeing the food untouched.

Anna knocked gently on the door frame.

"Is it time for my meds already?" Deb asked in her raspy, tobacco-saturated voice. And then, glancing toward the door, she let out a quiet, "Oh." Her eyes widened. "Anna. I was expecting the nurse. I... I wasn't sure if you'd ever come to see me."

Still holding Gabe's hand, Anna stepped into the room, tugging him along, keeping him close. "We're just here for a minute to say hello." She pressed a hand to Gabe's arm. "I brought someone for you to meet. This is—"

"I know who you are," Deb cut in. "Anna's boyfriend. I

recognize you from the photo in her apartment. A woman doesn't forget a face like that." She let out a sharp laugh and then began heaving a dry, wracking cough.

Gabe grabbed a bottle of water from a table next to the bed and hurried over to hand it to Deb. He hovered near, concern creasing his face as Deb took small sips. After a few moments, she pounded on her chest and gave a wave of her hand. "I'm fine. I'm fine."

"Are you sure?"

"Yes. Now, what's your name?"

Gabe offered his palm. "It's nice to meet you, Ms. Campbell. I'm Gabe."

Deb stretched her frail arm in Gabe's direction and gave his hand a weak shake. "You're Anna's boyfriend; you should call me Deb."

Anna stepped farther into the room. "He's my fiancé, actually. We're getting married today."

Deb blinked, her gaze sliding to Anna's ivory dress and then over to Gabe's suit. "You're getting married?" she repeated. "Today?"

Anna nodded.

"And you came to see *me*?" Deb's eyelashes fluttered, over and over, as if she were trying to clear something burning there. "Well, I certainly never expected to warrant that kind of attention."

Anna crept closer. "I have something for you. I don't know if you'll want it, but..."

Gabe grabbed a chair from the far wall and placed it in front of Deb so Anna could sit. And then he took the other chair, sliding it just close enough that she could feel his warm presence beside her. Anna reached in her dress pocket to pull out the cheap pawn shop jewelry box, and before she could overthink it, held it in Deb's direction.

Deb took the box in trembling hands, fumbling with the lid.

Anna leaned over to help snap it open, catching the faint scent of tobacco on her mom's skin. She sat back in her chair and watched Deb's eyes focus on the gold half-moon necklace. The pendant was the mirror of the one Anna had sewn into the seam at the waistband of her wedding dress. It was her "something old." A symbol of all that she'd overcome in her past to get here today.

Deb gave another blink, her head bent over the jewelry box. "I really was the worst mother in the world abandoning you the way I did."

Anna took a deep, shaky breath. And then she finally asked the question that had been burning inside her since she was fourteen years old. "Why did you? I understood why you left. But why didn't you ever come back?"

Deb ran a crooked finger over the necklace. "I'd planned to, I really did."

"But..." *But you didn't.*

Deb looked up. "I'd planned to do the job I'd gone out to California for and then come home. But the guy I was with had some friends living in a house in San Francisco. He said I could stay with him and there would be more opportunities for jobs." Deb shook her head. "Part of me really believed that if I stayed for work, I'd be doing something to take care of us. You and me."

"And the other part of you?" Anna asked, wrestling with her voice until it was flat and emotionless. Like she didn't care at all.

"The other part of me just wanted my next fix." Deb slowly lifted a shoulder. "And that part usually won out."

Anna closed her eyes, but before the sadness could overwhelm her, Gabe's arm slid around her shoulder, warm, firm, and so solid. She leaned into him, his woodsy scent dispersing any lingering smell of tobacco.

"And then, there was the guy, too," Deb continued. "I stayed for the guy."

Anna opened her eyes.

"He was mean and controlling, but I thought I loved him, and I didn't know how to be alone." Deb looked down. "Growing up, I never saw a relationship that wasn't full of violence and anger." Her gaze slid from Anna's eyes to Gabe's arm wrapped around her. "I really don't know how you turned out so differently. I certainly never showed you any kind of normal, healthy relationship."

Anna grasped at the fading memories of her childhood, those days when it was just her and her mom. "You did show me, a little." Anna's voice shook. "You cared for me, and you were loving. I do have good memories."

Deb's eyes welled up. With a deep breath, she picked up the necklace. "Well, I appreciate this. I really do." Her bent fingers fiddled with the clasp. "And I'm going to keep it on this time. I promise."

Anna turned that word over in her head. *Promise.* She didn't need promises from Deb, not anymore. But for some reason, Anna believed her this time. Maybe it was because the older woman only had a few months left to live, or maybe she really did feel remorse for abandoning her only daughter. Anna sensed a sincerity and gratitude in her mother for this small chance to reconnect.

Gabe leaned in and gently took the necklace, sliding open the clasp and securing it around Deb's neck. Deb reached up and smoothed the gold pendant against her pajama top.

Anna stood. "We should be going. We're already a little late."

"Yeah." Deb coughed out a laugh. "You don't want to miss your own wedding."

Gabe moved their chairs back into place against the wall and turned to Deb. "I'm really happy to meet you."

Deb's gaze slid from Gabe to Anna and then back. "I'm really happy to see that my girl found a good guy."

Anna's heart squeezed and her eyes burned.

"If you want to come back again, you know where to find me," Deb said, her voice rising in inflection, like it was a question. *Like she's asking us to come.*

Anna glanced at Gabe, and he nodded in encouragement.

"Sure," Anna said. "Next week?"

"That would be—" Deb's voice cracked, and she pressed her fingers to the pendant around her neck. "That would be great."

Anna moved her hand to her hip, feeling her own necklace tucked away in the seam. "We'll see you soon."

They arrived at city hall to find the family gathered outside in a giant swirl of warmth and laughter and good-natured jokes. When they spotted Anna and Gabe coming down the sidewalk, the Weatherall hive buzzed in their direction.

"I can't believe you were almost late to your own wedding," Leah scolded, checking over Anna's dress, smoothing out a wrinkle.

"Is being late bad luck, too?" Anna couldn't help teasing.

"I don't know!" Leah bit her lip. "I hope not."

"While we waited, we took a wager on what held you up," Rachel said. "I knew it wasn't because Anna was fiddling with her hair, but I'd definitely bet money that Gabe was fiddling with his."

Gabe propped his hands under his chin in an exaggerated model pose. "Can't have a hair out of place."

Leah continued to fuss with Anna's dress. "Do you have everything you need? Something old? Something new?"

Anna nodded. "I have a special pendant that's old; my dress is new." She held up a foot, waving the strappy gold heel that Julia had lent her. "My shoes are borrowed. And—"

"Her underwear is blue," Gabe cut in.

"You're not supposed to know about her underwear yet!" Leah cried, pressing her hands to her temples.

"Okay, we're veering into TMI territory, here." Rachel held up a hand.

Matt slid up next to Anna, leaning in to faux whisper in her ear. "You're sure you want to go through with marrying this guy?" He hitched a chin at Gabe. "Say the word and I'll drive the getaway car."

Gabe's mouth dropped open. "Dude! You're literally *my best man*."

Elizabeth moved into the mix to tug on her eldest son's arm. "Don't give your brother a hard time on his wedding day."

Matt nodded, stroking his chin. "So, you're saying I can give him a hard time as long as it's *not* his wedding day?"

Elizabeth sighed the sigh of a woman who'd given up decades ago. "I suppose so."

Matt clapped his hands together. "Deal."

At that point, John stepped in, waving Anna and Gabe toward the doors to city hall. "If we don't get this moving, there's not going to be a wedding."

Gabe held out his arm to Anna. "Should we go ahead and get married?"

She nodded, looking into his eyes, a shining silver-blue like storm clouds with the sun peeking through. It was an apt description for everything he had been to her for all these years. Her light in the darkness, her calm in the eye of a tornado.

He gave her a sideways smile. "Ready to officially become a Weatherall?"

Anna slid her hand through the crook of his arm. "I literally can't wait."

And then she turned and headed into city hall to marry her best friend.

# A LETTER FROM MELISSA

Dear reader,

I'm so happy to share this book with you, and I want to say a huge thank you for choosing to read it. If you enjoyed the story and connected with the characters, I would love it if you'd keep in touch. Please reach out over social media, email me from my website, or sign up for my newsletter to receive information on my latest releases. In addition, I always appreciate a short review, which helps new readers discover the book.

*www.bookouture.com/melissa-wiesner*

Most authors have a book they consider the book of their "heart." Sometimes it's the first book they've ever written, or it's the book that taps into something deeply personal, or it's the one that made them laugh and cry and feel like their heart would break while they were writing it. *It All Comes Back to You* is completely, irrevocably the book of my heart. It's the book that reminds me again and again why I fell in love with writing and how certain characters stay with you forever. Thank you for coming along on this journey with Anna, Gabe, and the entire Weatherall family.

Best wishes,

Melissa Wiesner

## KEEP IN TOUCH WITH MELISSA


www.melissawiesner.com

facebook.com/MelissaWiesnerAuthor
x.com/Melissa-Wiesner
instagram.com/melissawiesnerauthor

# ACKNOWLEDGMENTS

*It All Comes Back to You* has been seven years and about a hundred revisions in the making, and all the people who have impacted it during that time are too numerous to name. This book would not exist without all the supportive individuals I met in online writing communities during its early drafts. I am constantly blown away by the many, many writers who are willing to share their advice, experience, critiques, encouragement, commiseration, and friendship in order to help other writers succeed.

My enormous thanks to Brenda Drake and the entire team behind Pitch Wars for the countless hours you volunteered in order to lift up new and aspiring writers and to foster supportive writing communities. Though I was never a Pitch Wars "mentee," the program literally changed my life, and I know there are hundreds of other writers out there with similar stories.

Thank you to the judges behind the 2019 RWA Golden Heart in the Mainstream Fiction category for giving me a boost of confidence to keep going with this book, even when I wasn't sure if I should. And, more importantly, thank you for giving me the most amazing, supportive "in real life" writer's group I could ever ask for.

A huge thanks to everyone who critiqued this book, but especially to Maureen Marshall, who gave me some very hard-to-hear and necessary-to-hear tough-love feedback on my writing, a long time ago. And to Elizabeth Perry, who gave me some hard-to-hear and necessary-to-hear tough-love feedback on this story in particular.

Thank you to Amy Trueblood and Michelle Huack for the incredible time and effort you put into the Sun vs. Snow contest. And thank you to Jody Holford, my mentor in that contest, who helped me to perfect the first pages of this book, and who, almost six years later, is still answering my emails and offering wisdom and encouragement.

Thank you to Julie Dinneen, who loved Anna and Gabe as much as I do.

To Sharon M. Peterson—thank you for always being a (usually frantic) message away, even when you're on a deadline.

To my agent, Jill Marsal—I am so fortunate to work with you. Thank you for your incredible skill in navigating this business so I can focus on writing.

To my editor, Ellen Gleeson—I probably sound like a broken record with how often I repeat that I adore you and admire your amazing talent. I mean it sincerely every single time. I could not imagine publishing this book with anyone other than Bookouture or you as my editor. Thank you so much for believing in my writing and this book.

Thank you to everyone at Bookouture. You are truly the best at what you do.

To my husband, Sid—I would have to write a whole other book to tell you how much I love you. Someday I will, and I'll be sure to make it smutty.

As always, thank you my wonderful Brusoski-Wiesner family, for your encouragement and support.

And finally, my most sincere gratitude to my readers. I appreciate every single one of you.

Made in United States
North Haven, CT
17 October 2024

59029922R00211